## The Transformation

'Zach took some shots of you this afternoon, didn't he?' asked Lydia.

'Yes.'

'Those will be our "before" shots, then. I want to take you to a proper stylist so that we can completely rework your image.'

Nicholas couldn't quite believe what he was hearing. Why on earth did this sexy woman want to put *him* in her magazine? He could feel the heat coming from her body and the close proximity of her was making him feel light-headed, almost drunk with arousal. He glanced at her, unnerved that she was staring at his chest. 'What?' he asked.

'I was wondering what you looked like under that horrible jacket of yours,' she said. 'You're quite well-built, really, aren't you?' She reached out and took off his glasses. 'Let's not call this a makeover. That's too much of a girly term. Let's call this a transformation.'

# The Transformation

## Natasha Rostova

In real life, always practise safe sex.

This edition published in 2006 by
Cheek
Thames Wharf Studios
Rainville Road
London W6 9HA

Originally published in 1998 by Black Lace

Design by Smith & Gilmour, London
Printed and bound by Mackays of Chatham PLC

ISBN 0 352 34025 8
ISBN 9 780352 34025 2

# Contents

For Will,

With many thanks

# Introduction

The stories of *The Transformation* are inspired by three traditional fairy tales. Such tales often originated as stories told by women, and many of them have been adapted and sanitised over the years. Frequently, the original tales contain a dark, erotic undercurrent, including themes like bondage and domination. They often allude to societal issues and even address more gruesome elements such as murder and rape. Love doesn't always conquer all, and human emotions like selfishness and greed can go unpunished, but the tales provide lessons to be learnt nonetheless. In *The Transformation*, three friends encounter the themes presented in fairy tales by the Brothers Grimm and Hans Christian Andersen. Along the way, the women learn some of the same lessons.

*Lydia's Transformation* is based on *The Frog Prince*, written by the Brothers Grimm in 1812. *The Frog Prince* tells the story of a self-centred princess who loses a golden ball in a pond. A frog offers to retrieve her ball, but only if she will make him her companion and allow him to eat with her at the dinner table and sleep in her bed at night. The princess agrees, but is loath to keep her promise until the king reminds her that her selfishness is wicked. The princess thus makes the frog her companion and wakes up one morning to discover that he has become a handsome prince. The prince tells her that he had been under the spell of a malicious fairy and was fated to remain a frog until a princess rescued him from the pond and took him as her companion. Having broken the spell, the princess and her new prince marry. In a contemporary revision of this story, Lydia Weston discovers that her personal reservations about a rather rumpled bookshop owner are preventing her from knowing him completely.

*The Princess and the Pea* is a short fairy tale written by Andersen in 1835. The story focuses on a prince in search of a princess to marry. One stormy night, a wet and bedraggled woman shows up at his door. Despite her appearance, she claims to be a princess. The prince and his mother, determined to put the woman to the test, take all the bedding off the bed and put a pea on the bedframe. They then stack twenty eiderdown mattresses on the frame and tell their guest to sleep there for the night. In the morning, the woman complains that she slept very badly because there was something hard in the bed. The prince realises that she is indeed a princess, since only a real princess could be that sensitive. In *The Discovery of Molly*, Harker Trevane seeks to prove that Molly Radcliffe is not a princess, but a real woman according to his own standards. To do so, he puts her to the test.

*Becoming Cassie* is based on the 1835 Andersen tale *Thumbelina*, the story of a tiny maiden born in a tulip flower. Much to Thumbelina's dismay, an ugly frog decides that she will make a perfect bride. Luckily, several fish, feeling sorry for Thumbelina, rescue her from the frog's marsh and leave her free to wander through the marshes and forest for a year, where she makes friends with a field-mouse and heals a sick swallow. Later she encounters an old mole who is also determined to make her his wife, but the thought of living in the subterranean darkness makes Thumbelina despondent. The swallow, wanting to repay her for her kindness, carries her away on his back and leaves her in a field of flowers. There, Thumbelina finds within a flower a tiny companion just her own size. Likewise, Cassie Langford contends with several unusual assignations before discovering her own ideal companion.

# Part 1
## *Lydia's Transformation*

# Chapter One

The elevator doors slid open. Lydia Weston stepped into the bustle of the *Savoir Faire* magazine offices as if she had just parted the Red Sea. Immaculately dressed in a Chanel suit that hugged every curve of her lush figure, she strode past the receptionist's desk and headed for her office. Her straight dark hair, cut in an elegant and sophisticated bob, brushed her shoulders as she walked. The heels of her Italian pumps beat a tattoo across the marble floor. She passed her assistant's desk, not breaking her stride as she picked up the cup of coffee waiting for her on the edge of Mona's desk.

'Good morning, Mona.'

'Lydia, the Calvin Klein people called fifteen minutes ago,' Mona said, before Lydia was out of earshot. 'They arrived at San Francisco airport a few hours ago, but they'll be on time for your nine o'clock meeting. And Zack is –'

'Thank you.' Lydia pushed open her office door and stepped into her sanctuary. Only after she had let the door close behind her did she notice the man lounging on the leather sofa.

'Zack.'

'Hello, love.' Zack lifted his gaze to her, his blue eyes sweeping approvingly over her. 'How are you?'

'You're not allowed in my office unless I invite you in,' Lydia said coldly, making a mental note to have a word with Mona about keeping people at bay.

She went to her desk and set her coffee mug on a coaster. Her office was her own private domain, a haven she had decorated herself in rich shades of cream and rust with glossy oil paintings on the walls and an imported, teakwood desk. A large window covered an

5

entire wall, providing a view of bustling Market Street. Lydia did not appreciate having her sanctuary invaded, particularly by an upstart fashion photographer who fancied himself God's gift to womankind. Ignoring him, she sat down in her custom-made, ergonomic chair and proceeded to check her e-mail messages.

'I've found a great spot for a shoot I'm doing on that new line of fall clothing,' Zack informed her. 'Remember you said you wanted an antique store atmosphere or something?'

Lydia peered at him. 'Yes. Lots of beige and browns in that line. I want a scholarly look.'

'There's a funky, little antique bookshop just off Chestnut,' Zack said. 'It's called Libri Antiqui. Lots of leather chairs and high bookshelves with those rickety old ladders. Sort of haphazardly organised, but the place has hardwood floors and fabulous, high ceilings. There's even a ladder leading to an upper loft where the owner lives. We'd have to bring in lots of lighting, but the atmosphere is fantastic. We could never recreate it in a studio.'

'Have you spoken with the owner?'

'I have an appointment with him on Thursday,' Zack replied. 'Do you want to come? You'd love the place.'

'Yes, if I don't have any other appointments.' Lydia returned her attention to her computer. 'Now, if there's nothing else, Zack, I have a great deal of work to do.'

'We having a meeting with the Calvin Klein honchos at nine,' Zack reminded her.

Lydia's gaze flickered to him again. He was sprawled on the sofa like a lazy panther, his long, lean body encased in worn jeans and a black, turtleneck sweater. His blue eyes glinted with a hunger she had seen before.

'That's half an hour from now,' Lydia reminded him.

'I like to get an early start.'

'I know.' Lydia smiled slightly. She was well aware that Zack perpetually woke up in the morning sporting an impressive erection.

'What are you wearing underneath that sexy suit, Ms Weston?'

Lydia's lips parted on an inaudible sigh, even as Zack's

husky purr sent a ripple of pleasure over her skin. She had never made it her policy to avoid sexual relationships with the members of her staff, and Zack was no exception. They had indulged in several voracious liaisons over the past few weeks, and Lydia had found Zack to be a greedy but also generous and obedient partner.

In her view, if her staff wanted to gossip about her sexual appetite with the young men on staff, then so be it. Her sexuality was hardly something of which she was ashamed. She commanded respect with both her attitude and her total comfort with herself, and she wasn't about to let some antiquated notion of business protocol rob her of her appreciation of sensuality. Besides, she made certain that the men were quite clear of their positions with respect to her. Sex with her was never something with which they could barter for favours or raises. And she was always the one on top.

Lydia leant back in her chair, tapping a manicured fingernail on her desk. 'Zachary, I am not at your beck and call.'

'No, ma'am.'

Lydia scowled. 'And don't call me "ma'am".'

He gave her another grin. 'Yes, ma'am.'

'Shame on you for goading me,' Lydia murmured.

'You just seem a little tense.'

Lydia sighed again. She was tense. Circulation of the magazine had been falling, and lately her staff seemed unable to come up with anything but the most mundane story ideas.

Her gaze slid to the clock on her desk. The Calvin Klein people would be here on time, and she desperately wanted their account. However, Zack's hungry sexuality was beginning to affect her. She had been unable to indulge in her usual self-pleasuring that morning, opting instead for another fifteen minutes of sleep. As a result, she was more rested, but also rather irritable.

Heaven forbid the Calvin Klein people would think of her as irritable.

Lydia pushed herself out of her chair in a languid movement and crossed the room. She locked the door and turned to look at Zack, who hadn't moved. His eyes, however, had that slow burn she had seen before, like molten lava on the brink of overflowing. She approached him slowly, pinning him to his place with her gaze as she grasped her skirt in her fists and began to draw it up over her thighs.

Zack stared at the luscious revelation of her stocking-clad thighs, the shadowy cleft barely hidden from him. He reached out impatiently to unsnap one of her suspenders, but Lydia swatted his hand away.

'No,' she said firmly. 'You don't touch.'

Zack swallowed hard, the movement of his throat muscles appearing highly erotic. Lydia bent down and stroked her tongue into the hot hollow at the base of his throat, liking the salty tang of his skin and the way his body shivered.

Drawing away, she put her foot on the coffee-table, giving him a full view of her shapely leg and thigh as she unsnapped the suspender. She repeated the move with her other leg, amused by Zack's entranced gaze. She hooked her fingers under the elastic band of her silky underwear and drew them over her thighs, feeling her heart start to pulse with arousal. There was nothing like having a man hunger for her to spark her own desires. She lifted her skirt further, allowing Zack a glimpse of her shaven mons. Excitement prickled her skin.

'Well, Zachary,' she murmured, 'do you want to please your boss?'

His lips parted, his chest heaving with his rapid breaths. 'Oh, yeah.'

'Good.'

She put her hand on Zack's shoulder and straddled his thighs, lowering her body just enough so that her sex brushed against the straining bulge in his jeans. A thrill shuddered through her body at the intimate contact. She pressed her vulva against him more firmly, enjoying the sensation of his rough jeans against her inner folds. She rocked back and forth, increasing the pressure, feeling the juices of her arousal begin to flow. Lowering her head, she took Zack's earlobe between her lips and sucked, drawing a low gasp from him.

'Lydia...' Zack manoeuvred his hands between them, fumbling to unzip his jeans and also stroke Lydia.

Under other circumstances, Lydia would have ordered him not to touch her yet, but they didn't have much time. She bit down gently on his earlobe.

'All right, Zack,' she whispered. 'Do it.'

His forefinger thrust upward as Lydia brought her body down, sinking on to his finger with a gratified sigh. She was already slick and ready, hungry for more than just Zack's finger inside her. His thumb swirled around the hard nub of her clitoris, evoking a shower of pleasurable shivers down her spine. Twisting her hips, she rode his finger, clenching her tight heat around him. She rubbed her breasts through her suit jacket, wishing they had time to strip completely. Her body felt tense and ravenous for a long, indulgent release, particularly since she had denied herself an orgasm that morning. However, quick and hard would have to do for now.

She undid the buttons of the jacket quickly, baring her ample breasts clad in a sheer demi-bra. Her nipples pressed painfully against the fabric, and Zack's eyes drifted half closed as he leant forward to capture one between his lips. The sensation of his sucking through the thin fabric felt delicious, tightening the ropes of tension around Lydia's lower body. Still, it wasn't enough, she was too constrained. She pushed Zack away so that she could unsnap the front clasp, baring her breasts to the hungry pleasure of his lips and tongue. With a groan of pure rapture, he licked at her hard nipples, winding his tongue around the areola of one breast as he massaged the other with his fingers.

Lydia moaned with pleasure, adoring the sensation of his hot breath on her sensitive flesh. She would have delved her fingers into his hair, but he had obviously spent time slicking it and styling it with a plentiful amount of hair products, and she didn't want to muss it before their meeting. Instead, she dug her fingernails into his shoulders and arched her back to give him better access to her breasts. Zack nuzzled and bit at her, little pants emerging from his lungs as he pushed his bulging erection up towards her.

Taking pity on him, Lydia reached between them to unzip his jeans, moving away slightly so that he could lift his hips. She tugged his jeans and shorts over his hips just enough to reveal the gorgeous length of his hard penis. She grasped the thick member in her hand, stroking it from base to tip and eliciting a groan from Zack. His skin was hot and throbbing, silky smooth to her touch. The sight of her coral-tipped fingers manipulating his stalk never ceased to inflame Lydia's arousal. Her sex swelled with moisture in readiness for delicious penetration. Adjusting her body over him, she closed her eyes and guided his cock into her tight passage, immersing him in her body with a slow sensuality that made them both gasp.

'Oh, Lydia, please,' Zack gasped. 'Ride me.'

Lydia smiled at his desperation. She loved driving men to the brink. She put her hands on his shoulders and began to lift her body up and down, letting him slide almost completely out of her before sinking back down. Her face grew flushed, her breath coming in rapid gasps. He was delectable, hard and pliable, and so, so willing to please her. She increased the rhythm, her knees sinking into the plush leather of the sofa as she drove her body down on to Zack's throbbing erection. His hands came around her to cup her buttocks, his fingers digging into her flesh as his features tensed in an obvious attempt to fight the urge to orgasm.

Pleased with his restraint, Lydia rubbed her fingers over her shaven mons, loving the sensation of her smooth, damp skin. She slipped her fingers just inside her labia to caress the swollen knot in which all her pleasure was centred. Tension wrapped around her body, tightening every nerve as she stroked her clitoris and let her other fingers drift over the oily hardness of Zack's cock. Faster and faster she rode him, spurred on by Zack's grunts, by the wet slapping of their bodies. Her breasts rocked and swayed in time with each accelerated submersion.

'Lydia.' The strained note in Zack's voice told Lydia that he was on the edge.

She wished she had time to torment him further, but she told herself that there would be plenty of time later that night. She commanded him to wait as she arched her body voluptuously, writhing and twisting her hips as she pleasured herself on his cock. A cry escaped her lips as pleasure skipped lusciously along her nerves and caused her body to shudder with violent waves of rapture. Instinctively, Lydia clamped her inner walls around Zack's penis, immersing him in her wet heat as he let out a hoarse shout and convulsed inside her.

'Good boy,' Lydia murmured.

She pulled her underwear back over her legs and reattached the suspender clasps to her stockings. She walked to the adjoining bathroom, buttoning up her suit jacket. After washing her hands and running a brush through her hair, she patted her face with a towel and checked her reflection in the mirror. A little flushed, but the added colour made her look vibrant.

When she returned to the office, Zack was still sprawled on the sofa. A knock sounded at the door, causing him to jump.

Lydia frowned, putting her hands on her hips.

'Go into the bathroom and make yourself decent,' she ordered.

Zack fumbled to stand, tucking his penis back into his pants as he hurried to the bathroom and closed the door. Lydia smoothed down her suit and fixed a smile on her face as she walked to the door, fully prepared to negotiate a profitable deal.

'Hello, Harlan.' Lydia smiled at the *maître d'* as she walked into the La Scene restaurant. She dined here often, enjoying the French-inspired food and bright, theatrical atmosphere.

'How nice to see you again, Ms Weston,' Harlan said warmly, reaching out to take her wrap. 'Your friend is already here. I have your usual table ready.'

'Wonderful. Thank you.' Lydia followed him across the room, drinking in the rich scents.

Sketches of theatrical actors and costume designs lined the walls, and glossy, potted plants gave the restaurant an elegant touch. The air rustled with the low murmur of voices and the clink of silverware.

Lydia glanced towards her usual table in a private corner of the room. Cassie Langford was already there, her attention concentrated on an open book. She was dressed in a beige, silk blouse and brown slacks that didn't exactly display her petite figure, but that looked trim and neat. Her brown hair was clasped at her neck with a silver clip, her fine-boned features accentuated with a minimal amount of cosmetics.

A smile tugged at Lydia's mouth. She adored Cassie just as she was, but that couldn't stop her from thinking that Cassie could be stunningly sensual if she would only make more of an effort.

Cassie turned, smiling with delight at the sight of Lydia coming towards her. 'Lydia.'

'Hello, precious.' Lydia bent and hugged the younger woman. 'You look lovely. Harlan, we'll have a bottle of Pinot Noir, I think.'

'Right away, Ms Weston.' Harlan hurried off to fulfil the order.

'You've not been here long, I hope,' Lydia said as she settled into her seat.

'No, I arrived early.' Cassie pushed the basket of warm bread towards Lydia 'How are you?'

'Wildly busy.' Lydia crossed her long legs and broke off a piece of the bread. 'I'm so glad to get away and talk with you. I cut a new advertising deal with Calvin Klein just this morning.'

Cassie's eyebrows lifted. 'Calvin Klein himself?'

Lydia chuckled. 'No, doll, the company. I met with his advertising people. What about you? How are classes?'

'Good. I've also spent the week applying for a research grant for the book I'm writing about William Blake.'

'Girls, I'm sorry I'm late!'

Both Lydia and Cassie looked up to find their friend Molly Radcliffe dashing across the restaurant towards them, a distressed Harlan following in an effort to take her cape. Molly's auburn curls, even curlier due to the foggy day, bounced with each step. Her slender figure, encased in an exotic-looking Chinese jacket and silk pants, drew more than one glance.

Both Lydia and Cassie stood to receive Molly's enthused embraces as Harlan stood by patiently waiting to execute his coat duties. Molly slipped out of her cape and handed it to him along with a dazzling smile.

'Oh, I'm exhausted.' Molly sank into her chair and gave an exaggerated sigh. 'I'm supposed to be planning a debutante ball for a group of young ladies, but times have changed so drastically since we were young. I really don't know what children want nowadays.'

She made it sound like they were all a hundred years old. Lydia and Cassie exchanged smiles over Molly's dramatics.

'Well, you must relax for the next couple of hours.' Lydia squeezed Molly's hand. 'You look incredibly exotic. Wherever did you find that outfit?'

Molly glanced down at herself as if to remember what she was wearing. 'Oh, isn't this gorgeous? I found it on a shopping trip to Hong Kong about a year ago. I meant to tell you both about it, in case you want me to get you one the next time I go.'

She reached for her wine and took a long draught. 'I'm flying to Milan next week, did I tell you that? Let me know if you want anything.' She glanced at Cassie. 'Sweetie, wouldn't you love me to pick you up an Italian suit?'

Cassie smiled and shook her head. 'Molly, I can't afford an Italian suit.'

'I'll buy it for you. An early birthday present.'

'That's very generous of you, but no.'

'Cassie, if you'd just give me your measurements, I know a wonderful designer who would create something just for you.'

'No, Molly, I really can't.'

'It doesn't have to be ridiculously expensive, but something that would just caress that cute little figure of yours.'

Amused, Lydia sipped her wine and listened to her two friends bantering back and forth, letting her mind drift back into the past.

She thought about how long they had known each other, how their strong friendship had been formed in the adverse circumstances of boarding school. Lydia and Molly had been twelve years old and the undisputed leaders of their class when Cassie, a skinny, nervous ten-year-old arrived at the school. Rumours and whispers had started about her immediately, how her mother was an alcoholic and her father had walked out on her. An uncle had paid for Cassie to live at the boarding school, a place normally reserved for the upper crust of San Francisco society. No one knew how Cassie's uncle had managed to get his niece accepted into the school, but it was clear from the start that Cassie hardly belonged.

Out of her element among girls bred in sophisticated, cultured households, Cassie had withdrawn. She spent her first few weeks alone, ignoring the other girls until several of the nastier ones decided that she would make a good target for ridicule. She became the brunt of their jokes and their games, although no one else paid much attention to her. That is, until one day when Lydia found Cassie sobbing in the bathroom because someone had flushed a photograph of her mother down the toilet.

Lydia's twelve-year-old heart had cracked at the new girl's sheer dismay. She had helped Cassie smooth out the wet, ruined photograph, and then they took it to the headmistress to see if it could be fixed. Cassie had been so grateful, and Lydia found herself genuinely liking the skinny, gauche girl. She and Molly, who had always had a soft spot for hurt creatures, had been more than willing to take Cassie under their respective wings. And once it was known that Molly and Lydia had become firm friends with Cassie, the pranks stopped. Cassie lived out the rest of her years at boarding school in peace. She had been upset when Molly and Lydia graduated, and even more distraught when Lydia left to attend university, but she excelled in her classes and made other friends.

Still, the three of them remained oddly close. Cassie and Molly spent most of their free time together as Cassie finished school and Molly flitted from job to job. They were always thrilled when Lydia returned home for weekends or holidays, making a point of spending as much time with her as possible. Cassie entered a university close by to earn her doctorate, and they never lost touch with each other. Lydia moved to New York for a few years as she worked her way up the ranks of the magazine, but returned to San Francisco when *Savoir Faire* opened an office in the city.

'Ms Weston, are you ready to order?' The waiter's voice intruded into Lydia's thoughts.

She looked up, realising that three pairs of eyes were watching her expectantly. 'Oh, yes. I'll have the monkfish ravioli, please.'

'Very good.' The waiter wrote down the order and glided silently away.

'You're OK, Lydia?' Cassie asked, a slight frown of worry between her eyebrows. 'I hope you're not working too hard.'

'No, I'm fine. The magazine could use some help, but I suppose all businesses go through peaks and valleys.'

'What kind of help?' Molly asked. 'Money? Do you need financing? You know my father would gladly invest in the magazine if I asked him.'

'Thanks, love, but no,' Lydia replied. 'That's not it. We need something interesting, something to boost sales and move ahead of the competition. Our story ideas are starting to get repetitive, and our photography is downright mundane.'

'Even with that photographer you introduced me to?' Cassie asked, her brown eyes sparkling with a hint of mischief.

Lydia's mouth curved into a wry smile. 'Yes, even with Zack,' she said. 'Although, I must say, it's only his photography that's mundane.'

Molly giggled. 'Lucky you, getting to spend all your time with such hunky creative men.'

'Well, Zack happens to be one of the few hunky creative men who isn't gay,' Lydia replied. 'Unfortunately, that also means he has a penchant for the women he photographs.'

'Tell him to photograph some men,' Cassie suggested.

Lydia looked at her friend. 'Men?'

'Sure. Put a men's photo spread in the magazine.'

'Cassie, women don't want to look at men in a fashion magazine,' Molly interjected. She flashed another smile at the waiter as he placed their food in front of them.

Lydia gazed at Cassie thoughtfully. 'That might not be a bad idea.'

Cassie looked surprised. 'Really?'

'Yes. Perhaps accompanied by an article about what women can do with men.'

'Some of us know quite well what to do with men, thank you,' Molly said, earning a chuckle from Cassie.

Lydia gave Molly an amused look. '*You* know what to do with men, Molly, but many women don't. Maybe we could do a spread about how women can bring out the best in their man.'

'That's easy,' Molly said around a mouthful of roasted duck, orange vinaigrette, and walnuts. 'You just said it. Do a spread.'

Cassie laughed. 'Molly, you're incorrigible.'

'What if we devoted an entire issue to men?' Lydia asked, warming to the topic. 'With different subjects pertaining to relationships, sexuality, fashion, entertainment. We could interview men from different businesses to find out what they're looking for in a woman, and do a photo spread on how to help a man dress properly.'

Molly pointed her fork at Lydia. 'Now there you have something. If there's anything a man *doesn't* know how to do, it's dress properly. I mean, it doesn't take much imagination to match a tie to a suit jacket, but how many men can do that?'

'Why don't you gear the entire issue towards men?' Cassie asked. 'An issue that women would buy for their man to read?'

Lydia stared at Cassie. 'Darling, you're brilliant. Totally and utterly brilliant. Would you come and work for me?'

Two pink spots of pleasure appeared on Cassie's cheeks. 'You think that would work?'

'Work? My God, it's pure genius. Men would never buy a fashion magazine, but if we could get women to buy it for them ...' Lydia's voice trailed off at the magnitude of the idea. A burst of adrenalin rushed through her veins, a feeling terribly close to the physical thrill of an orgasm. Any tediousness she had been feeling disappeared in the face of the excitement of a new project, a new idea.

She reached out to squeeze Cassie's hand. 'Cassie, you've saved me. I'm forever grateful.'

Cassie smiled.

## Chapter Two

'Here it is.' Nicholas Hawthorne took a book from the high shelf and grabbed a handkerchief from his pocket. He wiped a thin layer of dust off the book cover, sneezed, and stuffed the handkerchief back into his pocket. Tucking the book under his arm, he descended the ladder.

His customer, a distinguished, grey-haired man wearing a suit and bow tie, held out his hands eagerly. 'Well, my boy, I'm delighted. I never thought you would have this. Poor old Hendrik van Loon is difficult to find nowadays.'

'Let me know if there's anything else by him that you're looking for, Professor,' Nicholas said. 'I'll be happy to do a search for you.'

The professor looked down at the book, stroking his hand lovingly over the cover.

'Olive will ring it up for you.' Nicholas glanced towards the front desk, hoping to find his flirtatious employee actually working rather than filing her fingernails.

Olive was a student at the local university who had convinced him that her major in English literature made her an ideal candidate for a part-time position as a sales clerk. Nicholas suspected that the sight of Olive's abundant cleavage rather than her knowledge of literature had played more of a role in his hiring of her. He now paid a daily penance for letting his hormones dictate his business decisions.

'Olive,' he called. 'Professor Martin has a purchase.'

Olive looked up from her careful nail filing and snapped her gum. 'Okey doke, boss. How's it going, Professor?'

'Fine, dear, fine.' Even the professor's gaze slipped down to the generous valley revealed by Olive's low-necked sweater.

Nicholas sighed and adjusted his tortoiseshell glasses. One of these days, he was going to hire a friendly, little old lady who wore lace collars up to her neck, smelled of camphor, and whose last sexual experience had taken place during World War Two.

He turned and climbed back up the ladder to rearrange the books and fill the hole created by the professor's purchase.

'He's gone, boss.' Olive called from below.

Nicholas looked down at her from his perch, only to discover that she was standing next to the ladder. She was a pretty, plump blonde girl with a mischievous sparkle in her blue eyes, which were currently upturned and gazing at him. 'Good, Olive. Now, if you could please finish doing the inventory on the history section, I'd appreciate it.'

'Sure thing.' She didn't move.

Irritated, Nicholas shoved the books back into place and descended a few steps. 'Olive, when I give you a job, I expect you to do it.'

'I know.'

Nicholas immediately realised his mistake in pausing halfway down the ladder, as Olive was now at a perfect eye-level with his crotch. Worse, she was staring directly at it.

To his horror, he felt his penis start to swell with arousal. His position gave him a full view of the tops of Olive's creamy breasts, which only served to remind him how long it had been since he'd been with a woman. He could see the hard points of her nipples pressing against the front of her sweater. The deep crevice created by her full mounds fairly begged to be filled with the length of a hard cock... Oh, damn. Nicholas winced and gripped the sides of the ladder as his trousers tightened further and his penis began to throb. Mentally, he told himself to get off the ladder, but he couldn't seem to move.

Maybe because Olive's gaze was fixing him to the spot. Her blue eyes lingered on the growing bulge at his crotch as she snapped her gum. She lifted her eyes to him, a small smile playing about her full, red lips.

'You know, boss, I've been thinking that you should put together an erotica and sexuality section,' she remarked.

Nicholas swallowed hard, willing his body under control. 'Um, erotica?'

'Uh huh. Erotic classics like the stories of the Marquis de Sade, *The Story of O*, some of that fabulous Victorian smut.'

'We have some of that.'

Olive's eyebrows lifted. 'Do we? Where?'

Anything to get her away from such close proximity to his groin. 'Over in the fiction section.'

'Hmm. Maybe I can be in charge of organising certain titles into a specific erotica section.'

'Great. Why don't you go get started?'

'OK.' She didn't move, but her gaze slipped back down to his erection. 'Some of that Victorian erotica is pretty hot, don't you think?'

'I wouldn't know.'

'You mean you've never read it?'

'No.' Nicholas's hands tightened on the ladder. This was insane.

'Pity. Maybe I'll have to read some to you sometime. It's quite raunchy, all that repressed sexuality suddenly bursting forth in these amazingly orgiastic scenarios.'

Nicholas coughed and sought to regain his composure and his position as her employer. 'Olive, this is highly inappropriate.'

'Your trousers don't seem to think so.' With a wicked little grin, Olive lifted her manicured hand and pressed it against the protrusion in his pants, her fingers cupping and caressing it.

A layer of perspiration broke out on Nicholas's forehead at the sensation of the luscious pressure. 'Olive –'

'Relax, boss. I'm supposed to be helping you out here. I mean, you're not paying me to file my nails now, are you?'

She winked up at him and took the zipper of his

trousers between her fingers, slowly pulling it down. The raspy sound filled the air. Nicholas looked hurriedly towards the front door. There were no customers in the store, but someone could walk in at any moment. A shudder of excitement ran through Nicholas's body, and his fingers dug into the ladder when Olive slipped her hand into his open fly and began fondling the length of his penis.

'My, my, you really are the big boss, aren't you?' She grinned.

'Olive . . .' For the life of him, Nicholas knew that he would never be able to stop this, not when Olive's warm fingers were touching his cock and easing it out of his trousers. His heart began to pound violently, his breath escaping him in rapid gasps.

Her expression both hungry and aroused, Olive murmured a series of low sounds of approval as the length of Nicholas's erection came into view. Her tongue flickered out to caress her lower lip. Nicholas nearly lost control at the delectable sight, his entire body suddenly aching for the sensation of her pink tongue on his cock. Olive's fingers wrapped around his bursting shaft, and she squeezed him lightly, drawing her cupped hand up and down the length with slow, sensual movements.

'What a waste to hide such a magnificent specimen under those baggy trousers you wear,' she murmured, her eyes gleaming as she traced the thick veins on his penis, rubbing her fingers over the hard knob.

Oh, Christ. The sensation and sight of her fondling was almost more than Nicholas could stand. He'd been relying on his own devices for longer than he cared to remember, and a perfectly luscious woman now appeared to be enraptured with his cock. He stared down at her, gripping the ladder so tightly he thought the wood would crack and splinter under the pressure. His glasses fogged.

'I'll bet you taste just delicious.' Olive smiled up at him before she leant forward and encased the head of his penis between her pouty lips.

Nicholas drew in a sharp breath. The feeling of her hot, wet mouth slowly enclosing him was an exquisite torment. His entire body pulsed with need. With an expertise he could not help but notice, Olive began to slide the length of his penis into her mouth as her other hand dipped down to caress the tight sacs between his legs. She rubbed her fingers over the crinkly skin, creating such a rush of sensation that Nicholas fairly trembled. Heat prickled along his skin, and he had to gasp to draw in a breath. Pressure built at the base of his cock, signalling an imminent orgasm, and he managed to croak out Olive's name in warning.

Olive's tongue licked up his shaft, dipping into the indentation at the tip as she slowly pulled away from him. Her pale skin was flushed with arousal, blooming a lovely reddish colour on her cheeks. She looked up at him, her breath emerging in hot, little bursts to torture his aching penis.

'Would you like to fuck my tits, boss?' she asked, her voice husky and raw.

Nicholas stared at her, stunned that she had fairly read his earlier thoughts. His throat worked as he tried to formulate a reply.

'I see you staring at my breasts,' Olive said, slipping one hand down to finger her hard nipple through her sweater. 'Nice, aren't they? I've been wondering what you think when you look at them. Don't you imagine what it would be like to thrust your cock between them?'

Nicholas could hardly breathe. Sweat trickled down his back, and flames seemed to encase his entire body. His cock was so hard it hurt.

'Come down a step.' Olive's fingers moved to the buttons of her sweater, and she began to unfasten them, revealing her breasts clad in a bra that seemed too small to contain her abundant flesh. The sight was a glorious one, and Nicholas descended another step in a daze, his penis jutting out in front of him like a rigid pole.

'One more.' Olive reached out to tug his trousers down his legs, then slipped out of her sweater and reached behind her to unfasten her bra clasp.

Her breasts spilled out like gorgeous, ripe fruits, topped with round, pink nipples that jutted forth. Nicholas nearly came right then and there, and only the thought of burying his cock between such delicious breasts reined in his control. He stepped down another rung, his chest heaving as Olive took his oiled cock in her hand and guided it between her breasts.

A shiver of pure sensuality rippled through his body as Olive cushioned his erection between her warm, resilient flesh. She cupped her hands underneath her breasts, her fingers stroking her nipples as she pushed them together to create a deep valley. Nicholas thought he could have quite happily died right then and there. His shaft pulsed and throbbed against Olive's hot skin, burrowed in total, sensual pleasure.

Still gripping the ladder to maintain his balance, Nicholas drew back slightly and began to thrust his penis back and forth between Olive's breasts. She gave him a slow smile, pressing her globes even tighter around him. Nicholas's entire body tensed with sheer excitement. God, it was amazing, her voluptuousness totally wrapped around a raging erection, surrounding and immersing it as if in imitation of a more intimate kind of enclosure.

'That's right, lover, fuck them hard,' Olive urged, bending to lick at the head of his penis as it appeared in sporadic, rapid thrusts between the crevice of her cleavage. 'Ah, you have no idea what it feels like to have such a thick, long cock moving between my tits.'

Nicholas's mind spun with sensation and heat. He worked his hips back and forth with an increasing rhythm, unable to take his eyes off the sight of his shaft thrusting back and forth between Olive's breasts. The luxurious friction of Olive's soft skin and his cock increased his intense arousal, and the intermittent lick of her wet tongue nearly drove him over the edge.

Pressure seemed to envelop his entire body, centring in the aching swell of his penis, and then he could no longer stand it. With a pained shout, he rammed his cock upward, feeling Olive squeeze her breasts tighter around him as jets of semen spurted out on to her creamy flesh. Pleasure wracked Nicholas's entire body, making him shake with the intensity of it all.

'Jesus, Olive.' He could barely catch his breath.

She smiled up at him again, reaching up to slide her fingers over his moist penis as it began to soften and slide out of the warm valley in which it had so happily been nestled. Nicholas closed his eyes and leant his forehead against the ladder, his chest heaving.

'I knew you'd been wanting to do that,' Olive said. 'I've been wanting you to, you know. That and much more.'

Nicholas opened his eyes and looked down at her. 'You have?'

'Mmm.' Olive began rubbing the damp trails of his seed into her breasts, making her skin shine with his arousal. 'I had a feeling you were a sexy man, boss. I mean, you're a complete nerd, but I knew something was simmering underneath all your geekiness.'

Nicholas gave a hoarse laugh. 'Thanks. I think.'

He pulled out his handkerchief and handed it to her, but Olive grinned and shook her head, still stroking her glossy breasts. 'Semen is good for the skin, you know. Lots of protein.'

'Olive, you're a very wicked girl.'

Olive laughed. 'Yeah. Lucky for you.'

'Hello?' The bell heralding a customer's entrance into the store tingled suddenly, making Nicholas start.

He turned and stared over the bookcases to the front of the store, horrified to find a man and woman standing there. Belatedly, he remembered his appointment with a photographer from a fashion magazine.

The man spotted him over the shelves and lifted a hand. 'Zack Donovan from *Savoir Faire*,' he called. He began making his way towards them.

'Wait!' Nicholas shouted.

The abruptness of his command made both the man and woman stop. Nicholas realised that the bookshelves hid his state of undress, but he and Olive would never be decent in the time it took the couple to cross the store.

'I'll be with you in a minute,' Nicholas called. 'Help yourself to some coffee. It's right by the door.'

'Great.' The man and woman exchanged looks over his odd behaviour, but Nicholas didn't care what they thought as long as they didn't try to approach him right now. Quickly, he descended the ladder, adjusting himself and zipping his pants.

Giggling, Olive slipped back into her bra and sweater. 'Imagine if they'd come in five minutes ago,' she whispered, her eyes sparkling. 'They would have seen you thrusting your hips like a wild man.'

'Thank heavens for small favours,' Nicholas replied, embarrassed by the mere thought of such an incident.

Olive glanced down at his groin. 'Well, I wouldn't call it a *small* favour,' she said.

'Olive, behave yourself.'

'Sure, boss. For now.' She gave him a saucy wink and headed off to greet the couple, the luscious swell of her hips swaying.

Nicholas took a deep breath, straightened his glasses, and tried to regain his composure. He would have plenty of time later to think about what had just happened, but now he had a meeting. He walked to the front of the store, where Zack and the woman were waiting near the coffee machine.

'I'm Nicholas Hawthorne, the owner of the store,' he said, holding out his hand. 'This is my associate, Olive.'

'Lydia Weston, senior editor of *Savoir Faire*.' The woman took his hand and gave it a firm shake, then turned to greet Olive.

She was a striking, sophisticated woman with a cool, dark gaze, and attractive features made all the more elegant by the rather imperious way she carried herself. Her eyes slid from Nicholas to Olive, taking in their flushed features and rumpled appearances with a keen perception that made Nicholas hugely uncomfortable.

Quickly, he turned to Zack and shook his hand. 'I understand from your message that you want to do some photography here.'

'That's right,' Zack said. 'Your store has a great atmosphere for a line of clothing we're going to highlight.'

'And we're looking to do more shoots on location around the city,' Lydia Weston added. She glanced around the book-filled store, and Nicholas suddenly wished he had taken the time to straighten up and do a little dusting.

'Sorry, Ms Weston, we've been doing inventory so it's kind of a mess.'

Lydia Weston's gaze went back to him. 'Call me Lydia, please, Nicholas. Your store is lovely. Reminds me a bit of an old library or a gentlemen's club.'

Nicholas was embarrassed by how pleased he was at her compliment. 'Thanks. Um, do you want to just look around?'

'Yes, we'd like to take some preliminary photos and see if this will work for us,' Zack said.

Nicholas frowned slightly. 'Then after you're finished looking, we can talk about whether or not your fashion shoot will work for me.'

Lydia Weston looked at him for a moment. A hint of something appeared in her eyes, and Nicholas didn't know if it was admiration or annoyance.

He blushed anyway. 'I just mean I don't want to inconvenience my business.'

'Of course not,' Lydia replied smoothly. 'We would never think of intruding.'

She nodded at Zack, and the two of them began browsing around the store and discussing the possibilities of a shoot. The sound of Zack's camera clicking echoed through the store.

Nicholas let out his breath in a sigh. Lydia Weston was obviously a sharp woman who had picked up on the fact that he and Olive had been engaging in a tryst. For some odd reason, the thought annoyed him, although he didn't think that his irritation was based on embarrassment. No, it was more the idea of Lydia Weston thinking that he was the kind of man who got off on regularly banging his employees during business hours.

'Well, they're very avant-garde, aren't they?' Olive had resumed her position behind the counter, and she gave Nicholas a grin. 'They seem like the kind of people who might have joined us.'

Nicholas shook his head. 'Olive, you're unbelievable.'

'So I've been told.'

'Would you please act professional right now?' Nicholas said. 'I'd prefer that people don't think this bookshop is a front for an orgy club.'

'Hey, now, there's an idea,' Olive said.

Nicholas gave her a dark look just as the bell rang to announce the entrance of another customer. Relieved, Nicholas turned his attention to the customer and soon became engrossed in a discussion of first editions of Steinbeck novels.

He spent the next hour with several customers, but was constantly aware of the presence of Zack Donovan and Lydia Weston as they meandered about the store and discussed lighting and locations. After the customer left with three books, Nicholas approached Zack and Lydia.

'If you'd like to talk, I have some free time right now.'

'Perfect,' Lydia said. 'We love your store, and we'd love to use it for one of our shoots. Unfortunately, we'd like to do the shoot during the day, and I see from your schedule outside that you're open seven days a week.'

'Yes, but I'm willing to be flexible as long as I have adequate prior notice.' Nicholas wondered why Lydia Weston looked as if she were dissolving into an apparition, and then he realised that his glasses were fogging up again. He took them off, wondering why he was getting so warm, and cleaned the lenses on his jacket sleeve.

'Maybe we can discuss dates.' He replaced his glasses on his nose, glancing up to find Lydia looking at him strangely. 'I'm sorry, is there a problem?'

She shook her head, seeming to pull herself together. 'No. No problem. Is there a quiet place where the three of us can sit down and talk?'

'My office is in the back. I'll bring coffee.' He gestured to the door at the rear of the store and returned to the coffee machine. 'Olive, please call me only if it's urgent.'

'Sure, boss. Urgency is my speciality.'

Nicholas sighed as he walked to his office with the coffee. Clearly, his relationship with Olive would never be the same again.

*   *   *

Lydia crossed her legs and took a sip of coffee from the recyclable paper cup Nicholas Hawthorne had given her. She glanced around his cluttered office. A small desk with a computer sat in the corner, and the rest of the space was filled with file folders, inventory sheets, and books. An entire leather-bound collection of Greek and Roman authors was stacked on the floor, and the walls were covered with photographs of famous authors.

She liked it. The place had a comfortable, intellectual atmosphere, not unlike Nicholas Hawthorne himself. She let her gaze settle on him. He was wearing corduroy trousers, a wrinkled linen shirt, and an old suit jacket that had holes in the lapel and elbows. His shoes were a scruffed pair of loafers that looked a hundred years old. His dark hair, badly cut and ruffled, brushed his collar. His face was obscured by a pair of tortoiseshell glasses and a scraggly beard. However, Lydia had been quite surprised when he had removed his glasses and revealed beautiful, dark eyes, thickly lashed and with well-arched eyebrows.

She wondered just what he had been doing with that lush associate of his. They had both looked as if they'd been exerting themselves quite heavily. Lydia suspected that they hadn't been hauling books around.

Nicholas looked up suddenly to find her watching him. A charming flush rose to colour his cheekbones. 'Um, do you want more coffee, Ms ... I mean, Lydia?'

Lydia glanced down at her nearly full cup, not wanting to hurt his feelings by telling him how awful the coffee tasted.

'No, thank you. I'm trying to cut back on caffeine.' She placed the cup on the desk and leant forward. 'Nicholas, we're willing to pay you well for letting us invade your space for a day. Of course, we'll have to move some things around, but everything will be put back. We will need you to temporarily close the store, but the compensation will be worth it.'

He was staring at her lips as she talked. Then, he nodded. 'Yes. Yes, I can see that.'

Lydia felt as if he had touched her lips rather than

merely looked at them. She lifted her fingers to her lips, aware of an odd tingling sensation. 'Good,' she murmured, telling herself she was being utterly foolish. 'Then it's all set. We'll plan for a week from Monday.'

She rose and extended her hand. 'Thank you for your time, Nicholas. We'll be in touch.'

'Would you ... um...' Nicholas's voice trailed off as another flush covered his face. 'Would you like to have dinner sometime?'

Lydia was startled. 'Dinner? With you?'

'Yes.'

Lydia could only imagine what it would be like going out with Nicholas. She didn't consider herself to be incredibly shallow, but as the senior editor of a fashion magazine, she did have standards. Standards that not even this odd sexual attraction could overcome. 'No, Nicholas, I'm afraid that wouldn't be possible.'

'Oh. All right.'

Lydia tried to quell the discomfort that rose in her stomach. She looked at Zack, who was barely repressing a grin. 'Come along, Zack.'

They said their goodbyes to Olive, who gave Zack a wink, and returned to Zack's Mercedes.

'Can you even believe he asked you to dinner?' Zack said. 'The nerve!'

'Stop it, Zack. He was just being polite.' Lydia settled into the leather seat. 'Good scouting, by the way. I like the idea of finding obscure places for photo shoots.'

'Yeah, those obscure places give the proprietors some privacy as well.'

Lydia looked at him. 'What does that mean?'

'Oh, come on. You know that Nicholas fellow was shagging his yummy little piece when we walked in.'

Lydia frowned at Zack's crudeness, discovering that she didn't like the idea of him knowing what Nicholas had been doing. It was one thing for her to speculate, but quite another for Zack to do so.

'Zack, he was standing on a ladder.'

Zack shrugged and eased the powerful car out into the traffic. 'Maybe she was giving him a hand job or a blow job or something. You saw them, Lydia. They both looked pretty ravished, and two of her buttons were undone.'

'You're overreacting. You have a one-track mind.'

'Do I?' He grinned at her devilishly.

'Yes.' Irritated, Lydia crossed her arms and stared out the side window. An image of Nicholas Hawthorne and Olive indulging in a hot quickie while standing up against the bookshelves appeared in her mind. It was not an image she liked.

'I don't know what she would see in him, frankly,' Zack continued. 'I mean, he looks like he just crawled out of a hole.'

'That's enough, Zack.'

Zack glanced at her. 'Are you coming back to the office with me, or do you want me to drop you off at home?'

Lydia glanced at her watch. Four in the afternoon was usually far too early for her to go home, but she didn't relish the idea of returning to the office. For some reason, she was restless. 'Leave me at home.'

Zack manoeuvred the car through the streets to Lydia's stately home in the posh Pacific Heights section of the city. He pulled up in front of the Italian-style mansion and stopped the car.

'Want me to come in with you?' he asked suggestively.

'No.' Lydia retrieved her briefcase from the backseat. 'Tell everyone at the office I don't want to be disturbed unless there's an emergency.'

'OK.' Zack leant over to kiss her cheek, but Lydia pulled away so that his lips brushed her hair.

'We'll talk tomorrow about the shoot,' she said. 'Thanks for driving.'

She hurried away from the car and went into her house, feeling an immediate rush of relief at being back in her sanctuary. She had made a point of decorating the home with warm antiques and paintings to give it an elegant but welcoming atmosphere. Her decor, enhanced by the bay views at each of the four levels, also made the house a perfect place for entertaining.

The housekeeper had gone for the day, leaving the faint scent of furniture polish in the air. Lydia dropped her briefcase on the foyer table and kicked off her shoes as she headed up the plush, carpeted staircase to her bedroom.

After checking her answering machine, which contained three messages from Molly in dire need of advice for her debutante ball and one from Cassie asking her to dinner this weekend, Lydia stripped off her suit and went into the bathroom. She turned on the shower and glanced at herself in the full-length mirror as she waited for the water to warm. She was proud of her body, liking the way the lean lines of her curved hips complimented her full breasts and large nipples, and the way her shaven mons left nothing to the imagination.

Stepping into the shower, Lydia tried to let the tension of the past few weeks wash away. She pumped a generous amount of bath gel into her palm and stroked it over her abdomen and breasts, swirling the tips of her fingers around her hard nipples. Another image of Nicholas Hawthorne and Olive came into her mind, only this time it wasn't disturbing, but arousing.

Warmth flooded into her area between her thighs as she imagined what Olive's pretty plumpness would look like naked. She could picture it in her mind's eye, the two of them, Olive and Nicholas. Olive's leg would be wrapped around Nicholas's thigh as he pushed her up against one of those rickety, old bookshelves, pumping his penis into her as he bit at her voluptuous breasts. Olive's nipples would be hard and rosy, rubbing against Nicholas's hairy chest as her body shook with each subsequent jolt.

Lydia bit down on her lower lip, smoothing the bath gel over her belly and dipping her fingers between her legs. Her labia was moist with arousal, her clitoris twinging at the light brush of her fingertips. She wanted to bury her fingers deep inside her body, but she forced herself to take her fingers away. With slow, deliberate caresses, she stroked the gel over her firm, rounded buttocks, sliding her fingers into the crevice between her cheeks. Her body began to feel hot and languid, her mind filled with images of Nicholas and Olive thrusting and pumping against a backdrop of literary genius and leather bookcovers.

What would they sound like, she wondered, thinking of Olive's clear, pure voice when she had spoken to them. Her voice would deepen with passion, certainly, becoming a low purr in Nicholas's ear. And what would he say to her while he was sliding his hands under her luscious thighs, opening her fully for his penetration?

*Yes, you're hungry for it, my Olive, hungry for the feeling of my long cock inside that sweet little pussy of yours. Come on, I want to hear you moan and beg. Tell me how much you want it, tell me . . .*

Lydia shivered, her blood throbbing at the thought of Nicholas Hawthorne murmuring such lewd phrases. Her skin was hot as she stroked gel over the curved length of her legs, then rotated luxuriously underneath the shower spray to rinse her naked body. She reached out and turned off the shower, then grabbed a towel from the heated rack. She wrapped the towel around herself and went into her bedroom, her sex aching with the need for release. She took her vibrator out of a drawer in her night table and switched it on, then stretched out on her bed and let the towel fall open.

Ah, God, she couldn't remember the last time she had been so aroused by a fantasy. Letting her eyelids drift closed, she pictured them again, the slick slide of Nicholas's hard penis stroking in and out of Olive's spread channel. His tight balls slapped against the young woman, evoking the wet, delicious sounds of sex. Olive's breasts shook and bounced with the force of his thrusts, her high cries of pleasure spurring him to thrust harder, faster, deeper.

Lydia parted her lips and moaned, stroking the phallus over her breasts and nipples, over her belly to the painful centre of her need. Her damp skin prickled with cold, but the air only served to heighten her senses and her arousal. She slipped the dildo between her legs, her body jerking with pleasure at the feeling of the vibrations against her velvety folds as she slowly began to push it into her vagina. Longing pulsed in her blood, colouring her skin with the reddish flush of passion, evaporating the lingering droplets of water on her body.

'Oh!' She arched her back, thrusting the vibrator in further, revelling in the sensations against her inner walls, sensations that trailed along every nerve ending. Her loins constricted with the advent of pleasure.

Nicholas was now lifting Olive's legs over his arms, spreading her so far apart that Lydia had a clear view of the thick root of his penis, well oiled by Olive's abundant juices, slipping back and forth. He stroked his fingers over Olive's swollen clitoris, eliciting a cry of ecstasy from the woman as she clung to his shoulders and received the full extent of his frenzied plunges.

Lydia grasped the base of the phallus, stroking it in and out of her body with increasingly rapid movements. Her hips pumped wildly to match her strokes, her mind filled with the sounds and sights of Olive and Nicholas fucking in the bookshop. He thrust into her again and again and again, making her sob with rapture and orgasm after orgasm until a burst of intense colours exploded in Lydia's body.

She cried out, shoving the vibrator up into her body and clenching her muscles around it as she succumbed to the vast, intense wave of her climax. And then suddenly, it was no longer Nicholas and Olive in her fantasy, but Nicholas and Lydia, and she was riding out her pleasure on his penis with his broad hands gripping her thighs and his hot breath on her breasts.

'Lydia, I have some of that wine you like.' Cassie stood on tiptoe to reach into her cupboard. She was dressed in jeans and an oversized shirt that made her look even more petite. 'Cabernet from the Hundred Acres vineyard in Napa.'

'Love, you know you don't have to buy wine for me,' Lydia said in dismay, aware of how expensive the wine was. She knew Cassie didn't make much money as an English literature professor, and she didn't like the thought of Cassie wasting her money just to please her.

'I know I don't.' Cassie began peeling off the cap of the bottle and flashed Lydia a quick smile across the threshold that separated the kitchen from the sitting room. 'But I like to.'

Lydia returned her smile, forcing herself not to say anything and hurt Cassie's feelings. Cassie had refused to let her bring anything to dinner, and the delicious scents of pesto and tortellini drifted from the kitchen.

'Did you find out about that research grant?' Lydia asked.

'Not yet.' Cassie poured wine into two glasses and came into the sitting room. 'I should hear by the end of the semester. If I get it, I'll have enough money to travel to London for research. Hopefully for an entire year.'

She handed Lydia one of the glasses and perched on the edge of an overstuffed chair. Lydia thought that Cassie looked extremely comfortable in her surroundings. Her friend lived on the second floor of a two-storey, Victorian building on the fringe of Russian Hill, a lovely, bright place with bay windows and hardwood floors. Molly, being the premiere shopper, had helped her decorate it with good-quality, inexpensive furniture and prints. Both Lydia and Molly would have loved to help Cassie out more financially, but they knew that Cassie's pride would never allow it. Even now, Lydia had to bite her tongue to prevent herself from suggesting that she fund Cassie's research trip to London.

'What's happening with that men's issue of the magazine?' Cassie asked.

'I have most of the staff writing stories already,' Lydia replied. 'That really is a wonderful idea, Cassie. Zack is even looking forward to photographing some male models.'

Cassie grinned. 'Maybe he's not quite as straight as you thought.'

Lydia chuckled. Cassie was probably right, but as long as Zack could still satisfy her, then she didn't particularly care about his extracurricular activities.

'Well, he gives me fantastic orgasms, so that's all I'm concerned about.'

Cassie was quiet for a moment. 'Lydia?'

'Hmm?'

'You're sure you're not just using Zack to, you know, fill a void?'

Lydia gave her a wicked smile. 'Of course I am, darling. He fills it quite nicely.'

A becoming flush coloured Cassie's cheeks. 'No, that's not what I meant. I mean, don't you think you're using these men when you're really looking for a soulmate?'

Lydia groaned. 'Good Lord, Cassie, the last thing I need is a soulmate. I'm a busy woman with very little time for a man. A satisfying fuck works for me just fine.'

'Maybe you're just trying to convince yourself of that,' Cassie said quietly.

'Cassie, I'm not like you,' Lydia snapped. 'I don't harbour dreams of romance and living out my old age with some decrepit man by my side.'

'All right, I'm sorry,' Cassie said. 'It's none of my business.'

Lydia sighed. She hated arguing with Cassie. 'I didn't mean to snap at you. I just don't like having my sex life put under scrutiny.'

Cassie reached out to refill their wine glasses. 'What about that fashion shoot you mentioned on the phone?'

'You mean the one at the antique bookshop?' Lydia took another sip of wine, relieved at having the subject changed. 'I went there with Zack on Thursday to meet with the owner. He turned out to be an interesting fellow.'

'Interesting how?'

'Well, he's extremely unsophisticated and appears quite homely at first,' Lydia said. 'But he's very intelligent. I was eavesdropping on him when he was talking to customers, and his knowledge of literature is vast.'

Cassie looked up. 'Really?'

'You and he could probably find a million things to talk about,' Lydia replied, realising that she was rather disconcerted by the thought.

'What does he look like?'

'Like a dishevelled, absent-minded librarian who sleeps in his clothes and fixes his glasses with masking tape.'

Cassie laughed. 'Not really.'

'Yes, really.'

'So, did he agree to let you use his store?' Cassie asked.

'Yes. We're doing the shoot on Monday.'

'Can I come? I'd like to meet him.'

'You're sure you'd want to? It's terribly boring to sit around and watch a fashion shoot.'

'I'd love to. I don't have classes on Monday. And I'm always on the lookout for a good bookshop. I won't get in the way.'

'No, I know you won't.' Lydia mentally chastised herself for being so reluctant. Heaven knew that she would never be interested in someone like Nicholas Hawthorne, but Cassie might find him fascinating. 'Of course you can come. I'll come pick you up.'

'Great.' Cassie smiled and padded back to the kitchen to check on the tortellini.

Lydia left around one in the morning, promising to pick Cassie up at eight on Monday. She drove back home, thinking about Nicholas and Cassie together. They might work quite well as a couple. They both adored literature, and Cassie was never picky about the way a man looked. Lydia stopped at a red light and bit thoughtfully on her thumbnail. Yes, they might work quite nicely, Nicholas and Cassie.

# Chapter Three

Lydia pushed aside a stack of books and leant her hips against a low shelf as she watched Zack arrange a model's position. In the span of a few hours, the Libri Antiqui bookshop had been transformed into a veritable state of chaos with models, make-up artists, hairdressers, and assistants running around like rats in a maze. There was, however, a method to the madness, and Lydia had no concerns that everything wouldn't be completed on time.

Nicholas Hawthorne apparently didn't feel the same way. He was standing near the front door, his brow furrowed as he watched two men pushing aside an entire bookshelf to make room for a light stand. Lydia took pity on him and walked across the store, hitching her satchel strap over her shoulder.

'Relax,' she said. 'We've done this hundreds of times.'

Nicholas looked at her, his dark eyes worried behind his glasses. 'You have, maybe,' he said. 'But I haven't.'

Lydia smiled. 'Well, at least one of us is experienced, then.'

His gaze slid away from her, a slight flush creeping over his neck. Lydia continued looking at him, taking in the lines of his profile and the strength of his jaw.

'Have you ever considered shaving your beard off?' she asked.

Nicholas's hand went to his scraggly beard as if he was making certain it was still there. 'My beard? Shave it off?'

'Yes. You have very nice features, and that beard is terribly unsightly. It doesn't suit you.'

'I've never really thought about it.'

'No, I imagine you haven't,' Lydia murmured. Her eyes moved down to his shoulders and chest, both of which were quite broad and well-shaped. At least, from what she could discern underneath that awful, torn jacket of his. 'Maybe you should also think about investing in a new wardrobe.'

'Now, Lydia, don't try and fix the poor man.' Cassie appeared at Lydia's side with two muffins and two cups of coffee on a tray. She handed one of the coffees to Nicholas. 'He's trying to live up to the classic image of a cerebral scholar.'

Nicholas gave her a grateful smile. A spark of unexpected irritation appeared in Lydia's stomach. She frowned. Cassie and Nicholas had been chatting all morning about literature and God knew what else. Lydia reminded herself that was exactly what she had intended.

'Cassie, being scholarly is no reason a person shouldn't look their best,' she said, looking pointedly at Cassie's tailored slacks and collared shirt.

Cassie bit into her muffin. 'Now, don't start on me, too.'

'There's nothing wrong with the way you dress, Cassie. You always look very neat.'

Cassie rolled her eyes at Nicholas. 'How complimentary.'

They shared a conspiratorial smile that made Lydia's nerves tense. What in the world was the matter with her? She thought it would be wonderful if Cassie and Nicholas started a relationship. Didn't she?

Annoyed, she spun on heel and went outside. She paused in front of an art gallery window and gazed at several paintings on display. She hadn't been herself lately. Her concern about the magazine had made her extremely edgy, so it was no wonder she was taking her frustrations out on people around her. Her edginess had nothing to do with what Cassie had said about her sex life a few nights ago.

'Lydia, the designer for the business suits just called!'

Lydia looked up to find Zack standing at the door of the bookshop, a cellular phone in his hand.

'And?'

'Do you want to talk to her?'

'Not if she doesn't need to talk to me,' Lydia replied.

Zack spoke into the telephone, gave Lydia a wave, and disappeared back into the store. Lydia sighed. She wished Zack wasn't so busy right now. She could have used a quick, intense fuck with him. Something just to take the edge off.

She glanced back towards the front of the store again, her gaze falling on Nicholas and Cassie heading out to examine the offerings of the caterers. Damn it! Why was she feeling so uneasy with this whole set-up all of a sudden? Was it just because the two of them seemed so cosy within the span of a few hours?

'Hey, Lydia, what do you think of putting that owner in one of the shots?' One of the assistants, Roger, approached her, tucking a pencil behind his ear.

Lydia's eyebrows lifted. 'Nicholas Hawthorne?'

'Yeah, him. He'd be a great contrast to the models, sort of a "nerd with a babe" scene.'

'No.'

'No?' Roger looked surprised. 'Zack thought you'd love the idea.'

An idea began to take shape in Lydia's mind. 'Has he taken any photographs yet?'

'Not that I know of.'

'Never mind, I'll talk to Zack myself.' Lydia strode past Roger and went back into the chaos of the bookshop. She found Zack changing the lens on one of his cameras.

'Zack, have you taken photographs of Nicholas Hawthorne yet?'

'No. I was waiting to see if you wanted to.'

'I do, but not with the models. When they leave, take some shots of Nicholas. Don't do his hair or make-up or change his clothes. Just photograph him as he is.'

Zack grinned. 'The beast in his natural environment?'

'There is no need to be rude.'

'Has he agreed to this?'

'Not yet, but he will,' Lydia replied.

'Lydia, it'd be such a great spread if we photographed him with the models. Talk about beauties and the beast.'

'Zack, you keep Nicholas Hawthorne out of this, all

41

right?' Lydia ordered in a low whisper. 'Take the photographs when everyone else is gone so he isn't uncomfortable. And keep him away from the models.'

'All right, all right. What's the matter with you? You hot for him or something?'

If they hadn't been in a room full of people, Lydia might have hit him. Instead, she gave him her most authoritative glower.

'Don't speak to me like that ever again,' she ordered. 'You'll regret that remark.'

She turned and went back outside. She searched the throng of people until she spotted Nicholas and Cassie nearby, involved in an earnest conversation.

Lydia fixed a smile on her face and approached them. 'Sorry to interrupt, Nicholas, but you and I have some business to discuss.'

'Oh. Right now?'

'No. Why don't we meet for a late dinner tonight? I have a proposal for you.'

He blinked. 'OK. Where should I meet you?'

Lydia reached into her purse and pulled out a business card. She wrote her address on the back. 'Come to my house around ten. I'll have my cook fix something light. And I've spoken to Zack about taking some pictures of you when everyone else is gone.'

'Pictures of me?' Nicholas repeated.

'Yes. Nothing extravagant. We'd just like some photographs of you in your store. I'll explain tonight.'

Without giving him a chance to protest further, she turned her attention to Cassie, who appeared totally unconcerned with the fact that her best friend had just invited her prospective romantic involvement for a late dinner.

'Are you going to stay for a while?' Lydia asked.

'Yes, I think I will,' Cassie replied. 'Nicholas wants to show me some first editions he has.'

'All right. Then I'll see you both later.' Lydia turned and walked to her car.

\* \* \*

Nicholas wondered what he was doing here. He got out of his car and closed the door, staring at Lydia Weston's mansion. Spotlights displayed the palatial, Italianite façade and dark traces of a carefully manicured lawn. He glanced down at the address she had written on the back of her business card and shook his head. He couldn't remember ever having been in this area of Pacific Heights, except maybe to gawk at the mansions. He didn't belong here any more than a penguin belonged in the Sahara desert.

Still, he had promised her. He pushed up his shirt sleeve and looked at his watch. Five minutes to ten. It was now or never. Taking a deep breath, he walked up the flagstone path to the front door. He smoothed down the dark suit he was wearing and pressed the bell.

Within seconds, the door opened. Lydia Weston stood there, dressed in a silky gown that caressed every inch of her savoury body. The foyer lights glowed on her dark hair.

'Nicholas. Come in.' She pulled the door open to let him in, her gaze sweeping over his suit. 'Goodness. You didn't have to pull out your best suit for me. This is just an informal dinner between friends.'

Nicholas cleared his throat and adjusted his necktie as he glanced up at the chandelier that dominated the foyer. 'I wasn't sure what you had in mind.'

'Well, let me at least take your jacket.' She slipped behind him and removed his suit jacket, then tossed it over the staircase banister. 'And loosen that tie, for heaven's sake.'

She reached up and pulled at the knot of his necktie. Her close proximity sent a wash of sensations through him as he gazed down at her fine features and full, red lips. A sweet, warm scent wafted from her body, something that jolted straight to his groin. It took him a moment to process the fact that Lydia Weston smelled vaguely like sex.

'Your home is beautiful.'

She smiled. 'Thank you. The views are the best part of

it. From each of the four levels, you can see the Golden Gate, Alcatraz Island, and Angel Island. I'll show all of the views to you after dinner.'

'Thanks.'

'There.' Lydia finished loosening his tie to her satisfaction and patted his chest. 'Come into the kitchen.'

She led him through a lavishly decorated dining room and into the kitchen, which contained two industrial stoves and a square, wooden central island. Batches of herbs hung from the rafters, scenting the air with spice, and copper pots and pans caught the light. It was both practical and comfortable, a place in which meals could be prepared for two or twenty.

Nicholas's eyes went to Lydia's buttocks as she turned from him to open the steel refrigerator. An uncomfortable heaviness started in his trousers. He suspected that she wasn't wearing anything underneath that filmy gown, which meant that she must have thrown it on recently. His groin tightened further, and he moved behind the central island when she turned. She put some covered plates into the oven, then took a bottle of wine from the refrigerator.

'I have a perfectly lovely chardonnay chilled,' Lydia said. 'Do you drink wine, or would you prefer something more spirited?'

'No, wine is fine, thank you.'

Lydia smiled at him. Lord, but she was sexy. He had seen women who were more conventionally beautiful, but none who exuded self-possession and sensuality the way that Lydia Weston did. He watched her uncork the bottle with fluid movements and pour them both a generous amount. She handed him one of the glasses and clinked hers against his.

'Cheers. To a budding friendship.' She swallowed some wine, and they went back into the dining room to sit down. 'So, tell me, what did you think of my friend Cassie?'

Nicholas looked up in surprise. 'Cassie? She's nice. Very intelligent.'

'Mmm. She's brilliant.' Lydia leant back in her chair

and crossed her legs, tracing the edge of her wine glass with a lavender-tipped finger. 'Are you planning on seeing her again?'

'You mean socially?'

'Yes.'

'I don't know.' Christ, he felt like such an awkward imbecile around this woman. He shifted in his chair and took a swallow of wine as he thought about Cassie Langford. She was extremely nice and pretty. He was lucky as hell that she'd even spoken to him for as long as she had, and now Lydia was asking about his intentions with her. 'Maybe.'

Lydia gazed at him for a moment, reaching up to run her elegant fingers through her hair. 'Good. Although, you've noticed that she's a classy lady? Conservative, but classy.'

'Yes. Can I ask you where this conversation is going?' He hadn't meant the words to sound so blunt, but he was getting tense.

To his relief, Lydia smiled. 'Just a little warning, Nicholas. I don't want my friends to get hurt.'

'Oh, I would never hurt Cassie.' Nicholas shook his head emphatically. 'Never.'

'No, I didn't think you would. Wait here. I'll bring in our food.' She rose and returned to the kitchen, then came back with a tray holding plates of angel-hair pasta, a basket of foccacia bread, and Caesar salad. She put a plate in front of Nicholas and resumed her seat. 'I suppose you're really wondering why I asked you here.'

'Yes.' He pushed his glasses back up on to the bridge of his nose. The food looked and smelled delicious.

'*Savoir Faire* is working on an upcoming issue dedicated to men,' Lydia explained. 'We're going to gear each of our articles and our photo spreads towards men.'

'That sounds interesting.'

'Yes. Of course, women will be the ones purchasing the magazine, but we're going to tailor the marketing so that they'll buy it for their men.'

Nicholas bit into a shrimp. 'Does this have anything to do with the photographs you told Zack to take of me?'

'Yes, actually, it does. I want to do a make-over on you.'

'A make-over?'

'Zack took some photos of you this afternoon, didn't he?'

'Yes.'

'Those will be our "before" shots. Now I want to take you to a proper hair stylist and a tailor so that we can completely rework your image.'

Nicholas couldn't quite believe what he was hearing. Why on earth would she want to put *him* in her magazine? 'I'm afraid I don't quite understand.'

'Let's not call it a make-over,' Lydia said earnestly. She wound a swirl of pasta on to her fork. 'That's too much of a girly term. Let's call it a "transformation".'

'Lydia, I really don't know why you want me involved in this.'

Lydia's gaze swept over him pointedly. 'You're a perfect candidate, dearest. I don't mean to insult you, but you really need to work on your appearance.'

Nicholas shook his head. 'This isn't in my league,' he said. 'I don't want to be made over or transformed or anything.'

'We'll pay you, of course,' Lydia said. 'Handsomely. And everything we purchase – clothes, shoes, suits – will be yours to keep. I promise you it will be a substantial amount.'

'I'm that much of a lost cause?' He didn't know whether to be flattered or insulted.

Lydia laughed, a light, clear sound that sent a pleasurable tingle over his skin. 'Oh, you're anything *but* a lost cause, Nicholas. That's why I want to transform you. You have extraordinary potential.'

'I do?' No one had ever said something like that to him before.

'Of course.' She looked at him for a moment, then reached across the table and removed his glasses. She promptly disappeared into a foggy blur. 'How well do you see without these?'

'Not well, I'm afraid. I'm quite near-sighted.'

'You have absolutely beautiful eyes. Have you ever worn contact lenses?'

He felt a flush creep over his neck at her compliment. 'No, I haven't.'

Lydia's fingers drifted over his cheekbone and paused at his beard. 'This really has to go, Nicholas. It's not an attractive look for you at all. It makes you look very dishevelled.'

'I've never thought about shaving it.'

'You don't think about yourself very much, do you?' Lydia mused.

'I guess not.'

'Wait here.' She stood in a blur of silken colour. 'I'll be right back.'

A light clink indicated that she left his glasses on the table. Nicholas fumbled for them as soon as he heard her footsteps in the foyer. He put them back on and turned his attention back to his food, feeling not only out of place, but also rather dazed by Lydia's charismatic sensuality.

'All right.' She returned a few minutes later, holding a bowl of steaming water and a small basket, with a towel slung over her shoulder. 'Let's give you a shave.'

Startled, Nicholas dropped his fork. 'A shave? Right now?'

'Yes.' Lydia smiled at him. 'Relax, sweetie. I've shaved a man before. And not only his face.'

When her meaning sunk in, Nicholas blushed to the tips of his ears. Yes, he was definitely a fish out of water here.

Lydia laughed. 'I meant his chest, but you look so charming when you blush.'

He had to get out of here before he really humiliated himself. 'If you really want me to shave, I can do it myself.'

Lydia pushed aside their plates and put the bowl on the table. 'I'm sure you can,' she murmured. 'But don't you trust me?'

Nicholas swallowed hard. 'Um, yes. Of course I do.'

'Good. Push your chair back from the table.' She took a razor out of the basket, along with a stick of lather. She dipped the brush into the water and worked up a rich foam. 'I'd hate to ruin your shirt. Why don't you take it off?'

Nicholas soon realised that he would never win in the face of Lydia's seductive manner. Embarrassed, he took off his tie and unbuttoned his shirt, then slipped it off and hung it over the back of his chair. He glanced at Lydia, unnerved to discover that she was looking at his bare chest.

Her gaze lifted to his. She gave him a wink. 'I was wondering what you looked like under that horrible jacket of yours. Do you play sports?'

'I play rugby on weekends. And I go on camping trips often. Nature fascinates me.'

'You're quite well-built.' She reached out and took off his glasses again, disappearing into a blur.

'Uh, thanks.'

'I wouldn't have pegged you as an athletic type.'

'I'm not, really. But I've always believed that to exercise your mind, you have to exercise your body.'

'Isn't that the truth,' Lydia murmured.

'It's the reason I keep in shape.'

'You're going to be full of surprises, Nicholas, I can just tell.' Lydia picked up the scissors and came closer, bending slightly as she began to trim his beard. The scent of her wafted into his nostrils, filling his head with images of what she had been doing before he arrived. He groaned inwardly when he felt himself start to get hard again. This was not exactly the time to display an erection.

Lydia reached for the brush and stroked a generous amount of lather over his jaw and down to his neck. 'Now hold still, love.'

She put her fingers under his chin, tilted his face up to her, and began to shave him. Nicholas thought that he had never experienced anything quite so subtly erotic in all his life. He gazed at Lydia's lovely face, which was close enough for him to see clearly, the slight crease between her eyebrows and the adorable way she bit her lower lip in concentration. Her touch was smooth and even, and she paused intermittently to cleanse the razor.

His cock grew even harder when she slipped his knee between her legs, bringing her breasts close enough to touch, close enough to kiss. Yes, she was definitely naked underneath that gown, her dusky nipples pressing against the thin material. He could practically feel the heat rising off her body. The sensation of her proximity made him slightly light-headed, heightening to almost a drunken feeling.

His fingers itched to clutch her hips, to drag that silken cloth off her body and expose her lush naked body to his gaze and his touch. He wanted to grasp her nipples between his teeth and suck on them until she squealed with delight. Christ, his penis felt like it was made of iron. He sent up a silent prayer that Lydia wouldn't look down and see the aroused state to which she had reduced him.

The ribbon that held Lydia's gown together at the neck slipped open slightly, revealing a tantalising bit of white, soft skin. He had never wanted to touch a woman more, and his heart began to thud with the advent of need. He was barely aware of the scrape of the razor as she rasped it over his skin, but when she stepped away from him, it seemed as if the entire procedure had taken less than a second.

'There.' Lydia wiped the remaining lather off his face and stepped back to view him with a critical eye. She stood there looking at him for so long that Nicholas grew uncomfortable.

'What?'

Lydia shook her head and smiled. 'You're a very handsome man, Nicholas. Strong features, well-defined. And an extremely sensual mouth. Too bad you hid it underneath that scraggly beard for so long.'

She reached out and stroked her warm fingertips over his jaw, pausing at his mouth. Her touch was feather-light and sensual as she rubbed her thumb over his lower lip, sending another arrow of heat right to his groin. He drew in a breath, closing his eyes in dismay when the movement of her head indicated that she was glancing down at his pants.

Humiliation washed over him in a wave. Silence filled the air between them in a thick curtain. Feeling intensely unguarded, Nicholas fumbled for his glasses, relieved when the world was once again well-defined.

'Nicholas, look at me,' Lydia commanded, her voice slightly husky.

He opened his eyes to find her gazing at him, her expression filled with something very akin to desire. He could hardly believe it.

'Sorry,' he said hoarsely. 'It's just that you're very ... um, sexy.'

'So are you, you know,' Lydia murmured. 'You just don't know it yet.'

Nicholas had the distinct feeling that there was a number of things he didn't know yet. 'Thanks.'

'We'll go to my optician and get you some contact lenses tomorrow,' Lydia announced. 'I refuse to allow you to wear those glasses any longer.'

'I ... I have to work tomorrow.'

'We'll go on your lunch break,' Lydia said. 'I'm sure that delightful associate of yours can take care of things for an hour or two. What was her name again?'

'Olive.' Nicholas's penis throbbed at the mention of the voluptuous Olive, no doubt in memory of the way it had been embedded between her breasts.

Lydia settled her hands on his thighs. 'Yes,' she said. 'Olive. She's lovely, but I'm sure you know that already.'

Startled, Nicholas glanced up at her, only to find her watching him with a hint of shrewdness. He remembered the way she had looked at him and Olive the first time they met, as if she had known what just transpired between them. His face grew even warmer.

'Yes,' he mumbled. 'She's very pretty.'

'What were you and Olive doing right before Zack and I walked in last week?' Lydia asked softly, her dark gaze never leaving his face. 'You both looked rather, shall we say, spent.'

Nicholas couldn't reply. Hell, he could barely breathe.

Lydia's hands slid up his thighs, stroking them with slow, seductive movements as they neared his groin. She leant towards him, brushing a kiss of such feather-light softness across his lips that he didn't know if it was real or imagined.

He was stunned when she went down on her knees in a lissome movement, her hands getting dangerously close to the bulge in his trousers. He grabbed her wrists suddenly to halt their progress.

Lydia looked up a him, a slight frown of confusion on her brow. 'What?'

'P-please,' Nicholas stammered. 'I don't know what you want from me, but whatever you're doing, please stop it.'

Lydia's eyebrows lifted. 'You want me to stop touching you?'

'Why are you doing this? So I'll agree to go along with your crazy idea of transforming me?'

Lydia gave a throaty laugh. 'Nicholas, I'm sure I don't need to suck your cock to persuade you, do I?'

'God, no, of course not.'

'Haven't you already agreed?'

'I – I guess I have.'

'Then what's the problem?'

Nicholas stared at her. Her eyes simmered with slow hunger, her luscious lips parted slightly as if waiting to draw the length of his prick into her mouth. His entire body thrummed with arousal at the thought.

'I thought ... I thought you were setting me up with your friend Cassie.'

'This has nothing to do with my friend Cassie.' She pried her wrists out of his grip and put her hands on his thighs again. 'For heaven's sake, Nicholas, relax.'

She cupped her hand over the raging bulge in his trousers, flashing him a small smile as her fingers closed over the zipper and tugged it down gently. A sheen of perspiration broke out on Nicholas's forehead. Lydia's hand delved into his shorts, a low murmur escaping her throat as her fingers touched the length of his penis. She tugged his trousers down further, easing his erection out of his briefs. He was so painfully hard he was embarrassed, but nothing could diminish the intense simmer of excitement throbbing in his blood.

'Like I said,' Lydia murmured, eyeing the length of his shaft. 'I knew you'd be full of surprises.'

Nicholas swallowed hard. 'Seems like you are as well.'

She laughed. 'Oh, you have no idea.'

As if to prove her point, she leant forward and enclosed the head of his penis between her lips. Nicholas drew in a sharp breath at the sensation of her mouth enclosing his rigid flesh. Her fingers traced the veins that lined his erection, pressing them lightly and causing his every nerve to tighten with anticipation. His hand curled around the edge of the table as he watched her luscious lips sliding down his shaft. God, it was like sinking into a warm ocean of sensations as her tongue flicked expertly over the tip, evoking a quiver that rushed through his entire body. He let out a groan.

Lydia glanced up at him, a wicked gleam in her eyes as if she knew exactly what she was doing to him. She slipped her hand down to the twin sacs nestled so tightly between his thighs, rubbing her fingertips over the crinkled skin. A tight rope of tension began to encircle the base of Nicholas's penis as he succumbed to Lydia's erotic ministrations. His head filled with the scents of shaving cream, of Lydia, of the ripe scent of bread, of his own burning heat. His hips jerked forward involuntarily as Lydia continued to enclose his erection in her mouth, wrapping one hand around the base to facilitate her movements. Nicholas watched her in stunned arousal as she started to move her head back and forth, letting him slide with ease in and out of the hot cavern of her mouth. A flush coloured her cheeks, and her eyes drifted half-closed. She eased back and swirled her tongue around the hard knob of his penis, her breath hot against his achingly sensitive flesh.

'Oh my, Nicholas,' Lydia murmured. 'Has anyone told you that you taste delicious?'

He couldn't reply. His chest heaved as both pleasure and frustration tightened his nerves. Why in the hell did they call it a 'blow job'? What an unattractive, harsh term for an act that a woman like Lydia could perform with such exquisite finesse. Why not something like a 'lip-and-tongue stimulation caress'?

'Nicholas?'

Nicholas forced his attention back to Lydia. 'No,' he gasped. 'No one ever has.'

'You do, you know.' Lydia stood up slowly, grasping her gown in both fists as she drew it up over her legs and hips.

Nicholas watched with uninhibited fascination and desire as the flimsy material began to rise like a curtain to reveal the length of her legs and the delectable, shorn apex of her thighs. Nicholas swallowed hard, his rapid breaths making his chest tight as he gazed at the unconcealed evidence of her need. Droplets of moisture clung to the plump lips of her outer labia, eliciting an intense craving in Nicholas to taste the sweetness of her. He began to lean forward, but Lydia put her hands on his shoulders and gently pushed him back.

'Wait,' she whispered. 'There's plenty of time for that later.'

'But I want to please you.'

Lydia smiled. 'Oh, darling, you do please me. Very much.'

She straddled his thighs, reaching down to slip her tapered fingers over his turgid penis. Nicholas could hardly believe what was happening, could hardly believe what this delicious woman was doing to him. Lydia positioned the head of his cock at the opening of her body, then bent to press her lips against his as she sank slowly down on to him. Nicholas groaned, stunned by the sensation of her full breasts brushing against his chest, her soft lips stroking his, her tight heat surrounding him. He moved his hands to her rounded hips, digging his fingers into her skin as if to make certain she was real.

And, oh yes, she was real, she was all heat and woman, her inner walls clenching around him as she began to lift and lower her body. Nicholas gasped at the intermittent sensations of air and humid warmth as Lydia slid up and down on his erection. Her breath became rapid, her hands sinking into his hair as her body moved with increasing frenzy. Her breasts shook with such enticing movements that Nicholas couldn't help himself from leaning forward and pulling open her gown, revealing her breasts. Instinctively he captured one of her hard nipples between his lips.

Lydia's back arched, her throaty murmurs spurring them both on towards the final release. Nicholas was so aroused, his desire for Lydia having been kindled the moment she stepped into his bookshop, that he knew within minutes that he wouldn't last long. The ache in his penis augmented to unfathomable degrees, and he pulled away from Lydia long enough to choke out a warning.

'Lydia, I –'

'It's OK, love.' Lydia slipped his erection out of her body and began to stroke his shaft with rapid movements. Nicholas felt as if his entire being was centred in the tension of his cock as his pleasure exploded in jets of molten semen. He groaned as Lydia's fingers tightened around him, unable to stand the intensity of what this woman could do to him.

Lydia's rapid breaths brushed against his lips as she leant her forehead against his. 'My turn,' she whispered.

'Christ, I'm sorry.' A rush of shame threaded through him at the realisation that Lydia's pleasure hadn't been fulfilled.

'No need to apologise, darling.' Lydia moved back slightly, slipping her legs over his until she was straddling his right thigh. She lowered herself until her hot, damp folds brushed against his hair-roughened skin. A jolt of pure awareness shuddered through Nicholas as Lydia began to ride his thigh. He thought then that he'd never seen anything quite so beautiful as Lydia moving up and down, her breasts wantonly exposed, her silky gown slipping off her shoulders, her face flushed with pleasure. Her clitoris pressed against his leg, her moisture bathing his skin as she spurred herself to the heights of pleasure. She let out a cry suddenly, her body quivering and vibrating as the tempest inside her peaked. Nicholas gripped her hips, pressing her down on to his thigh as the final waves of pleasure coursed through her body.

Lydia's writhing movements stilled slowly, but she didn't make a move to get up. 'Oh, yes, Nicholas,' she murmured breathlessly. 'You are indeed full of surprises.'

Nicholas had the distinct feeling he was in for a few more surprises himself.

'Not too short, Abigail.' Lydia's fingers threaded through the hair at the back of Nicholas's neck, causing a warm shiver to rain down his spine. 'I like it a bit long, but it certainly needs shape.'

The hairdresser snapped her gum and nodded as she ran a comb through Nicholas's hair. Her own hair was shorn completely at the back. The top was moulded into spiky points tipped with purple and gold that matched her eyeshadow. Nicholas wasn't thrilled with the idea of this woman cutting his hair, but Lydia seemed to be completely comfortable with the idea. He caught her eye in the mirror. She winked at him.

Nicholas shrugged to himself and settled back in the chair. Apparently, Abigail's own personal taste in avant-garde hairstyles didn't mean that she was going to dye his hair blue and carve it into the shape of a duck.

He watched in the mirror as Abigail began to wield her scissors under Lydia's watchful eye. His reflection looked so different to him. Just that morning, Lydia had taken him to her eye doctor for a contact lens prescription. The lenses themselves were quite comfortable, but Nicholas felt distinctly odd without his glasses. He thought briefly of Olive, wondering if she was managing to run the store properly or if she'd closed it for the day and gone off to the movies.

'Nice hair you've got, Nick,' Abigail announced through the popping noise of her gum. 'Thick and workable.'

'Like other things,' Lydia murmured.

A slight flush coloured Nicholas's cheeks. No one else seemed to notice Lydia's suggestive words, which wasn't a surprise. Zack's camera crew had set up a number of lights and equipment around the shop, and the place was packed with other hairdressers and people from the magazine. A buzz of voices hovered in the air, accompanied by the occasional click of the camera and burst of a flashbulb as they documented this momentous occasion.

The crowded, stuffy atmosphere made Nicholas slightly claustrophobic and the scent of hair products was giving him a headache, but all he had to do was look at Lydia and remember last night and suddenly nothing else mattered. He had never had quite such intense feelings about a woman in such a short period of time. Of course, he knew his feelings were partially based on their physical attraction, but he also just plain *liked* her a great deal. He couldn't wait for tomorrow evening, when Lydia had suggested they go out to dinner. Just the two of them.

A flashbulb popped in his face, momentarily blinding him. When his vision cleared, he saw Zack standing there, adjusting his camera. The other man did not look happy.

'So, Lydia, are we still on for tomorrow night?' Zack asked.

Lydia rested her hand along the back of Nicholas's chair. 'No, I'm afraid I have to cancel.'

'You have plans with him?' Zack asked.

'Zack, please continue working,' Lydia replied. 'You're getting paid.'

'Funny. I seem to get paid for doing other things besides working.'

Lydia frowned, her eyes hardening. 'Don't get snippy, Zack.'

The tone in her voice said it all. Zack turned away, a petulant twist to his mouth. Abigail grinned.

'A little jealousy there, huh?' she asked.

'Don't worry, Nicholas,' Lydia said, ignoring Abigail. 'He's harmless, really.'

'I'm not worried.' Nicholas wondered if Lydia was taking it for granted that he would be her new lover. Apparently, Zack's novelty was wearing off.

Flecks of hair flew off his head, sliced off neatly by Abigail's scissors. She moved around his head, cutting, snipping, and combing with such swift movements that the scissor blades flashed in the light of the occasional flashbulb. Then she took a hair dryer and wielded it like a weapon, aiming it at sections of his head as she brushed, fluffed, and sculpted his hair into position. Lydia stood a short distance away, her arms crossed against her chest as she watched the event.

Finally, Abigail thrust the dryer back into its holder, gave Nicholas's hair one last flick, and stood back with a flourish.

'There!' she pronounced. 'Done.'

'Perfect.' Lydia moved to stand behind Nicholas, sliding her fingers underneath his ears to his jaw as she lifted his head slightly. 'Just perfect. Look at how brushing your hair away from your forehead brings out those gorgeous cheekbones. And without those glasses to hide your eyes, all of your best features are enhanced.'

'All of them?' Nicholas asked.

Lydia chuckled, running her fingertip down his cheek. 'Well, almost all of them.'

Nicholas looked at himself in the mirror as Zack continued snapping photographs of him. He looked different, not like himself at all, and he felt almost naked without his glasses and his hair falling over his forehead.

'Thank you, Abigail, darling.' Lydia leant over and kissed the spiky-haired woman on the cheek as she slipped several bills into her hand. 'We'll be back.'

'Bring him with you.' Abigail winked at Nicholas as she unclasped his apron.

Nicholas thanked her and followed Lydia out of the shop as she cut a path through the chaos of camera equipment and magazine lackeys. Lydia tossed him a smile as they stepped out into the fresh, clean air.

'Now, we'll get you fitted for some clothes. We've set up another camera crew at the clothing store. Then on Thursday we'll take some final shots of you at the studio. You do look gorgeous, Nicholas.'

'I don't feel like me.'

'Oh, but you are you,' Lydia murmured. 'Like I said, you just don't know it yet.'

'I don't understand why you're putting all this effort into changing me just for part of a magazine article.'

'Nicholas, you're not *only* going to be part of a magazine article.'

'I'm not?'

'No, darling. You're going to be our cover boy.'

# Chapter Four

'This one is wonderful.' Lydia tapped her finger on a photograph of Nicholas standing in front of the Palace of the Legion of Honour. A slight breeze rustled his hair, and he looked more relaxed than he did in some of the other photographs.

'I took a few more of him inside among the art work,' Zack said, shuffling through the dozens of photographs spread out on the table. 'Makes him actually look rather cultured.'

Lydia shot Zack an annoyed look. 'He *is* cultured, Zack. He just didn't look as if he was.'

Zack rolled his eyes. 'Please, Lydia. He couldn't order decent wine at a restaurant if you pointed at the bottle yourself.'

'You're wrong,' Lydia replied. 'I hired an oenologist to teach him. We went out for dinner last night, and Nicholas was perfectly elegant.'

'Why didn't you want me to come along and take photos?' Zack asked.

'We'll set up a restaurant set if we need to,' Lydia replied. Photographers had been snapping photos wherever she and Nicholas went, and the constant chaos was beginning to make her weary.

Lydia returned to her office and closed the door behind her. She was surprised at how much she was looking forward to having another evening alone with Nicholas. The other night, she hadn't been able to resist indulging in the erotic pleasure of shaving him, and then taking his erection into her mouth ... A shiver of delight rained down her spine. She had been spending a great deal of time with him over the past few days. In the process, she discovered to her surprise that not only did he arouse her, but she also completely enjoyed his company. And as reluctant as she was to admit it, Lydia suspected she could get quite used to Nicholas's unaffected, genuine personality.

The buzz of the intercom jarred her out of her thoughts. She pressed the button. 'Yes?'

'Lydia, your friend Cassie is here to see you,' Mona's disembodied voice reported.

'Cassie? Oh. Send her in, please.'

Seconds later, Cassie came through the door. She looked fresh and vibrant in a blue silk suit with a matching scarf holding her hair back. She gave Lydia a smile. 'Hello, Lydia. I was passing by and I thought I'd stop and see if you were free for lunch this afternoon.'

'I'm sorry, dear, but I'm just overwhelmed with work right now. The men's issue of the magazine is taking up all my time.'

'I understand. What about dinner?'

'No, I . . .' Lydia's voice trailed off. For some reason, she didn't want to tell Cassie about her plans with Nicholas. 'I'm afraid I have another business dinner.'

'Oh. Well, maybe another time then.'

'Of course. I want you and Molly to come to dinner when this is all finished.'

'I'd love to,' Cassie said. 'Well, I suppose I should leave you to your work.'

'I'm sorry. There's just so much to do.'

'Don't apologise, Lydia. I understand.' Cassie turned and started towards the door, then stopped and glanced back at Lydia. 'Um, Lydia?'

'Yes, dear?'

Cassie hesitated, her gaze shifting down to the floor before returning to Lydia. 'Have you seen Nicholas lately?'

'Nicholas? Yes. We've been, as we like to call it, transforming him for the photo shoots.'

'Has he . . . said anything about me?'

Lydia winced inwardly. She looked at the papers on her desk and suddenly became very busy straightening them into neat stacks. 'He said you were very nice and pretty.'

'Really? Well, that's lovely. Tell him I said hello, would you?'

'Of course. I'll give you a call later this week.'

'OK. Thanks.'

Lydia didn't look up until the door clicked shut again. Then she sighed heavily and sank down into her chair. What was she thinking? She wanted Cassie and Nicholas to be together, didn't she? They had much more in common than Lydia and Nicholas did, not to mention being far more alike in personality. So what in the hell had she been doing sucking on Nicholas's cock as if it were an appetiser and then fucking him in her dining room?

Lydia groaned. This was starting to get beyond her control. And she didn't like it one bit. She liked the idea of having Nicholas as a sexual companion, but she suspected he would want more from her. More than she was willing to give.

With a sigh, Lydia turned her attention back to her work. Not even thoughts of Nicholas and Cassie could prevent her from finishing up reports and meeting three deadlines. She left the office around six and started the drive home, but took a detour and ended up in front of Libri Antiqui. Lydia slid her car into a parking space across the street and waited for Nicholas to emerge. When he came out the front door and paused to lock it, Lydia pressed the horn.

Nicholas looked up, caught sight of her, and hurried across the street. A familiar warmth and pride filled Lydia as she watched him. He moved with more self-confidence now, his clothing fitted him properly, and he simply looked damn good.

'You hungry tonight?' Lydia asked.

Nicholas grinned. 'Depends on what you're offering.'

'Get in. You'll find out soon enough.'

Nicholas slid into the passenger seat. Lydia eased the car out on to the street and headed for the Marina. Van Ness was packed with cars, so she took several side streets that led to a covered parking lot.

'Where are we going?' Nicholas asked.

'Just for a short walk.' Lydia buttoned her coat and began walking. A thick layer of fog hovered over the bay, but the chilly air hadn't stopped both residents and tourists from taking over Fisherman's Wharf. The scent of fish and crabs greeted them as they neared the wharf, along with the rising din of voices. People crowded in front of tables piled high with fresh seafood as vendors scurried around preparing packages.

'This doesn't seem like your kind of environment,' Nicholas observed.

Lydia shrugged. 'It's not. However, I like it because it's so anonymous.'

She paused next to a vendor and purchased a warm loaf of sourdough bread wrapped in a crinkly paper wrapper. She gave Nicholas a smile and tucked her arm through his as they made their way through the crowd. The wharf was lined with tacky tourist shops selling San Francisco mementoes, but it was a lively place. Street lamps glowed on the water and music drifted from the numerous cafés, restaurants, and street performers.

They walked in silence for several minutes before Lydia took Nicholas's hand in hers and led him towards the boats lining the harbour. They walked down to the docks, and Lydia paused next to a small yacht emblazoned with the name *Mae Belle*.

'This is your boat?' Nicholas asked.

'No, but I'm in the market for one.' A chain barred the gangplank, but Lydia simply removed it and walked up on to the boat. She paused to look back at Nicholas.

He stared up at her in surprise. 'Lydia, you're trespassing.'

'I know. Come along, darling. You'll earn a reward if you follow me.'

Nicholas glanced around him uncomfortably, as if expecting a security guard to appear at any moment. He walked up the gangplank after Lydia.

'Lydia, I don't think this is such a great idea.'

'Oh, you will soon enough.' Lydia went to the bow and gazed out over the bay. Voices still hovered in the air from the wharf, and the sound of laughter drifted from passers-by. 'Haven't you ever made love on a boat before?'

'Um, no, I can't say that I have.'

Lydia turned and leant against the railing, letting her gaze drift over Nicholas. He really was quite a dear. He lacked finesse in the sexual department, of course, but oh, did he have potential. She pulled a piece off the sour-dough loaf she held and popped it into her mouth, enjoying the sensual pleasure of freshly baked bread.

'What do you want out of life, Nicholas?'

'Just to be happy, I guess.'

'Mmm. That's what I want, too.' Lydia turned and gazed out at the harbour. 'Only sometimes it feels like all of my ambition is leading to financial success and nothing else. That I'm running and running with nothing else in sight.'

'It doesn't have to be like that.' Nicholas's voice was oddly gentle.

'Sometimes I worry that I'm going to wake up one morning and be eighty years old. And I'll look back on my life and nothing will have mattered.' Lydia almost couldn't believe that she was confessing this to him.

She felt Nicholas's hands slide around her waist suddenly, pulling her against his chest. 'Your friends will have mattered.'

Lydia smiled. 'Very true. In fact, Cassie and Molly will no doubt be hobbling over to my place for tea and scones every Saturday.'

She let herself relax against his body. Nicholas's mere closeness stimulated Lydia's nerves, creating a luscious wash of heat through her. She dropped the bread and turned, curling her arms around Nicholas's neck. Pulling him towards her, she favoured him with a deep, wet kiss. Nicholas gave a murmur of pleasure and cupped her head in his hand, but Lydia put her hands on his chest and pushed him gently away.

'Wait there.' While he watched, she slipped her coat off and began to unfasten the buttons of her suit.

Nicholas watched her with a hungry expression, then glanced hesitantly towards the wharf. 'Uh, Lydia . . .'

'You want me to stop?' Lydia gave him a smile and took off her jacket. She unzipped her skirt, letting it fall to the ground, and stepped out of it. The frozen sea air fluttered against her skin, heightening all of her senses and making her intensely aware of the flimsy silk of her lingerie. Her nipples hardened beneath her midnight-blue bra, and her sex swelled with anticipation.

'Come here, darling,' she murmured. 'I want you to kiss me all over. When you make love to a woman, that's what you must do. Utterly make love to her. Absorb yourself in her pleasure.'

Nicholas came to her and bent his head to kiss first her lips, then her neck. His mouth was warm and smooth as his slid his lips over the curve of her shoulder, his tongue flickering out to lick trails of fire along her skin. The delicious contrast of cold air and sexual heat stimulated Lydia's desire as she closed her eyes and let Nicholas work his magic. Ah, he was a fast learner, thank heavens. His fingers curled around the straps of her bra as he captured one of her nipples between his lips. Heat flowed from his mouth through the blue silk, eliciting another delicious contrast of sensation.

To Lydia's surprise, Nicholas went down on his knees in front of her as his mouth moved lower, dipping into the indentation of her navel. Lydia gasped with pleasure, letting her body lean against the railing for support. She curled her hands around the railing, intensely aroused by the sight of Nicholas on his knees in front of her. She expected him to strip off her blue silk panties, but he didn't. Instead, he put his mouth against her and let his hot breath stimulate her sensitive flesh. Moisture and heat gathered between Lydia's legs as she watched him pleasure her.

Nicholas reached up to push aside the thin material and allow him to arouse her directly. The instant his tongue touched her, Lydia let out a groan of sheer excitement. There was nothing like this, nothing like the illicit pleasure of indulging in erotic activities in a semi-public location. They were partially hidden by the cabin of the boat, but anyone could glance up at the right angle and see them. The boat rocked slightly in the water.

Steadying herself on the railing, Lydia parted her legs further to allow him more intimate access. Nicholas dipped his tongue into her sex with a ravenous kind of hunger. Lydia stroked her hand through his hair.

'Gently, precious,' she whispered. 'There is a time and place for swiftness, but pleasuring a woman should be approached with finesse and sensitivity.'

Nicholas let his tongue trail over the crevices of her labia and up to her swollen clitoris. Ah, yes. Definitely a fast learner. Lydia shivered as a rush of cold air wafted in from the bay and fluttered over her skin. The chill stood in delightful opposition to the growing fire in her body. Her nerves began to tighten with the need for release as Nicholas slid his tongue gently into her and began to thrust it back and forth.

'Oh, yes, just like that,' Lydia murmured. She slid her fingers over her shaven mons to her clitoris and began to massage it gently. 'Just like that...'

An orgasm broke through her body like a wave, causing her to tremble violently and cry out in pleasure. A rush of moisture flowed from her sex. Nicholas licked up the fluids of her arousal, draining the final sensations out of her. Lydia's body went weak with stimulation, her chest heaving.

Nicholas clutched her hips, his eyes hot as he gazed up at her. 'I want to fuck you,' he said hoarsely.

The blunt rawness of his words sent a thrill of excitement through Lydia. She sank down on to the deck, her hand going to the hard, prominent bulge in Nicholas's trousers.

'Do it, then. Prove that you're a man.'

Nicholas didn't appear to miss the challenging note in Lydia's voice. He unclasped her bra, letting her full globes fall into his palms. He ran his thumbs over her nipples, teasing the stiff peaks and creating a new cascade of quivers through Lydia's body. She had thought that she would need to instruct him more thoroughly, but Nicholas's own instincts appeared to have taken over quite nicely.

He guided her gently on to her back, and a flame lit in Lydia's belly, painting her skin with the reddish blush of passion. Her heart thudded hard as Nicholas began to pull her panties over her hips. To her surprise, his hands slipped between her thighs as he pushed her legs apart to fully expose her nakedness to his gaze. The intimacy and pure wantonness of the exposure thrilled Lydia to unfathomable degrees. The cold air cooled her, but her arousal was intensely accelerated by Nicholas's control. Who would have thought he had it in him, she thought.

She drew in a sharp breath when she felt his tongue sliding over her labia again and into the crack between her buttocks. His fingers dipped into her sex, stroking and massaging her as he coaxed excitement out of her once again. Lydia's entire body tightened, aching with the need to be filled completely. Stretching her arms over her head, she listened to the sound of Nicholas unzipping his trousers, and then she felt the glorious sensation of his penis probing her. He slid the hard, hot knob around her damp pussy, over her clitoris, teasing her with a eroticism she hadn't known he possessed.

'God, Nicholas,' Lydia gasped. 'Put it in me. Fuck me like you said you wanted to.'

His penis slipped into her with a tantalising slowness, throbbing against her inner walls and sending heat into her very blood. Lydia moaned and reached out to hold on to the railing as she spread her legs wide. The boat rocked, rolling underneath her with an erotic shift. Slowly, Nicholas's penis pushed into her until he was fully embedded in her body. And then he began to thrust back and forth, sliding almost completely out of her before he sank into her once again.

Ah, God, how delicious it was to feel his thick cock pumping into her with increasing speed. She bit her lip and closed her eyes, savouring the sensation of his rapid thrusts, the sound of their sexes slapping together, his hands clutching her buttocks. Her bare breasts swayed with each hard thrust, and then Nicholas leant over her and cupped her breasts in his hands. He squeezed and massaged the twin globes, rolling her nipples between his fingers and arousing her beyond all belief. Grunts of pleasure emerged from his throat. Lydia tightened her muscles around his cock, evoking a pained groan from him.

'Lydia, don't –'

'Come on, Nicholas,' Lydia hissed. 'Don't disappoint me. Make me come again. Oh!'

A cry broke from her throat as his thrusts increased in pace. He splayed one hand over her breast and dipped the other into the scorching area between her legs. His fingers spread over her clitoris, rubbing the swollen jewel until Lydia felt as if her body would explode with pleasure. Nicholas's body was so hot, hard, and good against hers, in hers. She gripped the railing so tightly that her hands hurt, but then a wash of convulsions wracked her body with a swiftness and intensity that surprised even her. Nicholas continued thrusting his penis into her until her shudders waned, and then he pulled out. He groaned deep in his chest as wet spurts of semen jutted out on to Lydia's belly. Neither one of them moved for a long minute as they let their harsh breathing slow.

Lydia opened her eyes slowly, meeting Nicholas's rather stunned gaze.

'See, darling? The world is just full of erotic possibilities. Not to mention locations.'

'Jesus, Lydia,' Nicholas gasped. 'I've never met anyone like you.'

Lydia smiled and stretched out on the deck, waiting for her body to cool down. 'There is no one like me, sweetie.'

'I think I could fall in love with you,' Nicholas said.

Lydia stared at him in surprise, but he didn't appear to notice her shock. He simply began to adjust his clothes as if he hadn't said anything earth-shattering.

After a moment, Lydia began to dress. Clearly, Nicholas was getting more involved in this than she had intended.

'Nicholas, I hope you don't plan on getting possessive,' she said.

He looked at her. 'Possessive?'

'Or of actually falling in love with me.'

'What does that mean?'

Lydia hooked her bra and reached up to run her fingers through her hair. 'Really, Nicholas. We're just having fun. I'm not about to be committed to you in any way.'

The hurt look in his eyes created an unexpected rush of guilt in her. She turned away from him and picked up her blouse.

'Sorry,' Nicholas said. 'I guess I misunderstood the fucking part.'

'Apparently, you did.'

'So, I'm just your project, is that it?'

'Nicholas, don't act as if you didn't know what this was all about.'

Lydia didn't look at him for fear of how his expression would make her feel. Why on earth did she feel so horrible about this? It wasn't as if she owed him any-thing. She'd transformed him from a complete loser into an actual man, not to mention giving him sexual self-confidence. He should be damn grateful.

'I guess I didn't know what this was all about,' Nicholas said. 'But I do now.'

Nicholas pushed the book back into place and climbed off the ladder. They had received a shipment of books yester-day, and the shelves were looking nice and full. Removing his glasses, Nicholas rubbed them on the front of his shirt and went to the front door.

'Closing time already, boss?' Olive asked, looking up from the computer.

'Yes. You're actually working, are you?'

Olive gave him a cheeky grin. 'I'm changing the shelf locations for the books I put in our new erotica section. You know, we've already sold about twenty books from that section?'

'Great. You obviously have your fingers on the erotic pulse of the public.'

Olive chuckled. 'So I've been told. Hey, what happened to your contact lenses? You look better without glasses.'

'The dust irritates my eyes when I wear the lenses,' Nicholas replied. 'Besides, I'm used to my glasses.'

'Hey, when is that issue of the magazine coming out?' Olive asked. 'I want to see you all polished up and spread over the glossy pages.'

Nicholas shrugged. Lydia hadn't contacted him for at least a week now. He had been trying to put her out of his mind, which was proving to be a more difficult task than he had anticipated. She was the most exciting woman he had ever known. And now, a tight knot of hurt seemed permanently lodged in his gut, along with anger at himself for not realising earlier what Lydia's intentions had been. Of course, she had only been out to use him, to change him into her ideal. And once that task was finished, she would move on to someone else.

Nicholas went to lock the front door, pausing when he saw Cassie Langford walking towards the store. She smiled and waved. Nicholas pulled open the door to let her in.

'Cassie, how nice to see you,' he said with genuine pleasure.

'Thanks. And you as well.'

'You know my associate Olive.'

'Of course.' Cassie smiled warmly at Olive. 'We've talked often.'

'Cassie, in fact, was one of our erotica purchasers,' Olive reported, giving Cassie a wink.

'Olive, don't embarrass her,' Nicholas scolded, despite being rather intrigued by this revelation.

'No, no, that's all right,' Cassie interjected. 'Olive helped me pick out some classics, all of which were quite enlightening.'

The two women exchanged smiles, leaving Nicholas feeling as if he were missing something.

'Cassie, we received several orders yesterday,' he said. 'If you want to go back and rummage through the boxes to see if yours arrived, I'll be there in a minute to help you.'

'Great. Thanks.' Cassie headed towards the back of the store.

Olive shot Nicholas a grin. 'She's rather delicious, isn't she?'

Nicholas's breath nearly caught in his throat. 'What?'

'Cassie. So delicate-looking and lovely.' Olive laughed. 'Don't look so shocked, boss. Women are delectable creatures, even for other women. There is something delightful about being with someone so soft and receptive, particularly if you're just not in the mood for a hard man. Not that there's anything wrong with a hard man,' she added hastily.

'Olive, I hope you're not planning on . . . I mean, Cassie is . . . well, she's . . .'

'Oh, relax, boss.' Olive reached underneath the counter and retrieved her bag. 'I'm not going to seduce Cassie out from under you. I just know how to admire an attractive, intelligent woman, that's all.'

She slipped on her sweater and slung her bag over her shoulder as she headed around the counter. She paused by the door and looked at Nicholas seriously.

'But you be careful with her, OK?' Olive said. 'She's . . . you know. Sensitive.'

Nicholas nodded. 'Good night, Olive.'

Olive waved and headed out the door. Nicholas closed and locked the door behind her and went in search of Cassie. He found her rummaging through a box near his office.

'Find anything?' he asked.

'No, and there's no packing slip either.'

'Olive probably put them on my desk. I'll see if I can find it.' Nicholas went into the office and sat down at his desk to search through the papers. 'It was another William Blake book, wasn't it?'

'Yes, by Reginald Thornton.' Cassie entered the office and paused to peer over his shoulder. 'It's gone out of print.'

'I had one of our book search services looking for it. I'm afraid it's difficult to find. I might have to put in another search request.'

'That's all right. It's not a book I need right away.'

'The erotic books are though, huh?' The words were out

of Nicholas's mouth before he could stop them. Horrified, he turned to Cassie with an apology forming on his lips. To his surprise, she was smiling.

'I guess they are,' she admitted, then laughed. 'Don't look so upset, Nicholas. You didn't offend me.'

'I didn't?'

'No. I'm not a fragile little bird, you know. Of course, I've never been as lusty and adventurous as Lydia or Molly, but I've always had my own needs.'

Nicholas cleared his throat. 'I'm sure you have.'

'That's why I was looking for erotica. I'd been doing some research into Blake's possible desire for a *ménage à trois* with Mary Wollstonecraft and Henry Fuseli, and the idea intrigued me. I wanted to find out about the psychological background to such desires.'

His skin was growing warm. 'I see. Did you find what you were looking for?'

'Somewhat. Of course, one can never know these things without trying them, but it's interesting to read about. Arousing, too.'

Nicholas wondered if he was being dense or if Cassie Langford was making a move on him. A brief image of Lydia appeared in his mind, tightening his gut with anger and bitterness. Lydia had done her duty, transformed him into the man she wanted him to be, and she had made it all too clear that she was now finished with him. Just like Zack, Nicholas was now no longer a novelty.

'Yes,' he said. 'I can see how that would be arousing.'

'You've never . . .' Cassie's voice trailed off.

'What? Oh!' Nicholas flushed as realisation dawned. 'No. No, two people, myself included, are enough for me. Usually more than enough.' He smiled weakly.

Cassie laughed. 'I like you, Nicholas. It's no wonder that Lydia saw something special in you.'

*Something special.* Sure she did. Nicholas blocked off another image of Lydia and reached up to slide his hand around the back of Cassie's neck. She gave him a smile that bolstered his courage. He pulled her gently down towards him to press his lips against hers. The kiss was nice and warm, stimulating a gentle rush of desire in him. He realised then that he was comfortable with Cassie in ways that he could never be with Lydia.

Tugging Cassie down on to his lap, he slipped his fingers through her silky hair and angled his mouth more firmly over hers. Cassie responded with a little murmur, wrapping one arm around his neck. She shifted her bottom on his lap with a sly little movement that made Nicholas's body respond almost instantly. His penis hardened underneath his trousers as he slid his hand up to cup one of Cassie's small breasts. Cassie never wore clothing that displayed her petite figure, which merely intensified his curiosity as to what her body looked like underneath her modest suit. He fumbled with the buttons on her jacket, pushing it over her shoulders with a quick movement.

Cassie pulled away slightly, her face flushed. Nicholas thought that she had changed her mind, but Cassie began to unfasten the buttons of her shirt. She flashed him a quick smile and slipped the shirt over her shoulders, exposing her small breasts cupped in a lacy, white bra. Arousal speared through Nicholas like a flame at the sight of the rosy tips of her breasts peeking through the lace. His erection stiffened even further, pressing against the globes of Cassie's bottom insistently.

'You take it off,' Cassie invited.

Nicholas was only too happy to oblige. He unhooked the front clasp of her bra, pushing it aside to reveal the most delightful breasts topped with small, berry-red nipples. Unable to resist, Nicholas bent his head and captured one of those nipples between his lips. He sucked lightly, the motion eliciting a gasp of sheer pleasure from Cassie. She squirmed impatiently in his lap.

'Quick,' she whispered, moving off his lap. 'Take off your clothes too.'

'Why don't you take them off for me?'

Cassie grinned. 'Stand up.'

Nicholas did, albeit a bit unsteadily. Between him and Cassie, they rapidly shed his clothes. He was almost embarrassed by how hard he was, his penis jutting forth like a ramrod. He pulled Cassie into his arms and pressed his lips against hers again, feeling the heat rising off her body as their tongues danced together. Nicholas slid his mouth down to her neck, flicking his tongue into the salty hollow of her throat where her pulse beat a heady rhythm. He unsnapped her trousers and pushed them over her gently rounded hips, then helped her step out of them.

For a moment, he stepped back and let his gaze roam over the slim pale beauty in front of him. Her body was proportioned perfectly for her size, with her sex concealed by a dusting of light brown hair. A becoming flush coloured her skin at his scrutiny. Nicholas sought to alleviate Cassie's self-consciousness by giving her a gentle smile.

'You are so incredibly pretty,' he said, suspecting that she was far more apprehensive about this encounter than she was letting on. 'I never realised just how pretty you are.'

He took her in his arms again, sliding his hands down her heated body. Her legs parted slightly, allowing him access to the damp folds of her sex. Nicholas sank his forefinger into the warm, wet passage of Cassie's vagina, nearly gasping at the sensation of her inner muscles tightening around him. An ache began to build at the base of his penis. He slipped his finger out of her and stroked his hands down her back to her buttocks. In one movement, he tucked his hands around the backs of her thighs and lifted her against him, then carried her to the desk.

'Goodness, Nicholas, I never realised just how masterful you are,' Cassie said, her eyes filled with both amusement and desire.

'I've been watching a lot of Tarzan movies lately,' Nicholas replied.

The sound of Cassie's laughter warmed him to the bone. He rubbed his palms over her thighs, stimulated further by the friction of her skin. Gently, he pushed her legs apart to allow him access to her innermost secrets. To his surprise, Cassie gasped and tried to close her legs.

'Nicholas, no one has ever . . .'

73

'Aw, Cassie, it's OK.' Nicholas continued stroking his hands soothingly over her thighs. 'It'll be good for you, I promise.'

He didn't move until he felt her start to relax again, then he urged her thighs apart and lowered his mouth to her sex. Ah, God, she smelled delicious, musky and all woman. Heat and moisture emanated from her body. Nicholas stroked his tongue lightly over the crevices formed by her labia, licking her just the way Lydia had taught him. His body quivered at the taste of her. Cassie gave a little yelp of pleasure, her hips jerking upward as his tongue began to explore further.

Nicholas slipped his hands upward to caress Cassie's breasts as her legs widened, allowing him total access. He pushed his tongue deep into her pussy, sipping at droplets of cream as he moved up towards her swollen clitoris. He stroked his tongue around the little nub before taking it gently between his lips and sucking. Cassie screamed with delight as her body tensed and vibrated violently underneath his sensual ministrations. A fresh rush of moisture bathed Nicholas's lips and tongue.

Cassie reached down to twine her fingers through his hair, her eyes dazed. 'Nicholas ...'

Nicholas pulled himself up, his own body burning for release as he guided his erection between Cassie's legs. She shifted impatiently, pushing her body up towards him. With a groan of sheer pleasure, Nicholas sank his penis into Cassie's achingly taut channel. She wrapped her arms around his neck, urging him closer as he began to thrust inside her. Heat throbbed through his blood, heat and pure desire for the delectable woman before him. Her inner walls clenched around him, stimulating the tightness in his groin to unfathomable proportions.

Nicholas gripped Cassie's thighs and hooked them over his forearms, his senses swimming with the feel of her, the sight of her bouncing breasts and passion-filled features. She clutched his arms, broken moans spilling from her throat as another orgasm shattered through her body. As her muscles tightened around him again, Nicholas could hold back no longer. He pulled out of her, grasping his stalk in his hand and pumping hard as streams of semen coated Cassie's mons.

Nicholas drew in a harsh breath. His body shook with the intensity of his climax. He leant over Cassie, propping himself up on his forearms as he gazed down at her. A sheen of perspiration coated her features. She gave him a languid smile.

'Who would have imagined this between you and me?' she murmured, running her fingers through his hair.

Unexpectedly, another image of Lydia flashed in Nicholas's mind. He almost winced. Pressing his lips against Cassie's forehead, he pulled slowly away.

'Nicholas?' Cassie hitched herself on to her elbows and peered at him. 'Are you all right?'

'Yes.'

Cassie slipped off the desk and began to dress. 'It's Lydia, isn't it?'

'Probably.' Nicholas glanced at Cassie. 'I'm sorry.'

Cassie didn't look at him, but shook her head. 'Don't be. It's not your fault. Lydia is quite fascinating to men. I've always known that.'

'It doesn't matter anyway,' Nicholas said. 'She doesn't feel the same way about me at all. I was just a project to her.'

Cassie put her hands on her hips. A flicker of anger appeared in the depths of her eyes. 'Oh, that's good.'

'What?'

'Your martyrdom. Poor you, the abandoned lover. You might want to take control of the situation, Nicholas. Lydia doesn't like men who aren't in control. Unless, of course, they're in her bed.'

Nicholas sighed and put on his glasses. 'I don't know how, Cassie. That's just not me.'

'Then you have no one to blame but yourself.'

# Chapter Five

'Lydia.'

Lydia looked up from her desk to find Cassie standing at the open door of her office. 'Cassie, hello.'

'Why didn't you tell me that Nicholas was falling in love with you?'

Lydia stared at her friend as her heart plummeted. Cassie's expression was neutral, but her brown eyes were filled with betrayal.

'Oh, Cassie.'

'It wouldn't have bothered me if you'd told me,' Cassie said. 'The trouble is that you didn't.'

'He's deluded.' Lydia walked around her desk and approached Cassie. She closed the office door and put her hand on Cassie's arm. 'He just thinks he's falling in love with me.'

'Is he? Or is that simply your view of the whole situation?'

'Sit down, Cassie. We need to talk about this.' Lydia went to the sofa and sat down, suddenly feeling very tired. 'Nicholas and I have had fun together. It's been very rewarding to see him gain self-confidence and poise. However, he is completely not my type. Surely you know that.'

'Yes, and that must be the reason you were having an affair with him.'

'Cassie, really. My affairs are none of your business.'

'They are when you give me the impression that you want *me* to be with Nicholas.'

'I don't know what to tell you. He's been fun, but it's over.'

'Not according to him it isn't.'

'Nicholas is just very sensitive,' Lydia explained. 'He'll get over it, believe me.'

'Lydia, you can be very unkind, did you know that?' Cassie's hands clenched into fists at her sides. 'You change him into the kind of man you want him to be, seduce him, and then dump him when he no longer suits you. That is downright cruel.'

Lydia was taken aback by Cassie's words, as her friend had never spoken to her so harshly. 'Cassie, I never made any promises. He's an adult. I didn't mislead him into thinking we would be together for ever.'

'So why did you get rid of him, then?' Cassie asked.

Lydia's eyebrows lifted. 'Why? Because he's ... well, I don't ... he ... Dammit, Cassie, I don't owe you any explanations!'

A glint of satisfaction appeared in Cassie's eyes. 'No, you don't. But has it ever occurred to you that you might feel more for him than you expected to and that scares you? Getting Nicholas out of your sight would be one way of denying what you feel.'

'Oh, Cassie, for God's sake, I'm not falling in love with Nicholas Hawthorne,' Lydia snapped.

'Are you certain of that?'

Lydia sighed. She wasn't quite certain of anything any more. 'Yes,' she said. 'I'm certain. And I'm sorry I didn't tell you I was seeing him. I know I thought you would be good together.'

'I'm not so much upset on my own behalf as I am on Nicholas's behalf,' Cassie said. 'Yes, I had sex with him and yes, I like him, but I wasn't emotionally involved yet. However, what makes me angry is that you knew from the beginning that he was a sensitive, rather naive man who wouldn't have the same view of sexuality that you do. And you completely disregarded that.'

'Cassie, I don't need a lecture from you.'

'Apparently you do. You've hurt a very good man. If that doesn't make you feel lousy, then you're not the Lydia I know.'

With that, Cassie turned and left the office, leaving Lydia staring after her. Cassie had never used such vehement words with her, which meant that she felt very strongly about what she said.

And Lydia did feel lousy. In fact, she felt worse than she had in a long time. She didn't want to hurt Nicholas. She simply didn't want to be committed to him. To anyone, for that matter.

Knowing that attempting to work would be futile, Lydia told her secretary that she would be leaving for the day. She called Zack and ordered him to meet her at her house, then drove home. She had always been in control of her feelings. Complete control.

When she got home, Lydia went upstairs and took a hot bath before slipping into a sheer silk caftan. She walked downstairs, enjoying the sensation of the smooth material against her bare legs. The doorbell rang just as she was pouring herself a glass of wine. Lydia opened the front door to let Zack in. He was still dressed in his work clothes of jeans and a black T-shirt, but he had an energetic gleam in his eyes that told Lydia he was ready to play.

'You've given up on your boy-toy, have you?'

'Don't be rude, Zack.'

Zack grinned. 'Now you need me to satisfy that lusty itch of yours.'

Lydia frowned. 'Go upstairs.'

'Can I have a drink or something?' Zack asked.

'No. Go.'

Zack made a point of complaining, but went up the stairs with little hesitation. Lydia followed, admiring the way his jeans hugged his tight buttocks. They went into her bedroom, which she had illuminated with a series of dark blue and rose taper candles. Shadows danced across the walls, the candle flames jumping and twisting with the slightest breath of air.

Lydia approached Zack from behind and ran her palms over the expanse of his back. He started to turn, but she dug her fingers into his waist to prevent him from moving. Slowly, she slipped her hands around to his chest, sliding them underneath the hem of his T-shirt. She stroked upward to his bare chest, finding the hard, flat coins of his nipples and tugging them between her fingers. She felt his breathing increase in pace, and she lulled him into a sense of security for a moment with her gentle caresses. Then, she grasped one of his nipples between her thumb and forefinger and gave it a strong tweak.

'Ow!' Zack yanked himself away from her. 'That hurt!'

Lydia put her hands on her hips. 'Good. Perhaps next time you'll think twice before speaking to me so crudely.'

Zack scowled and rubbed his nipple. 'You know I didn't mean it.'

'I don't care if you meant it, I care that you said it,' Lydia replied. She pointed to the bed, tossing her hair back over her shoulder. 'Take off your shirt and lie down.'

Still scowling, Zack sat down on the edge of the bed and removed his shirt, shoes, and socks. He lay down on the bed, his apprehensive gaze on Lydia as she pulled open a drawer and removed two pairs of soft leather handcuffs.

Zack groaned. 'Oh, come on, Lydia.'

She knew Zack disliked being restrained, but she also knew that he derived an intense dark thrill from it. She knelt next to him on the bed, reaching for his wrist. She fastened one handcuff to his right wrist and attached it to the bedpost, then did the same with his left. The sight of him lying there with the candle shadows flickering on his half-naked body sent a shudder of pleasure through her.

'Lydia...' Zack shifted, trying to pull himself up.

Lydia put her hand on his chest and pushed him back down, pleased to notice that his jeans were beginning to bulge with his arousal. 'Don't move, precious.'

She went back to the drawer and picked up a soft leather whip, sliding her long fingers over the length of it as she turned back to face Zack. The knowledge that she had him under her power was a heady one, as much for her as for him. Heat flowed through her entire body, centring at the juncture of her thighs and causing her sex to swell and dampen.

'Lydia, for Chrissake –' Zack's protest was halted by the sting of the whip as Lydia brought it down across his abdomen.

She knew that Zack's moan of pain was exaggerated. She was an expert at handling a whip, and she knew exactly how to use it to deliver a minimum amount of pain – or a maximum amount. However, she had no desire to truly hurt Zack, so she brought the whip down again with enough pressure to bite, but not enough to really hurt. Zack winced.

'Such a disrespectful boy, you are,' Lydia murmured. She reached up and ran a hand through the dark, glossy strands of her hair, letting her breasts press against the thin fabric of her caftan.

Zack's gaze went immediately to the hard points of her nipples tenting the material, and his hips bucked involuntarily.

Lydia gave a throaty laugh. 'Aren't you, Zack?'

He drew in a shaky breath. 'Yes, Lydia.'

Lydia strode to the other side of the bed and administered a series of light, stinging slaps to the expanse of his abdomen, which caused Zack to complain and twist his body to escape the strikes. He grunted with every twitch of the mild pain as narrow welts appeared on his tanned, muscular flesh. His penis, however, could not hide the extent of his arousal, and the bulge in his jeans soon looked as if it would burst his zipper. Lydia leant over and caressed his erection through his jeans, scratching at his painful torment with her fingernails. Shallow, harsh pants escaped Zack's throat, and he pushed his hips towards her in a silent but unmistakable plea.

Lydia slowly drew his zipper down and tugged his jeans off his legs, smiling at the sight of his thick penis springing free from confinement. Zack moaned with relief and closed his eyes as Lydia wrapped her fingers around his stalk and began to stroke it from base to tip. It was warm and throbbing, the hard knob glistening with a drop of moisture. Lydia rubbed her thumb over the tip, massaging the liquid back into his skin.

Zack groaned and began to pump his hips up and down, trying to derive more stimulation. The candlelight flickered off the sheen of sweat that broke out on his chest, highlighting the red marks on his abdomen. Lydia reached out and put her palm on his belly, enjoying the feeling of his hot, bruised flesh. She slipped her fingers lower and caressed the tight sacs of his testicles, then lower still to the puckered ring of his anus. Ignoring his low gasp of protest, she probed him with her fingertip, invading him in the only way a woman can invade a man.

'Lydia . . .' Zack's hoarse voice told her he was on the edge.

Feeling mischievous, she stroked her hand up and down his thick erection until she sensed he couldn't hold back any longer, and then she circled her thumb and forefinger around the tip and squeezed. Zack groaned, his entire body tensing with frustration.

'Now,' Lydia said softly. 'You wouldn't dare come before I tell you to, would you?'

Zack closed his eyes. 'No.'

Lydia grasped the material of her caftan and began pulling it up over her legs, revealing full, rounded thighs and the juicy cleft of her vulva. She straddled Zack's waist and slid her body upward until her knees were positioned on either side of his head. A tingle started in the pit of her belly, the heady rush of control that stimulated her on both sexual and intellectual levels. Reaching out to grasp on to the headboard, she lowered herself slowly over his mouth, pleased when his tongue flickered out immediately to caress her.

'Go on,' she commanded softly. 'Deeper.'

Her head fell back, her eyes drifting closed as the delectable sensation of Zack's tongue began to probe along the crevices of her pussy, circling the tight hole. In one movement, Lydia stripped the caftan off her body, writhing her hips to encourage Zack's penetration. Oh, he was good at what he did. His tongue plunged into her channel, making her shiver with pure, sensual delight as her fingers slipped down to rub her clitoris. Her body revelled in the physical pleasure, although her mind couldn't shake the thought that she wished it was Nicholas underneath her rather than Zack.

'That's it, Zack,' Lydia whispered, trying to push

thoughts of Nicholas from her mind. She loved the sensation of Zack's harnessed body twisting underneath her, his eager mouth sucking and licking at her sex. Her blood rushed with heat and fire, stimulated by the wicked restraint of her captive and the sensual dancing of the candle flames.

She splayed her fingers over the swollen knot of her clitoris, tightening the ribbons of luscious tension around her body. Zack thrust his tongue in and out of her as if silently begging to be allowed to do the same with his aching penis. Lydia arched her back, squirming over his mouth, lost in her own lavish pleasure as the ribbons broke around her. Vibrations and fervour sparked along her nerves, delicious explosions of satisfaction that made her cry out. She gripped the headboard, moaning when Zack's lips closed around her sensitive clitoris and sucked the last, sweet pulses out of her body.

Lydia stroked her hands into Zack's hair as she manoeuvred herself off him, bending to kiss his shiny lips. The taste of her secretions sent a jolt of gratification through her, and she drove her tongue into his mouth to drink fully the flavour of herself. Zack opened his eyes to stare at her, his expression filled with both adoration and desperation. Every muscle in his body was rigid with carnal pain, his skin burning at the slightest touch.

'You're so good, darling,' Lydia murmured. 'I'll take care of you. You know that, don't you?'

Zack nodded, groaning in relief when Lydia straddled his hips. His desperation elicited a new wash of heat through her, as she knew that she was the only one who could relieve his torment. She grasped his penis in her hand, adjusting her body over his again as she began a lush descent on to him. He felt glorious, all throbbing maleness and rigidity pulsing against her inner walls. Bracing her hands on his chest, she began to ride him, lifting her hips up and down as pressure built achingly in her loins again. She fell over him, her breasts pressing against the expanse of his chest as her lower body began to work in a frantic rhythm.

Ah, how she adored the lewd feeling of his cock sliding

in and out of her, and the moist sounds of their carnality. She increased the pace, slamming down on to him so that his entire length filled her. Strange, little noises spilt from her throat as she rocked her body on him, pleasuring herself to the utmost extent. Another orgasm shuddered through her body before long, and she pressed her clitoris against him to derive every ounce of pleasure.

Only after she had stopped shuddering did Zack thrust his hips upward in a pained attempt to succumb to his own desire. Lydia slipped his cock out of her body and wrapped her fingers around his oiled shaft, stroking him hard as a cry broke from his throat. Streams of semen spurted out on to his groin and lower belly, falling like pearl droplets.

'Oh, Lydia.' Zack's body went limp, his chest heaving as he drew in ragged gasps. 'Thank you.'

Lydia stretched her sated body alongside his, letting her leg fall between his thighs. 'Now, you'd better not insult me on a regular basis in the hopes that this kind of thing will continue,' she chided.

Zack turned to look at her, the handsome planes of his face flushed and sweaty. 'Not if you promise me that it will.'

Lydia didn't reply, irritated by the nagging thought at the back of her mind. She slid her hand over Zack's chest and shifted to get off the bed. Yes, other men could provide her with physical pleasure. She knew that already. So why was she still thinking about Nicholas?

'Where are you going?' Zack asked.

'To make a telephone call.' Lydia slipped her discarded caftan over her head. 'I'll be right back.'

'Lydia, will you get these handcuffs off me, please?' he asked in frustration.

Lydia shook her head. 'No, I won't. You can just stay there for a while.'

'What's going on?' Zack complained, twisting against his leather restraints. 'You can't leave me like this.'

'Of course I can.' Ignoring Zack's protests, she went downstairs to her office. She closed the door and sank into the leather chair behind her desk. She dialled Molly's telephone number, nibbling impatiently on her fingernail as she waited for her friend to answer. 'Molly?'

'Hi, Lyd, darling. How are you?'

'OK. Have you heard from Cassie?'

'Yes, she called me a few hours ago,' Molly replied. 'She's rather hurt.'

Lydia sighed. 'Tell me something I don't know.'

'She'll get over it soon enough,' Molly said reassuringly. 'She wasn't completely enraptured with Nicholas, you know. She just thought he was a nice man.'

'He is a nice man.' Lydia thought of Nicholas's gentle, brown eyes and sensitive hands. She had never known anyone quite like him. Her lovers had always been sophisticated, often arrogant men who expressed their sexual devotion to her, but certainly never love or an equivalent emotion. 'I don't know what to do, Molly,' she confessed.

'How do you feel about him?'

'I don't know. I thought he was just a diamond in the rough.'

'He was, wasn't he?'

'Yes, but I didn't want him to have thoughts about love, for heaven's sake.'

'Why does that bother you so much?'

'Molly, I don't want him to be in love with me!' Lydia said in exasperation.

'Why not?'

'Well, because ... because he's ... I mean, I'm ... Christ, Molly, I just don't want any man to fall in love with me!'

'That's not much of an answer.'

'What am I supposed to do with a man if he falls in love with me?'

'I don't know. Fall in love right back?'

Nicholas pushed a book back on to the shelf, trying to ignore the persistent and annoying sound of Olive's gum snapping. He climbed off the ladder and went to his office where a dozen unopened boxes sat waiting for his attention. With a sigh, he picked up a knife and slit the tape on the first box, pulling apart the flaps to reveal a stack of erotic fiction novels.

'Olive!' Nicholas shouted.

'Yes, boss?'

'Did you order an entire shipment of erotic books?'

There was a moment of silence, then Olive appeared next to him, a chagrined look on her face.

'Well, I did tell you that the erotica section was selling a number of titles,' she said defensively. 'I thought it would be good for business if I expanded it a little.'

'A little?' Nicholas said. 'All of these boxes are filled with erotica, aren't they?'

'I'm only trying to help you,' Olive replied. 'You need to get yourself out of the dusty, leather-bound world of dead old men and start living a little.'

'Olive, I do not need your advice on living, thank you.'

'Nicholas, the only difference between you and those frumpy, old intellectual authors is that you're not old yet,' Olive informed him. 'At least Lydia Weston made an effort to update you a little.'

'I'm not a computer, dammit. I didn't need updating.'

Olive didn't reply, but her dubious expression said enough. Nicholas glared at her, wondering how she had managed to shift this conversation from an overload of erotic novels to his relationship with Lydia.

'You think differently, do you?' he asked.

'I think she was good for you, if you want to know the truth.'

'Sure she was. The trouble was that I wasn't good enough for her.' The minute the words were out of his mouth, Nicholas wanted to take them back. The last thing he needed was for Olive to assume he was in need of therapy. Of course, she immediately assumed exactly that.

'Oh, Nicholas,' Olive murmured. 'She really hurt you, didn't she?'

'No, she had nothing to do with it,' Nicholas replied. 'I simply made some inaccurate assumptions.'

'About her?'

'I really don't want to discuss this.'

'She had all of your best interests in mind,' Olive reminded him. 'She thought you could be a better man than you were.'

'She was wrong, then.'

'Was she?'

'For God's sake, Olive. She wanted to turn me into the kind of man that I'm not.'

'Oh, you poor thing.' Olive's voice was suddenly laced with sarcasm. 'A beautiful woman shows you how to improve yourself and suddenly you're a martyr when she doesn't want to live happily ever after with you.'

'What in the hell do you suggest I do, then?' Nicholas snapped. 'Carry her off on my stallion?'

'Couldn't hurt.'

'She made it quite clear that she wasn't interested in that kind of romance.'

'Every woman is interested in that kind of romance, Nicholas. Some of us just don't like to admit it.'

'Lydia Weston is not "every woman".'

'And she didn't think you were just any man either.'

Nicholas hefted the box of erotic books on to the floor and began tearing open the box underneath. 'This discussion is finished.'

Olive shrugged and began to look through the erotica. 'Whatever you say, boss.'

Nicholas gave her a wry look. 'Now I'm "boss" again?'

'You're only Nicholas when you're being an idiot,' Olive replied cheerfully. She lifted a book out of the box. 'Hey, have you ever read this? *The Lusty Adventures of Alexei the Cossack*. He was quite a fellow, you know. You could learn a thing or two from him on how to capture the woman of your choice.'

'I'm sure I probably could.'

Olive opened the book. 'He struts about making love with all sorts of women, making them want him, and then he takes control sexually until the women simply whimper and moan with desire for him,' she said. 'Listen to this. "Alexei strode towards the woman, his expression dark with lust and heat as he gazed down at her nakedness. She was utterly willing and ready for him, her legs spread wide to expose the dampness of her sex to his eyes. His entire body craved her, wanting to sink into her hot, wet depths until he had submerged himself in her so fully, so completely that all reason would become subordinate to need. His cock throbbed with the intensity of his –"'

'Olive, that is quite enough,' Nicholas interrupted, aware of his increasing flush. 'Alexei the Cossack deserves to have some privacy, I think.'

Olive chuckled. 'That's what you need, boss. To subordinate your reason to need.'

'I did that once and look where it got me.'

'Hopefully there can be a happy medium between both reason and need.'

The sudden female voice made both Nicholas and Olive look up in surprise. Nicholas felt his heart nearly leap out of his chest.

'Lydia.'

She smiled at him, then at Olive. 'Hello, Nicholas. Olive.'

Nicholas wondered how much of the conversation Lydia had heard. He stared at her for a moment, rather entranced by how lovely she looked dressed in a pair of faded, worn jeans that hugged her legs and an old Stanford University sweatshirt. He couldn't recall ever having seen her dressed so casually.

'What are you doing here?' he asked.

'I came to talk to you,' Lydia replied. 'We parted on rather negative terms last time, and I never like partings to end that way.'

'Olive, would you please leave us alone?' Nicholas requested.

'Sure. I'll be at the counter if you need me Nicholas.' Olive flashed him a teasing smile and gave Lydia a curious look before picking up a pile of erotic novels and heading for the counter.

Nicholas paused, feeling his heart thudding hard. He gestured towards his office. 'Do you want to sit down?'

'No. I can say what I need to say standing up.'

'Then please do.'

'Nicholas, when I decided that you would make a worthy candidate for our magazine, I had no intentions of having sex with you, let alone somehow causing you to have rather strong feelings for me. I assumed that breaking things off would make things easier on both of us, but clearly they haven't.'

'Why would they need to be easier for you?' Nicholas replied. 'I understand, Lydia. I was your piece of clay and you were the sculptor. You transformed me into your ideal, then you discovered that your ideal might actually have a mind of his own.'

'Don't get philosophical on me, Nicholas. And stop acting as if you're the victim. It's a very unattractive quality, you know. You knew from the beginning that I was a no-commitment kind of woman, and yet you chose to get involved with me anyway. And don't even think about saying that I seduced you or that you didn't have a choice because you know damn well that you did.'

'Of course I did. But do you remember when I asked you to dinner the first time we met? You turned me down. It was only after my appearance met your standards that you changed your mind.'

Lydia had the grace to look ashamed. 'I know, Nicholas. I'm not proud of the way I've treated you, but please understand that this has never happened to me before.'

'Or to me.'

Lydia looked at the floor suddenly, her teeth sinking into her lower lip. To Nicholas's surprise, he realised that she was nervous. 'I still can't promise you anything, Nicholas. I don't particularly care for the confinement of relationships, and yet I intensely dislike the thought of losing you. I don't expect anything from you, and I need to make it clear that you shouldn't expect anything from me, but I would very much like to be both your friend and your lover again.'

Nicholas looked at her for a long time. He had assumed she'd come here to tell him off. Instead, she wanted to be his friend and lover? He had the strangest feeling that Lydia Weston had never said those words to another man in her life. She hadn't needed to.

'I don't get it, Lydia. You made me into the kind of man you wanted me to be. I look better on the outside, but I'm exactly the same person. There is nothing essentially different about me.'

'I know.'

'So now do you think you can change me on the inside?'

'No. I don't want to. I like who you are on the inside. Very much.'

'How do I know that you don't want to change me?'

'I suppose you don't.' Lydia shook her head and sighed. 'I don't know how to do this, Nicholas. I just told you everything I possibly can. Beyond that, it's up to you.'

'And if I do fall in love with you?'

'Then I'll be enormously flattered. And who knows? Maybe I'll surprise both of us and fall right back in love with you.'

A smile quirked Nicholas's mouth. 'Well,' he said. 'I did know from the beginning that you were full of surprises. And you didn't disappoint me.'

'Of all the things I try not to be,' Lydia replied, 'disappointing is at the top of the list.'

'You succeed admirably.'

'Well, then,' Lydia said. 'What do you say? Should we try again?'

'I don't know,' Nicholas hedged. 'I might need a reminder of why I should deign to be your lover again.'

Lydia arched an eyebrow. 'Deign to be my lover?'

'Yeah. I'm a pretty good fuck, you know. If I do say so myself.'

'You must have had a most excellent teacher, then.'

Nicholas had to smile. 'She was pretty damn amazing.'

'Maybe you need to teach her a thing or two for a change.'

'Maybe I do.'

It took Nicholas all of two steps to cross the space between them. He reached out and grasped Lydia's hips, pulling her body against his in one movement. She drew in an audible breath at the contact. Nicholas decided that this would be an excellent opportunity to take advantage of Lydia's lovely, parted lips. He bent his head and captured her mouth with his, sliding his tongue between her lips to explore the warm cavern of her mouth. A slight moan emerged from Lydia's throat, and the sound seemed to resound through Nicholas on a direct path to his groin. His cock started to harden almost immediately, induced by the sensation of Lydia's full breasts pressing against his chest, and the curves of her hips tucked snugly in his palms.

He waited for the subtle signal that would indicate her taking control of the situation, but the signal didn't come. Instead, she simply slid her tongue against his, clutched his forearms, and let him do the seducing. And as he began to move his hands over Lydia's buttocks and underneath her sweatshirt, Nicholas began to feel the power of that dominating Cossack. Making them want him. With one hand, he clutched the back of Lydia's head and angled his mouth more firmly over hers, while the other hand slipped under her sweatshirt to explore the satiny smoothness of her skin. Ah, yes, sexual control was a heady sensation.

'Come here.' Nicholas guided Lydia to a narrow ladder that led up to his loft. He pushed her gently up the ladder ahead of him, enjoying the sight of her swaying buttocks as she climbed. When they were in the loft, Nicholas tugged Lydia back against him. He slid his hands around to cup her breasts in his hands. Her hard nipples poked through the thick fabric of her sweatshirt, eliciting another rush of heat through his body. He nuzzled the back of her neck and smiled when she shivered. Pressing his pelvis against her buttocks, he rotated his hips so that she would feel the full force of his erection.

'Well, lover,' Lydia murmured. 'What are you going to do with that?'

'What do you want me to do with it?' Nicholas whispered, darting his tongue out to taste the warmth of her skin.

He grasped the hem of her sweatshirt and pulled it over her head, smiling at the sight of the skimpy, lacy bra she wore. He would expect no less from Lydia. He unhooked the bra from the back and let her bare breasts spill into his hands. His penis stiffened further as Lydia's tight nipples pressed against his palms. He took great delight in massaging her breasts and rolling her nipples between his thumbs and forefingers. Lydia's breathing grew harsh and her body began to squirm against him.

'Does that feel good?' Nicholas said softly, grasping her earlobe between his teeth.

'Mmm.'

Nicholas slid his hands down to the waistband of Lydia's jeans, then made quick work of the button and zipper. He pushed them over her hips and told her to step out of them. Without turning her around to face him, Nicholas moved his hands across her belly and down to the lacy nothingness of her panties. He dipped his fingers underneath the elastic, his blood quickening as his fingers encountered the satin of her shaven mons. His fingers explored lower and lower until they met with a rush of moisture from Lydia's sex. Slowly, he slid his fingertips into her, circling the swollen nub of her clitoris. Lydia let out a moan of sheer pleasure, thrusting her hips against his hand as if begging for him to touch her clitoris directly.

Nicholas didn't oblige her. Satisfied with the extent of Lydia's pleasure so far, he moved his hand away from her sex and pulled her panties over her legs. And then she was naked in front of him. She started to turn around so that they would be face to face, but Nicholas grasped her shoulders to stop her. He pointed to a full-length mirror on the other side of the room.

'There,' he commanded softly. 'Let's go over there.'

They went to the mirror, Nicholas still behind Lydia, and stared at their reflections with a sense of heightened anticipation and arousal. Nicholas rubbed his hands over her nakedness, taking great pleasure in the sight of his hands on her body. Lydia's nipples jutted out sharply, her shorn cunt allowing no seclusion or mystery as it glistened with the evidence of her desire. Nicholas loved that about Lydia. There was no mystery about her. She put everything right out on the table, letting people know exactly what they were getting into when they chose to deal with her. As he had known. Only Nicholas suspected that most people didn't ignore Lydia's clear signals the way he had. He grasped her breasts in his hand, admiring greatly the way that her nipples poked out between his fingers, and the way her expression grew languid and hot as she watched his hands move on her body. Nicholas slipped one hand back down to Lydia's vulva.

'Spread them,' he commanded.

She parted her legs, allowing him full access to her sex. Nicholas traced the moist ring of her pussy before submerging one finger deep inside her. Lydia gasped, letting her head fall back against his shoulder.

'Oh, yes, darling,' she whispered, her voice husky. 'Fuck me with your finger.'

Nicholas did, thrusting his finger back and forth while his thumb rolled over her clit. Their gazes were locked to their reflections in the mirror as Nicholas rubbed her to completion. When she climaxed, she let out a squeal of pleasure as her body shook with vibrations, and her fluids coated Nicholas's fingertips. She looked so stunningly beautiful in the mirror, her skin painted with the reddish blush of passion, and her eyes filled with sated sensuality, that Nicholas's heart skipped a beat. God, he did love her – loved her more than anything – only he would say nothing of that to Lydia until she had learnt to accept not only that love, but to admit her own feelings as well. Lydia did love him. Of that, Nicholas was certain. He simply knew now that it would take her a longer time to realise that.

Lydia arched her back, thrusting her breasts more fully into his hands as she put her hands behind her head to run her fingers through his hair. 'Oh, how wonderful you are.'

'I'm not finished yet,' Nicholas murmured. 'I want to fuck you from behind.'

A shiver of excitement shuddered through Lydia's body. 'I love that.'

'So do I.' Nicholas stepped away from her. 'Kneel on the bed.'

Christ, his cock was as hard as stone. He almost winced from the pressure as he unzipped his jeans and allowed his erection to spring free. Lydia climbed on to the bed, spreading her lovely legs wide as she positioned herself on her hands and knees. Her sex was fully exposed, damp with moisture, and Nicholas simply gazed at it for a moment, constantly in awe of the physical pleasures a woman could bestow upon a man. He stripped off his shirt and grasped his jutting penis in his hand.

'Can I see?' Lydia asked.

'No,' Nicholas replied. 'You'll just have to feel.'

Lydia moaned softly, bending and burying her face in a pillow. Her body quivered, her breasts dangling like ripe fruits below her. Nicholas situated himself behind her, rubbing one finger over her pussy and up to the tightly puckered ring of her anus. Lydia pushed her hips backward as if attempting to impale herself on his finger. Nicholas pushed his forefinger slowly into the lubricated hole, nearly gasping himself at the sheer tightness of it.

'Nicholas,' Lydia gasped. 'Put it in me. Please.'

'Here?' Nicholas rotated his finger in her anus.

'Anywhere!'

Nicholas's cock jerked in anticipation, as if of its own volition. He grasped it in his hand and slowly stroked it from base to tip as he teased the folds of Lydia's labia with the hard head. Fluid dripped from the tip as he slid his knob down one crevice and back up the other side. Her clitoris sprouted out from underneath its protective hood like a tiny blossom. And then slowly, ever so slowly, Nicholas began to push it into her, thrilling at the sensation of her hot heat surrounding his flesh.

He closed his eyes as another groan of pleasure shuddered through Lydia's body. Her inner muscles tightened around him, gripping him as if she would never let him go. He continued submerging himself in her until he could go no further, and then he gripped her upturned buttocks in his hands and began to thrust. He could hardly believe the intensity of the sensations that rocked through him as his hard cock was consumed by her soft humidity. His testicles slapped against her, eliciting the wet smacks of lust that spurred them both to higher levels of pleasure.

Nicholas worked his hips more rapidly, leaning fully over Lydia's back to clutch her swaying breasts in his hands and tease her nipples with his fingers. Loud moans punctuated her harsh breathing as her body pushed back against his to increase the depth of his thrusting. Nicholas straightened and grasped her jiggling buttocks, thoroughly enjoying the sight of his slick cock moving in and out of such a haven of pleasure. He had never taken a woman in this position before, but oh what a thrill it was. He pumped faster, harder, evoking squeals of pleasure from Lydia as she arched her back and spread her thighs apart even wider.

Nicholas pressed his finger against Lydia's anus, watching in aroused fascination as the tight ring widened to accommodate his finger, then contracted around it again. An intense tension built in his lower body. Sweat broke out on his forehead, his fingers digging into Lydia's buttocks. When he could stand it no longer, he pulled out and grasped his oiled penis, rubbing it hard with his hand as an orgasm vibrated violently through his body and streams of come jetted out on to Lydia's buttocks and back. Rubbing his cock into the crevice between Lydia's bottom cheeks, Nicholas leant over her again, slipping his hand into the scorching area between her legs so that he could bring her off. Lydia groaned as her body began to shake again with waves of pleasure. She collapsed on to the bed, her body heaving with the force of her rapid breaths.

'Ah, yes,' she murmured, her voice muffled by the pillow. 'That's the kind of loving I can appreciate.' She rolled on to her back and looked at him, her expression one of complete satiation. 'That kind of loving when it comes from you.'

'At the rate we're going,' Nicholas said, 'I think I'm going to be providing you with that kind of loving for quite some time now. Suppose you return the favour?'

Lydia gave him a slow, languid smile. 'Oh, darling. Believe me, I intend to.'

Lydia typed another title into the computer automatically, her mind a million miles away. Her entire body still tingled from the sheer physical pleasure that she and Nicholas constantly managed to create together. She still didn't know what kind of future, if any, they had together, but she did love their compatibility. As different as they were, it often seemed as if their differences were what drew them so closely together; they saw in each other the qualities they lacked in themselves. And Lydia knew now that their compatibility was one she wasn't willing to give up.

She looked up from the computer as another customer entered the store. A smile broke out across her face at the sight of Cassie Langford, belying her sudden tinge of wariness.

'Cassie, how lovely to see you. How are you?'

'I'm fine, thanks. Have you quit your position as a high society fashion magazine editor to work at Nicholas's bookstore?'

'Not quite. Olive wanted the day off today and, since it's Saturday, I was happy to help out.'

Cassie paused by the magazine rack at the front of the store and picked up a copy of *Savoir Faire*. 'Nicholas looks good on the cover.'

'Yes, but don't tell him that unless you want to see him turn beet-red. He actually tried to get me to cover the front with other magazines so that his face would be hidden.'

'Modesty isn't a bad quality in a man.' Cassie replaced the magazine and gave Lydia a smile. 'In fact, it can be quite appealing.'

'Yes, I know.' Lydia hesitated for a moment. 'Cassie, I'm terribly sorry about the way things turned out. I know I thought you and Nicholas would make a wonderful couple. I wasn't aware of the fact that I wanted him for myself. At least, not until that possibility became clear.'

Cassie lifted her slender shoulders. 'Don't worry about

it, Lydia. I told you that I liked him, and I did. But that was all. My heart wasn't broken. Far from it, in fact.'

'I still didn't mean to steal him away from you.'

'You didn't, Lydia. He was never mine to steal.'

'You told me you had sex with him.'

'I did. That didn't make him mine.'

Lydia nodded. She knew all about non-possessive sex. How odd it was, though. She had the strangest feeling that her relationship with Cassie had changed in some way. The trouble was, she couldn't pinpoint exactly what that way was. 'Cassie, you know you mean more to me than anything, don't you? You and Molly. I'd give up everything if I thought it would ruin our friendship.'

'I know, Lydia. You'd never let a man come between us. And neither would I.'

'Then we're OK?'

'We're fine.'

'Why don't I feel like we're fine?'

Cassie shook her head. Her delicate features suddenly looked somewhat worried. 'It's not you, Lydia. It's me. I'm just a little confused right now.'

'About what?'

Cassie smiled wryly. 'If I knew that, I wouldn't be confused.'

'Can I help?'

'Not right now. I'll be fine, Lydia, please don't worry about me. If I need your help, I'll ask. I always have before.'

'You won't stop asking, will you?'

Cassie smiled again and shook her head. 'Never.'

She crossed the small space between her and Lydia and reached out to hug her friend. 'If you and Nicholas end up getting married, I hope you'll consider me for maid of honour.'

'You'll be the first in line.' Lydia pressed her lips against Cassie's cheek. 'Although the thought of marriage gives me hives.'

'Yes, well, you also once claimed that the thought of a steady relationship produced the same malady,' Cassie reminded her dryly.

Lydia grinned. 'Touché.'

'Take care, OK? I'll call you next week and maybe we can have lunch.'

'I'd love that. Please do.' Lydia watched Cassie leave. Her heart was troubled over her friend's obvious uncertainty, but Cassie had always worked herself out of troublesome situations and relationships. And Lydia knew that whatever the problem was, Cassie would find a solution in the end. A solution that would allow no compromise.

Lydia looked at the computer screen for a moment before she heard the office door close. She glanced up, her heart warming at the sight of Nicholas walking towards her, his attention totally focused on the book in his hands. He was wearing a faded pair of jeans and a flannel shirt, and his glasses were perched on the edge of his nose. No, he wasn't the sophisticated, air-brushed gentleman who appeared on the cover of *Savoir Faire*, but Lydia no longer wanted him to be. She wanted him in all his rumpled, guileless glory, looking mighty tasty in those worn jeans.

'Lydia, this is a first edition of *The Wizard of Oz*.' Nicholas didn't even look up as he approached the counter. 'Have you any idea how rare these are?'

'Rare enough, I imagine,' Lydia murmured.

'You know, I need to get a moisture-controlled glass case to display items like this,' Nicholas remarked, finally tearing his attention away from the book to look around the store. 'Maybe we could put it behind the register, or even against that side wall so that people would be able to see them. Although, then we might have problems with the sun. I don't want any of the books to fade.'

'I'm sure you'll find a brilliant solution.'

'Mmm.' Nicholas started to return his attention to the book, but Lydia reached out and took it from his hands. Nicholas looked at her in surprise. 'What?'

'Nothing. I just happen to think you're pretty cute.'

Nicholas grinned, manoeuvring behind the counter to slide his hands around her hips. 'You do, huh?'

Lydia nodded. She reached up and pressed her lips

against his, loving the way he pulled her closer as if he couldn't get enough of her. Just as she was becoming aware of her own insatiability concerning him. 'Nicholas.'

'Hmm?'

'I think I could fall in love with you.'

Nicholas pulled back slightly and stared at her. 'What?'

'You heard me. You once said those words to me, so now in all honesty, I'm saying them back to you. I'm not promising anything, but simply telling you the truth.'

A slow contented smile broke out across Nicholas's face. 'I love the truth.'

Lydia returned his smile. 'So do I.'

Their lips met in another kiss. After a minute, Nicholas pulled away again, but this time it was only to lock the door and hang the CLOSED sign in the window.

# Part 2

## *The Discovery of Molly*

# Chapter One

Molly stared up at the chandeliers. They were common enough objects, especially to someone like her, with free and frequent access to opulently decorated establishments. But today the chandeliers appeared to her as if in a lucid dream. Such fragile things, made safe only by the strict tether that attached them to the ceiling. A paradox, fragility protected and enhanced by strict almost rough attachment.

'Didn't you go out with a new man last week, Molly?' Lydia asked, her voice breaking through Molly's thoughts. 'Was he any good?'

Molly shook her head as she recalled her evening with a businessman from Milan.

'He was incredibly gauche,' she answered, flipping back her auburn curls and pursing her lips in disgust. 'He wanted me to talk to his penis, if you can believe that. During sex! What did he think I was, a marionette? It was as if he wanted me to pull the strings and make the damn thing dance.'

Cassie laughed. 'And did you?'

'Lord, no. I rolled right out of bed and out the door. Then he called me the next day as if nothing was wrong, asking me if I would dress up looking hot to go to a party with him. I mean, please. One day I'm a cock psychologist and the next day I'm an arm decoration. I told him never to call me again, then I hung up.'

Lydia leant back in her chair, curling her long fingers around her wine glass. 'Was he Italian?'

'Of course. I do so love Italian men. This one, however, lacked the genteel quality required of men – Italian or otherwise – I allow to take me to bed. I've decided to go

103

back to Piero. At least he knew how to treat me like a woman.'

'Well, we all make mistakes,' Lydia murmured. 'Meaning the talking penis man, of course. And what about the rest of your social activities?'

'Oh, the usual.' Molly tried to ignore Lydia's slightly derisive tone. 'Organising the debutante ball for next year, in addition to several fashion shows and parties galore. I do hope you'll both be attending my parents' Christmas party this year. Last year, it was terribly dull without you.'

'I'll be in San Francisco this year, so of course I will,' Lydia said. 'Speaking of attending parties, you're both coming to my place on Friday, aren't you? Nicholas is beside himself with glee about meeting Harker Trevane, so I've gone above and beyond the call of duty to organise a fabulous party for him. I've planned it around a Japanese theme since Harker Trevane's book takes place mostly in Japan. The party, however, will be terribly exclusive. I'm expecting that it will end up the subject of several newspaper and gossip column articles. I've only invited a hundred people, and the dinner will be sit-down as opposed to buffet.'

'It sounds wonderful. I'd love to come to the book signing as well,' Cassie said. 'I have a colleague who studies contemporary American fiction and popular culture. She would love a signed copy of Trevane's book.'

'Please do come, then,' Lydia said, glancing at Molly. 'Are you interested in attending the signing, Molly?'

'Yes, I think it would be fascinating,' Molly replied. She turned her attention to her food, feeling more than a little upstaged by her friend. She had never before felt as if she and Lydia were in competition, but lately with Lydia's magazine skyrocketing in sales and her bliss over her relationship with Nicholas, Molly was beginning to think that her friend had adopted a condescending tone.

Either that, or her own insecurities were bobbing to the surface. She took a bite of her Caesar salad and let her gaze settle momentarily on Cassie. At least Cassie was the same. It was comforting to know that certain people could be counted on not to change.

'When is the signing?' Molly asked Lydia.

'Friday, starting at noon,' Lydia replied. 'We're expecting that the shop will be packed with people. It might be best if you both came through the back. Just ring the delivery bell, and I'll let you in.'

'Have you met him yet?' Molly asked. 'Harker Trevane?'

'Not yet, but his publicist claims that the main character in his novels is based on him,' Lydia explained. 'Harker used to be an investigative reporter before he turned to fiction writing, so much of his work is autobiographical. Or so the publicist claims.'

'What is this new book about?' Cassie asked.

'About a private detective who goes to Japan to battle a gang of terrorists responsible for having killed his parents,' Lydia replied. She rolled her eyes in evident disdain. 'He infiltrates the world of Asian gangs and drug trafficking. Packed with testosterone, obviously. However, I did read the book. Not only is it incredibly well-written, but it's also highly intriguing and suspenseful. I have to give Harker Trevane credit for keeping my attention throughout the entire novel. And the hero, Nevin Rafferty, is quite fascinating.'

'Well,' Molly murmured. 'There's nothing wrong with "packed with testosterone".'

'No,' Lydia agreed. 'Nothing wrong with that at all.'

'Not that Nicholas is anything like that.'

Lydia gave Molly a slight smile. 'You'd be surprised. Mastery can be taught, you know.'

'Now that's a man.'

Molly glanced at Olive, who had sidled up next to her. The bookshop employee looked like her usual perky self, dressed in a short, pleated skirt and a soft blue sweater that snugly cradled her ample breasts. Molly wondered vaguely if Nicholas had ever succumbed to Olive's unmistakable charms.

'He apparently has a very intriguing past,' Olive continued.

Molly rested her shoulder against the edge of the bookshelf and gazed thoughtfully at the man seated at a table near the front of the store. His brown hair was streaked with strands of sun-bleached gold, his profile hard as he looked down to sign another book. He wasn't particularly handsome; there was something too rough about him. Deep grooves bracketed his mouth, and creases fanned out from the edges of his eyes. Molly's gaze travelled down to his shoulders and his arms. He wore a soft chambray shirt that was rolled up at the sleeves to reveal tanned forearms. He did have beautiful hands, strong and broad with tapered fingers. Nicholas stood next to him, greeting eager customers and keeping the line moving.

'What kind of intriguing past?' Molly asked.

'Oh, all sorts of adventures as an investigative reporter,' Olive replied. 'Parts of his book are based on his own experiences.'

'Well,' Molly murmured, 'he does appear to have stamina.'

Olive chuckled. Molly returned her gaze to the author.

How many books had he signed so far? Customers had been lining up outside since early that morning for the noon book signing, and the line had only grown since then. Molly picked up a copy of the book from a stack on the floor. The title *Red Sun* was emblazoned on the glossy black cover in red letters accompanied by the name Harker Trevane.

'Well, loves, it appears that this is a success,' Lydia said as she stopped next to Molly and Olive. 'Nicholas is delighted.'

'I still don't know how you managed to convince a best-selling author that Nicholas's store was the place to do a major book signing,' Molly said.

'With a little encouragement, anyone can be persuaded to do anything,' Lydia replied. '*Savoir Faire* is going to promote his books for a female audience. The publishers have been disappointed in the female demographics for Trevane's books, so hopefully we can help change that.'

Molly looked at the book again and flipped through

the pages. She scanned a few sentences, written in a terse blunt style that lacked the merest hint of flowery prose.

'Why don't you read it and write up a report?' Lydia asked. 'Favourable, of course. We'll print it in the next issue.'

Molly's eyebrows lifted. 'You want me to write a book review?'

'Why not? You might enjoy it.'

'I guess I can try.' At least, Molly thought, it would give her something to do. She had been rather bored lately.

'Wonderful.'

'What time is the party tonight?' Molly asked.

'Eight. You'll be there, won't you?'

Molly's gaze drifted to Harker Trevane again, who was shaking hands with an adoring fan. After handing the book to the woman, he glanced in Molly's direction as if he felt her gaze on him. Startled at the sudden contact with his cold blue eyes, Molly took a step backwards. Their gazes held for the briefest second before Harker Trevane resumed signing books, effectively dismissing her.

Molly frowned. She was not used to being dismissed. 'Yes, Lydia. I'll be there.'

That evening, she took special care with her appearance, choosing a white silk slip dress that flowed around her body in soft folds. She left her auburn curls loose and applied a subtle coating of make-up. As she looked in the mirror, she silently dared Harker Trevane to dismiss her now.

Her limousine driver dropped her off at the front of Lydia's house, the outside of which was decorated with strings of paper lanterns. Molly left her wrap with the maid and went into the drawing room.

'You look wonderful, Cassie.' Molly made her way over to Cassie and hugged her friend, delighted with the way the soft grey silk suit complemented Cassie's adorable figure. She had helped Cassie pick the suit out several months ago and paid for it as Cassie's birthday present. 'Have you met the infamous author yet?'

Cassie shook her head. 'Not yet. Molly, you look lovely. I haven't seen you in that dress before.'

'No, it's new. I bought it in Paris last week.' Molly scanned the crowd for a glimpse of Harker Trevane. She couldn't locate him, but suspected that he was at the centre of the large crowd gathered near the French doors.

Lydia, as usual, had gone to great lengths to provide her guests with a lavish yet elegant party. Sequins and silk created an undulating sea of sparkle as people moved about the rooms like slow-moving ships, savouring the delicacies of the hors d'oeuvres. Voices and laughter, lubricated with plenty of expensive wine and champagne, rose above the crowd.

'Lydia seated you next to him for dinner,' Cassie informed her.

Molly stared at her friend. 'Who?'

'Harker Trevane. She thought you might want to talk to him since you're writing that review.'

'I think she's just trying to give me something to do,' Molly muttered.

Cassie grinned. 'With Harker maybe?'

'He wouldn't be a bad thing to do.' Molly caught a glimpse of Harker as he moved away from his crowd of admirers.

He wore a black-and-white tuxedo, and moved with a kind of masculine grace that belied his tough-guy persona. He glanced in her direction, and their eyes met again. A rush of warmth pooled in her sex simply from the visual contact. Yes, Molly thought, Harker Trevane was definitely intriguing.

'Excuse me, Cassie, I'm going to go outside and get some air.' Molly picked up a glass of champagne from a passing server and walked towards the French doors. She stepped on to the terrace that overlooked the bay and the Golden Gate bridge. Salty air drifted against her skin. She loved the bridge – it was so elegant in design and appearance, and yet so strong, built to withstand winds of over a hundred miles an hour. She curled her hands around the marble railing, enjoying the cold, erotic sensation against her palms.

She heard Harker Trevane before she saw him. His shoes clicked against the stone as he approached and stopped directly behind her. Molly refused to turn around, but she could feel his presence as if he were touching her.

'You're Molly, aren't you?'

'Yes. You're Harker, aren't you?'

'So they tell me.'

How close was he standing? Molly imagined that she could feel his body heat through the flimsy silk of her dress. And then, ever so lightly, Harker Trevane's finger trailed down her spine. Molly shivered.

'Nice dress.'

'Thank you. It's from Paris.'

'I figured. What are you doing out here?'

'Just looking at the bridge,' Molly replied.

'Mmm. Quite a sight. Did you know that the Golden Gate is the longest single-span suspension bridge in the world?'

'And one of the strongest.' Molly felt his finger trail up her spine again. The chandeliers again came to mind, strength and suspension.

'What is it that you do, Molly?'

'I'm very active in the community,' Molly replied.

'I hear your father is a newspaper magnate,' Harker said. 'And that you travel quite frequently.'

'That's correct.'

'You're a socialite, hmm?'

Molly turned, her eyes flashing with irritation over his derisive tone. 'Excuse me?'

A smile tugged at Harker's mouth. 'I know your type. You jet-set around the world, dining at the finest res- taurants, doing some superficial charity work, but with a total lack of contact with the real world.'

Molly was so surprised that for a moment she could only stare at him. 'Who in the love of God do you think you are, talking to me like that? You know nothing about me!'

To her further surprise, he grinned. 'I know you have spirit.'

'Are you trying to goad me?'

'I just asked around about you, princess, that's all.'

Molly frowned. 'Why?'

'I wanted to know who you were.'

'And you decided that I was a superficial socialite?' Molly knew she shouldn't be rising to his bait, but she couldn't help it.

'I decided you were one hell of a sexy woman.'

'You had to ask around to figure that out?'

'It didn't hurt.'

Molly was trapped between the closeness of his body and the terrace railing. She reached behind her to steady herself on the railing, highly aware of the way her nipples were hardening against the silk of her gown. When Harker's gaze slipped down to her breasts, she flushed. The air grew charged between them, an electric sexual heat augmented by the sensation of Harker's breath against her forehead.

Molly swallowed hard. 'I think we should go in for dinner.'

'Good idea.'

Molly slipped past him, her heart pounding hard in her chest, and went into the dining room. Round tables decorated with elaborate sprays of flowers were placed around the room, and a server stood waiting next to each table. Molly spied Lydia and Nicholas standing at the front of the room, guiding the guests towards their respective places. She admitted to being surprised that they had been together for so many months, but they appeared to be completely happy together.

'Please, sit down.' Harker pulled Molly's chair out for her, then took his own seat.

'Well,' Molly said. 'I didn't expect such courtesy from the dangerous Harker Trevane.'

'Surprising, isn't it?' He flicked out his napkin and spread it in his lap. 'I'm an honourable man.'

Molly chuckled. She didn't know if he was honourable, but he was certainly seductive. Her skin simmered with attraction simply because she was seated next to him.

'So,' she said, as the room settled down and the servers

brought out the first course. 'I hear you just have all kinds of adventures to tell.'

Harker lifted his shoulders in a shrug. 'I've been around.'

'Enough to know a socialite princess when you see one?'

He flashed her another grin. 'You said it.'

'You think that simply because I travel frequently and throw parties, I'm frivolous?'

'Don't get upset, Molly. I happen to have a thing for socialite princesses. As frivolous as they are.'

Molly shook her head at him. She didn't know if he was teasing her or being serious, but she would no longer give him the satisfaction of reacting defensively.

'You're a very strange man.'

'Mmm.' He broke open a hot roll. A spiral of steam rose from the split bread. 'Tell me, Molly, what you find erotic.'

Molly drew in a breath. 'Erotic?'

'Yes.' A slight smile curved his lips. 'For instance, I find bread to be quite sensual. Warm, textured slices of bread with soft, yielding centres and a heady aroma that seems to invade your body and makes you want more and more . . .'

His voice trailed off as he bit into the steaming roll with white, even teeth. Molly stared at him, aware of the pounding of her heart, of the warmth gathering between her legs.

She tore her gaze away from him, wondering what was the matter with her. She couldn't remember *wanting* a man with such pure carnality. She tried to focus on the bowl of soup in front of her, but her appetite was certainly not directed towards food.

'So, Molly?' he repeated, his voice deep and caressing. 'What about you?'

'If we're talking about food, I would have to say rich, buttery chocolate,' she said. 'Or else, flowers and blossoms that open and spread at the touch of the sun's heat.'

She reached for her wine glass, glancing at him sideways through her eyelashes. His dark eyes were hot.

'Delicious, isn't it?' he murmured. 'Eroticism can be found everywhere if you just look at things the right way.'

Although Molly was aware that they were both being rude by ignoring the dinner companions on either side of them, she really didn't care. She felt like she was sinking into a gauzy cocoon of sensuality with this man. And despite his derisive teasing, it was a place in which she wanted to stay.

'Is that something you always do?' she asked. 'Look for the erotic in everything?'

'Most of the time, it just seems that way,' he replied. 'Or else something or someone just exudes sensuality.'

His eyes slipped down to rest on the upthrust of her small breasts created by her tight bodice. Molly flushed.

'You're a born seducer, aren't you?' she asked.

'Ah, Molly. Only to those who want to be seduced.'

'And you think I do?'

'Don't you?'

God, yes, she did. Molly sipped a spoonful of soup, painfully aware of each movement of his body next to her. She couldn't help her gaze from drifting down to his lap, wondering if he was getting as aroused as she was. Unfortunately, his napkin hid whatever evidence might be mounting in his trousers.

Molly made a point of turning to the woman on the other side of her. After all, she didn't want to add to this man's arrogance by giving him her complete, undivided attention.

'Mrs Edwards, how was your trip to Rome?' she asked politely.

'Oh, just lovely, dear,' Mrs Edwards gushed. She launched into detailed descriptions of the restaurants she and her husband had frequented and the Italian upper-crust families they had visited.

Molly listened with as much attention as she could muster when she suddenly felt Harker's hand on her thigh. The heat of his hand burnt through the thin silk of her dress, flowing into her very blood. She didn't stop him when he grasped a fistful of material in his fingers and began to pull the skirt up her legs. Molly's heart thudded hard.

'So, you can imagine with all those fountains in Rome, the cleaning expenses are just exorbitant,' Mrs Edwards continued, waving her bejewelled hand in the air. 'So the Rossettis have these absolutely marvellous benefits and fund-raisers.'

'How wonderful.' Molly fought the urge not to squirm in her seat as Harker's hand touched her bare skin. His palm was warm, his fingers slightly rough and callused. His hand slid up her rounded thigh, pausing dangerously close to her heated apex.

Without warning, his fingers dipped between her thighs, brushing against the mound barely concealed by the flimsy silk of her panties. Molly gasped, stunned by the force of such light contact.

'Dear, are you all right?' Mrs Edwards asked, a crease appearing between her painted eyebrows. 'You look rather feverish.'

Molly almost choked on her soup. Harker chuckled.

'I'm fine, Mrs Edwards,' Molly replied, relieved when they were distracted by the arrival of the second course.

The tablecloth hid the inappropriate touching occurring in her lap, and Molly struggled to maintain a semblance of composure as the server removed her soup bowl. Harker edged his forefinger under the silk of her panties, causing her entire body to jerk in response as he touched her slick folds.

He glanced at her, his dark eyes amused. 'Delicious Molly, I want you.'

Feeling wicked, Molly put her hand in his lap, searching beneath the napkin for the evidence of his own need. Sure enough, a hard thick bulge greeted her seeking fingers. A little sigh escaped her lips as she cupped her palm around the large protrusion and massaged it gently.

'So you do,' she murmured.

She smiled when he grimaced and reached down to remove her hand. 'Careful, sweetie. As I said, this could become scandalous.'

Molly laughed. 'I'd venture to say that it already is.'

She had done some wanton things in her time, but never had she sat at a dinner party and allowed a virtual stranger to touch her intimately. Still, she didn't protest when his finger swirled around the hard nub of her clitoris, evoking tiny shivers of pleasure. A feeling of bereftness filled her when he eventually took his hand away, but not before sliding his palm lingeringly over her thigh.

Molly was barely aware of the conversation drifting around her or of the taste of her food. All she wanted to do was drink in the raw sensuality of the man next to her. Her gaze kept drifting to him, captivated by the succulent way that he ate. His every movement was purposeful and direct, and he clearly savoured each morsel. Molly trembled at the thought that he would make love with the same sort of relishing precision.

By the time dessert arrived, she was tense with unfulfilled longing and slightly light-headed from a lack of food and too much wine. Still, her senses were clear and alert as she licked a dollop of whipped cream from her fork and thought about a far more substantial dessert that would surely follow.

Smiling to herself, she watched the guests start to disperse. She glanced at Harker.

'Have you seen Lydia's library?' she asked. 'It's quite extensive.'

'I haven't. Would you care to show me?'

'Certainly.'

She pushed her chair back and stood, aware of him behind her as she walked back through the hall and into the foyer. Without a word, they went down a corridor lined with oil paintings to a room closed off by carved, wooden doors. Molly opened the door and went inside, tugging him after her. She closed the door behind her.

Lord, but Harker was sexy. All tall rugged maleness made enticingly mysterious by her lack of knowledge about him. Molly's heart thrummed a primitive drumbeat, her body slipping into the natural rhythms of lustful attraction. A smile played about her mouth as she moved past him into the library. Leather-bound books lined the walls, and the room was dominated by a large oak desk covered with folders and papers. Molly went to a cabinet behind the desk and opened it to reveal an array of liquor bottles.

'Would you like a drink?' she asked. 'Brandy?'

'Nothing, thanks.'

Molly turned to look at him. He still stood near the door, his gaze never leaving her.

'Come here, Molly,' he said, his voice slightly husky.

Slowly, her body feeling oddly light and free, Molly closed the liquor cabinet and crossed the room. She locked the library door and turned to look at him. Her breathing shortened at the look in his eyes. She didn't move when Harker approached her, backing her up against the door as his hands slipped down to clutch her hips.

His mouth descended on hers so swiftly that she barely had time to take a breath. But, oh, what an incredible pleasure to feel his lips pressing against hers, tactile and slightly rough. Molly sank back against the door, letting him hold her in place as her nerves began to simmer with arousal. She opened her mouth to let him in, revelling in the sensation of his tongue sliding across hers, stroking the glossy surface of her teeth, licking the corners of her lips. His kiss was demanding and probing, evoking her response as if he were tuning a fine musical instrument.

Harker's fingers grasped the folds of Molly's skirt and began to draw them up over her legs until he could touch the bare skin of her thighs. Molly shivered when she felt the first contact of his hands on her skin, sliding around to the backs of her thighs and cupping her bottom. The heat of his palms burnt through the thin silk of her panties, stirring her fires by rapid degrees. Without thinking, she wrapped one leg around his thighs, bringing their lower bodies into contact. The hard bulge in his trousers pushed against her belly so potently that she could practically feel the blood rushing through him.

Her head fell back as the kiss deepened, as their tongues explored each other's mouths with growing frenzy. He tasted delicious, like crisp wine and chocolate, and the flavour of him augmented Molly's awareness of all her senses. She stroked her tongue across his lower lip, wanting to eat and drink him all at once, her breath emerging in rapid, desperate gasps.

She slipped her hand between their bodies, stroking her fingers over the length of his cock. Harker's fingers moved under the elastic of her panties, finding and exploring the deep crevice of her buttocks. Molly started when he began tracing the puckered ring of her anus with his forefinger, even as a quiver of delight trailed over her skin. She clutched his arms, drawing in a breath when his mouth slid down to her neck, his tongue flickering over the rapid pulse beating underneath her skin.

'You are luscious,' Harker murmured. 'Succulent.'

His fingers closed around her panties, and then he ripped them off her in one, swift movement. A thrill of pure excitement skipped over Molly's nerves, and she tightened her leg around his thighs, opening her body up to him. His fingers dipped into the warm wet crevice between her legs. He gave a husky laugh.

'Hungry, aren't you?'

'Mmm.' Molly squirmed against him, silently pleading for the penetration of his fingers.

He seemed determined to tease her, sliding his fingertips leisurely over her silken folds, tracing the opening of her sex, circling the swollen nub. His touch was light and tormenting. And very clever. A delicious rope of tension and frustration wound about Molly's lower body. With a muffled groan, she reached down to grasp his erection again, her mind swimming with anticipation over what his hard length would feel like in her body.

She fumbled to unfasten the zipper of his trousers and tucked her hand into the opening. Her entire body shuddered with pleasure at the sensation of his throbbing penis against her palm. She rubbed her fingers over his shaft, trailing them across the veins pulsing with blood and heat. Feeling Harker tense at her touch, she glanced up at him through her eyelashes. His expression was tight, almost pained, as if attempting to retain control over himself.

A little feeling of triumph rose in Molly. She drew his

cock out of his trousers, flicking her tongue rapaciously across her lower lip as she gazed down at it. She wanted him to drive into her immediately, filling her to the hilt, but he made no move to enter her. Instead, he grasped her bodice, pulling it down over her shoulders and exposing her bare breasts. Molly's nipples were so hard and aching that they jutted forth without shame, crowning her creamy breasts with sharp evidence of her desire.

Molly let her eyelids drift closed as Harker bent to take one nipple between his lips, sucking at it with such expertise that Molly's tension expanded to unfathomable degrees. Her sex constricted, craving him in there. Ribbons of fire flowed down a path from her nipples to her sex, becoming so heated that perspiration broke out on her skin. She braced her hand on his shoulder, moaning with pleasure as he took her other nipple between his thumb and forefinger. He pulled and tugged at it so lightly that Molly's entire body went weak. She opened her mouth to draw in air.

'Oh, come on,' she murmured. 'Fuck me. Do it now.'

She grasped his cock again, rubbing her thumb over the bursting, plum-coloured tip. Spreading her legs farther apart, she guided him towards her, stroking his erection over the wet folds and her swollen clitoris.

Suddenly, Harker's hands clutched her thighs, pushing them apart as he simultaneously lifted her off the ground. Molly gasped, sliding her legs around his waist and gripping his shoulders as she tried to maintain her balance. Beneath the layers of smoky desire, his dark eyes twinkled with amusement.

'I thought I'd sweep you off your feet.'

'Fine, but just make sure you fuck me as well.' Molly pushed her pelvis towards him in frustration, unable to bear the growing pressure and tension.

To her utmost relief, Harker sank into her with a lush slow ease, filling her centimetre by delicious centimetre. His shaft rubbed against her inner walls, filling her body with heat. She closed her eyes, her chest heaving as she savoured the sensation of him inside her. Still holding her thighs, he began to thrust into her with long strokes, creating a slick easy rhythm that made her blood burn. His testicles slapped against her and filled the air with the wet sounds of lust.

Whimpers of pleasure escaped Molly's throat as she rubbed against him, delighting in the glossy heat of his cock. His thrusts increased in pace, his breath ragged against her neck. The ripe friction of their union began spiralling Molly towards intense pleasure, and her hands tightened almost desperately on his shoulders. Her body shook with the force of his repeated plunges. The contrast of the unyielding wooden door against her back and the pliable flesh inside her stimulated her lustful ache to extreme degrees.

Harker lowered his head to her neck, his whiskers scraping deliciously against her skin as he licked and kissed the juncture of her neck and shoulder.

'Come for me, Molly,' he whispered, his voice gravely with carnal pleasure.

His hand slipped down between their damp bodies to caress the nub of her clit. The light pressure sent Molly over the edge, exploding her pleasure into a series of intense convulsions. She cried out, gripping his cock inside her as she rode out her climax. She felt his body tense as he pulled out of her. She reached to grasp his oiled penis, then stroked it hard to urge his own release. Harker groaned as he surrendered to his own need, shuddering violently. Spurts of come coated Molly's hand as she milked him to the final spasms of rapture.

The sound of their harsh breathing filled the air. Slowly, Harker's hands slipped away from her. Molly's legs were so weak that, for a moment, she thought she would collapse against the door. She clutched his arms to steady herself, lifting her gaze to his face. His dark eyes glowed.

'I don't know you,' Molly whispered, suddenly shaken to the core by the intensity of what she had done with him.

'No, but I know you,' Harker replied, bending to brush his lips across hers.

Molly bristled. 'You do not.'

He chuckled. 'Don't fool yourself, princess.'

'You're a bastard.'

'Yeah, but a harmless one.'

Harker stepped away from her as they straightened their clothing. And then he left the room, closing the door behind him. Molly stood staring at the closed door for a moment.

No, she thought, he was anything but harmless.

# Chapter Two

Molly slammed the door of her flat and kicked off her shoes. Her blood boiled with annoyance at Harker Trevane and anger at herself. Who did he think he was dealing with here? She wasn't angry that she had indulged in her desire for him – heaven knew she was not above satisfying her desires – but she disliked intensely being the object of a superior attitude. She was having a hard enough time dealing with that from Lydia, and the last thing she needed was to take it from Harker Trevane.

Scowling, Molly poured herself a glass of red wine and flopped down on to the sofa. She glanced around at her flat almost defensively, as if Harker Trevane were waiting in the wings to criticise her expensive tastes. Her flat was appointed with bronze antiques and warm woods, with bay windows which provided a stunning view of the city. Dawn was just beginning to break, decorating the sky with ribbons of orange and gold.

Under normal circumstances, Molly's surroundings had the power to calm her frayed nerves, but not this morning. This morning, her restlessness simmered underneath her skin like the bubbling source of a river. So, Harker Trevane thought she was a spoiled, flighty jet-setter did he? Well, damn him to hell, then. He had no idea what kind of important work she did attending charity functions and heading committees on art restoration. Not to mention trying to plan party after party for all her various societies and theatre organisations. And then there was the matter of debutante balls, etiquette lessons, and organising exclusive tours of Europe's most fashionable locales for the young ladies of society. Maybe it did seem frivolous to someone like Harker Trevane who apparently spent all of his time exposing corruption and waging war against violent gangs, but her work was no less important.

Molly tossed back a swallow of red wine. Oh, who was she kidding? Next to Lydia, who ran a hugely successful magazine, and Cassie, whose brilliant scholarship was changing views of late eighteenth-century literature, and Harker Trevane, Molly felt as if she were doing nothing more than playing dress-up. She scowled again, suddenly feeling somewhat sorry for herself. She had never had 'direction' in the conventional sense of the word, but then she had never really had a reason to. As far as she was concerned, she had done the best with what she knew how to do. Not that that was very much at all.

Molly poured herself another glass of wine. She'd show Harker Trevane she was no marshmallow. She had a backbone. She had a resilient streak like everyone else. She would show him that she could take whatever he dished out. Of course, she had no idea just how she would show him that, but she would find a way. Right now, she needed a salve for her wounded pride. Reaching for the telephone, she dialled a number and waited impatiently for an answer.

'Hello?' Piero's voice sounded sleep fogged and fuzzy.

'Come on over here, Piero darling,' Molly murmured. 'I need you.'

'Molly, *cara*, you know how much I adore you, but –'

'Piero,' Molly dropped her voice an octave. The wine was beginning to flow into her blood, making her feel both languid and rather sexy. 'I really need you.'

'Do you?' He was starting to sound more awake now. 'Give me fifteen minutes.'

Molly smiled and hung up the telephone. She went into her bedroom and took a quick shower, then slipped into a long camisole and a matching robe. Exactly fifteen minutes later, the doorbell rang. Molly smiled at the sight of Piero, hastily dressed in jeans and a polo shirt, his hair still dishevelled from sleep. He looked perfectly adorable and delicious.

'Come in, Piero. I'm so glad you're here. I didn't want to be alone.'

'Whatever is wrong, my precious one?' Piero's Italian accent made everything he said sound so terribly romantic. 'You had an evening that was not so good?'

Molly thought about his question for a moment. On the one hand, her evening had been very good. On the other hand, it had left her feeling both lousy and inadequate. She shook her head. 'No. It wasn't very good. And you know my penchant for making love at dawn.'

He gave her a slow smile, displaying strong white teeth that appeared to have been custom-made to match the devilish twinkle in his dark eyes. 'Ah, yes. That is one of your more becoming penchants.'

Molly closed and locked the door behind him, waving her hand towards the wine bottle. 'Help yourself to some wine, if you would like.'

'No, thank you. I would rather drink in the sight of you.'

Molly smiled rather wryly. She could have lived without Piero's corny compliments – in fact, she would have preferred it if he would simply murmur Italian phrases and avoid English altogether. She had no idea what he was saying when he spoke Italian, but it sounded so lovely. 'Thank you, darling.'

Her eyes drifted down his body, across the expanse of his chest, down to his groin and his long legs. He had a marvellous body, one perfectly suited to physical adventures. The son of a shipping tycoon, Piero had little motivation beyond playing on the beaches of the French Riviera and visiting the finest restaurants in the most exotic of cities. Molly tried to ignore the fact that Piero's sense of direction was uncomfortably like her own. Oddly enough, the chandeliers again came to mind, but the heat that was beginning between her legs dispatched the images as quickly as they had appeared.

She crossed the room to Piero, pressing her hands against his chest as she leant in to kiss him. His body was solid and good beneath her palms, and she could feel the steady beat of his heart. The shape of his mouth fit hers perfectly as his tongue slid powerfully between her lips. He was shorter than Harker Trevane, making their union that much easier as Molly only had to tilt her head up to return his kiss. Pushing thoughts of Harker Trevane to the dark corners of her mind, she fairly melted against Piero. Piero didn't think she was a frivolous princess. Piero knew that she was all woman. As if to prove that fact, Molly rubbed her breasts against his chest, letting the friction stimulate her nipples into tight points of arousal. He murmured something against her mouth, stroking his tongue deliberately across the inside of her lower lip.

Slipping her hands underneath Piero's shirt, she smoothed her palms over his hair-roughened chest. His muscles were sculpted to perfection thanks to numerous workouts with personal trainers. Molly loved the tactile sensation of moulding her hands against his perfect form. She stroked her fingertips around his nipples, delighting in the way they peaked at her touch. She stripped his shirt off, then unzipped his jeans.

Her heart throbbed with excitement as she tugged his jeans over his legs to reveal the most promising bulge in his briefs. If she could count on Piero for anything, it was for producing an erection on command. Molly traced the length of the bulge with the back of her hand, then took hold of it and massaged it gently, smiling when Piero let out his breath in a groan. There were few things she loved more than having power over a man. Having him by the balls, so to speak.

She went down on her knees, hooking her fingers around his briefs and sliding them down his legs. His penis sprang free, half-hard with surging blood and arousal. Molly slipped her hands around the backs of his thighs as she leant forward and enclosed his erection with her lips. The urgent sensation of a man's cock pulsating in her mouth was, for Molly, one of the most intense aphrodisiacs. Her eyes drifted closed as she began to take him fully into her mouth, letting the hard tip slide across her tongue. He tasted salty and delicious.

Piero's hands threaded through her hair, his fingers clutching at her scalp as the pleasure heightened. Molly urged him forward and pulled playfully on the sparse hair that grew on his testicles. She liked to draw sensations out of men by making them intensely aware of each and every thing she did. Rubbing the crinkly skin, she simultaneously absorbed him into her mouth, tracing the veins on his shaft with her tongue. When she had almost taken him in completely, she began to pull back and licked her way back to the darkened knob. Flicking her tongue into the small indentation at the tip, she glanced up at Piero with a smile. He gazed down at her with heavily lidded eyes and an expression flushed with desire.

'Ah, *cara*. No one is like you.'

'I should hope not,' Molly replied. God, he made her feel so sexy, so powerful. She rose, stroking one hand down her belly to the juncture of her thighs. 'Touch me here.'

Piero put his hand over hers, pressing her fingers into her sex.

'You,' he husked. 'You touch yourself there. I want to watch, yes?'

'Oh, yes.'

Molly moved away from him and stretched out on the sofa, grasping her camisole in her fists. She slid it up over her hips, revealing her well-shaped legs and the trimmed triangle of her mons. Dipping her fingers into the creamy wetness of her sex, she let out a luxurious sigh and sank back against the pillows. She could feel Piero's hot stare on her, and it made her all the more conscious of her own arousal. She pulled her camisole up only to her waist, then spread her legs to reveal the moist flower of her vulva. Her clitoris fairly throbbed with arousal as she rubbed her fingers around the swollen bud. Ribbons of heat and tension coiled lusciously around her body, centring on the increasingly tight ache in her gut. She parted her thighs wider, allowing Piero a full view of her pussy as she continued to pleasure herself. Ah, how good it was to slide her fingers over the damp crevices and circle the hole of her sex.

She pushed her forefinger gently into herself, loving the way her body accepted – no, craved – the narrow digit. It made her wonder what a man must feel when he buries his cock in such warmth and heat. Yes, it must be quite an experience. Molly began to leisurely thrust her finger back and forth as her thumb revolved around her clitoris. With her other hand, she massaged the tips of her breasts, revelling in the sensation of the silky material against her sensitive nipples.

Her gaze drifted to Piero. She was pleased to see that his penis had stiffened to its full glorious length, the shaft still damp from being in her mouth as well as from the first advance droplets of semen. A shiver of pure sexual heat fluttered over Molly's skin. She lifted her hand to her lips and slipped her fingers into her mouth to taste her own musky fluids. The gesture caused Piero to groan aloud.

'Ah, Molly, love, how aroused you make me.'

'Come here, then,' Molly whispered.

He approached her, grasping his cock in his hand as he guided it between her legs. Molly gasped at the first touch of his heavy knob pushing teasingly against her, leaving the rest of her channel burning for more. She pumped her hips upward, urging him to thrust fully into her, but Piero seemed determined to torment her. His dark eyes fairly burned with lust as he gazed down at her. His hot breath bushed against her lips. Molly reached out and gripped his forearms to draw her closer.

'Fuck me, damn you. Fuck me now.'

Piero slipped his hands underneath her thighs, pushing them fully apart as he plunged into her with one hard, delicious thrust. Molly let out a cry of sheer delight, raising her legs to hook them over his shoulders and allow him to penetrate her to the fullest extent. As much as she loved being in control when she made love, there were also times when she thrilled simply in lying back and letting the man do what he did best. And, oh, could Piero work those lean hips of his, pumping his cock into her as if his life depended upon it.

Molly smiled and stretched out, loving the sheer physi-

cal sensations of being thoroughly fucked. She knew that
Piero would not stop until she was ready for him to. Her
breasts bounced with the force of his thrusts, her entire
body aflame and accepting. An orgasm rocked through
her within minutes, but she was so aroused that she
knew others would soon follow. Piero's thick shaft felt
like hot wax inside her, evoking untold gratifications.

And as he continued to pump into her, a hazy thought
flitted across Molly's mind that she wished it were Harker
Trevane on the other end of that cock and not Piero, but
then another orgasm began to build, tying her nerve
endings into delicious knots, tighter and tighter, and not
even thoughts of Harker Trevane could diminish her
pleasure.

Harker tore open the cellophane on yet another gift
basket, hoping to find something other than champagne
and chocolates. He would even welcome a decent piece of
fruit. But, no. As predictable as the USA being eliminated
from the World Cup, three boxes of gourmet chocolates
and a magnum of champagne stared up at him. With a
sigh, Harker opened one of the boxes and shoved a few
pieces of chocolate into his mouth. He debated on
whether or not to call room service for at least an ome-
lette or something, then decided against it. What he
needed now was sleep. Four weeks of jetting from city to
city on this book tour didn't bother him, but today's
signing, Lydia Weston's party, not to mention the delectable Molly Radcliffe, all seemed to have worn him out.

He popped the top on the champagne bottle and put it
next to the bed, then stripped off his tuxedo. His shirt
was redolent of Molly Radcliffe's perfume, which sent a
sudden rush of heat through his tired body. Stretching
out naked on the bed, Harker sipped some champagne
from the bottle and grimaced at the familiar, almost
empty aridity of the spirit. Why couldn't someone send
him some decent liquor, like bourbon or Scotch? He'd
even settle for a bottle of wine – a potent Hungarian
Bikaver, perhaps – rather than this constant supply of
champagne. The hotel had sent up the first bottle, appar-

ently thrilled at his presence in one of their luxurious suites, followed by more bottles from his publisher, agent, and then from Nicholas Hawthorne and Lydia Weston.

Ah, Lydia Weston. Harker's mind drifted from the gold of the champagne to the lovely, dark-haired woman. She was a treat, that one. Nicholas Hawthorne hardly seemed the type to capture the affections of such a sex bomb, but apparently he had. More power to the man. After all, there was no telling what sort of sexual legerdemain was practised behind closed doors. Sexual legerdemain, Harker thought to himself and laughed at the images that came to mind, causing a tiny stream of champagne to issue from the corner of his mouth. The magician's 'sleight of hand' in creating illusion might transfer most effectively to a sexual scenario.

Harker placed the bottle on the bedside table and reached for the television remote control. He flipped through a few early morning news programmes and about a dozen advertisements before pausing at the hotel's porn channel. When was the last time he'd watched a porn flick? He peered bleary-eyed at the instruction card by the side of the bed, then pressed the button to access the channel. A movie was just beginning, and the screen was soon awash in picture-perfect bodies rubbing and thrusting against each other. Harker yawned. These were charlatans in the art of sexual legerdemain.

He rubbed his hand over his chest, bored by the perfect bodies, the champagne, the hotel room. He'd become a highly successful fiction writer, but he missed the adrenalin rushes and excitement that had so characterised his investigative reporting. Occasionally, he still found himself in some hairy situations when researching a book, but it wasn't the same. He needed something new, something different. He'd never give up fiction writing, but surely there had to be another avenue, another angle. Another vista from which to gain a novel perspective on life.

Harker chewed on another chocolate and stared at the television screen. The scene shifted. A woman with long reddish hair not unlike the colour of Molly Radcliffe's was busy sucking away at a prone man's big cock. A steady stream of moans emerged from her mouth as she licked the damn thing as if it were a lolly. To his surprise, Harker felt his own penis stiffen slightly in reaction to the graphic lust. Now rather intrigued, he continued watching the television. The redhead finished the blow job and stood up, displaying breasts so scientifically perfect they appeared to defy gravity. She straddled the man, wrapping her manicured hand around his shaft as she began to lower herself on to him.

Letting her head fall back, the woman arched her body so that her breasts were thrust out towards the camera and began to ride him. Harker's hand moved over his chest almost involuntarily and down to his groin. He grasped his penis in his fist and began to stroke it slowly, his gaze locked to the movements of the redhead's body. Her hips writhed back and forth, up and down, occasionally letting the man's cock slip out of her and expose the wet shaft. The sound of her intermittent groans, as staged as they were, seemed to stimulate Harker to further arousal. He rubbed his fingers over his balls and spread his legs slightly.

Damn, that redhead did look like Molly Radcliffe. Either that, or his imagination was working overtime. His heartbeat increased when another woman, a blonde, entered the action. She favoured the redhead with a long, wet kiss, then straddled the man on her hands and knees. Her knees were on either side of his head, but her pussy was thrust into the air, practically inviting the redhead to feast her lips on the sweet confection. The redhead, of course, did just that. The camera panned in to a close-up of her lips going to work on the blonde, lightly haired cunt. Her tongue darted out to oblige the swollen labia and the treasures that lay within. There were wet, sucking sounds, and then a long drawn-out squeal from the blonde.

Harker shifted as his cock thickened and stiffened in response to both the women's staged pleasure and his own stroking. The sight of the two women and the man brought back memories of the last time he had been with two women, which suddenly seemed like an extremely long time ago. Harker paused his stroking for a moment to gather the clear fluid that was gathering at the tip of his prick. He spread it over the length of his shaft and resumed, slowly, acutely aware of the pressure that was building in his loins. There was no pleasure in the world as exquisite as having two women to make love to at the same time. It was a common fantasy for many men, and Harker knew he was one of a small number who had actually lived that fantasy. More than once, in fact.

With that memory lingering in his mind, he began stroking his cock faster and harder as he watched the redhead rocking back and forth on her phallic horse, all the while licking away at the blonde's pussy. The scene also made him wonder what Molly Radcliffe would do if she were confronted face-to-face with another woman's wet, fragrant cunt. Ah, God. He rubbed his thumb over the tip of his penis, drawing in a quick, shallow breath at the intensity of the pleasure – or was it pain? – that such a touch provided his engorged glans. He pumped his hips up and down as the women's squeals grew louder. Harker's fist was a poor substitute for the humid, snug channel in which his cock had been embedded earlier that night, but his pleasure now was of a different kind. This was pure fantasy pleasure, imagining himself, Molly Radcliffe, and perhaps a lovely blonde entwined in a tangle of limbs and lust.

He stared at the actor's thick penis sliding in and out of the redhead's cunt, glistening with her juices. The man's hands clutched her gyrating buttocks, guiding her on his cock until his excitement became too intense and he pulled out, shooting his come all over her moist sex. As if on cue, Harker felt his own come rising inside him inexorably, like lava inside a volcano. The eruption was not long in arriving. Drops of semen coated his pubic hair and lower belly, and he continued to stroke himself slowly until the last of the sensations had ebbed. He thought of cleaning himself, but the events of the preceding day and night, together with this orgasm, conspired to guide him quickly to sleep.

The shrill ring of the telephone jolted Harker out of his sleep. With a groan, he fumbled for the receiver. 'What?'

'Harker? Lydia Weston. I'm downstairs in the lobby. Remember we had a breakfast engagement this morning?'

'Oh, shit.' Harker peered at the bedside clock. 'What time were we supposed to meet?'

'Nine, although I realise now that it was rather cruel of me to suggest such a time when our parties always go until the wee hours of the morning. Perhaps I should come back in several hours and we can meet for lunch.'

Harker rubbed his palm over his face and tried to think clearly past the foggy remnants of lust. 'No, no. That's OK. Just give me a minute to get ready. You might as well come up here and wait. They've put me in a suite that's big enough for a family of four.'

'Delightful. I'll be right up.'

Harker hung up the telephone and sank back against the pillows. He felt lousy. Another three hours of sleep might have helped, but that would mean succumbing again to dreams of Molly Radcliffe entangled in a lesbian harem. And Harker didn't think he could take much more of that. Glancing down at his cock, already bobbing once more with the telltale signs of need, he was certain that he couldn't.

He opened his eyes when a sharp knock sounded at the door. Muttering a string of swear words, he wrapped a sheet around his hips and staggered to the door. The sight of Lydia Weston, her black hair brushed into a shiny bob, her red power suit showing off her legs, her make-up flawless, made Harker feel like a toad confronted by a very modern Snow White.

'Sorry,' he muttered. 'Late night.'

'I know.' Lydia's gaze slipped down to his bare chest and then to his lower body that was barely concealed by the thin sheet.

Harker returned her look. He wondered if Molly had told her anything, especially since he'd gathered that the two women were pretty tight, but Lydia's expression gave nothing away. Harker pulled the door open.

'Come in. I need to shower, and then I'll be ready.'

Lydia walked past him into the hotel room, gazing around at the ornate furnishings, the five bouquets of flowers, and the gift baskets. Her gaze fell on an opened champagne bottle by the bed. 'I see you've earned some goodies.'

'Yeah. You want any champagne or chocolate? I have more than enough.'

Lydia smiled at his derisive tone. 'No, thank you. Perhaps I'll send you something a little more creative next time.'

'There's something to be said for creativity.'

'I quite agree.' Lydia sank down gracefully on to a chair and crossed her legs.

Harker let his gaze rove across the curve of her calf. 'I'll just be a minute.'

'I'll be right here.'

Jesus. Harker turned and went into the bathroom. The sheet was doing a poor job of concealing even the earliest stages of his arousal, and he wondered if she had noticed. He couldn't remember being this horny since he was sixteen. Back then, even old Mrs Pickford from next door had aroused him when she bent over her flower bed and unknowingly exposed the cleavage of her huge breasts. Although women like Molly Radcliffe and Lydia Weston were hardly old Mrs Pickford.

He turned the cold water on full blast, grimacing as he stepped under the icy spray. He stayed under for a full five minutes until he willed his body under control again, and then switched on the hot water and washed. He slipped into one of the hotel robes before going back into the main room, where Lydia Weston was busy examining the papers spread out on the desk. She glanced up with a guilty expression when he returned.

'I'm sorry. I'm prying.'

Harker shrugged. 'Those who pry often find exactly

what they're looking for, you know. But there's nothing much to pry into here. Just some notes for my next novel.'

'Set in the Amazon rain forest, I see. That sounds fascinating.'

'I hope so. Fascinating sells much better than insipid.'

Lydia laughed. 'I know all about the capitalistic virtues of fascination,' she said. 'Are you going to the Amazon?'

'Next year. The book will also be set in San Francisco, so I'm going to hang around the city for another week.'

'Your publishing company is paying for this suite, is it?'

Harker nodded. 'I lived in San Francisco a few years ago before I moved to Chicago. Maybe I'll move back one day.'

'Maybe?'

'Depends on whether or not something exciting happens.'

'You sound bored.'

Harker didn't reply, unwilling to admit to Lydia's perceptiveness. He bent and pulled some clothes out of his suitcase. He moved as if to go into the bathroom to change, but he stopped, suspecting that Lydia Weston wouldn't care if he stripped naked right here. In fact, she was probably expecting it. Harker almost grinned at the thought of performing a reverse striptease for this powerful, influential woman. He turned away from her and put on his briefs and trousers under the robe, then took off the robe and finished drying his chest.

'Your publicist mentioned that you based the protagonist in your novels after yourself,' Lydia remarked. 'Nevin Rafferty is autobiographical, is he?'

Harker turned to face her, smiling wryly. 'You know what Hemingway said.'

'No, what did Hemingway say?' she asked.

'The goal of fiction isn't realism, but to be truer than reality.'

'Oh, that is rather deep.'

Harker laughed. 'Nevin Rafferty is one hell of a lot more honourable than I am, Miss Weston.'

'Good heavens, call me Lydia, please,' Lydia said. 'Honour is the only characteristic that separates you from Nevin Rafferty?'

Harker shrugged. 'Honour, integrity, morality. All that Boy Scout stuff, excepting the part about knot-tying. One never knows when that can come in handy.'

Lydia clinched her lips together in a half-hearted reproach, but her eyes twinkled with amusement. 'Oh, you're being modest now. If I recall, Nevin Rafferty is hardly a modest man.'

'Neither am I.'

Lydia smiled. 'Harker, you are most decidedly odd.'

'I'll take that as a compliment.' Harker fished a clean shirt out of his suitcase and slipped it on. 'And you, Lydia, are most decidedly a sexy woman. If Nicholas hadn't staked his claim on you, then I'd be first in line.'

'Oh, believe me, no man "stakes a claim" on me, not even Nicholas.'

Harker raised an eyebrow and turned to look at her directly. 'No?'

'No. We love each other, but we have an understanding.'

'What kind of understanding?'

'One that involves other people in sexual situations.'

Harker tried, and failed, to imagine the mild-mannered Nicholas involved with another woman. He could barely imagine Nicholas involved with Lydia Weston. On the other hand, Harker could quite clearly imagine Lydia involved with any number of men. Himself included.

'You mean to tell me,' he said, 'that Nicholas doesn't have a problem with you fucking other men?'

'Not if he is completely aware of what's going on,' Lydia replied. 'He doesn't like it, of course, but considering he's fucked other women, it would be rather hypocritical to complain. Don't you think?'

'I imagine so.' Harker watched Lydia move around the side of the desk and approach him. 'Is he aware that you're here?'

'Of course.' She paused in front of him, reaching up to rub her thumb over his lower lip. 'Actually, he was the one who suggested it.'

'I see.'

'You look divine,' Lydia murmured. She slipped her bag over her shoulder. 'Shall we go? I thought we would have breakfast at a lovely place over on California Street.'

'As long as they have coffee, I wouldn't care if we were eating down at the docks with the sea lions.' Amused at Lydia's abrupt turnaround, Harker grabbed a lightweight jacket and followed her out the door.

True to form, Lydia had commissioned a limousine to take them to the restaurant. The sleek black car deposited them right at the front door, and a *maître d'* whisked them immediately to a table. To Harker's relief, the server was waiting with a silver carafe of coffee. She filled their china cups almost to the brim and handed them menus. Harker took a swallow of the rich, dark brew and nearly groaned with sensual pleasure. He glanced up to find Lydia smiling sympathetically.

'Hangover?'

'Not enough sleep.' Harker waited for the caffeine to take effect. 'So remind me why we're meeting.'

'I want to talk to you and your agent about working out a publicity deal with *Savoir Faire*,' Lydia explained. 'Excerpts of upcoming novels, advertisements, special discounts, and that type of thing.'

'Great. Why do you need me?'

'Your publicist informed me that you make most of your own business decisions,' Lydia said. 'I want to make certain that you're completely comfortable with the idea.'

'Your magazine is very impressive,' Harker replied. 'I suspect I would be comfortable with any proposition you toss my way.'

'How kind of you to say that,' Lydia said. 'I'll have our business manager work out the details. I think that your books would really appeal to a female audience if they were marketed correctly. I asked a friend of mine to write up a review of *Red Sun* for the magazine.'

An arrow of suspicion shot through Harker almost immediately. 'A friend?'

'Mmm.' Lydia sipped her coffee and pushed back her cuff to look at her watch. 'Molly Radcliffe. I think you know her. In fact, I've invited her to have breakfast with us. She should be here any minute.'

Harker knew he should have been surprised, but he wasn't. He was, however, irritated at being deceived. 'Molly Radcliffe, huh?'

'Yes.' Lydia looked at him with eyes as innocent as those of an ingènue. 'You do know her, don't you?'

'Oh, definitely. Didn't she tell you we fucked at your party last night?'

To Lydia's credit, she didn't bat an eye. Instead, she simply compressed her lips into a tight line. 'No, Mr Trevane. She failed to tell me that. She did, however, tell me that she had met you and that she found you rather intriguing.'

'I think she found me more than intriguing.'

'Well, I see that Nevin Rafferty gets his arrogance from you, if not his integrity and morals.'

Harker lifted his coffee cup to Lydia in a silent toast. 'Touché.'

Lydia glanced to the restaurant entrance. 'Here's Molly now.'

She stood to greet her friend, reaching out to clasp Molly's hands in hers as Molly approached the table. Harker tried to see Molly Radcliffe in a different light, a light unclouded by festivities, alcohol, and pure lust. He tried to convince himself that she had simply been putting on airs, that she had been as affected by the evening as he had been, and that their lust had been the result of circumstance. He completely failed to do so. Instead, Harker looked at Molly's gorgeous curls, the delightful sprinkling of freckles across her nose, her lean figure encased in tan slacks and a crisp, white shirt, and he felt a jolt of desire straight down to his groin. Damn.

'Molly, you know Harker Trevane.' Lydia kept her hand protectively on her friend's arm as they turned to Harker.

Molly held out her hand. 'Yes, we've met. Hello, Harker.'

'Molly.' He gave her hand a quick shake, remembering the way those tapered fingers had closed so insistently around his cock.

Molly sat down, flashing Lydia a smile as she reached for a cup of coffee. 'Your party was wonderful as usual, Lydia.'

'Thank you. It was, of course, for Harker's benefit.'

Harker suddenly felt as if he were being trapped. 'It was unnecessary for my benefit,' he said. 'But very kind of you.'

'I'm reading your book, you know,' Molly remarked. 'Lydia asked me to write up a review for her magazine.'

'So she told me.' Harker tossed back another swallow of coffee.

'I'm finding it intriguing, but a little too macho,' Molly went on. 'Macho posturing can be tiresome.'

Harker drained his coffee and stood. 'I suspect this involves something other than a business meeting,' he said. 'And since I have neither the time nor the energy to play games, I'll take my leave of you ladies right now.' He looked at Lydia. 'Send any information you want to my agent. She'll forward it to me.'

'Wait.' Lydia reached out and put her hand on Harker's arm. 'I've made a huge mistake. Harker, I was unaware of what had transpired between you and Molly, and I certainly didn't ask you here to make you uncomfortable. It's clear that you both have some things to work out, so I'm going to be the one to leave.'

'Lydia –' Molly began.

Lydia picked up her bag and shook her head. 'Molly, you know where to call me if you need me. However, this is currently none of my business.'

With that departing statement, Lydia walked out of the restaurant.

Harker sat back down. 'So,' he said. 'What's your motivation in coming here?'

'I don't have a motivation,' Molly shot back. 'Don't worry, Harker. I'm not going to claim you've impregnated me or anything. We had sex, and that's it.'

'Is it?' Harker replied. 'Then why are you here? You're going to threaten to give me a bad review?'

'I'm not quite so petty,' Molly snapped. Her eyes flashed angrily, darkening to a deeper blue. 'However, I have to tell you that I did not appreciate you accusing me of being a flighty princess.'

Harker stared at her, suddenly wanting to laugh. 'What? That's why you're mad at me?'

Molly frowned. 'Yes.'

Then Harker did laugh. 'Molly, you are a princess. A princess in denial. You've been fed with a silver spoon your entire life, you've never had an actual job, and you think that the world revolves around your life and your problems. You've probably never even challenged yourself.'

'Who do you think you are?' Molly hissed. 'You know nothing about me!'

'Oh, I know more than you realise,' Harker said.

'You do not!'

'Don't I? Then why don't you tell me about a time when you've challenged yourself, when you've pushed yourself to your limits just to see if you could take it? When you've done something for the sheer excitement of learning something new about yourself? When was the last time you did that, Molly?'

'I don't have to explain myself to you!'

Harker levelled his gaze on her. 'Then why are you here?'

'I'm here because I ... because ... well, dammit, maybe I did want to prove something to you!' Molly snapped. 'You're so condescending with all your adventures and stories to tell, looking down on anyone who has had a different life than yours.'

'I don't look down on anyone who has had a life different than mine,' Harker replied. 'Simply on those who don't do a damn thing with their life.'

'That's just my point! How do you know what I've done with my life?'

Harker was suddenly very weary. 'All right, Molly. I suppose I don't. Why don't you tell me, then?'

'I've done charity work, I've headed committees involved with art restoration and fund raising, I've donated money to hospitals and children's organisations –'

'How have you earned a living?' Harker interrupted, taking pleasant note of the rosy flush Molly's excited discourse had brought to her face.

'I've been lucky that my father can continue to support me, so I haven't had to earn a living. But, believe me, I don't take my position lightly.'

'So, to repeat my initial question,' Harker said, 'how have you challenged yourself?'

'Every task I undertake is a challenge.'

'That's a lousy answer.'

'It was a lousy question.'

Harker leant back in his chair, curling his hand around his coffee cup. 'Maybe setting your sights on men to conquer is your challenge,' he said. 'Is that how you push yourself to your limits? Sexually?'

Molly bristled, her lips tightening with anger. 'If that's the case, then you were a hell of an easy conquest.'

'Fair enough,' Harker allowed. 'But that still doesn't answer my question.'

'Men are hardly a challenge.'

'Maybe not,' Harker said. 'But you can still challenge yourself sexually.'

Arching an eyebrow, Molly settled her blue-eyed gaze on him. 'Do tell,' she muttered dryly.

They stared at each other as blue eyes clashed with brown, charging the air between them with a sexual force so powerful it was almost tangible. Harker brushed his knuckles across the top of Molly's hand, finding great pleasure in the soft smoothness of her skin.

'Why don't I show you?' he murmured. A surprising rush of adrenalin shivered through his body at the thought of showing Molly Radcliffe exactly what he meant.

'Show me what?' Molly's naivety was almost endearing.

'Do you trust me?'

'Not particularly.'

'You're going to have to.'

She eyed him suspiciously. 'What for?'

Harker leant closer to her, warming to the ideas taking

shape in his mind. He thought of all the delicious, dark pleasures to which he could introduce Molly Radcliffe, pleasures that would heighten every one of her senses and push her to limits she didn't know existed. However, he knew he could do nothing unless she trusted him.

'You're going to have to trust that I won't hurt you,' Harker murmured. 'And that I won't do anything that you don't want.'

Molly looked at him for a long moment. 'I do believe that,' she finally said. 'However, I don't see what this has to do with anything.'

Harker took hold of the delicate china cup and tilted it towards himself. There was but one swallow of coffee left. How fortuitous. He raised the cup in Molly's honour and said warmly and yet with the utmost seriousness: 'A toast to the man who invented the bowline.'

'The what?' Molly asked.

'The bowline. It's the knot a Boy Scout uses when he wants to be sure of holding something fast.'

# Chapter Three

Molly had never considered herself a reckless person. However, as Harker slid into the taxi after her and closed the door, she had a feeling she was about to embark on an episode that could be considered at least impulsive, if not utterly reckless. Chewing on her lower lip, she looked out the side window. She no longer knew if she was trying to prove something to herself or to Harker Trevane, but she suspected it was a little of both. OK, a lot of both. She looked at Harker.

'Where are we going?'

'You'll see.' He crossed his arms over his chest and gazed back at her. 'Are you scared?'

'Is that a taunt?'

'No, it's a question.'

'Then, no, I'm not scared,' Molly replied. She could not deny the importance of statement that she trust him, but still felt the urge to fight against those very words, to struggle against them as a prisoner struggles against his manacles. 'I am, however, rather curious.'

'There's only one thing you have to do, Molly,' Harker said. 'Whenever you want to stop and go home, all you have to do is tell me. Do you understand?'

What in the love of God was the man talking about? 'Stop what?' Molly asked in irritation.

'Do you understand?' Harker repeated.

'When I want to stop and go home, I just have to tell you,' Molly said. 'Of course I understand. And believe me, I'm not shy about asking for what I want.'

A smile tugged at the corners of Harker's mouth. 'So I gathered.'

Molly glowered at him and turned her attention to the window again. She knew they were turning in the direction of Haight-Ashbury, but for the life of her, she couldn't imagine why Harker would take her to the Haight. She hadn't been there herself in years. As far as she was concerned, the place had deteriorated into a bunch of biker shops and ugly clothing stores whose clients seemed to think that they were still living in the 1960s. Maybe Harker was going to challenge her wardrobe by making her buy plaid trousers and striped shirts.

'All right. We're here.' Harker paid the driver and got out of the taxi in front of a relatively harmless-looking store that had window displays of lingerie and body oils.

'This is it?' Molly asked. 'Your sexual challenge?'

Harker didn't reply. He curled his hand around hers and led her into the store. Molly looked around at the various displays. She reached out and rubbed a lace teddy between her fingers, nearly grimacing at the feeling of the cheap polyester material.

'Harker, is that you?' A throaty female voice made Molly look up in surprise.

A busty, dark-haired woman emerged from behind a curtain separating the front of the store from a back room. She wore a low-cut blouse and a leather miniskirt, and she moved with the ease of a woman who was completely comfortable in her body. 'It is you, isn't it? How long has it been since you've walked in here?'

'A few years at least, Glenda,' Harker said. 'It's good to see you. This is my friend Molly.'

Glenda gave Molly a quick once-over and smiled. Molly nodded in greeting. Glenda was quite an attractive woman, voluptuous and sexy with an aura of warmth and sensuality about her. She wondered what the other woman's relationship with Harker had consisted of, but she wasn't at all certain she wanted to know.

Glenda flashed Harker a smile. 'You look gorgeous, Harker. You want to come in the back?'

Molly's mouth nearly dropped open in shock. Was Glenda running a brothel here with the shop as a front? And would Harker Trevane frequent such a place?

'Yes, thanks. Molly will be coming with me.' Harker glanced at Molly. 'Unless she doesn't want to.'

Molly heard the underlying challenge in his voice. 'Of course I do.'

For some reason, she wished he would take her hand again, but he didn't. They followed Glenda around the counter and past the curtain to the back room. Molly stopped in her tracks, stunned at the plethora of leather goods and clothing that were displayed everywhere. Leather teddies, skirts, vests, and pants hung on racks, along with some very sleazy-looking lingerie. But what surprised Molly the most were the items hanging on the walls. Leather whips of all shapes and sizes, handcuffs, cattails, and other items that she didn't even recognise. She was starting to have an idea of what, exactly, Harker Trevane had in mind when he talked about challenging her sexually.

She felt him looking at her and met his gaze.

'Well, Molly?'

'Well, Harker?' Molly shot back. 'This is it?'

'Oh, no. Not by a long shot. I thought Glenda could help you pick out something to wear.'

Glenda smiled with delight. 'Are you kidding? I have some fabulous things for you. You're looking for skirts and vests, or something sexier like bustiers?'

'Definitely sexier,' Harker replied. 'And in leather.'

So Harker wanted her to deck herself out in leather. That was hardly a challenge either. Molly would have preferred fur, but that was so *déclassé* lately. Besides, she'd taken on anti-fur activism as one of her latest projects.

'Great,' she said. 'Where do I start?'

Harker settled into a chair and stretched out his legs, crossing them at the ankle. 'Then I'll just wait here and leave you ladies to find something. You know what I like, Glenda.'

She winked at him. 'Do I ever. Come with me, Molly. I'll show you some gorgeous bustiers and corsets.'

Molly followed Glenda to the back of the room and watched as the other woman began shuffling through racks filled with leather and more leather. She pulled out a bunch of skimpy items and marched to a huge, three-sided mirror against the wall.

'Now.' Glenda shook out an outfit that was cut down to the belly button. 'Try on this one first, I think.'

Molly looked at the leather doubtfully. 'Not much to it, is there?'

Glenda laughed. 'That's the idea, doll.'

'Where is the dressing room?'

'You're in it. I hope you're not shy. I've seen women's bodies before. Hell, I live in one.'

'No, it's OK.' Molly glanced at Harker in the mirror, relieved to discover that he was reading a newspaper and not paying the slightest bit of attention to her and Glenda. She didn't relish the thought of stripping in front of a strange woman, but she'd be damned if she would falter so early into this little exercise Harker had dreamed up.

Molly stripped until she was standing in her bra and underwear in front of the mirror.

'Keep your underwear on,' Glenda said. She reached out and plucked at the hook on Molly's bra. 'But take your bra off.'

Instinctively, Molly grasped at her bra as the hook gave way and it started to slip off.

Glenda chuckled. 'You are shy, aren't you? How refreshing.'

Despite her increasing flush, Molly disliked Glenda's 'aren't-you-sweet' tone. She was getting sick to death of people talking down to her. She pushed her bra over her shoulders, trying not to think about the fact that she was standing half-naked in a sex-and-leather shop with Harker Trevane only a room away and a strange woman getting ready to help her into a leather outfit.

'Step into it.' Glenda bent and helped Molly step into the outfit, then tugged it over her legs. 'This one rides a little high on the hips.'

'And a little low in the cleavage,' Molly observed. Good God, the thing consisted of two straps that were apparently supposed to cover her breasts. She almost flinched as Glenda tied the straps around Molly's neck, then moved around in front and started to arrange her breasts.

'Um, maybe I should do that.'

'You have nice breasts,' Glenda said, stretching the leather over Molly's nipple. 'Small and nicely shaped, the way a breast should be. Unlike these huge things.'

She gestured towards her own chest, then tucked Molly's other breast underneath the leather. She stroked her fingers so swiftly underneath the crevice that Molly didn't know if it was a caress or an impersonal movement. Either way, she was shocked to feel her nipples hardening against the leather as she became aware of the closeness of the other woman and the light scent of her perfume. She was relieved when Glenda stepped away, leaving Molly to examine herself in the mirror.

Molly flushed at the sight of her reflection. A huge V of skin was exposed all the way down to her belly button, exposing the curves of her breasts and waist. The small swell of her belly seemed gigantic in this get-up, and Molly had never before realised how big her thighs were.

'This isn't particularly flattering,' she muttered.

Glenda looked thoughtfully at Molly's reflection, tapping her finger against her cheek. 'No, it's not, is it? Let's try something else.'

Well, at least the other woman was honest, Molly thought ruefully. She tried on three other items, all of which seemed to draw extreme attention to body flaws that Molly wasn't even aware that she had. So far, Harker Trevane's sexual challenge was only serving to give her a serious inferiority complex. She sighed when Glenda held up a bustier with a series of leather laces.

'Glenda, I obviously don't have a body made for leather,' she said. 'Isn't there something else? Maybe something really long and flowing?'

'Molly, everyone has a body made for leather,' Glenda replied. 'It's simply a matter of finding the right leather. Come on, just this one more.'

Molly took the bustier from her and pulled it on. At least the bottom half was a little more concealing. It even seemed to shape rather nicely to her buttocks. The top was relatively simple, consisting of leather strips that covered her breasts and the lace ties. Molly let Glenda tie the laces, wincing when she pulled tightly.

'I'm not going to be able to breathe.'

'Of course you are.' Glenda tugged harder, and the movement pushed Molly's breasts upward, causing them to swell over the leather cups. When she was finished with the laces, Glenda fastened the leather collar around Molly's neck, then stepped back and smiled. 'There. Told you.'

Molly stared at her reflection. She did look pretty good in this one. It tucked in her waist, rounded out her bottom, and moulded lusciously over her curves.

'This one isn't too bad,' she admitted.

'Just wait,' Glenda replied. 'Once you put some fishnet stockings and heels on, you'll be a devastating femme fatale. Take that one off, and I'll find you some shoes.'

After admiring herself for another moment, Molly managed to pull the bustier over her hips. She put her clothes on, glancing over in Harker's direction again. He still didn't appear to be paying the slightest bit of attention to her or Glenda. Molly headed off in search of Glenda again, and the two women found some shoes and stockings. As they approached Harker, he rose from his chair.

'So you're ready?' he asked.

'As I'll ever be,' Molly replied. She reached into her bag for her credit card and handed it to Glenda.

'Wait,' Harker said. 'I'll pay.'

Molly shook her head. She had the distinct feeling that she would be giving up far too much control if she allowed Harker Trevane to pay for a leather bustier, of all things. 'No. I'd prefer to pay myself.'

Glenda rang up Molly's purchases. 'And Harker? Anything for you?'

Harker nodded towards a paper bag by the side of the counter. 'I've collected some things in that bag, thanks.'

'When did you do some shopping?' Molly asked.

Harker winked at her. 'When you weren't looking.'

'Molly, it was a pleasure meeting you,' Glenda said. 'I hope to see you both again soon.'

'You'll definitely see me again soon,' Harker replied.

'Whether or not Molly is with me . . . Well, that will be up to her, won't it?'

Molly thanked Glenda for her help and walked outside with Harker. 'You're going to introduce me to the world of leather and sexual games, is that it?' she asked derisively. 'That's your challenge?'

Harker shook his head almost in disappointment. 'This is your problem, Molly. You have a very narrow view of things. Particularly those things you know nothing about.'

'How do you know I don't know anything about the world of BSMD?'

Harker tossed her a wry look. 'Because it's called BDSM. Do you know what it stands for?'

'Sure. Kinky sex.'

'Bondage, domination, and sadomasochism.'

'Yes, like I said. Kinky sex.'

Molly figured she could handle a little kinky sex with Harker Trevane. Heck, she had a feeling she would thoroughly enjoy it. She might not ever have indulged in BSDM or whatever it was called, but there was a first time for everything. Yes, she could do this, she reminded herself firmly as she sat in a taxi with Glenda's package on her lap. She would prove to Harker Trevane that she was no frivolous princess. She would prove that she could take any challenge he could dream up. Even if it did involve leather and the tying of knots.

Molly was certain her heart had never pounded quite so hard. She slipped her feet into the high heels and adjusted her bustier in a vain effort to cover more of her cleavage. Funny how she had never before found it necessary to cover what little cleavage she had.

'Molly.' Harker's voice on the other side of the hotel room door sounded impatient. 'I'm tired of waiting.'

'All right, all right,' Molly snapped irritably. 'No need to rush.'

If she looked in the mirror again, she would definitely lose her nerve. Molly took a deep breath and opened the door, feeling Harker's gaze on her as if he were touching her physically. She stood in the doorway, suddenly afraid that she wouldn't meet his standards, that she wouldn't look the way he had expected her to.

She soon discovered that she needn't have worried. Harker's eyes grew hot, and he approached her with the determination of a man who knows what he wants. Sliding his hands around to her buttocks, he pulled her hard against him. 'Molly, you have no idea what you're getting into, despite all your flippant claims to the contrary. Tell me if you want me to stop.'

Molly shook her head, feeling her heart beating wildly. The pulse in her throat throbbed against the leather collar. 'No. I don't want you to stop.'

Harker pushed her against the wall, cupping her neck in his hand as he guided her mouth up to his. A charge of pure electricity crackled between them as their lips met again, and Molly sank into the hazy state of desire that only Harker Trevane seemed able to evoke. Heat fluttered across her body, heightening her awareness of the leather straps constraining her body, of the way her nipples pressed so insistently against the fabric. The sensations were unlike any she had experienced before, a combination of restraint and excitement.

Harker pushed his knee between her thighs and put his hands on her hips to guide her. Molly let her head fall back against the wall as her legs spread and her sex encountered the hardness of Harker's thigh. Her sex was already seeping with moisture, dampening the leather between her legs and causing the oddest sensations as it rubbed against her. Instinctively, Molly squirmed, wanting to ease the growing pressure in her sex. Harker gave a husky laugh.

'Oh no, Molly, my sweet. On to the bed with you. You don't get relief quite that easily.'

His words caused Molly to lift her head. He was denying her an orgasm? Since when did men deny her orgasms? They usually fell over their feet in their haste to give her one. 'Excuse me?'

'On the bed.'

There it was again, that challenging note in his voice. Molly gave him a mutinous glower, but went to the bed. She stretched out on her back, spreading her legs in the hopes that he would notice how wet and ready she was. The leather bustier hugged her hot body, feeling deliciously wicked against her skin. She suspected she could get rather used to the feeling. She let her eyes drift closed, hoping Harker would ask her to touch herself the way Piero had, but he didn't. Instead, she felt his hands grip hers, and then the rough, chafing sensation of rope on her wrists. Molly opened her eyes and looked up at Harker.

'You're tying me up?'

'Mmm. Do you like it?'

Molly waited until he had finished his knots. She fidgeted, trying to sort out her feelings of both helplessness and a dark, dangerous excitement. 'I don't know.'

'You want me to untie you? That's the great thing about the bowline. It's easy to tie, easy to untie, but it holds oh so fast.'

Molly squirmed again. Her breathing was growing so rapid that her chest heaved against the leather ties. She didn't think she had ever felt quite so vulnerable and secure at the same time. Like the chandeliers.

'No. I don't want you to untie me.' The thought of Harker fucking her while she was lashed to the bedpost caused an immense rush of heat to slide through her.

'The safe word is "dark",' Harker murmured. 'Say that word and I'll stop whatever I'm doing. Understand?'

Molly nodded. To her surprise, Harker didn't clamber on top of her. Instead, he sat next to her on the bed and trailed his forefinger down the side of her face. 'So, Molly. Why don't you tell me about one of your fantasies?'

Molly stared at him. 'You want me to tell you about a fantasy?'

'Yes. One of your most forbidden fantasies.'

A red flush coloured Molly's cheeks. 'Why?'

'Because I want to know. Are you afraid to tell me?'

'Why do you keep asking me if I'm afraid?'

'Are you?'

'No.' She was definitely wary, but not afraid. For some reason, she had an implicit trust in Harker Trevane that she didn't think she had ever had before with another man. 'I'm not afraid.'

'Then tell me.'

'I've had fantasies involving two lovers,' Molly said slowly.

'Go on.'

'That's it. Two lovers.' Molly wriggled, twisting her trapped wrists. Did he want details here? 'Two men are making love to me.'

'Are you on your hands and knees?'

'Harker!' Molly gasped in shock, her gaze flying to his. 'What kind of question is that?'

He reached out and put his hand on her forehead. 'Relax, Molly. See if you can do this. See if you can tell me in detail about this fantasy of yours.'

Could she? Molly wasn't at all certain. She lowered her gaze, her flush growing hotter. A long silence stretched between them before Molly spoke again. Her voice was very soft, even to her own ears. 'It's a fantasy I've had since I was a teenager. I don't know the men, and they don't know me. It starts with me lying on my back with my legs spread while one of the men fucks me, and the other one straddles me so that I can suck him.'

'Straddles you how?'

'Across my chest.' Molly forced herself to go on, realising that she was becoming more and more aroused by this recounting of one of her favourite fantasies. 'His buttocks rub against my breasts.'

Harker reached out and covered her breast with his hand, stroking his fingers over her nipple through the leather. 'Are your nipples hard?'

'Yes.' Molly couldn't believe she was doing this, and with Harker Trevane of all people. But, oh, how aroused she was. The entire surface of her skin was alive with stimulation and pleasure, and the leather strip between her legs rubbed deliciously against her labia.

'Go on.'

Molly's flush deepened. 'What else do you want to know?'

'How you feel.'

'In the fantasy?'

'Yes.'

'Aroused, of course.'

'Dominated?'

'Yes.' Molly risked a glance at him, her gaze meeting his hot eyes. 'You think that means I have some kind of hidden desire to be dominated, don't you?'

Harker shook his head. 'I don't think that, Molly. Although it's true that fantasies sometimes do indicate hidden desires. Do you want two men to fuck you at the same time?'

'I suppose it would depend on the men.'

'But you would like it.'

'Yes.' Molly parted her lips to draw in air, stunned at her own admission.

Harker stroked his hand over her breasts and belly, down to the wet apex of her thighs. His fingers slipped underneath the leather strap and into the creaminess of her vulva. Molly gasped, pushing her hips upward. Harker smiled and slowly trailed his finger over the crevices, swirling his thumb tantalisingly over her clitoris.

'Don't come yet,' he commanded, his voice husky.

A whimper escaped Molly's throat. 'But –'

'No. Don't. Turn around.'

The ropes were long enough so that Molly could turn on to her stomach. Her heart pounded violently as she did so, totally aware of the feeling of leather against her skin, the chafing rope around her wrists, the sound of her own breathing, the scent of her arousal. She closed her eyes on Harker's order. Never before had she been so excited, her body alive with anticipation over what Harker would do next. His palm moved over her buttocks, then he gently slapped one of her cheeks. Molly gasped in surprise and tried to rise, but the rope restricted her.

'Relax,' Harker murmured. He landed another slap on her buttocks, harder this time.

'Ow!' Molly twisted and shot him a glare. 'That hurt.'

'It's supposed to.' His fingers dipped into her sex again, stimulating her aching clitoris. 'You want me to stop?'

'No.' Molly's eyes drifted closed again, her body jerking as Harker landed another blow. A burning warmth began underneath the leather stretched over Molly's buttocks. She hadn't known that such a mixture of sensations were possible. As Harker continued spanking her, she became aware of the warmth spreading to her lower belly like a hot red flame. She moaned and squirmed, wishing he would manipulate her sex again and ease the tight ache. She gasped his name in a plea, then flushed again when he chuckled.

'My hungry Molly.' He put his lips against her ear. 'Would you like to fuck Glenda?'

Oh, God. Molly closed her eyes as she thought of the other woman's large breasts and lusty sensuality.

'Molly?'

The word 'yes' came out in a rush, shocking her when it resonated in her ears. Harker's hand stilled on her bottom. Slowly, Molly turned her head and met his gaze. She couldn't believe the things she was willing to tell him; the things she was willing to admit. And how free these admissions made her feel.

Harker looked at her seriously. 'Do you want me to stop?'

Molly shook her head. 'No.'

Molly woke with her body throbbing with need. She shifted, wincing when her arms stiffened in protest. She was still tied to the bed. Her mind cleared a little, evoking the memory that Harker hadn't let her have an orgasm last night. Molly groaned softly. Her entire being felt as if she had reached a new level of stimulation and awareness. She lifted her head and looked around for Harker. A flutter of fear went through her when she didn't see him. He wouldn't have left her. Would he?

The bathroom door opened, and Harker emerged dressed in jeans and a black T-shirt.

'There's my sleeping beauty.' He paused by the bed, reaching out to brush her hair away from her face. 'What's wrong?'

Molly swallowed hard and shook her head. 'I just ... I didn't see you right away.'

'I'd never leave you alone, you know that.' Harker leant over her and untied the knots in a surprisingly quick series of movements. He rubbed the red marks encircling her wrists. 'Are you sore?'

'A little, but not much.' Molly sat up slowly. The leather outfit no longer felt sensuous, but tight and hot. 'What time is it?'

'Three in the morning. How do you feel?'

'Hot.'

'Go and take that off,' Harker said. 'And come back here naked.'

Molly gave him a startled look. 'Completely?'

He nodded. Molly realised that he had never seen her naked. The thought was strangely unsettling. She climbed off the bed and went to the bathroom, relieved to strip out of the leather. She showered quickly and dried, hesitating before she went back into the bedroom.

Harker's gaze roved over her, skimming over her breasts and hips to her sex. Molly flushed, suddenly highly conscious of her body flaws. She fought the urge to cover herself.

'You're lovely, Molly.' Harker pulled a long lightweight coat out of the closet. 'Put this on.'

'That's all?'

'That's all.'

Molly slipped the coat on and belted it around her waist. She slipped her feet into a pair of heels Harker handed her. This was rather sexy, being completely naked underneath a coat.

'And now,' Harker said, pulling on a leather jacket, 'let's go.'

'Go? You want me to go out like this?'

'Don't you want to?'

Molly considered the idea, not surprised to discover that she found it highly erotic. 'Where are we going?'

'Come on.' Harker took her hand and led her to the door.

He didn't release her hand as they descended the elevator, a gesture for which Molly was grateful. They took a taxi to an address Molly didn't recognise. The streets were virtually deserted with lamps casting an eerie glow over the city. The taxi pulled up in front of a darkened building with an iron staircase leading down to the basement.

'What is this place?' Molly gave Harker a wary look, but followed him down the stairs.

Her hand tightened around his as they went through a narrow doorway and into a room filled with people. The place looked like a bar, only with clientele who were dressed in all manner of leather clothing, most of which exposed one body part or another. It was the strangest group of people Molly had ever seen, from a man wearing nothing but a leather bikini and a woman dressed head-to-toe in latex. She stared in shock as another woman walked past, leading a man by a leash. Loud music pounded through the walls.

'Harker, I'm not sure I like this.'

'I'm not going to leave you, Molly, I promise.' Harker guided her through the crowd and through another door. He closed the door behind him, shutting out some of the noise. This room was empty, save for a huge, round bed with a mirror on the ceiling and a number of leather implements.

'There you are, lover.'

Molly looked up to find Glenda rising from a chair, a smile on her face. She was fully decked out in leather and chains, her generous cleavage almost fully exposed by the V-neckline of her outfit. Molly remembered what she had confessed to Harker only a few hours ago and blushed deeply.

Glenda smiled at Molly, leaning over to press a light kiss against her lips. 'How are you, Molly?'

'OK.'

'Come and sit down.' Glenda moved over to the bed,

patting the seat beside her. 'Don't be afraid, Molly. No one will make you do anything you don't want to do.'

'Aren't you curious?' Harker murmured, brushing his warm lips across the back of Molly's neck.

Molly's breath caught in her throat. To her surprise, she was curious indeed. She released Harker's hand and went to sit next to Glenda. Her body was growing warm underneath the coat. She sat down, catching a light whiff of Glenda's perfume.

'You know, Molly, the scene really doesn't consist of a bunch of weirdos,' Glenda said. 'It's just ordinary people like business owners, journalists, accountants, all kinds of people who just like either giving up control or taking control in consensual sexual situations. And liking it doesn't make you twisted. Not by a long shot.'

Molly wasn't entirely convinced of that, but her ambivalence didn't overtake her curiosity. Far from it, in fact.

Glenda placed her hand on Molly's knee, slipping it between the folds of the coat to touch her bare thigh. A glimmer of excitement appeared in Glenda's eyes, but she moved very slowly as if not wanting to frighten Molly. Her fingers skimmed over Molly's thigh, creating a pleasurable series of trembles. Nerves tightened in Molly's stomach. She had never before been touched so intimately by another woman, and she wasn't certain she liked it.

When Glenda tugged at the belt of the coat, Molly flinched. 'I don't know about this.'

'We can stop whenever you want,' Glenda murmured, pausing in her movement.

Molly looked at Harker and took a deep breath. She wanted to do this, she was intensely curious about what it would be like, but her nerves were getting the better of her. 'I don't ... I mean, I've never ...'

'I know, sweetie,' Glenda whispered. 'It's all right. I find you so beautiful.'

She pressed her lips against Molly's, lightly at first, and then with increasing force. Arousal gathered in Molly's loins as the sensuality of the other woman began to take effect. Glenda felt so different from men, softer and completely filled with eroticism. She parted her lips under Glenda's mouth, letting their tongues explore each other's mouths slowly.

'OK?' Glenda asked.

Molly nodded, allowing herself to sink into the hazy environment of the other woman's lust. Her body began to relax. She had fantasised about making love with a woman, but she had never imagined that it would be like this. Her coat fell open, exposing her nakedness to Glenda's seeking hands and lips. Molly gasped with pleasure when Glenda began to nuzzle her breasts, licking the circle of her tight areolae. Molly was dimly aware that Harker was still in the room, that he wouldn't leave, and she didn't want him to. She felt safer with him there, safer to fully explore this new experience.

She sank back on to the bed as Glenda's hands slipped down to push Molly's thighs apart. Molly's breathing grew rapid. She gazed at Glenda with longing. 'Would you . . . I want to see you.'

Glenda smiled. 'You're such a dear.'

She stood and stripped off her outfit, exposing her lush, generous curves. Her large breasts were creamy white and topped with pink nipples that fairly made Molly's mouth water. She craved the sensation of Glenda's body against her own. Glenda leant over Molly, pressing their breasts together. Heat crackled between them. Molly moaned, entranced by the soft sensation of another woman. Instinctively, she spread her legs, allowing the other woman full access to the soft wet place between her thighs. Glenda kissed and licked a path down Molly's abdomen until she could explore Molly's pussy with her tongue. Molly gasped at the first touch of Glenda's mouth. With leisurely slowness, Glenda slipped her tongue over the crevices and into Molly's overflowing slit.

'Oh, God. That feels wonderful,' Molly said, her voice tremulous.

Glenda's hand moved between her own thighs. Her hips moved rhythmically as she began to masturbate herself while feasting on Molly. Her tongue grew more inquisitive. Molly closed her eyes and drifted into the sensations created by another woman. It was like knowing someone so thoroughly, so completely, that pleasure was simply a matter of doing. With Glenda, there appeared to be no guessing involved. She knew exactly what to do and where to place her tongue most aptly.

A shattering orgasm, having been building for hours now, rocked through Molly almost instantly the moment Glenda's tongue touched her clitoris. She cried out in rapture, her hips bucking off the bed. Glenda reached up and caressed Molly's breasts, her tongue still working industriously as she licked up the copious juices flowing from Molly's sex.

Her entire body vibrating like a strummed guitar string, Molly opened her eyes and stared up at the ceiling mirror. There was a swirl of light, a multitude of tiny, prismatic reflections that slowly resolved into an image of two lusty women on a bed. The sight of herself, spread wantonly on the bed with another woman between her thighs, excited her in a way and to a degree she never felt before. Was it simply the newness of the experience? Or was it the taboo? Right now, she didn't give a damn.

Molly turned her head and met Harker's gaze. He gave her a knowing smile. She had never imagined the pleasures to which this man could introduce her. And she had never imagined what she would do to prove herself to him. Would she do still more? Confusion momentarily gripped her, a dizzy swirl of disturbing yet spellbinding lights, but then Glenda began kissing her. Molly surrendered to the intoxicating excitement which coursed through her veins with redoubled fervour.

# Chapter Four

'You did what?' Lydia frowned, looking up from pouring cream into her tea. 'Molly, that's not a very safe part of the city!'

'It does sound a bit dangerous,' Cassie observed. She was sitting on the bay window seat, her expression one of concern. 'That's in the Tenderloin district, isn't it?'

'I know, but I was with Harker.' A shiver of pleasure travelled through Molly at the sound of his name on her lips. The very syllables were fraught with danger and the promise of passion. 'I feel very safe with him. I had no idea what this BDSM business was all about.'

'And you think you do now?' Lydia replied. She settled back in her chair and shook her head. 'I don't like this, Molly. Not one bit.'

Molly looked at her friend in surprise. 'What, that I'm fucking Harker Trevane?'

'No, that he's introducing you to certain activities that you might not be ready for.'

'How do you know I'm not ready for them?' Molly asked.

'I'm not saying that you're naive, sweetie,' Lydia replied. 'Just that Harker is a great deal more experienced than you.'

'You have personal knowledge of that, do you?' Molly gave Lydia an irritated look, feeling as if her friend were trying to upstage her again. 'I didn't ask for your advice on this. I'm simply telling you about my experiences with a very intriguing man.'

'That intriguing man is also dangerous,' Lydia said. 'And I don't want you to get hurt.'

'I'm not going to get hurt,' Molly retorted. 'Why are you so concerned about me all of a sudden? You've never been this bent out of shape over any of my lovers before.'

'Your previous lovers have never been like Harker Trevane.'

'That's my point! He's completely different, and I like that. No, I love it. I love what he's introducing me to. I loved being tied to the bed. I loved being with another woman, and I even loved being spanked.'

'You sound like you're trying to convince yourself as well as us,' Lydia said.

'I do love it!' Molly snapped, annoyed that Lydia's words were not only condescending but true. 'That shocks you, does it? Well, good. You're not the only one who can have an exotic sex life, you know.'

'Molly –' Cassie began.

'I don't have a problem with you exploring different things,' Lydia interrupted. 'Just with who you've chosen to explore them with. Molly, this is not the kind of man you let drag you around to the seediest parts of town.'

Molly was getting more and more annoyed. She was tired of everyone thinking they were somehow superior to her. 'I think you're jealous because Harker wants me rather than you.'

'Oh Molly, for heaven's sake.'

Molly glared at Lydia. 'Aren't you? For a change, a man is interested in fucking me rather than you, and you can't handle that.'

'If I'd wanted to fuck Harker Trevane to prove a point, I could have easily done so when I was in his hotel room the other day,' Lydia snapped. 'But, Molly, we're not in competition for men! We never have been! I'm trying to tell you that I'm concerned about what you're getting yourself into.'

'Molly, please don't get upset,' Cassie said, her tiny frame trembling slightly over the increasing rancour of the scene. 'Lydia is only looking out for you.'

'Well, she doesn't have to,' Molly retorted. 'I can take care of myself quite well enough.'

'I hope you can,' Lydia muttered.

'What did you say?' Molly asked, her forehead wrinkled angrily.

'I said, "I hope you can."'

'Stop acting as if we were back in boarding school,' Molly said. 'I'm not a schoolgirl any more, and I'm damn sure not the frivolous socialite everyone seems to think I am! I happen to be enjoying this exploration of the darker side of life. Why can't you accept that?'

'Because you shouldn't get involved with a man just to prove something. When you do such a thing and the man just happens to be Harker Trevane, then there are real dangers involved.'

'It's not just to prove something!' Molly shouted, and even as the words issued forth she doubted their validity. 'I like him a great deal, and he likes me, too.'

'You realise that you're only one of many, many women he's been with, don't you?' Lydia asked.

'Yes, I am aware that he doesn't exactly lead a cloistered existence.' Molly stood up, putting her hands on her hips. 'This conversation is over, Lydia. I don't care to discuss my relationship with Harker any further.'

'Now, both of you just wait one minute,' Cassie said firmly. 'I will not have you two fighting over this. Lydia, Molly certainly is intelligent enough to know what she's doing. And Molly, you should be grateful that Lydia is concerned about your well-being. There is no reason to fight.'

Lydia shook her head. 'I still don't like it. I don't trust him.'

'That's well and good,' Molly retorted. 'But you're not the one fucking him.'

Lydia glared at her and stood. She picked up her bag. 'I can see that talking to you in this state of mind is like speaking Turkish to one of your Italian lovers.' She shook her head and turned to go. 'Cassie, thank you for tea, but I think I should leave now.'

'Lydia, don't go.' Cassie hurried after Lydia to prevent her departure, but the front door was already closing with unmistakable finality. Cassie returned to the sitting room, her expression worried. 'Molly, this is silly. You know Lydia cares about you and is only trying to protect you.'

Molly sighed. 'I know, Cassie, but after a while such solicitude wears a little thin.'

Cassie shrugged her shoulders and sat down. After a few thoughtful moments she spoke. 'You really like it, do you?'

Molly looked at her friend. 'What? The things I've done with Harker?'

Cassie nodded.

'They're definitely exciting,' Molly said, her mind spinning back to the feel of the leather on her nipples and the rope on her wrists. Her sex tingled even now. 'I've never experienced anything like it before.'

'But do you like it? Are you comfortable with it?'

'Of course.' Again, Molly was painfully aware that her voice sounded unconvincing. 'Well, I imagine it takes some getting used to on a psychological level, but it's thrilling physically.' She gazed at Cassie, wondering about her friend's curiosity. 'Why do you ask?'

'I don't know. I've been thinking about some things lately.'

'Sexual things, I assume.'

Cassie nodded. She looked down at her hands, which were twisted in her lap. 'I had sex with Nicholas. Did you know that?'

Molly nodded. 'Lydia told me. She said it surprised her because it didn't seem like something you would do, even if she hadn't been involved with him.'

'It wasn't really something I would do.' Cassie sighed. 'I enjoyed it of course, but I guess I wanted to see if I could actually go through with it.'

Molly couldn't help wondering uneasily if her own relationship with Harker had the same motivation.

Molly knocked on the door of Harker's hotel room, nibbling anxiously at her lower lip. Her nerves were more than a little rattled, and now all she wanted was be with him. To her relief, he opened the door.

'Molly!' he said, offering her his familiar, conspiratorial smile. 'What a pleasant surprise.'

'Hello, Harker.' Molly drank in the sight of him dressed in a snug pair of jeans and a white, button-down shirt. His dark hair was damp and brushed away from his forehead, and he smelled like soap and shaving cream. 'Were you going out?'

'Not at all. Come in.' He closed the door behind her and put his hand on her shoulder, gently massaging it. 'Is something wrong?'

'Not really. Well, a little. I just had tea with Lydia and Cassie, and Lydia wasn't particularly happy about the fact that I'm seeing you.'

Harker lifted an eyebrow. 'And why is that?'

'I ... I don't know.' Molly wrung her hands. She hated arguing with Lydia, but she couldn't deny that there was a glimmer of truth, however slight, in what her friend had said. Not that she would ever admit that to Lydia. 'She doesn't like what you're ... um, I mean what *we're* doing.'

'She doesn't, does she? Well, is that her business?'

'No!' Molly said firmly, still quite defensive about any challenges to her independence. 'But she is my best friend, and I tell her and Cassie everything.'

'So what do you want me to do about this?' Harker asked, removing his hand from her shoulder and moving over to sit on the edge of the bed. 'You don't want to see me any more? Is that it?'

'I didn't say that. I'm just confused.'

Harker looked at her, a crease appearing between his eyebrows. 'You trust me, don't you?'

Molly nodded.

'You shouldn't have told Lydia.'

'I tell her everything.'

'Not any more you don't. I'm not happy with your conduct, Molly.' He flexed and stretched the fingers of his right hand. 'Come here.'

Molly approached him, relieved when he stood and took her in his arms, pulling her against him in a strong, masculine embrace. He bent his head to kiss her, sliding

his hands around to her buttocks. He gave them a
squeeze, and Molly gasped with delight. The firm presence of his hands on her ass reminded her of previous
events, of the rope which had held her hands, of the
leather – of Glenda. Harker's tongue slipped into her
mouth and over the surface of her teeth, invading her in
a deliciously seductive manner. Molly's blood warmed as
Harker continued to explore her mouth, assuaging the
unpleasantness of her argument with Lydia. Sometimes
there is no better counsellor than a man's tongue, she
thought hazily. Harker lifted his head slightly, his breath
brushing her lips.

'Take off your clothes,' he murmured. 'I want to watch.'

Trembling, Molly stepped away from him and unbuttoned her blouse, letting it fall to the floor at her feet. She
removed her bra, almost embarrassed at the fact that her
nipples were already so hard. So shameless they had
become. Just like me, she thought, and a crackle of excitement leapt through her. She stripped off her skirt and
panties, then stood before him naked.

'I think you need a bit of punishment.' Harker sat down
in a chair.

'What?' she said, her heart leaping with fear and yet
aware that the very sound of his voice pronouncing the
word 'punishment' was causing her sex to swell.

'You heard me.'

'I heard you, but I'm not sure I agree with your sen-
tence, Judge.'

Harker smiled. 'Oh, I think you do. You do agree that
you shouldn't have told Lydia about our activities, don't
you?'

Molly dropped her head and sighed. Lydia had always
been such a good friend, had helped her through so many
rough times, but dammit, she was just overprotective. So
condescending.

'Yes,' she said at last, so softly that Harker leant forward and put his hand to his ear.

'Yes,' Molly repeated. 'I was wrong.'

She swallowed hard as Harker took her by the hand
and tugged her across his lap so that she was lying across

his knees. The pale globes of her buttocks quivered, and Molly caught her breath in surprise when Harker landed the first loud smack on her backside. She gasped more from the shock of it rather than any actual pain, but her body jerked forward to escape the inevitability of the second blow. Harker's left arm clamped around Molly's waist to prevent her from writhing as she struggled against another slap. He spanked her again and again, each strike eliciting a moan of discomfort from Molly.

A rosy warmth covered her bottom cheeks, even as she wriggled around frantically to escape the hot stings of Harker's hand. She blushed hotly when he broke the pattern of his slaps to bend down and lay his tongue against the tortured flesh. It was so cool and wet against her. Such delicious contrast. Molly bit her lip as Harker continued to lick her bottom. This is punishment? she thought. But he must have been attuned to her thoughts, because no sooner did she think that than Harker resumed his spanking, beating a rhythmic tattoo of punishment over the rounded globes of his captive. The pain was sublime. Finally, his hand came to a halt. Molly tried to turn her head so that she could see what would happen next, but a sharp glance stopped her short.

'Don't you dare look me in the eye, you slut. Look at the floor.'

The words stung her to the quick. No spanking could ever have caused as much pain as that awful, hurtful word. Slut.

'You son of a bitch!' she cried out and tried to wrest herself from his grasp, but as she did, Harker lightly traced his finger over her pussy.

'Ohh,' she gasped, much too taken with the sensation to continue struggling.

'Yes, I think you do want this. And very badly, too.' He held his finger to her face. It glistened with the proof of his statement.

Without his having to tell her, Molly dropped her head and looked at the floor. Harker's fingers slipped down to the cleft which separated her cheeks, and he eased them apart. Molly felt a sudden rush of air on her most private

areas. She squeezed her eyes tightly shut at the completely humiliating position in which she now found
herself, her breasts dangling down like an animal's, her
anus suddenly exposed to heaven only knew what treat-
ment. But the humiliation and fear only served to
heighten her arousal. Harker's finger, wet with her own
juices, momentarily teased the tight little hole, but didn't
venture inside. Her sex now flowed freely with the thick,
hot evidence of its need. She arched her back, parting her
legs slightly, silently begging Harker to quell the fire
which was raging out of control. He extended his forefinger and tested her wetness, rubbing his finger against
her with exquisite cleverness. Then he pulled away.

'Harker, please –'

'Please what?' he replied, ever so lightly running his
fingers over her sex. 'Ah, how your sweet pussy quivers
for me.'

'Please, please, please . . .' Molly moaned, her voice trailing away. She felt as if she were suddenly climbing an
impossibly tall ladder. Up, up, up, into the thin air. A
feeling of light-headedness started to descend on her.

'Who is it that you trust?' Harker growled, pulling on
the damp hairs that covered her pussy. 'Me or Lydia?'

'I trust . . . I mean . . . Oh, Harker!' she panted, the earth
shrinking away to nothingness beneath her. She was as
light as a cloud. Her whole being was centred in her sex.

'Who, Molly, who?' he implored, simultaneously teasing and torturing her sex. 'Who?'

'You, Harker.'

'Good answer,' he said with a soft, devilish voice, at last
thrusting his finger into Molly's tight, hungry channel.

'Mmm.' A moan escaped Molly's mouth as her entire
body went limp with relief. She was floating in the
clouds. Her writhing movements shifted into luscious
wriggles as Harker's fingers explored her aching pussy.
Fiery prickles scorched the tender skin of Molly's bottom,
and an equally intense heat centred on the pulsing bud
of her clitoris. She bit her lip on a groan, unable to prevent
the thrusts of her hips as she started to work her body
against Harker's blunt fingers. Her senses swam in a

whirlpool of sensations created by his hard palm slapping against her buttocks, his fingers sliding into the humid warmth of her passage, his erection pressing obscenely against the flesh of her belly.

Poised on the brink, Molly closed her eyes, her breath coming in rapid gasps as she struggled vainly to force Harker's fingers deeper inside her. All she craved was the explosion of pleasure that dangled tauntingly just beyond her grasp. There it was, coming closer. The waves built higher and higher, faster and faster, bearing down on her inexorably, promising to wash her away with ecstasy.

But Harker lifted his hand from between her legs with a swiftness that startled her. Molly caught her breath, trying to turn and see what was the matter. Harker's strong hands clamped around her waist as he lifted her to her feet, his arm brushing against the swollen, tender flesh of her bottom. Molly gave a little yelp of pain, her hands automatically caressing the areas which had been the object of Harker's punishment. Her skin fairly flared with heat against her palms.

Harker pushed her towards the bed. 'Lie down and spread your legs.'

Molly looked at Harker, stunned by the burning hot expression in his eyes. Slowly, she lay back on the bed, wincing as she stretched out and her inflamed buttocks made contact with the coverpane. She had never been so aware of her body, of each little sensation that contributed to her arousal. She spread her thighs apart to cool her heated sex, left so cruelly on the precipice of release. Harker went into the bathroom, then returned with a bowl of water and a razor.

Molly stared at him. 'Harker . . .'

'Who is it that you trust?'

Molly nodded, even though a brief twinge of nervousness went through her. She suspected that this was one of the ultimate tests of trust. Harker put his hands on her knees, pushing her thighs farther apart. He spread a towel underneath her buttocks, then rubbed her damp sex with a corner of it. Molly gave a little sigh of pleasure at the friction, her tension heightened to unfathomable limits.

She closed her eyes and surrendered to Harker's ministrations. He dampened her pubic hair, then began stroking a generous amount of shaving cream over it. His fingers moved with lush ease over her sex, spreading the frothy lather. It felt so good that Molly nearly forgot about the razor as tension began to coil in the pit of her stomach and her blood hummed with the electricity of forbidden eroticism.

'Now hold still,' Harker said firmly.

Molly started at the first touch of the razor against her skin, but Harker drew it over her mons with such care that her initial fear quickly dissipated. In fact, she found his devout attention to her sex most arousing, particularly with the lingering prickles of heat still covering her buttocks. Harker wiped away the hairs of her mons, then scraped the razor gently over her labia. Molly was almost embarrassed by the fact that she was producing so much wetness, but it was erotic, this sensation of the steel blade against her sensitive folds and Harker's careful attention. It was more than erotic. It was the height of the erotic. She toyed with her left nipple, giving herself up to the sensual intimacy of this act.

Harker dipped the razor in a bowl of water, then reached for a bottle of lotion. He pumped some into his hand, and smoothed it over her shorn pussy. Molly moaned, pushing her hips up towards him as the rich lotion soothed her. Harker dipped his slick fingers into the valley of her pussy, thrusting two fingers deep into her slit.

'Oh, yes!' Molly squeezed her breasts together, rubbing her nipples between her thumbs and forefingers. Arrows of sheer pleasure rushed through her, as if her nipples were connected directly to her sex.

Molly's natural fluids mixed with the silky lotion as Harker massaged it into her shaven mons. He circled his thumb around her clitoris, then rubbed it directly. Shudders of rapture vibrated through Molly's body at long last, washing her in pleasure. She opened her eyes and looked at Harker, her chest heaving.

'You look lovely,' he said huskily. 'Do you want to see yourself?'

Molly nodded. Harker wiped away some excess lotion, then picked up a hand mirror and held it up to her sex. Molly gazed at the bareness of her swollen pussy for a long moment.

'It ... reveals everything, doesn't it?' she whispered.

'That's the idea,' Harker replied. 'That's what I want you to do with me, Molly. Reveal everything. Do you think you can do that?'

'I don't know.'

'Tell me what you're afraid of.'

'Myself.'

'You don't have to be.' Harker stripped off his clothes. Molly watched him, her arousal returning powerfully as she gazed at his naked body, his penis already bobbing.

'I'm afraid of what I feel when I'm with you,' she amended.

'You're learning more about yourself.' Harker leant over her, placing his hands on either side of her head. He lowered his head and kissed her, brushing his chest across her breasts. Molly squirmed, wondering what his erection would feel like against her new smoothness. She reached down and closed her fingers around his pulsing shaft, warm with blood and heat. Slowly, she rubbed the hard knob against the new-found silkiness of her labia. Shivers of pleasure rained down her spine. Oh, yes, everything was revealed.

She groaned as Harker's cock pushed against her tight, wet passage. She wrapped her arms around his neck, craving the complete immersion of his hardness in her body. He reached down and cupped his hands underneath her thighs, pushing her open for him as he sank into her. Molly gasped. She had never imagined just how erotic the sensation of smooth skin against a man's nether hairs would be. There were many things she never imagined or discovered before. As Harker found his rhythm, she thought to herself, what else is left to learn? What else is left to reveal?

'You feel so incredible, so slick and wet and tight,' Harker whispered huskily in her ear.

He began to thrust deeper, his testicles slapping against her roughly, animalistically, his oiled cock sliding in and out like pliable iron. Sporadic cries of pleasure came from Molly's throat as she clutched him to her. She tightened her inner muscles around him, feeling a rush of satisfaction at his own groan of pleasure. There was no disputing the honesty of such sounds. This honesty, this basic undeniable honesty, was a clarion call beckoning to her own sexuality. Instantly another orgasm roared through her body like a living flame. She clamped down on Harker's cock again and again, her mouth curling into a smile as she felt the fire invade his own body, rising quickly into a conflagration. With a final almost desperate thrust, he put the fire out. For the moment, anyway.

Harker collapsed next to Molly, flinging an arm over his eyes. 'Ah, Molly. You'll grow to love being pushed to your limits. And one day pushing other people to theirs.'

Molly looked at him. 'What do you mean?'

'Do you want to find out?'

'Yes.' The word came as a whisper. She rolled on to her side to face him, gazing at the hard line of his profile. Her bottom still felt scorched from his earlier slaps, and she pressed her palm against her hot skin. Between the spanking and her shorn vulva, she had experienced more sensations than she had known were possible. But hadn't she thought the same thing just the other night with Glenda? Yes, she had, but Harker's question – and her answer – promised that there were still more to discover.

'Get dressed, then.'

Molly didn't have to ask him what she should wear. She went to the closet and pulled out the leather bustier, slipping it over her legs. Her backside hurt like hell against the tight leather, but her smooth, already slick pussy felt delicious in its leather domain. She wrapped the coat around herself and slipped her feet into heeled shoes.

They went down to catch a taxi. Molly wasn't surprised when he directed the driver to the same Tenderloin address they had been at a couple of nights ago. Glenda was waiting in the same room, wearing a gaudy diamond necklace and a long, black gown that nearly caused her breasts to overflow from the cups. If not for the circumstances, Molly might have suspected that Glenda was about to head out for a night on the town. Molly smiled in greeting, surprised when Glenda didn't respond.

Harker looked at Molly. 'Are you ready for this, Princess Molly?'

Molly didn't know what she should be ready for. The lighting of the room was low, aided only by multiple flickering candles. The door opened, and about ten people filed into the room. Drinks in hand, they chatted amongst themselves and sat down in various chairs around the room. One of the women greeted Harker with a sloppy kiss. Unease curled in the pit of Molly's stomach.

Harker went to a cabinet and produced a blindfold. Without a word, he tied the blindfold around Glenda's eyes, then slipped his hand down to the juncture of the woman's thighs. He bent to kiss her, stroking his tongue over her lips and into her mouth. A rush of jealousy hit Molly so hard that she nearly reeled. Good god, was this part of the whole scene, watching one's lover with another woman? She couldn't help thinking about what Lydia had said earlier: 'You realise that you're only one of many, many women he's been with, don't you?'

Yes, yes, yes, Molly thought to herself and clenched her lips together.

'Thank you, master,' Glenda murmured in response to Harker's lewd kiss.

'On the bed, my pretty slave.'

Molly stared at the scene unfolding before her with both fascination and an increasing sense of shock. Harker guided Glenda to the bed, and she quickly situated herself on her hands and knees. Harker pulled her gown up over her hips, arranging it over the expanse of her back. Glenda's buttocks jutted upward, full and white, her legs spread enough to reveal her labia, plump and heavy, already beginning to open like the thick petals of a tropical flower. Her pendulous breasts dangled below, topped with the large, tight nipples Molly had seen before. Molly drew in a sharp breath when she saw another woman hand Harker a leather whip. Surely he wasn't going to whip Glenda? Spanking was one thing, but whipping?

Molly winced when Harker trailed the whip handle over the crease of Glenda's buttocks, then slid it into the creamy passage of her slit. Glenda let out a low moan, lowering her head to her arms.

'Oh, no,' Harker murmured. He put his forefinger underneath Glenda's chin and lifted her head. 'No hiding.'

He pushed the whip handle further in, eliciting another moan from Glenda. Her back arched, her buttocks thrusting back against the whip handle to coax it further inside. Harker slid the handle back and forth before removing it and holding it in front of Glenda.

'Suck,' he ordered softly.

Glenda's lips parted as Harker inserted the shiny handle into her mouth. Slowly, she sucked and licked her own secretions off the handle. Molly bit her lip, disliking what she was watching and yet unable to take her eyes from the scene. Candle shadows fluttered around the room, dancing on Glenda's white skin. The silhouetted figures of people shifted against the walls, making Molly aware of their presence.

'Now, tell me what you want,' Harker said.

Glenda swallowed, her throat convulsing. Her head turned slightly as if trying to see him, but her blindfold blocked her vision. 'Whip me, master. Please.'

The small crowd stirred, their voices rising in a murmur. Molly hugged her arms around herself as if trying to contain her increasing confusion. Why had Harker brought her here to witness this? Wasn't this supposed to be an exercise in Molly pushing others to their limits? To make matters even more disturbing, Molly became aware of the growing warmth between her legs as she gazed at Glenda's voluptuous body and her prone, submissive position. Her eyes went to Harker, the hard set of his face as he stroked his hand over Glenda's ass. An erection pushed at the front of his trousers. The thought that Harker was already so aroused so soon after fucking her infuriated Molly. And yet it made her pussy throb with greater urgency.

Harker lifted the whip and brought it down with expert precision over Glenda's buttocks. Glenda let out a cry of pain, her body jerking forward. Harker landed another blow, and the cracking sound made Molly recoil.

'Thank you, master,' Glenda gasped, as two red welts began to rise on her bottom.

Molly remembered her own spanking just a few hours ago, and the certain arousal that had resulted. The slaps of Harker's hand had hurt, but surely nothing like the sting of a leather whip. Even so, Molly lowered her gaze to Glenda's spread labia, which glistened with moisture, each little droplet shining in the candlelight like the prisms of a chandelier. The lash of a leather whip was exciting.

Molly cringed as Harker's whip landed again and again, creating a criss-cross of thin red lines on Glenda's previously unblemished buttocks. Choked moans and whimpers spilt from Glenda's throat in an unending stream, accompanied by gasped 'Thank you, master's whenever Harker paused in his lashing. Tears streamed down her face, but she didn't tell him to stop. In fact, she arched her back and thrust her bottom out to him as if asking for the lash of the whip. The movement earned a smile from Harker.

'Good girl.'

Finally, when he had landed a number of blows, he cast the whip aside and stroked his hand lightly over Glenda's inflamed cheeks. She yelped with pain, but pushed herself up towards him again. Harker slipped his hands between her legs, spreading her sex apart roughly, casting his glance backward at Molly as he did so. Molly swallowed hard. It was as if his hands were on her pussy instead, holding it open for the whole world to see. The thought thrilled through her, bright and dizzying. And terrifying.

'Now what do you want?' he whispered.

Glenda drew in a sharp breath. 'Fuck me, master. Fuck me, please.'

Harker stripped off his shirt, revealing his muscled torso made all the more intimidating by the candlelight flickering eerily over his skin. He unzipped his trousers and removed them, his erect penis emerging triumphantly like a conquering hero. Or a tyrant. An appreciative murmur rose from the women in the room. Molly glanced to her right, realising that some of the people were touching each other intimately as they watched the dark drama playing out before them. One woman rode another woman's thigh, as a man thrust his cock into the fist of a third woman.

Molly looked back at Harker, trying to quench the increasing disgust as she watched him sliding into Glenda's pussy. She couldn't believe this, couldn't believe what he was doing, what he was making her witness. The thick, veiny stalk of his cock slid halfway into Glenda's vagina, evoking a squeal of pleasure from the blindfolded woman. And then Harker thrust hard, sinking into Glenda with a groan of pleasure. The cushions of her bottom slammed against his lower belly as he pumped inside her again and again. Sighs and groans rose from the witnesses as they indulged in their own pleasure.

Molly watched Harker, the sheen of sweat that covered his skin, the tight expression on his face as he fucked Glenda with long, hard thrusts that caused her to whimper with rapture. At that instant, Molly knew that she was next, that she would soon be expected to do what Glenda was doing, to call Harker 'master' and allow herself to be whipped with a leather strap. Her chest constricted at the mere thought of herself in that position. Her sex was scorching, but arousal could not get the better of her fear and disgust this time.

Harker came, slumping forward on to Glenda so roughly that the clasp of her necklace gave way. The jewel bounced once on the bed and then landed on the hard floor with a dainty tinkle, but in Molly's ears it was the sound of a chandelier crashing to the floor.

She stood still, as if tied from head to foot in rope, unable to breathe. Harker's cold eyes, offset by the placid smile of a man who has just come, suddenly met hers. Molly stared at him for a long moment. And then she turned and fled.

# Chapter Five

Molly stepped out of the shower, finally feeling clean after half an hour under the steaming water. She wrapped her damp body in a robe and went to the telephone, dialling a familiar number.

'Lydia, it's Molly.'

'Hello, Molly.' Tension strained Lydia's voice, as if she was uncertain what to expect.

'Lyd, I wanted to apologise. Can you come over here? I need to talk to you.'

'Of course,' Lydia said, genuine concern evident in her words. 'Give me about twenty minutes, and I'll be there.'

Molly waited impatiently for her friend, then hurried to the door when Lydia knocked. Dressed in black trousers and a grey silk shirt, Lydia looked as refined and elegant as she always did. She gave Molly a smile and a hug.

'You're OK, aren't you?'

Molly sighed and nodded as they settled in the sitting room. 'Yes. You were right about Harker. I was wrong.'

Lydia frowned. 'Did he hurt you?'

'No. He didn't do anything I didn't agree to.' She hated having to recount what she had witnessed, but she forced herself to recount all the lurid details. Lydia listened silently.

'Well,' Lydia murmured when Molly had finished. 'It's clear that Harker Trevane doesn't know how to introduce a woman to BDSM.'

Molly looked at Lydia, intensely grateful that her friend didn't take advantage of the opportunity to condescend.

'I'm so sorry,' she said. 'You were right about him, about me. I was trying to prove something to him. To prove that I could take it. I guess I was also trying to prove it to myself.'

'You don't have to prove anything to anyone,' Lydia replied. 'BDSM isn't about proof, or even about pain necessarily. It's about control, and most importantly trust, Molly. It's another avenue to sexual gratification, but only through honesty and negotiation. If someone – someone like Harker Trevane – uses it as a way to derive pleasure from simply humiliating others or inflicting pain upon them, then that really isn't BDSM anymore. Not to me anyway.'

'What is it?'

'It's psychosis. I'm not a psychologist, but I'm sure there's a clinical name for it.'

Molly let out a long sigh, resting her head against the back of the sofa. She knew Harker wasn't the monster that Lydia made him out to be. 'I don't know. It seemed so exciting at first, something different. And then I just knew that he would want me to accept that whipping sooner or later.'

'He tried to move you much too fast,' Lydia said. 'Maybe he wanted to see how far he could push you in a short period of time. I think he's only in the city for another couple of days.' She paused. 'But there again, the very act of pushing is a dangerous thing. If you've never really been pushed before, it's easy to let someone push you too hard. And too far.'

'I guess so,' Molly mumbled.

'You're sure he didn't really hurt you? That he didn't force you to do something you didn't want to do?'

'I'm sure. I agreed to everything we did, but I finally discovered just how intense it can get. I don't like that at all.'

'It's definitely not for everyone,' Lydia said. 'I suspected that it wasn't for you, but every woman needs to discover these things for herself. I'm so sorry you had a bad experience, Molly.'

'It wasn't so much bad as shocking,' Molly said. 'The whole thing completely unnerved me. I don't want to get involved with whipping, for heaven's sake. I don't like that kind of pain.'

'Well, it sounds like you discovered your limits, then,' Lydia said. 'That's always a good thing.'

Molly looked at her friend. 'You like it though, don't you?'

'I like to be in control,' Lydia replied. 'And that's one way of being in total sexual control.'

'And what do the men being whipped get out of it?'

Lydia tucked her legs underneath her and rested her arm along the back of the sofa. 'They get the satisfaction of surrendering to a woman with total trust. They know they've pleased me, and for them it's a way of giving up control. A man has so many obligations in life that sometimes it's nice to let the woman lead the way.'

'But pain is pain.'

'You said you liked it when Harker spanked you,' Lydia reminded her.

'Well, that wasn't incredibly painful,' Molly said. 'That was kind of a mixture of pain and pleasure.'

'So is whipping, just on a different level,' Lydia said.

Molly shuddered. 'I don't know. That's just much too extreme. I mean, I admit that it was somewhat exciting to watch, but if that's something I would have to do...' Her voice trailed off.

Lydia ran her hand soothingly through Molly's hair. 'Like I said, you've discovered your limits. Everyone needs to do that at one point or another. I'm only sorry that it happened the way it did.'

'Well, it's my own fault. I agreed to go with him. I wanted to.'

'It's not your fault,' Lydia said firmly. 'He pushed you too fast. I think I need to have a talk with him.'

'No.' Molly shook her head. 'This is my problem, and I'll handle it. I just needed to talk to you.'

They both looked up at the sound of the doorbell. Molly's nerves tensed. She went to the door, unsurprised to find Harker Trevane standing there.

'I suppose it won't do me much good to apologise,' he said.

'Give it a try.' Lydia suddenly appeared behind Molly,

her eyes cold. 'How dare you subject her to something she wasn't ready for, you bastard! I have a mind to call the psych ward and have you picked up.'

'Lydia –' Molly began.

Harker's gaze clashed with Lydia's. 'I'm aware of what I did,' he replied. 'Molly is a grown woman. I told her that if she wanted me to stop, all she had to do was tell me. She knew I would.'

'She didn't understand the implications of what you involved her in.'

'Forgive my bluntness, but I fail to see why this is any of your business.'

'It's my business because she's my closest friend, and I love her very much,' Lydia said. 'She was trying to prove something to you, a need you obviously planted in her head. It's people like you who give the BDSM scene such a bad reputation.'

'Stop talking about me as if I'm not even here,' Molly snapped. 'Lydia, I know you were right, but I'm tired of being talked down to.'

Lydia's dark eyes shot daggers at Harker Trevane, but she didn't say anything else. Harker looked at Molly.

'We need to talk about this.'

'All right. Come inside. Lydia, I can handle it from here.'

'I'm not leaving you alone with him,' Lydia replied.

Molly tugged her friend towards the door as Harker disappeared into the sitting room. 'Please, Lydia. I need to handle this on my own. You can't constantly protect me.'

'Molly, after what he did, I don't want you to be alone with him!'

'He won't hurt me,' Molly said. 'If there's anything I know about him, it's that he won't hurt me.'

Lydia hesitated, obviously not as confident of Harker's self-discipline as Molly was. 'I'm about ready to call the police, Molly.'

'Lydia, please.'

Lydia bit her lip and nodded. 'All right. I know I have to let you take control of your own life. However, I have my cellphone with me, and I'm going to go right home. I want you to telephone me immediately if he makes you the slightest bit uncomfortable.'

Molly nodded. 'I will. I promise.'

The two women hugged each other tightly, then Lydia left. Molly took a deep breath and went into the sitting room. Harker was standing by the window, his shoulders slumped slightly as he stared out at the Golden Gate bridge. He turned to look at her. 'I manipulated you. I'm sorry.'

'You damn well should be.'

'After I spanked you and shaved you, after I felt how hot and wet it made you, I thought certainly you were ready to move to the next level.'

'You were wrong,' Molly said firmly, but with compassion. She could tell Harker was genuinely sorry for what he'd done, and she couldn't help suspecting that this sort of contrition was quite difficult for him.

'Yes, I was wrong. I subjected you to something you weren't ready for.'

'True enough,' Molly allowed. 'However, I am grateful in a masochistic kind of way.'

Harker lowered his head and laughed. 'Is that so?'

'Yes. As Lydia told me, everyone needs to discover their limits sometime.' She eyed him speculatively. 'When did you discover yours?'

'I don't even know that I have yet. I suspect you're one ahead of me in that respect.'

'Well, I've had more practice,' Molly replied, a suggestive smile animating her lips.

She crossed the room to him, reaching up to trail her forefinger over his whisker-roughened jaw. What a strange man he was to have introduced her to such dark desires, to have caused her both intense pleasure and confusion. 'Why did you want to get involved with me?' she asked.

'I thought you would be a challenge.'

Molly couldn't help laughing. 'Wanting to see if the princess could take it?'

Harker sighed. 'You're not a princess, Molly. I'm sorry I

ever thought you were. You're definitely a strong woman.'

'Yes, I know.' Satisfaction flooded through Molly at the sound of Harker's admission. 'I've always known that. But sometimes strength is revealed in surprising ways. Take, for example, a chandelier. A large, magnificent one, all coddled prisms and delicate ornamentation.'

He looked at her, lost in thought for a moment. Then he nodded his head and smiled. 'Yes, I see what you mean.'

'Do you?' She rubbed her thumb over his beautifully shaped mouth, then curled her fingers around the back of his neck. As she drew him down towards her, a heady sense of power filled her. For the first time with Harker, the swirling lights of the chandelier were inside her, not around her.

Harker didn't touch her, but his lips parted as Molly slipped her tongue between them. Her tongue slid over his teeth, and she pressed her hand against his chest to feel his heartbeat. It was rapid and warm against her palm. It was there, she could feel it, that barely restrained power that was such an implicit part of his personality. He didn't give up control, he took control.

Until now. She unbuttoned his shirt and pushed it off his shoulders, running her fingers through the dark mat of his chest hair. Her skin began to tingle as she thought of what she would ask Harker to submit to, of what discovery she might lead him to. He put his hands on Molly's hips as if to draw her against him, but Molly pushed him away.

'No,' she whispered. 'You don't touch.'

To her delight, his hands dropped away from her. He didn't move as she pulled and pinched his nipples, only grimaced slightly, an expression which made Molly laugh with wanton pleasure. Then she moved her hands to the waistband of his jeans. Slowly, she unzipped them, her heart pulsing at the sensation of the promising bulge pressing against her fingers. Stepping away from him, she eyed his groin.

'Take them off,' she ordered softly.

Harker did, sliding his jeans and shorts over his hips to reveal himself. His cock was already thick and pulsing with obvious need. Molly let out her breath in a sigh, highly conscious of the increasing warmth between her legs. The belt of her robe loosened slightly, revealing a V of damp skin to which Harker's eyes were drawn. Molly smiled. She felt as if she were establishing herself and her own sexuality again, only this time on her terms. Terms with which Harker Trevane could not argue.

Grasping his penis in her hand, she let her fingers slide over the throbbing shaft, causing Harker to draw in a sharp breath. Molly looked down as his cock grew and thickened still further, flicking her thumb over the moist, plum-coloured tip. Harker let out an anguished cry.

'Oh, my poor baby. Does that hurt?'

Harker bit down on his lip as she continued to rub his glans. 'No, no, it just feels ... so ...'

Molly tossed her head back with a glee she hadn't felt in a long, long time. She had reduced the famous writer to wordlessness.

'Now sit down.' Molly pointed to an upright chair. 'And don't move.'

He did as she told him. Perspiration broke out on his chest, making his skin glisten. Molly gazed at him for a moment as a thrill of pleasure rushed through her. Ah, yes, she was definitely starting to understand why Lydia so loved to have sexual control. Molly stripped off her belt, letting her robe fall open to reveal her breasts and smooth sex. Harker's eyes roamed hungrily over her nakedness, but he made no move to stand. His penis jutted forth between his legs, a gorgeous stalk of flesh that was harder than she had ever seen it.

Without removing her robe, Molly moved behind Harker. She wrapped the belt around his wrists and tied them to the back of the chair. Then she went into her bedroom and returned with two silk scarves. She knelt and lashed each of Harker's ankles to the legs of the chair. Rising, she surveyed her handiwork with an extreme sense of pleasure and satisfaction. Her clitoris fairly tingled between her legs at the sight of the masterful Harker restrained and helpless, his cock shamelessly advertising his desperate need. Moisture gathered in her sex and a familiar ribbon of tension tightened around her lower body. She put her hands on Harker's shoulders and leant forward.

'Go on,' she commanded softly. 'Suck them like a good boy.'

Harker's lips closed around the tight nub of her left nipple. An electric spark seemed to flow through Molly's body at the sensation of his mouth on her sensitive flesh. His tongue circled the areola, his teeth tugging lightly on her nipple. Molly straddled his naked thighs, arching her back as she pushed her breast towards him.

'Now the other one.'

Obediently, Harker turned his attention to her right breast, licking and sucking it with the same degree of devotion. Molly let out a small moan, leaning forward enough so that their bodies barely brushed against each other. Reaching behind her, she slid her fingers over Harker's engorged cock, taking a great deal of pride in having caused it to grow to such a degree. She let her hand drift further down, to his tight, lightly haired testicles and the sensitive skin between his thighs. With a mischievous smile, she took hold of his cock firmly and slid the hard knob into the crevice of her buttocks, feeling his hips jerk involuntarily.

'No,' she whispered. 'You don't move at all. Do you understand?'

Harker nodded, his eyes glazed with passion and heat. Molly bent her head to kiss him, sucking his lower lip between hers. Her blood pulsed hotly with desire for him, her mind swimming in a sea of dancing lights. She had always had control over her Italian lovers, but to take control with a man as independent and domineering as Harker Trevane was a stimulation unlike any she had experienced before. She rubbed her breasts against his chest, revelling in the friction of his chest hair against her smooth skin. Still holding his penis, she spread her legs further, pressing the moist flower of her vulva against his pelvis.

'Oh, Christ,' Harker whispered. 'Do it, Molly. Ride me.'

'All in good time.' Molly writhed her hips, stimulating the tight ache in her clit to even greater depths as she rubbed it against Harker's skin.

Slowly, she rubbed the head of his cock into her sex, shivering with excitement at the feeling of his hardness sliding against her. The moist knob elicited a delicious friction, and Molly's sex swelled and ached in anticipation of being fucked. She guided his cock to the entrance of her body, gazing down at him with hot eyes. She began to slide their sexes together. Her eyes drifted closed, and a groan emerged from deep inside her she sank on to his erection. Ah, God, how luscious it felt, the hard length throbbing against her inner self and sending heat directly into her veins. Harker's restrained body bucked underneath her with impatience.

'Don't fight it, Prince Harker,' she said, sweeping her eyes over his face with rapacious abandon.

Placing her hands on his shoulders, Molly lifted her hips and brought them down again, driving herself towards a fast, intense rhythm. Her breasts bounced, and she let the robe slide off her shoulders so that she was completely naked. The wet, slapping sound of their union resounded through the room as Molly increased the pace of her movements. Her skin burned with heat and arousal, stimulated even more by the knowledge of Harker's restraint, by the sight of his face, contorted incredibly by the intense pleasure she was giving him. Harker's hard cock slid with lush ease in and out of her oiled slit. Molly reached back to caress his testicles, eliciting a moan of pleasure from him.

Pressure began to build in Molly's loins like tight bands. She increased her movements to an almost frantic pace, slamming herself down on Harker's cock so that her buttocks slapped against his thighs. Suddenly, the bands broke and a wave of pure rapture rolled through her body. Her sex convulsed around him as she rode out her pleasure. She clutched his shoulders, her breathing harsh as the sensations began to ebb.

It took her a moment to realise that Harker hadn't yet

succumbed to his own orgasm. Molly pressed her lips against his forehead as she eased herself off him. She scooted back to his knees so that his penis was between their bodies, then grasped it, hard and slick, in her hand again. With slow movements, she began to stroke him, watching his heavily lidded eyes as she spurred him towards his release. Within seconds, a shudder coursed through his body and spurts of hot come squirted out on to Molly's hand and belly. Harker groaned, slumping in the chair as much as the restraints would allow.

Molly stood, wobbly from the lingering effects of the experience. She picked up her robe and wrapped it around her body. She knelt and untied Harker, tossing the belt and scarves on to a nearby table. 'Well, I can understand why that's exciting,' she murmured.

Harker rubbed his hand over his face. 'Christ, Molly. You have a real talent for the dominant role. An innate one, if I judge correctly.'

'Like your innate talent for the arrogant role?'

Harker chuckled and began to pull his clothes on. 'Touché.'

'I learnt a lot from you, Harker,' Molly said. 'I really did.'

'Oh? You mean my teaching you how to tie a bowline?'

She reached for one of the scarves and swatted him. 'No, I mean your teaching me that I needn't destroy my delicate side to be strong.'

'I don't think I taught you that. I think you taught yourself.'

'Well, the important thing is that I learnt it.'

'I'm glad that you did, Molly. I learnt a lot from you, too, you know. Most of it in the last fifteen minutes.'

Molly shrugged. 'Better late than never.'

'Thank heavens for that.'

Molly gazed at him for a moment. A strange thought suddenly occurred to her. What happened to the tether when it no longer fulfilled its purpose of securing the chandelier?

\* \* \*

Sun streamed in through the window, warming Molly's exposed skin gradually and with delicious ease. She rolled over in bed and nuzzled her face into the pillow. Sleeping late was one of life's very greatest pleasures, sex notwithstanding. Molly was drifting towards a dream, a dream in which a Venetian gondolier was reciting Italian verse to her. She couldn't understand the words, but the man's face was enchanting, and the tone of his voice told her that it was a love poem. A poem meant to seduce her. She squirmed in bed, easing her legs apart slightly so that the sheets rubbed against her bare cunt.

The phone rang, jolting her rudely from her reverie. Molly heaved a sigh. She let the phone ring three times and then started to reach for the receiver when her answering machine clicked on.

'Hello, Molly. It's Harker. I'm all packed and ready to go, but I did want to speak with you first. I thought we might have coffee or something before my plane left.'

Molly lowered her hand to the receiver, but she couldn't bring herself to take hold of it and lift it.

'Well, you must still be asleep. I wanted to let you know that I'll be back in San Francisco in about six months, doing some research for my next novel. I thought perhaps we could get together then.'

Perhaps, Molly thought. She wasn't averse to the idea, but six months was a long time. She had no desire to plan her life that far ahead.

'I guess I'll sign off now. Take care of yourself and keep your friend Lydia in line. Goodbye, Molly.'

A twinge spasmed in the pit of Molly's stomach when she heard the word 'goodbye'. She suddenly wished she had taken Harker's call, but just as quickly as the feeling appeared, it started to vanish.

Molly stretched her arms above her head and yawned. She rose from the bed and walked to the window. The sun sat on the treetops and flooded her room with golden light. She wrapped her arms around herself, completely comfortable in her body, and stood at the window for a long time. Sparkles danced on the surface of the bay, making the water appear as if it were covered with millions of tiny jewels. Fog floated lazily over the sky like soft, grey pillows. Soon, Harker's plane would be winging its way across that very sky.

Molly turned from the window, already thinking of the day ahead. After a quick shower and a cup of instant coffee, she made telephone calls to her various charities, then went to a board meeting at the San Francisco Museum of Modern Art. At around one in the afternoon, she drove to the *Savoir Faire* magazine offices. She strode into the building with quick, light steps, smiling at Lydia's secretary. 'Is she in?'

'Yes, I'll just let her know you're here.' Mona buzzed Lydia's office and spoke into the intercom. 'Lydia, Molly is here.'

Molly went into Lydia's office, closing the door behind her. Lydia rose from behind her desk and approached her friend with a smile.

'You look wonderful,' Lydia said. 'Very relaxed.'

'I feel relaxed,' Molly said. 'I don't know why, but I do.'

'No need to explain,' Lydia assured her, stepping forward and squeezing her arm. 'The look on your face says it all.'

'Thanks, Lydia.'

'You're welcome, sweetie.'

'No, I mean thank you. Really. For bearing with me this past week. I know it's been difficult.'

'You'd do the same for me, Molly. I know you would.'

Molly tilted her head and smiled. Lydia was right. Again. But this time, the thought didn't irk Molly. It was a warm, inviting, comfortable realisation. She wanted her relationship with Lydia to be just as it was before Harker Trevane had invaded her life. And yet she knew that something fundamental had changed. 'I'm thinking of giving Piero a call tonight. I could use someone unassuming for a change.'

'Wonderful! You know, Piero is quite a cutie. If Italian men are your cup of tea, of course.'

They laughed, freely and spontaneously, as they hadn't laughed in a long while. Molly reached into her bag and pulled out a file folder. 'This is my review of Harker's book.'

Lydia's eyebrows lifted. 'You've written it?'

'Don't worry, it's a good review. I enjoyed the book. Maybe I can write another review for the magazine sometime.'

'I'd like that.'

'Are you free for lunch?' Molly asked.

'I am now.' Lydia put the folder on her desk and pulled her coat on. 'My treat, OK?'

The two women walked out of the office into the gorgeous, northern California afternoon. Molly took a deep breath of crisp salty air, feeling oddly content after such a tumultuous week. The boredom she had once felt closing in on her inexorably had dissipated, as certainly and as magically as a valley fog. For the first time in months – no, years – she felt free to move to whatever task she chose to set herself, without the slightest need to make it seem more important than it was. And they were important because they belonged to her. Hers was an existence that reflected the light of life in diverse, enchanting and sometimes surprising ways. She intended to enjoy every sparkle to the fullest.

# Part 3

# *Becoming Cassie*

# Chapter One

Cassie turned off her computer and picked up a book from one of the many stacks piled around her desk. She doubted her fascination with William Blake would ever play itself out. His poetry was filled with such stunning fusions of religious, erotic, and mystical images that Cassie suspected she could study his work for years and never fully comprehend it. She could understand how a woman like Mary Wollstonecraft, a writer herself and a pioneering feminist, would have become so entangled in Blake's life.

Cassie leafed through the pages of *The Songs of Experience*. Wollstonecraft had apparently wanted to have an affair with the artist Henry Fuseli, while Blake had been in love with her. There was a possibility that he had not only wanted an affair, but a *ménage à trois* as well, while Wollstonecraft had wanted to live with Fuseli and his wife. As far as historians and deconstructionists were concerned, it was impossible to say for sure whether the *ménage à trois* had actually taken place, but the sexual implications among the three creative souls were evident.

Cassie put the book down and went to her overflowing bookshelf. Trailing her finger along the spines, she pulled out a large, thick hardcover. It was a book of Victorian erotic etchings, many of which consisted of a woman making love with two men. Cassie kicked off her slippers and sat down on her bed as she looked through the glossy pages. One etching in particular intrigued her. The two women were stretched out on the bed, one on top of the other, their breasts pressed together as a man penetrated one of the women with his thick penis. Warmth gathered between Cassie's legs as she gazed down at the picture, imagining herself as one of the women, her thighs parted, her small breasts pressing against those of another woman.

Letting the book slide to the floor, Cassie stretched out on her bed. She didn't surrender to many temptations, but her desire for collecting books and tiny throw pillows for her bed were two of her most extravagant. She sank back against the soft pillows, her eyes drifting closed as she pictured herself in such a scene. She opened her legs, pulling her nightgown over her hips and slipping her fingers between her legs. A rush of moisture bathed her labia, intensified by the pattern of erotic images flashing through her mind. What would it be like, to yield to the kind of fantasy that had doubtless made Mary Wollstonecraft's own sex wet, to allow two men to penetrate and touch you at the same time? Or to touch the softness of a woman, to feel her hard nipples brushing against yours, her smooth lips kissing your skin?

Cassie parted her lips on a sigh, one hand caressing her breasts as she thrust a forefinger deep into her slick vagina. Her slim finger should have been an inadequate substitute for the penis of a man like Nicholas Hawthorne, but Cassie didn't find it so. Rather, she thoroughly enjoyed the solitude of self-pleasuring, needing to focus on no one but herself. It wasn't that she disliked being with a man, but simply that when she was alone, she didn't have to worry about how she looked or what the man thought of her.

Spreading her legs even wider, she massaged the area around her swollen clitoris, welcoming the familiar tension that collected in her lower body. Behind her eyelids, her fantasy grew more explicit, the hot slide of skin against skin accompanying increasing moans of pleasure. She saw herself, mouth open, thrusting her tongue between another woman's lips as a man pumped his stiff cock into her from behind.

Utter animal pleasure conquered reason. Cassie had no idea who the man and woman were, nor did she care. Her chest heaved as she arched her back, pushing her hips up involuntarily as her body floated in the sea of pillows. She rotated her thumb and forefinger around her tight nipples, raining a series of shivers down her spine. Her fingers began to work frantically at her pussy, massaging the tiny aching bud in which all of her pleasure was centred. Her orgasm pealed through her body like a thunderstorm, quivers of rapture skipping over her nerves like little bolts of lightning.

Cassie heaved a deep sigh, milking the final sensations out of her body as the vibrations ebbed. She rolled on to her side, tucking a pillow against her as the warm envelope of fantasy and sleep surrounded her.

'Hello, darling!' Lydia rose from her crouched position on the floor, brushing dust off her jeans. 'How nice to see you. I'd hug you, but I'm a complete mess.'

Cassie smiled. Despite her torn jeans and T-shirt, Lydia looked both lovely and happy. 'Inventory?'

'Nicholas suddenly has all sorts of wonderful ideas about how to rearrange the store,' Lydia said. 'Of course, I found it necessary to volunteer my help.'

'What would Nicholas do without you?'

'Good question.'

Cassie turned at the sound of the male voice, smiling as Nicholas came up the aisle with an armful of books. His 'transformation' thanks to Lydia had clearly taken place on more than just a superficial level. Even Cassie recognised that while Nicholas's appearance was much more ordered and refined, he also acted with a great deal more self-confidence and poise. It was the kind of confidence that only a woman like Lydia could instil in a man.

He grinned at her in welcome. 'Hey, Cassie.'

'Hello, Nicholas.' Cassie thought back to the moment she had practically seduced him in his office simply to see if she could. He'd been so gentle and caring that she had enjoyed the experience, but she had known even as it was occurring that it lacked something. Probably the kind of feelings Nicholas had for Lydia. 'Do you have any new books for me?'

'Not yet, but I'll let you know if any arrive,' Nicholas replied as Lydia took the books from him. 'I think I have at least a dozen books on order for you.'

'You're still coming for dinner tonight, aren't you?' Lydia asked. 'It'll just be the three of us. Molly has a charity committee meeting late this afternoon, but she'll be there around seven.'

Just the three of us. The word caused Cassie's cheeks to warm as she recalled her recent fascination with the idea of *ménages à trois*. 'Oh, definitely. Do you want me to bring anything?'

'Only you.'

'Are you looking for any particular books right now?' Nicholas asked.

'No, thanks. I'll just look around.' Cassie moved into the other room of the store, rather furtively making her way towards the erotica section. She had purchased several erotic titles recently, all Victorian fiction that involved any number of sexual scenarios. She glanced over the titles, wondering if there was anything new.

'Can I help you?' Olive paused next to Cassie suddenly. She was dressed in a long, flowing skirt and a blouse that would have been modest if it weren't virtually transparent. Cassie had the fleeting wish that she were as comfortable in her body as Olive appeared to be.

'Hi, Olive. No, I'm just looking.'

Olive glanced at the erotica section with a sense of pride. 'You wouldn't believe the volume of business we've been doing from this section,' she said. 'Nicholas reorders books for it at least every other day.'

'I've mostly just read some of the Victorian erotica,' Cassie said. Olive had helped her pick out some titles recently, so Cassie felt comfortable discussing her new penchant for erotica with the other woman.

'Would you like me to help you find something different?' Olive asked. 'I've read dozens of erotic books, both fiction and poetry.' She examined the titles on the shelf and pulled out a thick paperback. 'This is a wonderful anthology of excerpts from literary erotic novels. I liked it because it includes authors from around the world, like Latin America and Japan.'

Cassie took the book and glanced through it. 'You do read a lot of erotica, don't you?'

Olive laughed. 'Well, I have a lusty soul.'

Cassie smiled, appreciating the rich sound of the other woman's laugh. 'Thanks for the recommendation. I'll take it.'

She paid for the book and said goodbye to Nicholas and Lydia before heading for the university. The campus of San Francisco University was dotted with grass and trees, a small oasis in the midst of the busy city. Cassie parked in the staff lot and went to her office. She was only teaching one class this semester, which left more time available for her book research.

'Good, Cassie, you're here.'

Cassie tossed her coat over her desk chair and looked up at the man standing in her doorway. Tall and lanky, her research partner Adler Smith was a man who appeared to be anything but a professor. He was a nice-looking man with a trimmed beard and thick, long hair that he wore pulled back into a ponytail. He also had a habit of dressing in tie-dyed T-shirts and bell-bottom jeans that had gone out of style three decades ago. Adler wasn't more than forty years old, but he had a distinct yearning for the psychedelic era of bygone days. However, his 'trapped-in-the-1960s' attitude belied his sharp mind.

'Hello, Adler. I wanted to tell you that I started taking notes on *America, A Prophecy*. I'm trying to understand how it fits in with public sentiment against King George.'

Adler came into the office accompanied by the vague scent of incense. He sat down, propping his feet against Cassie's desk. 'Great. We should get together and talk about that this weekend. I also want to discuss the figure of Orc as the spirit of revolution. Are you going to be around?'

'Yes, I was planning to work on it more this weekend. If you want to come over on Saturday, I can make dinner.'

Adler lifted an eyebrow. 'You can cook?'

Cassie gave him a look. 'I'm not completely helpless in the kitchen.'

'You can cook?' Adler repeated.

Cassie grinned. 'No, but if you want to take a chance, we might actually get some work done.'

Adler shrugged and scratched his left ear. 'I'm always willing to try something new.'

'Gee, thanks for the enthusiasm. Just for that, I might even try a new recipe.'

Adler reached out with his foot and poked the paper bag from Libri Antiqui that was lying on Cassie's desk. 'Is that a new book about Blake?'

Cassie picked up the bag, flushing slightly. 'No, just a fiction book I wanted to read.'

'What book?'

'Just a book.' Cassie opened her file cabinet and started to shove the bag inside, but Adler was by her side in less than a second.

'Come on, let me see,' he wheedled, reaching out to grab the bag from her.

'Adler, stop it! It's just a book.' Cassie clutched the bag and tried to hold it out of his reach.

Adler, however, was a good nine inches taller than her, and plucked the book from her hands with little trouble. He grinned in triumph.

'Adler!' Cassie glowered at him angrily as he opened the bag and pulled the erotica book out.

'*The Altar of Love: Erotica from Around the World?*' Both of Adler's eyebrows nearly shot up to his hairline. 'Since when do you read erotica?'

Cassie continued glowering at him. 'For God's sake, Adler, I'm not a nun. I happen to enjoy erotica.'

Adler opened the book and skimmed some of the pages. 'Who would have known that the sedate professor Cassie Langford was actually filled with the seething heat of lust?'

'Adler!' Despite her bright-red flush, Cassie couldn't help laughing. 'I would hardly say that.'

Adler gave her a leering look. 'Nothing wrong with the seething heat of lust, you know.'

'Oh, for heaven's sake.' Cassie snatched the book back from him and turned away, shoving it into the back of her filing cabinet. 'It's just a book. I don't frequent porn film palaces and strip clubs after hours, you know.'

'Damn. And here I thought we would finally be able to hang out together.'

Cassie shook her head at him. 'Adler, go back to your office. I have work to do.'

'OK. We're still on for this gourmet meal at your place?'

'Only if you promise to eat it.'

'Deal. Then maybe we can read aloud from that new book of yours.'

Cassie threw a pencil at him. Adler chuckled and ducked out of the office before the pencil made contact. Still flushing, Cassie settled into her chair and started to check her e-mail messages. She managed to get a sizeable amount of work done before her class, then spent the afternoon talking to students who came to her office hours. She took the erotica book from the filing cabinet before she returned home to shower and change for Lydia's dinner.

As she closed her eyes under the shower spray, she admitted that her composed image sometimes annoyed her. After all, Adler wouldn't have teased her if she didn't project a demure and sedate persona that never quite seemed to mesh with what she felt inside. It was an image she had perfected since her days at boarding school. She had known back then that if she made herself unassuming, then hopefully she could avoid being the target of teasing and cruel jokes. It hadn't really worked back then, at least not until Lydia and Molly had come to her rescue. It had, however, worked throughout her university days and her professional life. She was responsible, poised, and predictable. In other words, she was boring.

Wrapping a towel around herself, Cassie stepped out of the shower and padded into her bedroom. After hesitating for a moment, she dropped the towel and stood in front of a full-length mirror. She had a bad habit of comparing her figure to the lushness of Lydia's body or to Molly's slender proportions. Cassie looked at the reflection of her petite body, her small breasts topped with tiny nipples, the curve of her stomach and the shortness of her legs. She supposed she was well-proportioned for her size, but that didn't prevent latent feelings of inadequacy, particularly when she was with a man. As confident as she was in her intellectual and social abilities, Cassie had always had reservations about her sexual proficiency and her body.

Her thoughts drifted back to the experience with Nicholas. She had thought that he was a harmless, safe man on whom to practise some moves, only to discover that he was entangled in Lydia's sensual web. And understandably so.

Cassie picked up the towel and finished drying herself, then slipped into a pair of navy trousers and a crisp, white shirt that buttoned up to the collar. She drove to Lydia's house, smiling when Molly answered the door, dressed in a long, flowing caftan shot through with threads of gold. Her auburn curls shone under the foyer chandelier.

'Cassie, darling, how are you?' Molly enfolded Cassie in a warm hug. 'I feel like I was neglecting you during that business with Harker Trevane.'

'Whatever happened to him?' Cassie asked. 'You look wonderful, by the way.'

'Thanks. I picked this up in India a couple of weeks ago. Their cloth always has the most gorgeous colours.' Molly took Cassie's arm and led her into the sitting room. 'Harker went back to Chicago about a month ago. I don't know if he's going to return, but right now, I'm more than happy being back with Piero.'

'And what about the BDSM thing you were so mesmerised by?'

'I'm learning about it. Piero and I fool around with some light play, but that heavy stuff that Harker was involved in was far too much for me.' She smiled. 'And Piero is an extremely adept student. Oh, Lydia is in the kitchen if you want to say hello to her. I'm going to fix a drink, then I'll come in and help with the food.'

Molly squeezed Cassie's arm and drifted over to the

bar. Cassie went through the dining room into the kitchen. She found Lydia arranging a tray of hors d'oeuvres, her sleek, black hair falling forward to partially shield her face.

'Hi, Lyd.'

Lydia looked up, flipping her hair back. 'Hello, Cassie darling. How was your day?'

'Good. The usual work, but my class is going well.' Cassie picked up a glass from the counter and poured herself a glass of wine. 'I bought a new erotica book today.'

'Olive told me. Literary erotica, she said. Here, try some of this brie. It's unbelievably delicious.'

Cassie plucked a brie-topped cracker off the tray. 'Did you know that there's a possibility that Blake wanted to have a *ménage à trois* with Mary Wollstonecraft and Henry Fuseli?'

'Way to go, Blake!' Molly's chuckle preceded her as she entered the kitchen. She immediately went to peek into the oven at the roasting game hens.

'Wollstonecraft actually wanted to live with Fuseli and his wife in a free love relationship,' Cassie said.

'That's what this erotica book is about?' Lydia asked. '*Ménages à trois* and free love?'

'No, no,' Cassie said. 'It's just interesting, don't you think?'

'Sure. I always love knowing about the sexual lives of historical figures. Makes them more real somehow.' Lydia grinned. 'And I have respect for any woman who wants to have a threesome.'

Cassie popped the brie-topped cracker into her mouth. 'Have you?'

'Had a threesome? Sure.'

'Really?' Intrigued, Cassie leant her elbows on the counter and rested her chin in her hand. 'What was it like?'

Molly looked up from the oven. 'That's right, Lydia, you have had a few threesomes, haven't you? I forgot all about those.'

Lydia chewed thoughtfully on a cracker. 'Well, I had

one in college with two men, which was sort of a bungled mess since none of us knew what we were doing. Then I had two more, one with two men in France that was utterly incredible. There really is nothing like having two men totally devoted to your pleasure at the same time. And I had one several years ago that involved another woman.'

'What was that like?' Cassie asked. 'The one with the other woman?'

Lydia shrugged. 'It was exciting, of course. I hadn't been with another woman before that, so the newness of it thrilled me.'

'But did you like it?' Cassie pressed. 'Being with another woman?'

'I suppose.' Lydia ate another cracker and took a sip of wine. 'Touching another woman's body is very sensual, and we both gave each other oral sex. I don't know if I really loved it, but it was definitely fascinating.' She glanced at Molly. 'You were with another woman, weren't you?'

Molly nodded. 'I loved it when it was happening, but since it was part of the whole Harker Trevane experience, I wasn't so sure after it was over. I think being with another woman is lovely, but only under the right circumstances.'

'Would you do it again?' Cassie asked.

'Possibly. I think it would depend on the woman.'

Lydia looked at Cassie curiously. 'Why are you asking us this?'

'I don't know. I've just been thinking lately.'

'Of what?'

'My sexual experiences. Of course, they haven't been nearly as varied and interesting as yours and Molly's.'

'Believe me, Cassie,' Molly said. 'Variety also means that you have to experience a lot of disappointment.'

'Well, I've managed to experience that without any variety.'

Lydia drew her eyebrows together slightly. 'Really? You've had disappointing experiences?'

'Yes. A few.'

'What about with Nicholas?' Lydia asked.

Cassie flushed. She and Lydia had never discussed her encounter with Nicholas in detail, and Cassie wasn't at all certain that she wanted to.

'Well, no,' she admitted. 'That wasn't disappointing, but it wasn't really . . . well, fulfilling.'

Molly shrugged. 'Maybe you weren't emotionally ready for it. I know all about not being emotionally ready. In fact, I'm a pro at it.'

'I don't know.' Cassie sighed and took a swallow of wine. 'I've just been confused lately.'

'You've been confused for a while now, it seems,' Lydia murmured. She leant against the counter and looked at Cassie. 'Cassie, what's wrong? You really haven't seemed like yourself these past few months.'

'I don't know, Lydia. Like I told you, if I knew, I wouldn't be confused.'

'Are you thinking that you want to try a threesome?' Molly asked.

'Possibly. I mean, I fantasise about them.'

'That doesn't always mean you want to experience it in reality,' Lydia said. 'I think you just haven't met the right man. You've gone out with some real losers in the past, and that mess with Nicholas didn't help matters. Why don't you let me set you up with some men I know?'

'Oh, Lyd, I don't know about that . . .'

'That's a wonderful idea!' Molly interjected, a spark appearing in her blue eyes at the thought of playing matchmaker. 'I know some wonderful men who would just adore you, Cassie. Come on, let us help you out.'

'We know you very well, Cassie,' Lydia said. 'We know what kind of man would be right for you.'

Cassie knew that she would never be able to stop her two friends from going through with their matchmaking plans, so she relented. 'All right, but I don't want to walk into my flat and suddenly find myself confronted by two naked men.'

'Don't worry,' Molly said, shooting her friend a wink. 'I'm saving that scenario for myself.'

* * *

'I don't know what her problem is.' Lydia slipped her silk robe over her shoulders and climbed into bed next to Nicholas. 'She hasn't been herself at all.'

Nicholas removed his reading glasses and put his arm around her, tugging her against him. 'Is she having trouble at work?'

'Not that I'm aware of. I know the research for her book is going well.' Lydia splayed her hand over his chest, moving it in slow circles. 'I hope she'll be OK.'

'Sounds like you and Molly are doing what you can to jump-start her love life,' Nicholas observed.

'I think that's what she needs,' Lydia said. 'She hasn't had the most thrilling experiences, you know.'

'Hey.' Nicholas looked mildly offended. 'Should I be insulted?'

Lydia grinned. 'Her experience with you excluded, of course. She just needs variety, that's all. Or at least someone to explore variety with.'

'Like we do, huh?'

'Oh, most definitely.'

Lydia propped herself up on her elbow and leant over to kiss him. She and Nicholas had had a rocky beginning, but that made their current relationship all the sweeter. Urging his lips apart, she leisurely explored his mouth with her tongue as a familiar warmth began to unfold through her body. She circled her forefinger around his nipples, inciting them to peak with arousal at her touch. Lydia had once thought that she would become bored by one man, but Nicholas was constantly exciting to her. She never would have guessed all those months ago that his unassuming exterior hid such a deliciously wicked mind. Slowly, she stroked her hand over his chest and underneath the waistband of his pyjama bottoms. The skin of his penis was hot. Lydia trailed her fingertips over his shaft before taking him in her hand, thrilled with the way his cock began to stiffen at the light touch.

'Take them off,' Nicholas whispered, tucking his hand around the back of her neck to pull her closer.

Lydia's heart began to pulse hard in her chest as she hooked her fingers underneath his waistband and pulled his pyjamas over his legs. She pressed a series of kisses over his abdomen to his groin before taking his penis in her mouth. With lush ease, she allowed him to slide past her lips and over the velvety surface of her tongue. The salty taste of him stimulated her own arousal, her sex swelling with moisture and heat. Her nipples hardened and pressed urgently against the silk of her nightgown. Nicholas gathered the voluminous material in his fists and began to pull it over Lydia's body. Her full breasts pressed against his thigh, resulting in a delightful friction against her nipples. She murmured a low sound of approval.

'Ahh, Lydia...' Nicholas sank back against the pillows, his hand tightening on the back of Lydia's neck as she traced the veins on his shaft with her tongue. His cock stiffened in her mouth, engorged with blood and heat.

Lydia pulled back, her expression flushed with pleasure as she bent and took the twin sacs of his testicles in her mouth. How she loved giving him such gratification. She stroked her hands over the tops of his thighs and nudged her breasts urgently against him. Nicholas's hand slipped over her back, his fingers trailing down her spine to her buttocks. He caressed the rounded globes gently before exploring the fissure between them. Lydia squirmed, abandoning his erection to straddle his thighs. She braced her hands against the headboard, arching her back so that her buttocks pushed against his hands. He kissed her shoulder, his breath deliciously hot against her skin as his fingers delved into the shadowy cleft of her bottom and traced the ring of her anus.

'Oh, yes.' Lydia shivered, putting her mouth against his ear. She took his earlobe between her lips and sucked. 'Do it.'

Slowly, Nicholas dipped his finger into her wetness, then spread the moisture over her anus. He pushed his finger into the tight aperture, creating a river of sensations through Lydia's body. She moaned, pushing her body down so that he could penetrate her further.

'What do you want?' Nicholas whispered, his voice husky with desire. 'You want my cock there?'

'God, yes.' Lydia closed her eyes, pressing her damp forehead against his as their mouths met again. Thick heat spread over their bodies, enveloping them in a lust that blocked out all other thoughts.

Nicholas clutched Lydia's hips, lifting her off his lap and back on to the bed.

'Turn around.' He patted her lightly on the bum.

Excited beyond reason, Lydia grabbed a pillow and turned on to her stomach. Her past attempts at anal sex had been dismal failures, but then she had never trusted a man the way she trusted Nicholas. She tucked the pillow underneath her pelvis so that her bottom was thrust out towards Nicholas like a ripe melon. He let out a sigh of pleasure, bending to kiss the twin mounds before sliding his tongue into the crack between them. Lydia gasped and writhed at the delicious sensations. Her sex flowed copiously as her blood streamed with liquid fire. No man had ever provided her with the intensity of sensations that Nicholas did.

Lydia buried her face in the bedcover, parting her legs even wider. She heard a drawer close from the bedside table, then Nicholas's fingers slipped between her buttocks again. He stroked lubricant over her anus, which evoked a whole new series of shudders. Lydia lifted her head and glanced over her shoulder. The sight of Nicholas, his cock projecting out from the thick mane of hair, his eyes dark with heat, nearly made her climax then and there. She squirmed impatiently and tried to rub her swollen clitoris against the pillow.

'Nicholas,' she murmured. 'Hurry.'

He looked at her, reaching up to stroke his fingers through her hair. 'I like it when you beg.'

Lydia was only too happy to oblige him. 'Please,' she said throatily. 'Please fuck me.'

'Oh, I will.' Nicholas grasped his penis in his hand, pressing it gently against the unyielding ring of muscles.

Lydia gasped at the pressure, forcing her body to relax. Nicholas slipped his hand underneath her and spread his fingers over her throbbing clit. As he began to massage the bud gently, Lydia closed her eyes, stunned by the myriad sensations that mingled throughout her body. Nicholas pushed again, easing slowly into her. He paused, waiting for her body to get used to the unfamiliar tension.

'OK?' he whispered, his voice tight.

'Oh, yes.' Lydia had never felt so full and aroused in her life. The thick root of Nicholas's cock eased further and further into her channel, stimulating every nerve ending. Nicholas began to pump gently inside her, his pathway eased by the slickness of the lubricant, and Lydia moaned with sheer delight.

Nicholas dug his fingers into her bottom-cheeks, pushing them apart to open her even further to his penetration. His fingers worked ceaselessly at her clitoris, and then he pushed a finger into her wet passage, invading her doubly. Lydia cried out, stunned by how her body reacted to such pleasure. An orgasm shattered her almost instantly. She gripped the bedcover, her breathing harsh as incessant waves of rapture coursed through her. She heard Nicholas groan, easing his cock out of her as warm spurts of semen covered her buttocks.

He leant over her back, pressing his lips against her neck. 'You're OK?'

Lydia turned and wrapped her arms around his neck. She gazed up at him for a moment, totally sated. 'I'm wonderful.'

Nicholas grinned. 'Yes, I'd have to agree that you are.'

# Chapter Two

Cassie gathered her hair into a clip at the base of her neck, then examined herself critically in the mirror. The very idea of going on a blind date made her wary, but Molly had been so enthused that Cassie hadn't had the heart to let her friend down. The telephone rang, and Cassie went to pick up the receiver.

'Hi, it's Molly. Are you ready?'

'Yes, I'm just finishing getting dressed.'

'What are you wearing?'

Cassie glanced down at her clothing. 'A blue skirt and a white blouse.'

'Wow, sounds incredible. Be careful Brad doesn't lose all reason when confronted with such provocative attire.'

Cassie grinned. 'Point taken, Molly. However, I'm not about to deck myself out in a mini-skirt just for Brad.'

'I think you'll like Brad a lot,' Molly said. 'He's a fun guy. Call me tomorrow and let me know how it went, OK?'

'All right. Talk to you later.'

'Hey, at least wear those shoes I gave you last Christmas, OK? Those are sexy.'

'OK, I promise.' Cassie hung up the phone and went to finish dressing. She applied some light make-up, then slipped her bare feet into a pair of high-heeled, navy sling-backs with straps that wound around her ankles. As it was an unusually warm evening, she didn't bother with stockings. The doorbell rang promptly at seven, and she hurried to answer the door.

Taking a deep breath, she plastered a smile on her face and pulled the door open, only to find herself confronted by a huge spray of flowers to which a pair of legs was attached. 'Brad?'

Blue eyes peered through the space between a carnation and a daisy. 'Hi, Cassie. These are for you.'

'Thanks. They're beautiful and . . . um, big. Come on in.' She held the door open as Brad manoeuvred through the doorway with the flowers, leaving a trail of petals behind him en route to the sitting room. He placed the bouquet on her coffee-table and beamed at her.

Cassie returned his smile, reminding herself to give him a chance. After all, a gargantuan flower bouquet was a sweet gesture. Brad was a handsome man, tall with broad shoulders and thick, straw-coloured hair. He had a wholesome look about him, as if he'd grown up on a farm or at least in the Midwest.

'It's nice to meet you.' Cassie held out her hand. 'Molly speaks very highly of you.'

'You, too.' He shook her hand and brushed his hair out of his eyes, glancing down at her feet. 'Wow. Sexy shoes.'

An odd compliment, but a compliment nonetheless. 'Thanks. They were a gift from Molly.'

'She has great taste, doesn't she?' Brad said rhetorically. 'Should we go?'

'Sure.' Cassie retrieved her bag and went with him down to his car, which turned out to be a sleek red Corvette with a black racing stripe.

'Cool car, huh?' he said proudly.

'Yes,' Cassie agreed. 'Very . . . cool.'

'I thought we'd go to this great Mexican place on Mission,' Brad explained as they settled against the leather seats. 'OK with you?'

'Sure.' Cassie looked at his profile as he drove through the streets. 'Molly tells me you're a stockbroker.'

'That's right. I break stocks.' He grinned at his own joke.

Cassie smiled weakly. 'And what else do you do?'

Brad shrugged. 'I sometimes bike on weekends, and lately I've been getting into racing cars.' He glanced at her. 'What about you?'

'I'm an English literature professor.'

Brad raised an eyebrow. 'Is that a fact? Molly didn't tell me that.'

'How do you know Molly?'

'Oh, I was dating one of the girls in her etiquette class,' Brad explained, pulling into a parking lot near the restaurant.

'So you're not really friends with Molly?' Cassie closed the car door and walked with him to the restaurant.

'We've hung out, sure. I mean, we never dated or anything, but yeah, we're friends.'

The restaurant was both crowded and noisy, with a stale scent of beer lingering in the air. Cassie and Brad managed to find a table in the corner, and pushed their way through the crowd to get to it. Cassie wasn't sorry that it was almost too noisy to talk and spent most of the evening harbouring a sense of awe over the amount of food Brad managed to consume.

He leant across the table to yell into her ear. 'You want dessert?'

'No!' Cassie shouted back. 'I think we should probably go now.'

'OK!'

With the music pounding in her ears, Cassie followed Brad back outside. The cool air brushed against her face like a refreshing wind. 'Maybe we should call it a night,' she suggested.

'Already?' He looked surprised. 'Don't you want to go dancing or anything?'

'No, I don't think so.'

Brad shrugged and unlocked the car door. As they drove back to Cassie's flat, she thought that maybe she wasn't giving him a chance. After all, they had barely even talked, let alone learnt much about each other.

'Would you like to come up for coffee?' she asked.

'Sure, that'd be great.' Jingling his keys in his hand, Brad followed her up to the flat.

'So, did you grow up in San Francisco?' Cassie asked, gesturing for him to sit down when they were inside.

'No, Los Angeles. Beverly Hills, to be exact.'

Cassie went into the kitchen and put the coffee-pot on. 'What made you move to San Francisco?' she called.

'My job,' Brad replied. 'Plus, I thought it would be a cool place to live for a while.'

Cassie waited for the coffee to percolate and poured them both a cup. She went into the sitting room and handed a cup to Brad, then sat down next to him on the sofa. As she settled back, she realised he was looking at her feet.

'Those really are great shoes,' he remarked.

'Thanks again.' Cassie didn't think a man had ever paid such close attention to her shoes.

'Are they Ferragamos?' Brad asked.

Cassie looked down at her shoes. 'I think so. Molly bought them in Italy.'

'Those straps fit around your ankle perfectly.' Brad bent and brushed his finger over one of the straps. 'I mean, your ankles are really slim and pretty.'

Cassie looked at him for a moment. 'Thank you.'

He flashed her a smile, displaying white, even teeth. 'Do you think I can kiss you?'

'I don't know,' Cassie replied wryly. 'Can you?'

She doubted that she would ever see him again, but it certainly wouldn't hurt to kiss another man. After all, she needed to have some basis of comparison or she would never learn what it was really like to have a satisfying sexual experience. She leant forward, letting him brush his lips across hers. It was a nice kiss, warm and friendly, but not at all demanding. Cassie slid her hand into his hair, enjoying the coarse feeling of the strands against her palm. Brad moved his lips more insistently over hers, and Cassie sensed the growing tension in his body. It never failed to fascinate her, the sexual reaction of a man to a woman.

Brad pulled away slightly, his blue eyes darkened and his breathing rapid. 'Cassie, if I ask you something, don't think I'm weird, OK?'

'I'll try not to.'

'Can I take off your shoes?'

He appeared to really have a thing for her shoes. Oh, well, she did want variety, didn't she? 'Sure, if you want.'

Leaning back against the sofa, she put her legs on the coffee-table and waited for him to remove her shoes. Brad did so with the utmost attention, rubbing his finger over the leather straps as he unbuckled them and slipped them off her feet. Curious, Cassie glanced down at his crotch, her heart jumping as she noticed the unmistakable bulge pressing against his trousers. Good Lord, he was stimulated just by a kiss and touching her shoes? How bizarre. Cassie watched as Brad gently slipped her left shoe off and trailed his fingers over her toes and the sole of her foot.

'Ah, you have such a perfect, high arch,' he sighed. 'And what lovely toes.'

Cassie was fascinated. She'd never met anyone with an honest-to-god foot fetish, but Brad appeared to be a connoisseur. To her further surprise, she discovered that she was becoming rather aroused by such attention. Brad lifted her legs over his thighs and grasped her foot in both hands, stroking his thumbs against the arch. His erection pressed against her calf, and Cassie drew in a slight breath. Brad removed her other shoe with the same careful devotion. He circled her slender ankles, dipped his forefinger between her toes, and stroked his palm over her calves. Cassie watched him, surprised at the stimulating effect of his movements. Her sex grew damp, and trails of pleasure fluttered over her skin as Brad massaged her feet.

'What incredible little feet,' he murmured, his eyes glazed. 'So perfect.'

To Cassie's further shock, he bent his head to kiss her toes. She jerked instinctively, wondering if she was letting this go way too far, but then Brad actually sucked one of her toes into his mouth. The sensation of her toe enveloped by the warm wetness of his mouth sent a thrill of sheer delight over Cassie's legs and straight to her pussy. A moan escaped her involuntarily, which appeared to encourage Brad all the more. He took another toe into his mouth, sucking lightly enough to provide a most exciting degree of stimulation.

Cassie squirmed, her calf pressing against his prominent cock. Her skirt slipped over her legs to expose her thighs and the white cotton of her panties. Cassie fought the urge to slip her fingers underneath the cotton and into the humid warmth of her labia, to rub the tight knot that was beginning to ache with tension. She watched Brad turn his attention to her other foot, sucking with devout pleasure on each one of her toes as his hands continued to massage her arches.

'Cassie, forgive me, but I have to ... you're just so exciting...' Brad's face was flushed, a sheen of perspiration breaking out on his forehead as he clutched her right foot in one hand and began to unfasten his trousers with the other.

Part of Cassie was shocked by the ease with which she consented to this kind of strangeness, but the rest of her was undeniably aroused by it. No man had ever called her 'exciting' before, let alone been so rapturously turned-on by her feet. Enthralled, she stared at the jutting stalk of Brad's penis as it sprang free from his briefs. It was compact and thick, made all the more intriguing by a slight rightward tilt, and a drop of liquid glistened from the tip like a pearl. The head was darkened to a deep, reddish colour, and his testicles were tucked tightly between his legs.

An urge to touch him seized Cassie suddenly, but she forced herself to lie back and wait for his next move. She opened her legs further in an attempt to cool the heated flesh of her sex, and was unable to resist slipping a finger underneath the elastic of her panties. Slowly, she stroked her finger over her oiled labia, sighing with delight at the sheer, sensual pleasure.

His breathing harsh, Brad shifted so that he was kneeling on the sofa. Cassie gasped as he took her foot and rubbed it over his hardness. The feeling of the satiny skin of his cock against the sole of her foot elicited another rush of moisture between her legs. Staring at the sight before her, she started to move her foot against his erection of her own volition. She had never felt anything like this, the hard damp knob rubbing underneath her toes and over the arch of her foot. Lifting her other foot, she nudged her toes against his testicles, causing Brad to groan aloud in rapture.

Cassie's clothing felt extremely heavy, as if it were

weighing her down. The constraint, however, provided a rather delicious contrast to the freedom of her bare legs and feet. She pressed another finger into her pussy, whimpering as she brushed it over her swollen clitoris. Brad cupped her heels in his hands, his hips starting to work back and forth as he masturbated himself against her feet. She watched his cock slide back and forth, leaving a trail of glistening moisture on her foot. And then she completely abandoned herself to the moment by taking his cock between the soles of both her feet and massaging them together.

'Oh, yeah,' Brad groaned, his voice throaty with sensual pleasure. 'That's it, Cassie. Rub my cock like that, just like that between your sexy feet. I want to come all over them, all over your toes. Jesus, you don't even know what you're doing to me.'

His words stimulated Cassie's arousal to greater heights. She had a distinct idea of what she was doing to him, but she doubted he realised how excited she was by the whole scenario. By its very bizarreness. She worked her fingers around her sex, teasing herself as she was teasing him. Her clit bloomed against her fingers, tightening the nerves around her loins.

'Faster,' Brad husked, his eyes half-closed as he clutched her feet harder and thrust his cock against her. 'Faster.'

Cassie rubbed his cock faster, feeling the skin growing hotter as blood rushed through him. She pressed her fingers against her pussy as the rhythm increased in pace. Suddenly, Brad let out a shout, his entire body stiffening as his come spurted out of his cock and on to Cassie's feet. She watched in fascination as he continued rubbing against her, his expression relaxing in utter rapture as the final sensations pulsed through him. The dampness on her feet and Brad's evident ecstasy jolted through Cassie like lightning. She massaged her clitoris with a sense of desperation until her climax broke through her and consumed her with pure sensuality. Her body quivered violently, and then the only sound in the room was their hard breathing.

Cassie let out a long sigh, stunned by the strength of

her pleasure as well as the strange acts that had led to it. She looked at Brad, who had collapsed back on to the sofa, totally content.

Cassie sat up slowly, reaching for a napkin to wipe her feet. Well, she had definitely never experienced anything like that before. She reached out and put her hand on Brad's knee.

He opened his eyes to look at her. 'God, Cassie, you're amazing. Can we see each other again?'

'I don't know,' Cassie said honestly. 'I think you should leave.'

Brad tugged his trousers over his legs and zipped them up. 'I hope I didn't . . .'

Cassie shook her head. 'No. That was . . . interesting.'

Brad bent and kissed her cheek before he left. Cassie sat on the sofa for a long time, trying to absorb the lingering effects of the pleasure. Oh, yes, that had felt good. Very good. Cassie went into the bathroom and took a quick shower, looking down at her ordinary feet. She couldn't help smiling. At least Brad had found them to be highly sexy.

Wrapping a towel around her body, she went to the telephone and dialled Molly's number. 'Molly, did I wake you?'

'No, doll. How did it go? He's nice, isn't he?'

'Yes, but not really my type. He has quite a foot fetish.'

A shocked silence filled Molly's end for a moment. 'He told you that already?'

'He . . . um, demonstrated it.'

'Cassie! Are you serious?'

Cassie flushed, but couldn't prevent the slight rush of pride. Lydia and Molly weren't the only ones who could engage in different sexual practices. 'Yes. He was quite enthralled with my feet.'

'I can't believe this. Were you shocked?'

'Yes, but it was rather fascinating. I've never done anything like that before. I didn't even know that foot fetishes really existed.'

'I am stunned,' Molly declared. 'Honestly, Cassie, I

know Brad is a little dense, but I didn't think that he would introduce you to his kinks right away.'

'That was why you wanted me to meet him, isn't it?' Cassie asked. 'You thought he would eventually introduce me to his foot fetish kink as well as probably plenty of others.'

'Well, you did say you wanted variety.' Molly paused. 'You're not mad at me, are you?'

'No, not at all, but I wish you'd at least warned me. Brad isn't the kind of man I'm interested in having a relationship with, but that was a unique experience. And as unique experiences go, it was one of the safest, too.'

Molly chuckled. 'See? Fetishes can be the safest sex around. I have to say, you've completely surprised me. I never thought you would do that on your first date with him.'

'No, neither did I,' Cassie agreed. 'But maybe that's why I did.'


'Did you like it?'

Cassie looked up at the sound of Olive's voice and smiled at the sight of the other woman. Olive looked particularly pretty today, wearing a long purple dress and with her blonde hair held back by a scarf. 'Like what?'

'The book, of course. International erotica.'

'Oh, yes. I'm still reading it. There's a story by an East Indian woman that's wonderful.'

Olive nodded. 'Those stories prove that erotica can be sensual without being very explicit.' She grinned. 'Although there is something to be said for explicitness.'

'There most definitely is.' Cassie returned her attention to the books on the shelf. 'The history of literature is filled with erotic stories and poems, but they've usually been confined to the underground. I often run across erotica in my research.'

Olive leant her shoulder against the bookshelf and gazed at Cassie. 'Lydia told me that you're researching someone named William Blake.'

'Yes, he was a late eighteenth-century British poet and

artist,' Cassie said. She glanced at Olive, aware of the light scent of lotion that drifted from Olive's skin, and the way her brown eyes held a clear direct light. 'His work tends to have a number of erotic implications.'

'Is that what you're focusing on in your book?'

'In one of the chapters, I am,' Cassie said. 'I have a research partner who thinks I should write an entire book about it, so that might be my next project.'

'Is this partner writing your book with you?'

'No, I'm doing the main part of the research and all of the writing. He helps me with fact-checking and tossing around ideas and theories.'

'You know, you might be interested in some of our non-fiction titles, as well,' Olive said. She leant past Cassie to take a book off the shelf. 'Your friend Molly bought this one recently.'

Cassie started slightly as Olive's generous breasts pressed against her arm. The sensation was made even more intriguing by the fact that Olive's nipples were hard. Cassie could feel them through the thin material of her dress.

'This is it,' Olive said. 'It's about BDSM and fetishes.'

'Fetishes?' Cassie took the book and looked at the cover. Oh, who was she kidding? She didn't want to get involved in the world of fetishes, for heaven's sake.

'Olive, are you socialising or working?' Nicholas's voice emerged from the cash register area.

'Working!' Olive called back, giving Cassie a wink.

'I should go,' Cassie said reluctantly. She returned the book to its home on the shelf. 'I'm actually supposed to cook dinner tonight for my research partner.'

Olive arched an eyebrow. 'Sounds serious. Are you involved with him?'

'Oh, no.' Cassie had to smile at the thought of being involved with psychedelic Adler. 'No, we're just good friends. He wears sandals even in winter, tie-dyed T-shirts, and he worships the Grateful Dead. He's also trying to revive Woodstock for the new millennium.'

Olive grinned. 'He sounds delightful, but not quite your type.'

Cassie didn't bother to tell Olive that she was starting to wonder what, exactly, *was* her type. Not men like Brad or Adler, apparently.

She returned home and organised some of her work that she wanted to show Adler, then she started to prepare some lamb chops from a recipe Lydia had given her. The flat was just beginning to smell rather delicious when Adler arrived, sporting a plaid bow tie along with his T-shirt and torn jeans.

'Well, you're looking very dapper.' Cassie smiled at him and accepted the bottle of wine he handed her. 'You didn't have to dress up just for me.'

'I always like to impress a lovely lady,' Adler reported.

'Come and sit down. Dinner is cooking, but I wanted to go over some of the new information with you.' Cassie retrieved two wine glasses and poured them both a glass, then went to sit next to him in the sitting room. She had put all of her books and papers on the coffee-table, and Adler was busy shuffling through them.

'Blake's sex life was something else, wasn't it?' Adler picked up a page on which Cassie had written a number of sexual details. 'Did he ever actually have that threesome with Fuseli and Wollstonecraft?'

'Not that I've been able to discover,' Cassie said. 'I believe Blake and his wife did seduce Wollstonecraft at one point. Wollstonecraft also wanted to live with Fuseli and *his* wife in a free love relationship. But Fuseli's wife banned Wollstonecraft from their house when she proposed the idea between the three of them. Oh, I also found out that Blake used to teach his wife to read when they were sitting naked in the backyard. He thought that being naked would help his wife absorb the lesson better into her skin.'

'Wow. Want me to teach you how to read?'

Cassie grinned. 'Luckily, I already know how to read.'

She showed him some of the new information she had discovered, along with a new article she had found in an obscure journal. They discussed Blake's epic poem about the American Revolution, and decided to consult one of the eighteenth-century scholars in the Art History department about Blake's illustrations. So involved did their discussion become that Cassie forgot about the lamb chops until smoke began to invade the sitting room.

'No!' With a groan, she hurried into the kitchen. 'I forgot! Adler, why didn't you remind me?'

'Remind you? Hell, I don't even know what kind of food you're subjecting me to. Do you need help?'

'No, everything is under control.' Cassie grabbed a pot holder and pulled the pan out of the oven. She poked at the lamb chops with a fork, deciding that they looked a little dried out, but at least they weren't burned. She took two plates from the cupboard and put the chops on them, then filled two salad bowls with lettuce. The telephone rang from the sitting room.

'Want me to answer that?' Adler asked.

'No, the answering machine will get it,' Cassie called, pulling open the refrigerator. What had she done with the salad dressing? How could a person lose an entire bottle of salad dressing?

She found a couple of rather ancient carrots and started to slice them up to add to the salad. The beep of the answering machine sounded, and then a male voice drifted through the speaker.

'Hi, Cassie, this is Brad. I just wanted to tell you what a great time I had the other night. I haven't been able to stop thinking about your sexy feet and...'

Oh no! Cassie flung the carrots down so hard that one of them bounced into the sink as she dashed back into the sitting room and towards the telephone. Brad's voice continued to resound through the room.

'... how much they turned me on. You were so unbelievably hot...'

Frantically, Cassie pushed at the buttons on the machine to turn it off.

'... and every time I think about your toes, I can't help remembering how gorgeous they looked covered with my...'

Cassie grabbed for the answering machine plug and yanked it clear out of the wall. Thankfully, Brad's voice was curtailed before it could reveal further shameful details.

Aware that her face was bright red, Cassie glanced at Adler, hoping against hope that maybe he wouldn't even be there any more. He was sitting with his feet propped up on the coffee-table, wiggling his toes, and a grin a mile wide spread across his face. Cassie wished that the floor would open up and swallow her.

'Don't even say it,' she sighed, knowing that her request was futile.

'Well, little Cassie Langford surprises us once again,' Adler remarked, still grinning. 'Brad appears to have been quite stimulated by your feet.'

'Adler, this is none of your business.'

'If you tell me that you moonlight as a dominatrix, can I sign up for a session?'

'Adler!' Cassie's flush deepened even further. 'Stop it right now. Brad and I had a date the other night, and that's all you need to know. In fact, you don't even need to know that.'

'I suspect I already know more than that,' Adler observed. 'All right, all right. I'll shut up. However, if you want to know something embarrassing about me now, I'll tell you that I have a thing for women's bellybuttons.'

Cassie gave him a wry look. 'That's embarrassing?'

'Well, I like to ... you know ...'

'Lick them? Why, you pervert.'

'No, I like to come in them,' Adler said. 'They're such perfect little cups, you know?'

Cassie blinked. 'Oh.' She paused. 'You like to do that all the time?'

'Not *all* the time, but it's pretty arousing.'

'And that's your most embarrassing sexual urge?'

'That's the only one I'm going to tell you.'

'It figures.' Cassie headed back towards the kitchen. 'We might as well try to eat this shoe leather I've cooked.'

Adler got up and followed her into the kitchen. 'Is that what you served Brad the other night? Shoe leather?'

'Yeah, and he loved it.' Cassie thrust a plate at Adler

and pointed towards the dining table. 'And you're going to love it, too.'

Adler sat down, looking at her with a new-found respect. 'Cassie, if you don't already moonlight as a dominatrix, might I suggest you look into it? I really think you're a natural.'

'Does this mean you'll do whatever I say?'

'Oh, absolutely.'

'Good. Then shut up and eat.'

'Like I said, Miss Langford,' Adler stated, sawing diligently on the lamb chop. 'You're a natural.'

# Chapter Three

Cassie gazed across the table at Peter. He was an extremely handsome young man with a mop of curly black hair and the most intense green eyes Cassie had ever seen. She figured that, since she had given Molly a chance to set her up with a decent fellow, then she should do the same for Lydia. So far, Peter had proven to be a very pleasant dinner partner, with lots to say about his work as art director for *Savoir Faire*. And Cassie had little trouble admitting that he intrigued her sexually.

'Lydia tells me that you've spent a great deal of time in London,' he said, reaching over to refill her wine glass.

Cassie nodded. 'I love it there. I'm thinking of buying stock in the British Museum's library since I spend so much time there. Their archives are incredible.'

'Are you going there to work on research soon?'

'I hope so.' Cassie scraped up the final remnant of her chocolate mousse and sat back with a satisfied sigh. 'I should find out by the end of the month whether I am going to receive a research grant I recently applied for. If I do, then I'll have enough money to study in England for at least a year.'

'Wow. That's impressive.'

Cassie smiled. 'Well, it'll only be impressive if I actually get the grant.'

They chatted until they had polished off the bottle of wine, then decided to walk around Union Square. As they had agreed to an early dinner, most of the stores were still open. Shoppers meandered about the streets, heading in and out of expensive department stores. Cassie and Peter strolled around the square, talking and window-shopping, then went into Macy's to see one of their famous flower exhibitions. Flower bouquets lined the entire aisle of the cosmetics section, along with intricate displays in the windows.

'How long have you lived in San Francisco?' Peter asked, as they stepped back on to the bustling street.

'Oh, most of my life,' Cassie said. 'Lydia and I met way back when we were attending the same boarding school.'

'Hey, look at that.' Peter paused by a Neiman-Marcus window that displayed several mannequins wearing lingerie. 'That rose-coloured number.'

Cassie looked at the flowery lace bra and matching panties. 'That's lovely.'

'Would you wear something like that?'

'Sure. That's one of the advantages of being small. You can always find lingerie that fits you.'

'Do you want to try it on?'

Cassie eyed him warily. 'You're not going to get obsessed with my feet or anything, are you?'

'Your feet?' Peter glanced down at her shoes. 'They're very nice.'

Variety, Cassie reminded herself. Lydia and Molly had managed to experience it in their sexual lives, and it was about time she did too. And trying on lingerie was hardly the same thing as masturbating a man with her feet.

She took Peter's hand and led him into the department store. 'I'll try it on.'

They took the escalator to the lingerie department, which was nearly empty save for a few salespeople and some women in business suits. Cassie felt oddly nervous considering she had never been in a lingerie shop with a man. She approached a sour-looking saleswoman and asked about the rose-coloured lingerie in the window.

The woman pointed towards the far wall. 'You'll find all the sizes over there.'

Cassie glanced at Peter as they made their way over to the lingerie. She couldn't believe she was doing this, but it was definitely something that Lydia would do in her place. She looked through the bras and picked out her size, then chose the matching panties.

'Are you going to model them for me?'

Cassie shot Peter a smile, intrigued by the glimmer of excitement in his green eyes. 'Possibly.'

She went in the direction of the dressing room. Butterflies fluttered around in her stomach with increasing force. Cassie glanced furtively at the saleswoman, who was busy straightening a sale display.

'You wait here,' she whispered to Peter as they went towards the dressing room.

'The heck I'm waiting here,' he muttered.

'Peter!'

'OK, I'll wait in the next dressing room.'

Cassie couldn't help laughing. The dressing room guard was nowhere to be seen and the room itself appeared to be empty. Cassie ducked into a booth near the back, while Peter locked himself in the booth next to her.

'Are you undressing?' His low voice carried easily through the thin wall.

'Shh!' Cassie unbuttoned her blouse with shaking fingers and slipped off her bra. She put on the new rose one and then took off her skirt and panties to slide the lacy underwear over her hips.

'How does it look?' Peter's dark head appeared in the space near Cassie's feet between the two booths. 'Wow, fantastic!'

Cassie struggled to contain a fit of laughter. 'Peter, get away from there!'

'Are you kidding? You look amazing in that.' Peter crouched down further and started to climb underneath the barrier separating the booths. Within seconds, he had eased himself into her dressing room. He straightened and grinned at her. 'Really amazing.'

Cassie was laughing so hard that she completely forgot to be shocked that she was standing half-naked in a dressing room with a man. She forced herself to calm down as she became aware of the way that Peter was looking at her.

'OK, Peter, this has gone a little far.' Cassie wiped a tear of laughter away from the corner of her eye and glanced at herself in the mirror. Surprise flitted through her as she realised how provocative the lingerie was. Her nipples and the dark triangle of her pubis showed through the lace, and the push-up bra created a gentle swell of cleavage.

She looked at Peter, who was staring at her hungrily.

'Really sexy,' he murmured.

Cassie felt her nipples harden against the lace, and an echo of arousal coursed through her blood simply from the way he was looking at her. The knowledge that they were in a public place, that they could be caught at any minute, heightened her excitement. Peter moved closer to her and, considering they were in a tiny booth that allowed little room for movement to begin with, Cassie found herself backed up against the wall within a second. She didn't move when Peter bent to kiss her. The air thickened between them, and Cassie allowed herself to enjoy the heated kiss he pressed against her lips.

'This is crazy,' she whispered.

'Uh huh.' Peter slipped one hand down to her waist, rotating his pelvis slightly against her. He cupped her breast with his other hand and flicked his thumb over her tight nipple. 'You feel amazing.'

'Peter, anyone could walk in and hear us,' Cassie whispered. She didn't protest when his knee slid between her legs.

'I know.' Peter pressed his knee upward until her legs were spread and her sex was rubbing against his thigh. Cassie gasped at the sensation of his trouser leg against her humid warmth.

Peter lowered his lips to her neck, licking the hot hollow of her throat and the pulse that beat so rapidly there.

'Oh.' Cassie let her eyes drift closed and leant her head against the wall as she succumbed to the illicitness of the experience. 'Oh, that feels good.'

She splayed her hands over his chest, feeling his body heat through the thin material. She slipped her hands around the middle of his back and paused when her fingers encountered an elastic band.

'Um, Peter?' Cassie pulled away, her eyebrows drawing

together as it dawned on her exactly what that elastic band felt like.

He blushed. 'Sorry. I didn't think I would have to explain so soon.'

Cassie stared at him. 'Explain what?'

'Well, that I like women's lingerie.'

'All men like women's lingerie.'

Peter unbuttoned his shirt, revealing a navy blue bra wrapped around his chest. 'Not all men like to wear it.'

Cassie groaned, sinking her head into her hands. 'Don't even tell me. You're a cross dresser?'

'No! Cassie, I'm not a transvestite,' Peter said, his lips parting in a smile. 'I just dress like one sometimes.'

Cassie registered that what he had said should have been funny, but she was incapable of laughing.

'It feels fantastic, Cassie, that's all.'

'You were looking at this bra and panties for yourself, weren't you?' Cassie pushed him away and grabbed her skirt. What was she, a magnet for every weirdo in the city? At least Brad had been wearing men's briefs. 'Peter, I've had more than my quota of kink lately.'

'This isn't kinky!' Peter protested. 'Aw, come on, Cassie. I'm not a pervert.'

'Peter, I like to be with men who let *me* wear the bras,' Cassie snapped. She buttoned her blouse and picked up her bag. 'This is completely out of my league. I don't even know if it's the same sport.'

'Cassie, wait! I can explain this.'

'Don't bother.' Disgusted, Cassie stalked out of the dressing room and almost out of the store when she remembered she was still wearing the rose-coloured bra and panty set. She turned to go back up to the lingerie department to pay for the underclothes, but the thought of encountering Peter, no doubt with her own bra and panties in tow, made her nauseous. She looked about her quickly and left the store. Once outside, she hailed a taxi at the corner to take her home, then changed her mind and directed the driver towards Lydia's house. She rang the doorbell impatiently.

'Cassie?' Lydia pulled open the door. 'What's wrong?'

Cassie crossed her arms and glowered at her friend. 'You might have warned me that Peter was planning to wear women's lingerie on our first date.'

Lydia clapped a hand over her mouth, her eyes widening in horror. 'He didn't.'

'He most certainly did.'

'Oh dear.' Lydia took Cassie's arm and ushered her quickly inside. 'Cassie, I had no idea. I'm so sorry.'

'Yeah, sure you are,' Cassie grumbled. 'You and Molly. What is it with these friends of yours? Are kinks a prerequisite? Did you take applications when you were trying to figure out a blind date for me?'

'How did you find out about Peter's ... um, taste in clothes?'

'We were getting hot and heavy in the lingerie dressing room at Neiman-Marcus,' Cassie replied, slumping down on the sofa. 'Part of my endeavour to have a varied sex life, like you and Molly. Then I realised that not only was I expecting him to unhook my bra, but he was also expecting me to unhook his.'

Lydia smiled gravely.

'And do you know I had to shoplift just to get away from him?'

'You what?' Lydia asked, her eyes widening in shock.

'I didn't get caught, thank God. I was in such a hurry to leave that I forgot I still had on Neiman-Marcus lingerie. Imagine me getting plucked up by the police and then stripped to reveal the evidence of my crime.'

'Cassie, I am so sorry,' Lydia said. 'I honestly didn't know that Peter was into that. You know I never would have set you up with him if I'd known.'

Cassie sighed. 'Oh, forget it. I guess I did learn something.'

'And what was that?'

'A man in a bra just doesn't turn me on.'

Lydia smiled sympathetically and sat down next to Cassie. 'Well, it's like Molly and I told you, love. If you want variety, you have to accept the disappointments that invariably accompany it.'

'Yes, I know.' Cassie leant her head against the back of

the sofa and yawned. 'Well, I think I'm finished with variety for a while. I think I'm better suited to boredom.'

'Don't say that, Cassie. You're still just looking for what pleases you.'

'At Nicholas's bookshop, Olive has been helping me find some good erotic literature,' Cassie said. 'I've been reading one story about a threesome involving two women and a man which leads them all into a relationship. I was expecting that the women would start to get jealous over the man, but the exact opposite happened. They became best friends and lovers, while the man was left out in the cold. Seems they found in each other something that he couldn't give either one of them.'

Lydia was quiet for a moment. 'You're really fascinated by the idea of threesomes, aren't you?'

'Yes, I guess I am. I thought that was a wonderful story, that these two women aren't split apart because of a man.'

'I take it that means that Peter and his lingerie aren't going to split you and me up.'

Cassie chuckled. 'Not a chance. I do think, however, that I'm going to go back to the store and buy a book that Olive recommended about BDSM and fetish practices. I have no desire to get involved with it, but these two men have definitely made me curious about the psychology behind it.'

'It sounds like you're becoming good friends with Olive.'

'Oh, I like her a great deal. She's so friendly and non-judgemental.'

'Maybe you should ask her to have coffee.'

'Good idea,' Cassie said. 'Maybe I will.'

Cassie tucked her lecture papers back into her briefcase as she answered questions from lingering students. Glad it was Friday, she walked out of the lecture hall and returned to her office.

'Hi, Adler.' Cassie reached into her pocket for her key, spotting Adler coming down the corridor towards her. Because today was a lecture day, Adler had honoured his position by wearing mended jeans and socks with his sandals.

'You want to come over for dinner tomorrow?' Adler asked. 'We can smooth out that first chapter, and I owe you a delicacy of some sort for that delicious lamb you cooked.'

Cassie smiled wryly. 'You mean that dried-out slab of meat I nearly incinerated.'

'Never let it be said that I'm not a polite gentleman.'

'I would never say that,' Cassie promised. 'Sure, I'll come for dinner. Around seven?'

'Great. I live near the Haight.' Adler wrote his address on a piece of paper.

'Why doesn't that surprise me?'

'Haight-Ashbury happens to be the site of one of the most important cultural revolutions in American history,' Adler informed her. 'If not *the* most important.'

Cassie held up her hand. 'Sorry. I meant no disrespect.'

She took the paper from him and went into her office as Adler continued on his way. Checking her watch, Cassie realised that she could make it to Libri Antiqui before Olive left. She checked her e-mail messages quickly, then slipped on her light coat and hurried out to the parking lot. She drove down to Chestnut Street and parked close to the store. After dropping a few coins into the meter, she pulled open the door and went inside.

Olive was seated behind the cash register, burnishing her already-perfect fingernails. She looked up and smiled with delight at the sight of Cassie.

'Cassie, how are you? You haven't been here in a few days.'

'I'm fine, thanks.' Cassie was surprised to discover that her heart was beating rather quickly. She attributed the palpitations to her haste in getting here. 'You?'

'I'm great.' Olive grinned. 'Working up a storm, as usual.'

'I love that book of stories you recommended to me,' Cassie said. 'I told Lydia last night that the one about the *ménage à trois* between the two women and the man was particularly poignant.'

'Isn't that the one by the French author?' Olive asked. 'I liked that one, too. Very empowering.'

'Have you received any new shipments in the past few days?'

'No, but I can show you another book of short stories you might like.' Olive hopped off her stool and led Cassie back to the erotica section.

'Hey, Cassie, how are you?' Perched on a ladder as he shelved a few books, Nicholas gave Cassie a wave. 'Olive, get to work.'

'I'm working as hard as I can, boss,' Olive called. 'In fact, I'm thinking of putting in for overtime.'

Nicholas snorted. 'Don't you mean "putting out"?'

Olive laughed and shook her head at him. She turned to Cassie and whispered confidentially, 'If he weren't so darned cute, I might never have even thought of the idea of an erotica section.'

Cassie lifted her eyebrows in surprise. 'Nicholas inspired the section?'

'Well, it was before a little ... um, interlude that I thought of it,' Olive replied. She straightened a few books, pulling out a couple of history texts that had been misplaced.

'An interlude between you and Nicholas?' Cassie prompted.

'Sure. I mean, look at him. He's adorable.' Olive looked at Cassie, suddenly appearing to realise what she had just revealed. 'It was before he'd even met Lydia,' she said hastily. 'I mean, it's never happened since they got together. I'd never do that.'

'Oh, I never thought you would,' Cassie assured her. She was more than a little rattled by the image of Nicholas and Olive together, but she forced herself to push the thought out of her mind. 'So, what's the title of this other book?'

Olive pulled the book from the shelf. 'It's a collection of lesbian stories. I know that sounds like something you wouldn't be interested in, but they're beautifully written and very woman-positive.'

'You've read them?'

'Of course. I bought a copy for myself.'

Cassie took the book from Olive's hands and looked at it, intrigued by the thought of reading stories that focused strictly on women. The cover alone was erotic, a hazy black and white photograph of two female bodies pressed together. The lines of their breasts and hips curved in a motion that was visually poetic.

'Maybe I'll give it a try,' she said.

'The book, you mean?' Olive asked, a mischievous glint appearing in her brown eyes.

Cassie nodded, aware that she was missing something. As she and Olive returned to the cash register, she also realised that she was nervous about asking Olive to have coffee with her. It seemed completely ridiculous to be nervous over such a thing, but Cassie was. She watched Olive slip the book into a bag.

'Olive, would you like to have coffee one evening?' she asked, feeling her heartbeat increase again.

Olive smiled. 'Sure, that'd be great. When?'

'Um, sometime next week?' Cassie suggested, surprised at the quickness of the other woman's response. 'Tuesday?'

'That sounds perfect!' Olive scribbled her telephone number on Cassie's receipt and stuffed it into the bag. 'Why don't you meet me here since my slave driver won't let me leave early. We can go down the street to a terrific little bistro. They have salads and sandwiches, so maybe we can even have a light dinner.'

'OK. Thanks again for the book.' Cassie took her bag and went outside. Well, that wasn't so bad after all. She liked Olive and was certainly looking forward to the idea of spending some time with her outside the confines of the bookshop.

Cassie had never been to Adler's flat before, but she wasn't surprised when her theories about the place turned out to be true. Grateful Dead and Jefferson Airplane posters covered the walls, and beaded curtains separated the sitting-room, kitchen, and bedroom. The sitting room furniture consisted of several beanbags and a large futon, along with at least three lava lamps and a framed photograph of Allen Ginsberg. Cassie handed Adler a bottle of wine, looking around appreciatively.

'Interesting place, Adler. It's very you.'

'Thanks.' Barefoot and dressed in loose, drawstring trousers and a T-shirt emblazoned with the face of Jimi Hendrix, Adler looked as comfortable as a king in his castle. He waved towards a beanbag. 'Sit down. I have samosas in the oven.'

'Please tell me you didn't make them yourself.' Cassie sank into a beanbag and stretched her legs out in front of her. 'I'll experience a massive sense of cooking inadequacy.'

Adler grinned. 'No, they're from the store, but I did make dinner. Chicken curry and mango chutney.'

Cassie's eyebrows lifted. 'Where did you learn to cook Indian food?'

'I spent a year there when I was in my twenties,' Adler explained. 'Didn't you know that?'

'No. I knew you were interested in East Indian culture, but I didn't know you lived there.'

'Oh, I lived with a musician in Calcutta so that I could take sitar lessons.' Adler went into the kitchen and returned with several samosas on a plate. After offering one to Cassie, he flopped down in a beanbag across from her. 'His wife showed me how to cook. I also studied a great deal about the Hindu and Buddhist philosophies.'

'So why are you now studying eighteenth-century British literature?' Cassie asked. She bit into a samosa, enjoying the spicy flavour.

Adler shrugged. 'Just caught my fancy in college, and I thought it would be fun to work on it. I didn't really want to study Indian culture academically.'

'Well, I'm glad you didn't,' Cassie said. 'I'd have been completely stuck more than once on this William Blake research if it hadn't been for you.'

'Great, that means that your next book is going to be about Blake's erotic themes,' Adler said. 'Just like I want it to be.'

Cassie smiled. 'You won't get much argument from me on that.'

'I won't, huh?'

'None at all.'

'Does this have anything to do with Brad and his obsession with your feet? You want to make sure I'm going to keep the secret, don't you?'

'Adler, I am not going to discuss Brad with you again.'

Adler looked offended. 'What do you mean, again? You never did discuss him with me. All I know is that your feet turned him on.'

'If you don't be quiet about that, I'm leaving.'

'Aw, come on, Cass. I'm not trying to embarrass you, really.'

Flushing, Cassie shot him a sideways glance. Adler's brown eyes lacked his usual teasing light, and his expression was serious. 'The hell you're not.'

'I'm not, really.' Adler crossed his finger over his chest. 'Cross my heart. It's just a surprise that you have this interest in ... well, kink.'

'I do not have an interest in kink!' Cassie said indignantly. 'Brad happened to have this fetish, and I sort of went along with it. But I most certainly do not make a habit of it.'

'What do you make a habit out of, then?' Adler asked. 'Reading erotica alone?'

'Adler, why are you asking me this?'

'I'm just curious. I mean, you're so cool and professional that all these discoveries I'm making about you are very intriguing.'

'What, do you have a weird kink that you want to try out on me?'

'No, no kinks here.'

Cassie eyed him suspiciously. 'Because, if you really want to know the truth, after Brad and his foot fetish, I had to deal with Peter and his fascination with women's underwear. Wearing it.'

Adler's mouth dropped open slightly. 'He wore women's underwear?'

'Yeah. Imagine my surprise when we started to get sexy, and I discovered I was going to have to unhook his bra.'

'Oh, my.' A spark of amusement lit in Adler's eyes. 'You poor thing.'

Cassie remembered her shock over Peter's underclothing and tried to stifle a giggle. 'It wasn't quite what I expected.'

'Was it a training bra?'

'No, actually it was quite nice. Dark blue and lacy. Although I didn't stick around to see if he was wearing the matching panties.'

She and Adler looked at each other, and then they both burst out laughing. Cassie realised that she hadn't yet been able to see the humour in her experiences with Brad and Peter, and she was grateful to Adler for bringing it up in his usual droll manner.

'Well, Lydia and Molly have been fired from their positions as my matchmakers,' she said, still chuckling. 'Especially considering that all of their other friends appear to be hiding deep, kinky secrets.'

'Ah, well, those sound like pretty harmless kinks to me.' Adler crunched into another samosa and heaved himself out of the beanbag. 'Still, it sounds to me like you need a much more vanilla experience.'

'What, you're volunteering?' The words were out of Cassie's mouth before she could stop them, and then she flushed again. 'Wait! I didn't mean that.'

'I don't know, Cassie.' Adler padded into the kitchen to get their dinner. 'Considering I'm kink-free, I doubt I'm your type.'

'Hey!' Cassie was offended. 'What if you did have a kink? Then would you go for me?'

'Only if you'd promise to help me pick out a decent suspender belt,' Adler called from the kitchen.

'OK, I promise.'

'Then I'd be putty in your hands.' Adler grinned at Cassie as he returned with two plates piled high with chicken curry, rice, and chutney.

Cassie dug right into the delicious meal, highly impressed with Adler's culinary skills. Everything was seasoned perfectly. She glanced at Adler. She felt quite comfortable with him – much more so than she had ever felt with other men. She ate a second helping of curry as Adler got up to put a CD on the stereo.

Light exotic Indian music drifted from the speaker, sounding almost like a series of raindrops pattering on a windowsill.

'That's lovely.' Cassie put her empty plate aside and sighed with contentment. 'And your dinner was delicious.'

'This is sitar music,' Adler explained. 'Actually, this is Ram Banerjee, the man I studied with when I was there.'

Cassie leant her head against the back of the beanbag. These sacks were incredibly comfortable. 'What else did you study when you were there?'

'Hindu religion and Tantrism.'

Cassie's eyebrows lifted slightly. 'Tantrism? Isn't that about sex?'

Adler grinned. 'You're starting to have a one-track mind, aren't you?'

'Yes, well, with all my experiences with fetishism, I'm becoming quite worldly. I'm thinking of starting a news-letter called *Cassie's Kinks*.'

'The sexual aspect comes into play with Tantric yoga,' Adler explained. 'It focuses on the union of the male and female divine principles.'

'Just in principle?'

'No. In practice also. However, it also focuses on medi-tation and streams of energy throughout the body.'

'And what is the sex supposed to do?'

'Well, when done right, the idea is that you're releasing an energy that will help you attain a more spiritual state of being. You become more closely attuned to your mys-tical and inner self, and thus become more completely fulfilled.'

Cassie gave him a sceptical look. 'And you've done this?'

'It takes practice, but I've tried. You can't have one experience of Tantric sex and expect it to work. You need to be aware of things like the movement of your muscles when you have an orgasm, how to channel energies appropriately, and how to become aware of all your senses. The idea is to create a higher state of conscious-ness that leads to spiritual evolution.'

'Sounds complicated.'

'It definitely takes some thought and discipline.'

'So, have you ever attained this higher state?' Cassie asked.

Adler was quiet for a minute, and then he nodded. 'Once, I did. This beautiful Indian woman was my lover, and we must have been making love for hours when this incredible wave of energy and light seemed to course through me the instant before I had an orgasm. I'd never experienced anything like it, but I was still hard and we kept going. I felt the same thing again when I had another orgasm, like being transported into a river of sheer light in which we were completely united.'

Cassie stared at him in fascination. 'Wow. That sounds amazing.'

Adler nodded. 'It was.'

'And you never had that again?'

'No. Not even close. It depends a great deal on your partner and how in tune both of you are.'

'And you can only experience this through sex?'

'No, not necessarily. Meditation and massage can also release built-up energies.'

'You studied those too?'

Adler nodded. 'I meditate for an hour every morning. It gives me a great sense of peace.' He stood up and picked up their empty plates. 'And I can give you a massage, if you want. That'll give you an idea of what I'm talking about.'

'A massage?' Startled, Cassie looked at him. 'You're serious?'

'Sure. This isn't a come-on, Cassie. Like I said, Tantric sex takes time and practice. Even if you and I decided to try all night, we'd probably never reach that level of ecstasy. A massage, however, can often serve the same purpose of balancing energies.'

Cassie considered the idea. A massage did sound rather nice, and, unlike Brad and Peter, Adler was a man she could trust. 'OK. What do I have to do?'

'Nothing. I'll unfold the futon so you can lie down. You just have to lie there and relax.'

'That's what the guy who took my virginity said,' Cassie muttered.

Adler grinned. 'I'm not going to take your virginity,' he promised. 'But you are getting feisty lately, aren't you?'

'Men in women's lingerie will do that to me.'

Chuckling, Adler went to put the plates in the kitchen, then returned to spread the futon mattress out on the frame. He looked at her for a moment and scratched his head. 'Um, if it makes you uncomfortable, you don't have to do it, but it'll be better if you take off your clothes. I have a robe you can wear.'

Cassie hesitated, feeling more than a little gun-shy after her experiences with Brad and Peter, but then she went into the bedroom and changed into the robe Adler gave her. She thought about keeping her bra and panties on, but eventually decided that she might as well do this right. After taking off her underclothes, she pulled the robe around her and went back to the sitting room.

Picking up a pillow, she stretched out on her stomach, feeling oddly relaxed. The light scent of incense and curry drifted in the air, along with that lovely raindrop music that brought to mind silken robes, bejewelled turbans, and dark kohl-lined eyes.

'If you ever start to feel uncomfortable, just tell me, OK?' Adler said. He grasped her robe and tugged it over her shoulders to reveal her bare back. 'Take a deep, long breath through your nose and let it out through your mouth.'

Cassie filled her lungs with air and exhaled through her mouth. She gazed for a moment at one of the lava lamps, oddly soothed by the slow, spherical movements and deep blue colour. She closed her eyes and tried to relax. Adler began to massage his fingers against the top of her head, then touched the back of her neck gently, his long fingers prodding at the tense muscles.

'The idea of Tantric massage is to uncoil all of the pent-up energies that are causing you tension,' he explained, pressing his fingers down the length of her spine. His touch was so careful and precise that Cassie began to relax within seconds. 'The energy is called kundalini.'

'Mmm. What a lovely word.'

'It's described in yogic literature as a coiled snake,' Adler went on. His fingers touched the base of her spine and pushed. 'A snake resting at the base of the spine like a receptacle for the pure creative energy that runs along your back and to the top of your head. And this channel of energy is composed of several different centres called chakras, each of which corresponds to a vital part of your body like your heart, genitals, throat, and the top of your head.'

Slowly, his hands moved against her back, stroking hard over her muscles that connected to her spinal cord. He traced her spine, paying particular attention to the base as he pressed the heels of his hands against it. Cassie gave a sigh of sheer pleasure. Tension flowed out of her body like a river, leaving her feeling both pliant and relaxed.

'When your energy is released, then it can flow properly upward through your spine and chakras, thus giving you a feeling of total harmony and balance,' Adler said.

'I'm beginning to feel very harmonious and balanced,' Cassie mumbled.

She let her eyes drift closed as Alder's hands moved lower, pushing aside the robe to reveal her buttocks. Cassie didn't even think to protest and merely sank further into the delicious sensations evoked by his touch and the lovely scents and music in the air. Her breasts pressed against the futon mattress. She took another deep breath, imagining weeks of tension melting, loosening, seeping steadily from her body like water from a glacier.

Adler's hands flattened against her buttocks, kneading and prodding as they moved down to her thighs. His fingers slipped slightly into the crevice of her backside, but they didn't linger as they might have if the massage had had purely sensual designs. Cassie tensed slightly when she noticed that a degree of warmth was collecting between her thighs, but Adler's hands moved with such gentle devotion that she knew she had nothing to worry about. She relaxed, even allowing her legs to part slightly as a current of air cooled her heated sex.

'Your energies are seriously blocked,' Adler said. He rubbed his hands hard over her thighs and calves, pressing deep into her muscles and forcing them to pliancy. 'No wonder you're so tense all the time.'

Cassie yawned. She was feeling quite luscious. 'I'm tense all the time?'

'Cassie, you walk around as if you have a pole up your bum.'

She chuckled. 'What a lovely image.'

'You really need to stop being afraid of your potential and your emotions,' Adler said.

'I'm not afraid.'

She was, however, becoming rather aroused. Adler's hands created a rosy glow over the surface of her skin, a glow that seemed to penetrate into her blood. Her sex swelled with sheer pleasure over what was happening to her body, but it felt like such a natural reaction that Cassie didn't even think twice about it. Instead, she let the sensations submerge her. The gentle pulsing of her clitoris seemed a perfect indication that her energies were, indeed, being released.

'That kind of denial only contributes to the repression of energy,' Adler said. 'And repression of energy can lead to all kinds of problems. Even physical illness.'

'Why should I be afraid of my potential and emotions?' Oddly enough, this conversation wasn't bothering Cassie the slightest bit. Instead, she found herself quite willing to continue it.

'Maybe your experiences with the foot and panties men have something to do with that,' Adler said.

'Well, I suppose I am trying to find something,' Cassie murmured. 'I just don't know what.'

'That's because you haven't yet opened yourself up to infinite possibilities,' Adler said.

He knelt next to her, pressing the weight of his arms on to her back.

Cassie let out a groan of utter pleasure. Waves of heat radiated from her skin, augmenting the delicious feelings in her sex. The only tension which remained in her body was now focused completely in her clitoris. Cassie drew in a breath as her body began to pulsate. Her mind became so fogged with total relaxation that she was barely aware even of Adler any more. Once more, he pressed his hands against the base of her spine, stroking his fingers hard upward in a motion that mirrored the gentle, thrusting rhythm of intercourse.

Cassie gasped. A clear, fluttering orgasm rippled through her body like a bird taking flight. Sensation flew through her with such illumination that ecstasy shimmered from her very fingertips. She couldn't believe that it actually happened with a complete lack of direct stimulation, but the throbbing of her heart and pulsing between her legs told her otherwise.

Adler didn't stop his movements, continuing to press his fingers along her spine. Cassie had no idea if he even noticed what had happened, and she realised that she didn't particularly care. Absolute relaxation bathed her in a warm light. Every muscle in her body felt pliant and slack, and she suspected that she couldn't have moved even if she wanted to. Not that she had any intention of trying.

Adler's hands began to move with long, slow strokes over the entire surface of her back. Cassie murmured a low sound of approval, letting her mind empty of all thought as she descended into a dreamless sleep.

# Chapter Four

'No way.' Cassie handed Lydia the bowl of popcorn and settled down in front of the television. She glanced at Molly. 'I mean, Brad was unique, Molly, but I'd rather avoid a repeat scenario of both him and Peter. That's enough odd kinks to last me a lifetime.'

'I think odd kinks are underestimated,' Lydia replied. She popped a few kernels into her mouth and dusted the salt from her fingers. 'I mean, some people think that oral sex is an odd kink.'

'Lyd, thanks again, but I'm through with being set up,' Cassie said.

'Give it a shot, Cassie,' Molly said. 'What have you got to lose?'

'I promise, he's very nice,' Lydia assured her.

'So was Brad, and then he had an obsession with my feet.'

Molly grinned. 'I told you those shoes were fabulous.'

'No.' Cassie shook her head emphatically. 'No more set-ups. The only man I'm hanging out with lately is Adler, and that's strictly a research relationship.'

Molly and Lydia exchanged glances.

'Um, research for what?' Lydia asked. 'This is that hippie, right?'

Cassie glowered at her friend. 'Adler happens to be a very nice man with no kinks as far as I can tell.'

'Did you do anything with him?' Molly sat up eagerly.

'Actually, he gave me this amazing massage and told me a few things about Tantric sex, which he learnt about in India. It was great, but we don't have anything other than a professional relationship.'

Lydia frowned. 'Why not? Seems like you have a lot in

common with your mutual interest in William Blake and all.'

Cassie shrugged and stared at the movie unfolding on the television screen. Why didn't she want to be in a relationship with Adler? He was a nice enough man, and he certainly knew how to treat a woman.

'Cassie?' Lydia pressed.

'I don't know. It just doesn't feel right.'

'So what does feel right with you?' Molly sounded somewhat exasperated. 'You said you wanted to experience variety, and clearly you have. What is it you're looking for?'

Lydia looked at Cassie for a long moment.

'If you're waiting for a knight in shining armour, Cassie, then forget it,' Molly continued, flopping back on to the sofa as she tossed popcorn into her mouth. 'They don't exist.'

'Molly,' Lydia said softly. 'Be quiet.'

She reached out and gave Cassie's shoulder a gentle squeeze, then picked up the television remote control. 'OK, let's watch this Bette Davis movie. Nothing like watching a woman who knows exactly what she wants.'

'Hi, Cassie, I'm ready to go.' Olive hitched her bag over her shoulder. 'I just have to tell the Master of the Universe that I'm leaving.'

She peered into the other room of the bookshop. 'Hey, boss?'

'Yeah?' Nicholas's voice called back.

'Cassie's here, so I'm going to leave, OK?'

'You're coming in early tomorrow, aren't you?'

'Crack o' dawn.'

'There is no need to be sarcastic.'

Olive and Cassie exchanged grins. 'Hi, Nicholas,' Cassie called.

'Keep an eye on Olive, Cassie,' Nicholas replied. 'She only looks innocent.'

Olive rolled her eyes as she and Cassie left the store and headed to the bistro at the end of the street. 'He's become even worse since he met Lydia. Now he actually thinks that he owns the place.'

'Is he right?'

'About owning the place?'

'About you only looking innocent,' Cassie said.

Olive laughed. 'Yeah, he's right. To a degree, of course.'

The two women went into the bistro and found an empty table by the window. After ordering chicken sandwiches and café mochas, they settled down to eat. Cassie took a sip of her coffee, pleased to finally have a chance to talk alone with Olive. The other woman wore a knee-length, red dress with a scooped neckline that exposed a tantalising hint of cleavage. Her blonde hair fell about her shoulders in gentle waves, and Cassie found herself wondering about the texture of Olive's hair.

'You look good, Cassie,' Olive remarked. 'Rather relaxed if you don't mind my saying so.'

'Thanks.' Cassie forced her thoughts back to the present. 'A friend gave me a Tantric massage a few nights ago, and it worked wonders. I'm still feeling the effects of it. He also loaned me a book on meditation techniques that are supposed to keep my energy flowing smoothly. I've been trying them, and they really do seem to work. He said that energies shouldn't be repressed.'

'I'd have to agree with him,' Olive said. 'You say he's a friend?'

'Well, my research partner. His name is Adler.'

Olive's eyebrows lifted slightly. 'And you're not romantically involved with him?'

'Oh, no. I like him, but he's not exactly my type.'

'Lydia said that she didn't know what your type was,' Olive said.

'Lydia has talked to you about me?'

'No, she just mentioned that she set you up with some of her friends.'

'One friend,' Cassie corrected. 'And that was one too many.'

She told Olive about her adventures with Brad and Peter. Olive chuckled and shook her head.

'Oh, you know, all women have to deal with men's little quirks every now and then,' she said. 'Believe me, those are pretty mild compared to some. I was once with a guy who wanted to call me "mummy" and have me dress him up in diapers.'

Cassie stared at Olive in shock. 'You're kidding.'

'No. I'm very open-minded, but needless to say, I fairly kicked him out the door.' Olive chewed her sandwich and looked at Cassie thoughtfully. 'At least Adler sounds like a decent sort of chap.'

'He is, no question. Like I said, just not my type.'

'Maybe you could introduce him to me,' Olive suggested, her bow-shaped lips curving into a smile. 'I could use a Tantric massage.'

For some reason, Cassie was bothered by the thought of Olive and Adler together, just as she had been at the thought of Olive and Nicholas being intimate. She shrugged noncommittally and turned her attention to her sandwich. 'Maybe.'

'So, what made you go to Lydia for help with your love life?' Olive asked.

'She's my best friend. She offered to help, I didn't ask her. I was just curious about some stuff, particularly since I'd been reading about Blake's erotic adventures.'

'Which are?'

'Well, a possible *ménage à trois*.'

Olive's eyes widened. 'You're interested in that?'

'I was only curious,' Cassie said. 'There's no need to look so surprised.'

'I'm sorry, Cassie, but I am surprised. You don't seem like the type of woman who'd be interested in that.'

'I didn't say I was interested in trying it,' Cassie replied. 'I'm interested in why people would want to.'

Olive leant her chin on her hand and gazed at Cassie. 'That's why you liked that story about the man and the two women, isn't it?'

Cassie nodded. She took another sip of coffee, grateful to Olive for not making her feel uncomfortable about this kind of conversation. It was one thing to discuss it with

Lydia and Molly, both of whom knew everything about her, but another to discuss it with Olive.

She glanced hesitantly at the other woman. 'Have you had any experience with that?'

'Threesomes? No. The closest I've come to that is that I had sex with twins, only I did it six months apart. So that doesn't count.' Olive polished off the last bite of her sandwich and gave a satisfied sigh. 'Mmm, that was delicious. Hey, have you read any of the stories from that lesbian anthology I suggested?'

'I've read about three of them. They're wonderful.'

Olive smiled. 'Hot, too.'

Cassie nodded, remembering just the previous night when she had become quite aroused by reading one of those very stories. She had even indulged in a highly erotic fantasy about herself and another woman, only this time there was no man involved.

Olive glanced at her watch. 'Do you want to come over to my place for a while? I live just around the corner on Alhambra Street, and I have a bottle of wine I've been wanting to share with someone. I can also show you some of my other anthologies.'

Flattered, Cassie nodded. 'I'd like that.'

They finished their coffee, then walked to Olive's flat. She had a charming, one-room place decorated with a great deal of lace and chintz. A bookshelf overflowed with hardcovers and paperbacks, and the large bed was covered with lacy pillows. Cassie smiled.

'I have a couple dozen pillows on my bed, too,' she said.

'Aren't they wonderful?' Olive dropped her bag on a nearby table. 'Like sinking into a bed of clouds. Have a seat. I'm going to get out of this dress.'

She went to a closet and pulled out a long, white robe, then tossed it on to the bed. Cassie realised quickly that, since there was only one room to Olive's flat, there was nowhere for her to go. She sat down and picked up a magazine, trying to ignore the fact that Olive was undressing less than five feet away.

'I swear, one of these days, I'm going to join a bra-burning rally,' Olive said.

Against her better judgement, Cassie glanced at the other woman. Her heart leapt at the sight of Olive without her dress, her full breasts constrained by a white, lace bra. Olive's nipples poked through the transparent lace, and her cleavage swelled over the cups. Cassie couldn't stop staring as Olive reached behind her to unclasp the bra.

'I mean, it has to be healthier to be free, you know?' Olive continued. She pushed the bra off her shoulders, revealing her creamy white breasts crowned with rosy nipples. 'That kind of restriction must be damaging.'

Cassie's mouth went dry. Her heart began to thud hard, shocking her with her intense reaction to the sight of this woman.

'Probably,' she croaked.

'You're lucky that you don't have such large tits,' Olive said, hooking her fingers under her slip and pushing it off. 'They can be a real pain.'

'I think they're beautiful.' The words came out of Cassie's mouth almost involuntarily. Her eyes widened with horror as Olive turned to look at her. 'Oh, I didn't mean ... I just think ... oh, Lord ...' Her face flushed bright crimson. 'I'm sorry.'

Olive continued looking at her, not making a move to cover herself. 'Don't be sorry.'

'I'm not ... I mean, I'm not attracted to you,' Cassie stammered, unable to believe this was happening. 'I didn't mean it like that.'

'You're not?'

'No!' Cassie gasped. 'I'm not a lesbian.'

'You don't have to be a lesbian to be attracted to another woman,' Olive said. 'I'm attracted to you.'

Cassie stared at her. Her heart had never pounded so hard in her life. 'Y-you are?'

Olive nodded. 'I think you're lovely, so petite and delicate. I've wondered what it would be like to kiss you.'

'Oh. Oh, Olive, I don't ... this isn't what I ... I think I should leave now.'

Olive held out her hand. 'Wait, Cassie. Just wait. There's nothing to be afraid of.'

'I'm not interested in women!' Cassie said, her voice strained as she tried not to look at Olive's naked breasts again. She felt totally flustered. 'I'm not attracted to them.'

'You're comfortable with me, aren't you?'

'Of course.' So why was she freaking out when she'd dealt with a couple of kinky men like Brad and Peter without this kind of agitation?

'Cassie, I've been with both women and men. For me, there's something satisfying about both.' Olive approached her slowly, as if Cassie were a scared kitten whom she didn't want to frighten away. 'Why don't you let me kiss you? If you don't like it, I'll stop.'

'That's really not necessary.' Cassie swallowed hard when Olive paused in front of her, unable to take her eyes from Olive's lush nudity. She experienced a raging desire to close her lips around one of those juicy nipples and suck. Her heart hammered ceaselessly.

Olive went down gracefully on her knees in front of Cassie and reached out to put her hands on Cassie's knees. 'You've never been with another woman, have you?'

'No.'

'But you want to be.'

'Olive, I –'

'It's just a kiss,' Olive murmured. Her brown eyes darkened, her lips parting slightly as she leant towards Cassie.

Cassie couldn't move, clenching her hand around the arm of the chair as Olive's lips neared. And, oh, Olive did have luscious lips, full and shaped into a perfect Cupid's bow. What would those lips feel like against hers, Olive's tongue sliding into her mouth … Cassie drew in a sharp breath when Olive's mouth touched hers. Confusion fogged her mind as her body reacted to the inevitable stimulation. Olive's breasts brushed against Cassie, causing her to start slightly.

'It's OK,' Olive murmured soothingly. She began to slowly stroke her palms over Cassie's thighs. 'You're delicious.'

Cassie's blood grew heated as Olive began to explore

her mouth with her tongue. Her fantasies about this had never come close to the reality, the sensation of Olive's incredibly soft lips, the velvet taste of her tongue, the smoothness of her skin. Unable to stop herself, Cassie lifted her hands and cupped Olive's large breasts. Olive murmured a little sound of pleasure, leaning forward to push her breasts into Cassie's hands.

A sense of pure wonder washed over Cassie. She admitted now that she had been longing to touch Olive's breasts for some time, only she hadn't been willing to confess such a desire. Not even to herself. She stared at the other woman as one thought broke through the haze of her confusion. *I want her.* Adler's words from a few nights ago came back to her. *You haven't yet opened yourself to infinite possibilities.* Cassie thought that she had done so with men like Brad and Peter, but the possibility of making love to another woman was the 'infinite possibility' she had been craving on an innate level.

Slowly, she rubbed her fingers over Olive's nipples, delighting in the sensation of hardness and softness all at the same time. Olive's skin felt warm and slightly damp, scented with the light floral aroma of lotion.

Olive pressed a series of kisses against Cassie's lower lip, moving down to her neck. Cassie closed her eyes and succumbed to the pure enjoyment of the other woman. Olive's lips nibbled gently at Cassie's throat, licking the pulse beating wildly against her skin. Cassie drew in a deep breath, filling her nose with the clean scent of Olive's hair. Olive lifted her hands to the buttons of Cassie's blouse, then paused.

She looked at Cassie, her eyes heavily lidded and hot. 'OK?'

Cassie nodded. 'OK,' she whispered.

Olive began to unfasten the buttons, revealing Cassie's beige bra and the heated flush of her skin. Cassie's nipples pushed almost painfully against the lace of her bra. With one flick of her fingers, she unsnapped the front clasp. Her small breasts spilt forth. Olive reached up and rubbed her fingers over them, teasing the taut peaks of Cassie's nipples deliciously. A momentary sense of inadequacy gripped Cassie, but Olive looked at her with such desire that her anxiety soon dissipated.

'You're as pretty as I thought you would be.' Olive bent to press her lips against Cassie's breasts, licking her tongue slowly around the areolae of her nipples and taking the hard nubs between her teeth.

A rush of moisture made Cassie squirm, and when Olive abandoned her breasts, Cassie rotated her nipples between her fingers. Olive grasped the elastic band of Cassie's skirt and slid it off. Cassie wasn't wearing any stockings, and she flushed slightly when she realised that the crotch of her panties was already damp. Olive slid the panties down over Cassie's knees and then slipped her hands between Cassie's silky thighs, pushing them apart so that she could gaze at the luscious secrets of her sex. An infusion of pure desire filled Olive's eyes as she reached out to trail her fingers over the light curls covering Cassie's mons.

'I'm so glad you don't shave,' Olive murmured. 'You're so pretty just the way you are.'

Cassie's blood throbbed at the mere touch of Olive's graceful fingers dipping into her. Olive trailed her forefinger up the little crevice created by the folds, then around Cassie's aching clitoris. Olive rose on to her knees, gently pushing Cassie's hands aside as she leant forward and again captured one of her nipples between her lips. A quiver of sensation travelled from Cassie's nipple to her sex, which dampened even further with moisture. She gazed down at Olive's blonde head, her full lips and pink tongue sucking and licking with such affection that Cassie's entire being filled with warmth. She stroked her hand through Olive's hair and down her back, feeling the heat of her bare skin.

Olive's mouth moved to Cassie's other breast, her tongue sliding into the juicy crevice underneath it before trailing hungrily over her abdomen and belly. The soft, feathery touch of Olive's mouth felt like a butterfly's wings against Cassie's skin. Pressing a series of kisses around Cassie's navel, Olive urged her friend's thighs apart again to give her full access to the secret delights. Cassie had never before felt quite so exposed, not even during her experience with Nicholas. She gazed at Olive with utter fascination, her pretty mouth moving with such ardent pleasure. Exquisite tension tightened around her body, and she allowed herself to surrender.

Cassie's body went rigid with pleasure at the first touch of Olive's tongue on her pussy. She drew in a gasp of air, feeling perspiration break out on her skin. Olive's warm palms ran up and down her thighs, creating a delicious friction as she began to work more ardently at Cassie's sex. Olive knew how to use her mouth, and she stroked her tongue with precise dedication up and down the crevices of Cassie's labia, swirling it around her clitoris and around the tight opening of her sex. Cassie nearly held her breath. A sheen of perspiration broke out on her skin, and she cried out when she felt Olive's tongue pushing into her body. Ah, how different from the sensation of a man's rough thrusting. Olive was all softness, her mouth exploring Cassie with a curiosity borne of a desire to mutually please.

Ropes of tension constricted in Cassie's loins, augmented by her sheer joy over the fact that Olive was wholly hers at this moment. A low moan escaped her throat, her breasts heaving with the force of her breathing. Cassie relished the sight of Olive's head between her legs, her desire stimulated by intermittent glimpses of Olive's flickering tongue. Olive reached up to grasp Cassie's breasts, her fingers pulling and tugging at the tight nipples until Cassie felt as if her entire body was awash in flames.

'Olive,' Cassie whispered. 'I want to see you, too.'

Olive lifted her head and smiled. She pulled herself up and kissed Cassie, urging her lips apart. Cassie opened her mouth to let Olive inside, delighting in the flavour of her nectar upon the other woman's tongue. Then Olive stood slowly, her pale skin painted with a pinkish hue as she drew her panties over her hips. Cassie stared with uninhibited fascination at the sight of Olive's lush curves, the dark triangle of hair between her thighs and the moisture that glistened on her sex.

'Come here.' Olive reached for Cassie's hands and tugged her out of the chair and over to the bed. With a smile so gentle that Cassie's heart fluttered, Olive pulled Cassie against her. Their bodies pressed together as they sank on to the bed amidst the flurry of pillows. Olive stroked her hands over Cassie's abdomen, pushing her legs apart again. 'I want to make you come.'

Cassie drew in a sharp breath at the rawness of Olive's words. Olive knelt on the bed, looking incredibly succulent with her nipples jutting forth and her eyes glazed with passion. 'Do you want me to, Cassie?'

'Oh, yes. Yes. Make me come.' Cassie stretched her arms over her head in utter submission.

She opened her legs to allow Olive full access to her body again, crying out in pleasure when Olive's tongue plunged into her. Their previous gentleness gave way to urgency and desperation. Cassie bucked her hips underneath Olive's mouth, panting furiously as pressure began to mount.

'Come, Cassie,' Olive murmured against the musky heat of Cassie's vulva. 'Come for me.'

Cassie writhed, gripping a fistful of the bedcover as an orgasm broke over her, spilling a river of honeyed fluid into Olive's mouth. Both women moaned. Olive diligently continued to lick up the remnants of Cassie's lust as the final vibrations shuddered through her.

'Oh, Olive,' Cassie gasped, her chest heaving. 'You're incredible.' She lifted her head. 'I want ... you haven't.'

'I know, it's all right.' Olive pulled herself up alongside Cassie and gathered her in her arms. 'Just wait.'

'But, I –'

Olive gave her a lovely smile, her brown eyes filled with warmth. 'I wanted to pleasure you, Cassie. We have plenty of time, unless you need to be somewhere tonight.'

Cassie shook her head. She tucked her body against Olive's, revelling in the sensation of their nakedness pressed so closely together. She closed her eyes, saturated with the sensations and emotions evoked by another woman.

The scent of coffee woke Cassie with delicious ease. She opened her eyes, momentarily confused as to where she was, but then memories of the previous night flooded back to her. Smiling, she raised her arms above her head for a long, leisurely stretch.

'Good morning.' Olive came out of the kitchen, her hands wrapped around a coffee cup. Her blonde hair fell in dishevelled curls around her shoulders, and her full figure was loosely wrapped in a thin, white robe.

'Morning.' Cassie finished stretching and gazed at Olive's cleavage with hungry eyes.

Olive held up the coffee mug. 'Do you want some coffee?'

'Mmm, thanks, I'd love some.' Cassie rolled out of bed and stumbled into the bathroom. She brushed her teeth and washed, then returned to the main room. Olive was sitting on the bed, the length of her legs exposed through the folds of her robe.

Cassie climbed on the bed next to her, realising that for the first time she was completely unconcerned with her nudity in front of another person.

'Here you go.' Olive picked up a mug from the bedside table and handed it to Cassie. 'It's a French roast I picked up the other day.'

Cassie inhaled the scent deeply and took a sip, enjoying the rich flavour. 'Do you have to work today?' she asked.

'Not until noon,' Olive replied. She settled back against the pillow and smiled at Cassie. 'You?'

'I have office hours at three, but no classes.'

'Hmm, I guess we'll have to find something to do for the next few hours, then.'

Cassie grinned. 'I guess so.'

Olive took the mug from her and put it back on the table. Cassie sank into the other woman's arms, feeling like it was the most natural movement in the world. She opened her mouth against Olive's ruby lips and kissed her thoroughly. Last night, Olive had pleasured her, and now Cassie wanted to return the favour. She stroked her tongue over Olive's teeth and pushed apart her robe to reveal her breasts.

'I love your body,' Cassie whispered, rubbing her fingers over Olive's hard-tipped breasts.

'I'm too fat,' Olive murmured.

Cassie pulled away momentarily to stare at Olive. 'Olive, you're not fat,' she protested. 'You're perfect. You're so ... so lush. So tasty.'

'You're perfect, too.' Olive smiled and tugged Cassie back into her arms. Their lips met again, nipples brushing together and creating a most stimulating friction. Cassie smoothed her palms over Olive's creamy skin. She thought then that the time would never come when she would grow tired of the other woman's body. She captured one of Olive's nipples between her teeth, so caught up in sensations that she barely realised it when Olive sat up slightly.

'Cassie, turn around,' Olive murmured.

Cassie lifted her closed eyelids. 'What?'

'Turn around,' Olive repeated.

Cassie couldn't stand the thought of not giving to Olive what Olive had given to her. 'But, I want –'

'I know what you want,' Olive interrupted. 'You will, I promise.'

She sat up, pushing her robe over her shoulders. Cassie gazed hungrily upon Olive's nudity, her full breasts and sinuous curves. She wanted to pull Olive down to her again and feel the full length of their bodies pressing against each other, but Olive went to a cabinet at the end of the room. She took something from a drawer, then returned to Cassie holding a vibrator. Cassie's pulse beat heavily at the sight of Olive's fingers caressing the light brown phallus.

'Come, lover, turn around.'

Excitement licking at her nerves, Cassie turned around, bracing her hands on the headboard as she presented her rounded buttocks and spread sex to her friend. Her body quivered when she felt Olive's hands skimming over her globes and gently exploring the dark crevice between them. After what seemed like an eternity, Cassie felt the head of the phallus teasing the wet folds of her sex. She closed her eyes, drawing in a sharp breath of pleasure as Olive turned the vibrator on and began to push it slowly into her.

'How's that?' Olive asked, a smile in her voice as she pressed a kiss against Cassie's shoulder. 'Is that good?'

Cassie could hardly speak for the sensations wracking her body, but she managed a groan of delight that was unmistakable. The vibrations of the dildo beat heavily against her inner walls, evoking such intense delight that Cassie had the sudden thought that men might not be terribly necessary after all. The dildo was smaller than any decently endowed man, but she had certainly never felt a man's penis vibrate like this. Her lips parted on another moan as Olive began working the phallus back and forth slowly, twisting it as she pumped to stimulate all portions of Cassie's tight, humid passage. The glorious friction made Cassie's clit throb with the need for release, and she couldn't stop herself from sliding her fingers down to her sex.

'Wait.' Olive reached around to still Cassie's hand. 'Wait. It'll get better. I promise.'

Cassie didn't know how much better it could get, but she had unwavering trust in her friend. With a mutter of frustration, she leant on her elbows against the multiple pillows, closing her eyes against the intensity of sensations created by the dildo. The vibrations seemed to ricochet through her entire body, inflaming her ache to an extreme level. Her fingers clutched tightly at a pillow as she fought to retain control. She was unable to prevent herself from thrusting her hips backwards in an attempt to impale herself on the phallus.

Olive gave a husky laugh. 'Ah, Cassie, I adore you.'

Slowly, she pulled the phallus out. Feeling completely empty, Cassie turned her head to look at Olive in an unspoken plea.

'I know,' Olive said before Cassie could speak.

Olive's face was flushed with her own growing excitement over her role as director of Cassie's pleasure. She trailed her forefinger down the groove of Cassie's buttocks, lightly circling the ring of her anus. It took Cassie a moment to realise just what Olive had in mind, and she tensed automatically.

'Olive –'

'Relax, love. You trust me, don't you?'

'Of course, but –'

'Then you have to relax. It's not large, and it won't hurt.'

Olive dipped her fingers into Cassie's sex, coating them with viscous fluids. She rubbed them over Cassie's anus, then gently pushed the head of the phallus into the puckered aperture. Cassie gasped at the sensation of pressure, but Olive's movements were so slow and careful that there was indeed no pain. She didn't try to force it all the way in, but just far enough so that it vibrated against Cassie's rectal walls, eliciting an entirely new series of sensations. Cassie wasn't certain she liked it at first, but then as she began to relax, she became aware of how her body was reacting to the forbidden penetration.

Olive leant forward, her breasts brushing against Cassie's sweat-slickened back as she pressed her lips against Cassie's neck.

'Good?' she whispered.

Cassie gasped and nodded. Good, yes, it was good. Her blood seemed to be throbbing with the rhythm of the gentle vibrations, and her sex surged with a renewed rush of need. Squirming impatiently, she tried to silently let Olive know that the tension was too great, that she couldn't possibly let it build any more.

Olive seemed to sense the frenzy of Cassie's urgency. After pressing another lingering kiss on Cassie's neck, she slipped back down between her legs. Cassie couldn't see what she was doing, but within seconds, she felt Olive's lips working at her again. A cry of pleasure broke from her throat when Olive's tongue pushed deep into her. And then she could stand it no longer, her body couldn't take any more of this delicious double-assault. Her climax burst over her in waves of rapture so intense that her world became one of pure feeling. Thought vanished. It seemed so endless that Cassie wasn't even aware of Olive licking up the fluid evidence of her pleasure or removing the phallus.

Cassie fought to regain her breath as she turned stunned eyes on her friend.

Olive smiled. 'You've never had it up the bum, have you?' she asked.

Still unable to speak, Cassie shook her head.

'If you ever decide to let a man do it, you make certain he goes slowly.' Olive reached out to brush Cassie's damp hair away from her forehead. 'Don't let him force it or hurt you in any way, all right? And make sure it's someone with whom you can be completely relaxed.'

'The idea just never seemed appealing to me,' Cassie admitted, still finding it difficult to think and express herself after the intensity of her orgasm. She didn't even try to explain that she had little intention of going that far with a man. She collapsed back on to the bed, her breathing slowly calming. 'That's just never been a desire of mine.'

Olive shrugged and put the vibrator on the bedside table. 'It might be one of those things that you don't know you like until you try it.'

Cassie's gaze skimmed over Olive's damp, naked body. 'Come here.'

Olive smiled again and stretched her body over Cassie's, their breasts and sexes pressing together without the slightest barrier. With a swift movement, Cassie thrust her tongue into Olive's mouth as her hands drifted down the curve of Olive's back to clutch at her resilient buttocks.

'Have you let men do that to you?' Cassie whispered.

'Mmm, sometimes,' Olive replied, stroking her tongue over the inside of Cassie's lower lip. 'However, I still prefer the traditional way. They're both an entirely different set of sensations.'

'Your turn,' Cassie murmured, shifting slightly. 'I'm being too selfish.'

She positioned them both so that Olive was lying back on the bed and Cassie had access to her. Thrilled by the newness of this experience, she simply gazed at Olive's spread sex for a moment before kissing her gently. She loved the silky hair of Olive's mons underneath her lips, loved hearing the sound of Olive's groans as she began to caress her intimately. Cassie licked her way around the perimeter of Olive's outer labia, sinking two fingers into the wet passage. Olive's fluids tasted tangy and slightly sweet. Cassie delved in deep with her tongue, wanting to give Olive as much pleasure as Olive had given her.

Olive's hand stroked through Cassie's hair. Her body tensed with growing need as Cassie continued working diligently and lovingly at her sex. Cassie reached up to cup her lover's breasts in her free hand, alternately the left and right tit, plucking at her lovely hard nipples. She loved the sensation of Olive writhing and panting beneath her, knowing that she was responsible for her friend's pleasure.

Cassie buried her face in Olive's pussy, and captured the swollen clitoris between her lips. She sucked lightly, drawing sensations from her until Olive bucked underneath her. Her body jerked violently as she shrieked out her ecstasy. Cassie soothed Olive with her tongue, drinking up the final rush of moisture as her body shuddered through her climax.

'Oh, Cassie . . .' Olive went limp, her eyelids drifting closed as she sank back against the pillows. 'You are just so luscious.'

Smiling, Cassie eased her way up over Olive's body, lowering her head to give her friend a deep kiss. Olive opened her eyes and gazed up at Cassie affectionately.

'I've wanted you, you know,' she murmured. 'Ever since you started coming into the bookshop.'

Cassie lifted her shoulders in a mild shrug, concealing the rush of pleasure Olive's words brought. It was unspeakably wonderful to be wanted, to be desired by the beautiful woman. And wanted in a way that was completely free from the contrivance that men always seemed to mean. 'I never thought I would ever do this with you. I can't believe this happened.'

'Mmm.' Olive stretched in satiated enjoyment, rubbing

her hand lightly over Cassie's back. 'Sometimes it's just so nice to feel the softness of another woman.'

Cassie didn't bother asking how many other women Olive had been with. Instead, she shifted so that they were lying beside each other. Olive gave a little contented sigh as she settled into Cassie's arms. Cassie gazed down at Olive for a moment, realising that she had never before experienced a feeling of such fulfilment. Then she closed her eyes and nuzzled her face into the soft expanse of Olive's hair.

# Chapter Five

Cassie plucked a book from the shelf and examined the cover. She wasn't quite certain how to handle her newly discovered – or was it newly uncovered? – feelings about women, but hopefully she could find some answers. As it was, she didn't feel nearly as confused as she thought she should. On the contrary, she was filled with peace, a feeling not unlike the one Adler had been speaking of when he gave her the massage.

'Hi, Cassie.'

'Nicholas.' Cassie tucked the book against her chest to hide the title. 'How are you?'

'Good.' He looked quite handsome in a pair of dark slacks and a grey shirt, his brown hair brushed away from his forehead. 'Lydia was asking about you the other day since she knows you've been spending so much time here lately. Would you like to come to the jazz festival? Etta James and the Dirty Dozen will be at the Masonic auditorium this weekend, and I think Lydia has tickets for the entire concert series.'

'Thanks for the invitation,' Cassie replied. 'Can I let you know this week?'

'Sure.' Nicholas's gaze slipped down to the book Cassie held. 'Can I help you find something?'

'No, I'm just looking.'

Nicholas glanced at the shelf right in front of them, which was clearly labelled GAY AND LESBIAN STUDIES. Cassie flushed.

'You're sure?' Nicholas asked.

Cassie looked at him. 'What has Lydia told you?'

'Nothing. I just know you've been talking to Olive and that you've become very interested in erotic literature.'

'Has Olive said something about me?' Cassie asked.

'Not really. Several months ago, she did tell me to be careful with you. That was right before you and I got together. And I know Olive has been with women.'

Cassie hesitated, then glanced down at the book. She had never discussed her sex life with Nicholas, but she had always felt comfortable with him. Something about him put her at ease.

'Well,' she said, 'I'm sure Lydia has told you that I've been confused lately about some things.'

'She did mention that,' Nicholas said.

'After a couple of disastrous experiences with some men who were more than a little kinky, I ended up at Olive's place last night,' Cassie explained. 'And we had sex.'

She was grateful when Nicholas didn't bat an eye. 'Oh. I see. And you're comfortable with that?'

Cassie nodded. 'Surprisingly so. I keep expecting to be hit with a rush of confusion, but so far that hasn't happened. I was so confused before, and now everything seems clear.'

Nicholas rested his shoulder against the bookshelf and crossed his arms. 'What is it that's clear?'

'That there's nothing wrong with me,' Cassie said. 'I thought that there had to be some reason, some bizarre clinical dysfunction, that explained why I didn't glean any emotional fulfilment from my experiences.'

She remembered that one of those experiences had been with Nicholas, and lowered her head for a moment, afraid that the kind man would be offended. To her surprise, Nicholas gave her a gentle look and shook his head. 'Don't worry about it, Cassie.'

Cassie tilted her head and looked at him. 'They were usually physically satisfying, you know, but something was missing. And now I realise that it wasn't because there was any problem with me.'

Nicholas smiled. 'And you're so relieved to have discovered that there's no room for confusion over having made love to a woman.'

'Exactly! Oh, I'm so glad you understand.'

'Cassie, you have to do what makes you happy,' Nicholas said. 'And if there's anything you shouldn't be con-fused about, it's loving another woman. If you find pleasure in that, then celebrate it.'

'But society has so many problems with it.'

Nicholas lifted his shoulders in a shrug. 'Society has problems with just about everything, when you think about it.'

'I suppose it does.'

'Cassie, you know I like Olive,' Nicholas said. 'But keep in mind that she can be a little capricious. I'd hate to see you get hurt.'

'Oh, please don't worry about that. I like Olive a great deal, but I haven't fallen in love with her. I've been much too busy trying to work out my own feelings.'

They fell silent for a moment, and then Cassie stood on tiptoe to press a kiss against his cheek. 'Thanks, Nicholas. Do me a favour, would you?'

'Anything.'

'Don't tell Lydia about this. I'm going to tell her of course, but I'd like to do so in my own way.'

'My lips are sealed.'

Cassie arched an eyebrow. 'I don't know if that's good enough. Knowing Lydia, she can unseal those lips of yours in less than a heartbeat.'

Nicholas grinned. 'For you, Cassie, I can even withstand the temptation of Lydia's lips. But don't wait *too* long.'

'You said you wanted to meet him.' Cassie pulled three plates from the cupboard and gave Olive a pointed look.

'Well, that was before you and I made love,' Olive reminded her. She poured herself a glass of wine, looking as if she were on the verge of a sulk.

'Aw, come on, Olive.' Cassie leant over to press her lips against her friend's cheek. Despite Olive's sulk, she still managed to look perfectly adorable in a low-cut flowered dress that managed to be both demure and sexy at the same time.

'It's just Adler,' Cassie said, suppressing a desire to slide her hand underneath Olive's neckline. Or underneath the hem of her dress. 'He's harmless.'

'Is he cute?'

'Sure, in a 1960s, hippie beat generation sort of way,' Cassie replied.

'I thought you and I were going to try that Tantric massage thing tonight,' Olive grumbled. 'I've been look-ing forward to it all day. I even climbed a ladder to shelve some books today because I thought you were going to massage all my tensions away and release my energy. Nicholas was overjoyed with my productivity.'

Cassie chuckled. 'I'd be happy to release your energy once Adler goes home. Come on, Olive, I promise you'll like him.'

'OK, OK, I'll be on my best behaviour.' Olive swallowed some wine and peered into one of the pots on the stove. 'What are you cooking?'

'Pasta. I figured that if there's anything I can't screw up, it's basic spaghetti. Oh, there's the doorbell.' Cassie wiped her hands on a dishtowel and hurried to let Adler in. 'Hi, Adler.' Cassie paused. 'Is that a Nehru jacket?'

'Snazzy, huh?' Adler looked down at his T-shirt and jacket. 'Authentic, too. I got it in India.'

'Well, it makes you look very dashing,' Cassie said. 'Come in.' They went into the kitchen, and Cassie intro-duced Adler to Olive. 'Olive works in that bookshop I'm always telling you about.'

Adler and Olive exchanged pleasantries, and the three of them went to the sitting room.

'So, Cassie tells me that you're quite a masseur,' Olive said, settling into a chair and crossing her legs.

'Olive!' Flushing, Cassie shot Adler a quick look. 'I just told her that you gave me a massage, that's all.'

'A Tantric one, Cassie said,' Olive went on.

'You're supposed to be on your best behaviour,' Cassie reminded her.

Olive winked at Adler. 'This is my best behaviour.'

'It seems to have worked,' Adler observed. 'I haven't seen you this relaxed in ages.'

'Yes, I can definitely report that all of Cassie's energy is flowing in the right direction,' Olive told him. 'And other things have been flowing in the right direction, too.'

Cassie had a feeling she was in for quite an evening. She should have known that something interesting would happen if she introduced feisty Olive to mellow Adler. Grinning to herself, she went into the kitchen and filled three bowls with spaghetti. She handed one each to Adler and Olive, then fixed a bowl for herself.

'So, Cassie tells me that you're both interested in three-somes,' Olive said brightly, winding several strands of spaghetti around her fork.

Adler's eyebrows lifted. 'Is that right?'

'William Blake again,' Cassie said. 'Honestly, Olive.'

Olive smiled. 'That does sound like an intriguing thought, if I do say so myself. I mean, making love to two brilliant artists and writers like William Blake and Henry Fuseli. Imagine how creative those two men could get in the bedroom.'

'Yes, probably even with things like body painting,' Adler agreed. He leant back in his chair, stretching his long legs out in front of him. 'Although considering Fuseli's painting of the nightmare, you'd have to wonder about their darker desires.'

Olive licked pasta sauce off her fork. 'Nothing wrong with dark desires.'

'You have dark desires?' Cassie asked in surprise.

Olive glowered at her. 'Of course. Why shouldn't I?'

'What kind of dark desires?' Cassie was delighted when Olive flushed. She had no idea that anything about sex could embarrass Olive.

'Yeah, Olive,' Adler chimed in, 'what kind of dark desires? Cassie must have told you about her interludes with foot fetishes and cross-dressing men.'

'Those were the men's desires, not mine,' Cassie reminded him. 'Well, Olive?'

'I've wondered about the usual dark desires,' Olive replied. 'Spanking, bondage. Threesomes.'

'How many dark desires can there be, anyway?' Cassie asked. She stood and started to collect the dirty plates, shaking her head as Adler and Olive offered to help her clean up.

'You'd be surprised,' Olive muttered. 'Remember that

guy who wanted to act like he was a two-year-old. Sheesh.'

Cassie brought the plates into the kitchen and busied herself with cleaning, leaving Olive and Adler to their discussion of the diversity of desires. She scraped off the plates and put them in the dishwasher, then started washing the pots and pans. She suddenly realised that it had become oddly quiet in the sitting room. Cassie placed a pot on the drying rack and peered around the corner into the sitting room.

Olive was stretched out on the floor, her face buried in a pillow as Adler went to work on her back. Cassie went into the sitting room, reaching out to dim the lights.

'It might not work without Adler's lava lamps and sitar music,' she remarked.

Olive rolled over slightly to peer at Cassie. 'Wow. I can already tell that he has hands of magic.'

'He does indeed. Wait, I'll at least try to recreate the mood as best I can.' She looked through her CD collection, finally settling on Bach's *The Well-Tempered Clavier*. She put the disc into the player and soon harpsichord music was drifting from the speakers.

'Oh, lovely,' Olive murmured.

'Now this is supposed to release your repressed energy upward through the top of your head,' Adler informed Olive. He'd taken off his Nehru jacket and sandals and was making himself comfortable on the floor.

'Adler, shouldn't Olive take off her dress?' Cassie asked as she settled into a chair to watch the proceedings. 'There shouldn't be anything constricting her. Olive doesn't like to be constricted.'

Olive shot Cassie a suspicious look. Adler merely appeared surprised.

'Cassie, you really have relaxed, haven't you?' he said.

Cassie smiled and settled back. Oh, yes, she definitely had. The thought of watching Adler give Olive an erotic back massage intrigued her no end.

Olive shrugged and grasped her dress, pulling it up over her head. Adler stared at her.

'Um, don't you want a robe or something?' he asked.

'What for? You're not going to massage me though it, are you?'

'Well, no, but –'

Olive turned and slipped off her bra, then pushed off her panties and stretched out on her belly. Cassie gazed hungrily at the sleek lines of Olive's body and the white rounded globes of her buttocks, which just begged to be squeezed and kissed. She glanced at Adler, not surprised to see that his eyes had glazed over slightly. If Cassie expected any jealousy over Adler touching Olive, then she was to be disappointed. Instead, she watched them with a great deal of enjoyment and more than a little arousal.

His hands shaking only slightly, Adler massaged Olive's smooth back and rambled on about kundalini and chakras until she told him to just be quiet and rub. Cassie smiled, leaning her head on the back of the chair as she watched Olive's body descend into visible pliancy and relaxation. Her skin became heated to a rosy pink from the pressure of Adler's hands, and a stream of entranced moans issued from her throat whenever Adler pressed a sensitive area.

Cassie propped her feet up on the coffee-table and let her gaze drift to Adler. His face was tight with concentration, his lips clamped together as he kneaded Olive's full bottom. Cassie's mouth curved into a slight smile when she glanced down at Adler's groin and noticed the distinct bulge pressing against his trousers. She gave him credit for continuing the massage with such dedication. Few men would have been able to maintain their commitment to the massage when confronted with nakedness of Olive's standard.

'Oh, Adler, you're good,' Olive murmured throatily. Her eyes were closed, her lips parted suggestively. 'So good.'

Cassie squirmed a little in her chair, thinking that Olive's voice sounded much the way it did when she was awash in sensual pleasure. Of course, Adler's massages definitely did wash one in sensual pleasure, as Cassie had unexpectedly discovered.

She wondered if Olive was experiencing the same arousal that she had. The mere thought was enough to create a shiver of awareness down her spine. Cassie squirmed again and pressed her thighs together. Her sex began to pulse.

Olive let out another low moan as Adler's hands kneaded her thighs and calves. Her legs parted, giving both Adler and Cassie a direct view of the plump labia lips nestled between her thighs. Cassie stared with uninhibited pleasure at the sight of Olive's moist pussy.

Olive suddenly lifted herself up on an elbow and glanced over at Adler. 'So, are you going to do my front next?'

Adler gaped at her, sweat breaking out on his forehead. Olive grinned, giving Cassie a wink as she rolled over and stretched out on her back, spreading her arms to the sides. 'My front is tense too, you know.'

Her breasts swayed like pliant cushions as she arranged herself, lifting her knees slightly. Adler looked at Cassie with a degree of shock.

Cassie smiled. 'Adler, relax. Remember? Release your energy.'

'I didn't expect to release it like this,' he croaked.

'Yes, free love and all that,' Olive agreed. She slipped her hands underneath her breasts, lifting them. 'I'm tense all over, Adler.'

Not even a man of Adler's philosophical bent could resist such a luscious temptation as the one now presented to him. With a shuddering sigh, he moved forward, grasping her breasts in his hands. Olive's nipples, still soft from her massage, peaked when Adler began rolling them between his fingers. His eyes grew hot with sheer lust as Olive whimpered her approval.

Cassie watched them with increasing arousal. She could well understand why such an experience would have appealed to a woman like Mary Wollstonecraft. She fidgeted, pressing her thighs together harder until the pressure wasn't enough. Then she slipped her hand underneath her skirt and into her panties. The amount of her wetness surprised her, and she plundered the treasures of her sex as she gazed at her two friends. The air thickened with heat.

'Oh, yes, Adler,' Olive breathed. 'Massage me.'

Adler splayed his hands over the swell of Olive's belly, hesitating for only an instant before he bent to flick his tongue into the indentation of her navel. He seemed to lave it with more than a passing interest. His long fingers spread over her mons, twining through her pubic hair before finding the knot of her clitoris. With the same slow deep strokes he had used on her back, he massaged the bud until Olive gasped and reached down to still his hand.

'Wait,' she gasped. 'I don't want to come yet. Cassie . . .'

Cassie could barely stand for the tightness between her legs, but she craved nothing more than to feel Olive's body against hers again. Her hands shook as she slipped out of her skirt and blouse, then removed her bra and walked to Olive and Adler. How long had she been curious about this, about the pleasures that could derive from being with two people? She started to kneel next to Olive, but Olive wrapped her hand around Cassie's ankle. She urged Cassie's foot over her body so that Cassie was straddling her with her sex poised directly above Olive's face.

'Now,' Olive murmured. 'Take off those panties and come down here.'

With a quickening of excitement, Cassie pushed her underwear down over her legs. She lowered her body over Olive's mouth until she was positioned with her knees on either side of Olive's head. The touch of Olive's slow, stroking tongue against her inner lips caused her to gasp with sheer delight. She reached out and clutched on to a chair to steady herself as Olive began to eat with increasing abandon.

Cassie was vaguely aware of Adler behind her, still moving his hands over Olive's body. Her excitement began to peak with an intensity that surprised her, and she recognised through the haze of pleasure that part of her stimulation derived from the fulfilment of this long-standing fantasy of hers. Cassie shuddered when she felt Olive thrust her tongue into her taut channel, grasping Cassie's buttocks to hold her in place. Cassie drew in a rush of air, her heart thrumming wildly as she turned to look at Adler.

He was straddling Olive's thighs, and had stripped off his trousers to reveal a slender, compact penis that quivered with anticipation. His lightly haired testicles were drawn up tightly between his thighs. He grasped his penis in his hand and began to stroke it rapidly as he stared lustfully at the two women in front of him. Cassie eased herself off Olive's mouth, trembling with arousal as she stroked her hands over Olive's full breasts.

'So beautiful,' she whispered. 'You're so beautiful.'

Olive smiled, her brown eyes warm. She flattened her hand against her own belly and slid it through the curls of her mons to her pussy.

'Would you mind if Adler fucked you?' Olive whispered. 'I want to watch.'

A series of shivers rained down Cassie's spine. She looked at Adler, who was still stroking his throbbing erection, causing a clear thick liquid to stream out. 'Adler?'

'Cassie, I . . .' His voice was hoarse. 'Are you sure?'

Cassie couldn't recall a time when she had been quite so sure of both herself and her life. She nodded. 'Oh, yes.'

She turned around and approached him, presenting Olive with the sight of her buttocks as she reached out to touch Adler's cock. Lightly scratching her fingernails over the shaft, she drew him closer to her and into her mouth. Heat throbbed in her pussy at the taste of Adler's penis. He groaned, clutching a swath of her hair. Feeling a delicious sense of power, Cassie licked up the salty moisture that was oozing from the tip, then pulled him into her mouth until she could take him no further. She caressed his shaft with her tongue, then moved back and grasped the base of his penis. She manoeuvred her head lower, gently taking one testicle in her mouth and then the other.

With a start of surprise, Cassie felt Olive's tongue prodding at her again. A rush of excitement filled her unlike any she had known, excitement and utter carnal lust. She stroked Adler's cock hard as she pulled slowly away from him. She turned and gave Olive a slow, dreamy smile.

Bending her head, she pressed her lips against Olive's mouth, hungrily licking the other woman's lower lip. Olive tasted scrumptious, like wine and oregano made all the more potent by the heady flavour of lust. Cassie lowered her mouth to Olive's breasts and sucked. She rolled Olive's thick nipples against her tongue, loving the whimpers of pleasure evoked by her actions. Her palms skittered over Olive's body as she stretched out fully on top of her friend, pressing their breasts and sexes together. Cassie wriggled experimentally and smiled when Olive groaned.

'Don't you like this?' Cassie whispered, kissing Olive's lips again.

'Oh, I definitely like this.'

Cassie started slightly when she felt Adler's hands on her back. She realised that this was, indeed, very strange for her and Adler's relationship. Their eyes met as she glanced at him over her shoulder. Although lust was the predominant emotion in Adler's expression, he looked at her with both kindness and affection. Cassie relaxed as his hands touched the base of her spine and pressed, an echo of the massage he had given her earlier. Any tension in Cassie's body dissipated save for the luscious rope twining tighter and tighter in her loins. Her legs tangled with Olive's as she parted her thighs.

Adler kneaded his hands over Cassie's buttocks and dipped his fingertips into the fissure between them. With incredible ease, his hands moved down to her sex. He stroked her labia with a sensitivity that almost made Cassie smile. She would have expected no less from him. Adler's finger traced her clitoris, causing it to blossom out towards his touch, while another finger slipped into her damp passage. Cassie clenched her inner muscles around his fingers. Her skin burned, and Olive's hot breath brushed against her neck, stimulating her need to greater dimensions.

Pulling his fingers out of her, Adler rubbed the satiny skin of Cassie's inner thighs as he pushed her legs further apart. The head of his cock nudged against Cassie's sex with a delectable torment. Her body craved the complete immersion of his stalk, but Adler appeared to be in no hurry. He rubbed the hard knob back and forth, inserting it halfway into her before pulling out again and smoothing it over her clitoris. Cassie squirmed with delight over this unexpected teasing.

'Adler, come on,' she gasped. 'Do it. Fuck me.'

'Oh, do, Adler.' Olive's hands stroked over Cassie's back and clutched at her bottom. 'Fuck her.'

Adler's slender penis began a luscious slide into Cassie. At the same instant, Olive thrust her tongue into Cassie's mouth. Cassie moaned, her body tensing with delight at the incredible sensation of the soft, voluptuous woman beneath her and the hard cock inside her. She pushed her hips up as if trying to hasten their union. Adler continued pushing into her, bracing his hands on her buttocks. Cassie looked over her shoulder at him, thrilled by the sight of him starting to pump inside her. Olive held out her hands, and Adler gripped them tightly, his expression contorting with a pleasure akin to pain.

'God, you're tight, Cassie,' he gasped. 'So wet and hot.'

Cassie's body began to sway back and forth as his thrusts increased in pace, his testicles slapping against her. The sensation of her and Olive's bodies rubbing against each other's with such rhythmical precision made Cassie cry out. She ground her pelvis against Olive's, then reached between their bodies to find the slippery jewel of Olive's pleasure. She could hardly believe the exquisite sensations which wracked her entire being – disbelief over the fact that she was fulfilling one of her fantasies, and rapture because it was all so incredibly gratifying.

Cassie spread her fingers over Olive's clitoris and stroked hard, hearing Olive's breath quicken against her ear. She buried her face in the hot skin of Olive's neck as the wet, slapping sounds and intense scents of carnality filled the air. Their bodies continued to jerk rhythmically, and then Olive's hips bucked upward. With a cry, her teeth bit down on Cassie's shoulder as her climax broke over her. A rush of moisture bathed Cassie's fingers, and she continued rubbing Olive until the final shudders ebbed.

Adler's cock slid with slick ease in and out of Cassie, accompanied by grunts of lust as he spurred himself towards his own release.

'Kiss me,' Olive whispered hoarsely, her mouth open against Cassie's shoulder.

Cassie lifted her head and plunged her tongue into Olive's mouth, her entire body filled as Adler pumped harder and faster. The shaft of his cock throbbed against her inner walls, sending heat directly into her veins. She clenched her muscles around him. Adler groaned and pulled out of her in one movement. His penis pressed against her cleft as his hot come spurted over her buttocks. Cassie shivered at the wet, erotic sensation.

'Oh, lover, it's your turn,' Olive murmured. She slipped her fingers into Cassie's throbbing slit and simultaneously thrust and stroked to bring Cassie to the heights of pleasure. Overwhelmed by this experience and by such a multitude of sensations, Cassie came within seconds as her body quivered anew.

Cassie rolled off Olive, her chest heaving as she lay on her back and tried to recover. She glanced at Adler, who was sitting propped against the sofa, his eyes closed with utter repletion.

'So?' Olive reached out and threaded her fingers through Cassie's hair. 'That was your fantasy, wasn't it? Was it everything you imagined?'

Cassie turned so that she could look at Olive. The other woman's lovely skin was bathed with perspiration, her eyes exuding contentment.

Cassie smiled and nodded. 'Actually, it was more.'

Cassie pulled some folders and letters out of her mailbox in the Literature Department's main office. Glancing through them, she headed back down the corridor towards her office. Her heart leapt at the sight of one of the letters, the unmistakable return address in the corner. She hurried into her office and slammed the door.

Fingers shaking, she tore open the envelope and

removed the letter inside. For a heart-stopping minute, she almost couldn't read it. She closed her eyes and opened the letter, sending up a quick prayer to any deity who happened to be listening. Then she opened her eyes and scanned the letter quickly.

Cassie slumped into her desk chair and let the letter fall to the ground. She took a deep breath, but tears pricked the backs of her eyes. She couldn't believe it. After all this time, all this work. It was impossible to comprehend.

'Cassie?' A knock sounded on the door and it opened.

Adler's bearded face appeared around the corner. 'You OK?' he asked. 'I heard your door slam.'

Cassie wiped a tear away from the corner of her eye. 'Yes, thanks. I'm fine.'

Adler entered the room, frowning slightly. 'You don't look fine.'

Cassie bent and picked up the letter. She handed it to him, realising her fingers were still shaking. Adler read the letter, his mouth falling open in disbelief.

'Cassie!'

Cassie laughed. 'I know. Can you believe it?'

'You got the grant! Cassie, you got the grant!' Adler dashed around the desk to grab her out of her chair and give her a huge bear hug. 'This is fantastic! Congratulations!'

He danced around the room with her as much as the small size of her office would allow. Cassie laughed again, tears of joy streaming down her cheeks.

'I honestly didn't think it would happen,' she said, hugging him tightly. 'I can't believe it did.'

'Aw, Cassie, I knew you could do it.' Adler set her down again. His grin was a mile wide. 'Wow, Cassie, this is wonderful.'

Cassie smiled, flushed with pleasure. 'Thanks. I couldn't have done it without you, you know. You've been invaluable to me.'

'Well, I hope I still can be,' Adler said. 'Even though you're going to be on the other side of the ocean.'

Cassie pressed her hand against her chest, feeling her heart beating wildly. He was right; now, she would finally have a chance to immerse herself completely in research. 'I hope you're going to come and visit me.'

'I hope so too,' Adler said. 'I've become rather intrigued by Byron and his relationship with Shelley, so maybe I'll find a new avenue of research for myself.'

Cassie reached out and took his hand in hers, giving it a tight squeeze. 'Thank you, Adler. For everything.'

Adler looked at her. 'You don't regret anything, do you?' he asked. 'I mean, what we did?'

'Oh, no, of course not,' Cassie said. 'I thought briefly that it might make things awkward between us, but I doubt we could ever be awkward with each other.'

Adler smiled, leaning over to kiss her cheek. 'Let's have dinner this weekend, OK? There's a great new Caribbean restaurant in North Beach I want to take you to.'

'I'd love to.' Cassie watched him leave her office. She read the letter from the grant officials again, still trying to come to terms with the fact that she had received something she had worked so long and hard for. She picked up the telephone and dialled Lydia's office number. 'Mona, it's Cassie. Is Lydia in?'

'Hello, Cassie. No, she left for lunch. She said she was having lunch with Nicholas, so she might be at the bookshop.'

'I'll try her there. Thanks.' After hanging up the telephone, Cassie folded the letter and grabbed her bag. She hurried to her car and drove to Libri Antiqui. Hoping that Lydia would be there, Cassie went in the front door.

'Hey, you.' Olive smiled at Cassie from her position behind the cash register. 'What brings you here?'

'I'm looking for Lydia,' Cassie said. 'Is she here? I need to speak with her.'

'She and Nicholas just left for lunch, but they'll be back in an hour,' Olive replied. 'Why? What's going on?'

'Do you remember I told you that I had applied for a grant, one that would permit me to do the final round of intense research for my book?' Cassie asked.

Olive nodded.

'I received a letter today saying that I've been awarded the grant.'

Olive's eyes widened. 'No!'

Cassie smiled and nodded.

'Oh, Cassie, that's marvellous!' Olive hopped off her stool and ran to hug her friend.

Cassie returned Olive's embrace. 'Thanks. I'm still trying to decide if it's real.'

'Of course it's real! I knew they'd give you that grant.' Olive squeezed Cassie's hands, her eyes shining with pleasure. 'You deserve it. You applied so that you could research in London, didn't you?'

'Yes. I'll be able to go for the entire year.'

Olive hesitated. 'When?'

'Starting next September.' Cassie gazed at Olive, then reached up to brush a loose strand of hair away from Olive's face. 'I guess you and I never really talked about the possibility.'

The light in Olive's eyes dimmed a little. 'There isn't much we can do about it. I have to finish classes, and you certainly can't stay here.'

'Olive, I –'

Olive shook her head to stop Cassie's words. 'Don't, Cassie. We'll have all summer. And I don't think either one of us is looking for a serious commitment right now. You know, we both have things to do, places to go.'

Cassie nodded. 'Why don't we just enjoy what we have and then see what happens?'

'Good idea. I can definitely guarantee you a sizzling summer, if you're so inclined.'

Cassie laughed. 'Oh, I'm inclined. Maybe even reclined . . .'

She pulled Olive to her for another embrace. Her body was warm, fragrant, and accommodating. Accommodating. With a blissful sigh, Cassie tightened her arms around the other woman.

# Epilogue

A cold wind buffeted against Lydia as she gazed out at the vast expanse of sand, sea, and sky. She loved Marin County, the sloping hills and cliffs that all seemed to lead to the sea. Undulating waves splashed rhythmically against the shore of Drake's beach, coating it with frothy white foam. Seagulls sailed about, picking at the ropes of seaweed that had drifted on to the beach. A dismal fog covered the sky, which, when combined with the wind, seemed to be preventing people from spending the afternoon at the beach. At least, everyone save for her, Cassie, and Molly.

Lydia spotted her friends a distance away seated on a couple of large beach towels. She took one of Nicholas's shirts from her bag and slipped it on over her T-shirt, glad she'd had the foresight to consider the weather. Picking up her picnic basket, she slipped off her shoes and began walking through the coarse sand. The grains tickled the soles of her feet, feeling rather delicious between her toes.

Cassie and Molly lifted their arms and waved.

'Hi, Lyd!' Molly called. 'We weren't sure you'd show.'

'And miss such a gorgeous afternoon with my best friends?' Lydia smiled and handed Molly the picnic basket. 'Besides, I figured you ladies would be getting hungry.'

'We're starving,' Molly declared, opening the basket. 'Would you believe we went to the Point Reyes lighthouse and climbed down all those steps to get to the darned thing?'

'And then back up again,' Cassie added.

'There must be over three hundred steps,' Molly groaned, shaking her dishevelled curls. She took out a container of pasta salad and handed it to Cassie. 'Since when do you climb down a mountain to get to a light-house? I was *dying*.'

Lydia grinned and sat down on Cassie's beach towel. 'But, you did it. You'll even find some chocolate éclairs in there that you can have as a reward.'

'Oh, Lydia, I love you.' Molly handed out the plates and forks and opened the rest of the containers. Between the three of them, they managed to polish off most of the food, which turned out to be only slightly sandy as a result of the steady breeze.

Chewing on her second éclair, Molly reached out and nudged Cassie with her foot. 'Go on, Cass. Tell her.'

Lydia glanced at Cassie. 'Tell me what?'

'Cassie has some incredible news,' Molly said.

Cassie smiled. 'I was awarded the grant to study in London.'

Lydia stared at her, her heart suddenly leaping with excitement. 'Cassie, that's wonderful!'

'I received the letter the day before yesterday. I was going to call you, but I really wanted to tell you in person.'

'Oh, I'm so glad you did!' Lydia reached out to give Cassie a tight hug. 'Congratulations.' She pulled away slightly, thrilled over her friend's success. 'I'm so proud of you!'

Cassie flushed with pleasure. 'Thanks.'

'You realise this means that she's going to live in London for an entire year,' Molly said, looking slightly dejected by that fact.

Lydia smiled and stroked her fingers through Cassie's wind-blown hair. She suspected that a year in London would work wonders for Cassie. 'Well, all the more reason for you and I to fly to England to visit her.'

'Hey, good point! We can all go shopping at Harrod's.' Brightening visibly, Molly stood and brushed flakes of chocolate icing from her hands. 'Come on, you two. Let's go swimming.'

'Swimming?' Cassie repeated. 'Molly, the water is freezing.'

'Well, wading at least.' With a grin, Molly took off her beach sandals and rolled up the legs of her loose linen trousers. She dashed down to the ocean's edge and stepped into the Pacific waters, letting out a shriek of surprise when the waves covered her feet.

Cassie chuckled.

'Hey, it's invigorating!' Molly called, jumping in and out of the water. Her teeth started to chatter within a few seconds. 'Come on in!'

'Maybe later!' Lydia called back. She grinned at Cassie, pleased to see her younger friend looking both relaxed and happy. 'You look wonderful, Cassie. I'm so happy for you.'

Cassie smiled. 'Thanks. I've had quite a month.'

Lydia stretched out on Molly's towel, propping her head on her hand. 'You have, indeed.'

'I've also been meaning to tell you that I finally asked Olive to coffee,' Cassie said. 'We ended up doing dinner, and a little more as well.'

Lydia's eyebrows lifted slightly. 'A little more?'

Cassie nodded as two pink spots of colour appeared on her cheeks. 'We went back to her place and had sex that same night.'

'Ahh. Did you enjoy it?'

'Yes, I did. I couldn't believe how much. I didn't even realise how attracted to her I was.' Cassie eyed Lydia speculatively for a moment. 'You don't seem surprised.'

'I'm not,' Lydia said honestly. 'I've thought for some time now that there was something between you and Olive, even if it was unacknowledged.'

'You thought I might be attracted to women?'

'I was almost certain that you were, but I didn't want to be the one to tell you.' She smiled. 'I thought it would be best if you made the discovery yourself.'

'Wow.' Cassie shook her head. 'I had no idea I was that transparent.'

'Oh, love, you're not transparent.' Lydia reached out and put her hand on Cassie's knee. 'Not at all. It's just that I know you so well.'

Cassie drew her knees to her chest and hugged her

arms around them as she gazed out at Molly playing in the waves. 'I haven't minded being with men, and sometimes I've certainly enjoyed it, but being with Olive was unbelievable. I'd never known that an attraction to someone could be so exciting and fulfilling. So magnetic. I loved everything about it.'

'Do you think it's Olive or women in general?' Lydia asked.

'I think it's women in general, but I haven't had enough experience to figure that out yet. I do know that being with a woman feels incredibly right to me. More right than anything I've ever felt before.' Cassie glanced at Lydia hesitantly. 'That doesn't bother you, does it?'

'Why should it bother me? All I want is your happiness, you know that. I've hated seeing you so confused these past weeks and, frankly, I'm delighted that you've discovered something I've been suspecting for some time.' Lydia sat up, putting her hand on Cassie's shoulder and giving it a gentle squeeze. 'You're my heroine, you know that?'

'I am?'

Lydia smiled and nodded. 'I've often wanted to be more like you.'

'Really?' Cassie's mouth dropped open in surprise. 'You're kidding.'

'Of course I'm not kidding. You've always managed to find your way with both strength and such a degree of quietude. I envy that about you.'

'But, you're ... you're Lydia!' Cassie said. 'Everyone wants to be like you. You're so comfortable with yourself.'

'Not always. Remember Nicholas? I didn't know whether I was coming or going with him.'

'I'd bet you were definitely coming,' Cassie said with a grin.

Lydia chuckled. 'OK, bad metaphor. I didn't know what I wanted with him or how I was feeling until it was almost too late. Luckily, he is infinitely patient and was willing to give me another chance.'

'You may consider yourself lucky to have him,' Cassie said. 'But I think he's far luckier to have you.'

'Oh, you're such a doll.' Lydia stood and brushed sand off her legs. 'Have you told Molly yet?'

'No, not yet. I will soon.'

Their gazes went to their red-headed friend, who was busy poking gingerly at a slimy rope of seaweed with a stick.

'She's OK now, isn't she?' Cassie asked.

Lydia nodded. She was so relieved that Molly had not only weathered her storm, but that she had discovered more about herself in the process. 'She's fine. She'll always be fine. She has an incredible resiliency.'

She reached down and grasped Cassie's hand to help her to her feet. 'However, we'd better make certain she doesn't go too far or she's liable to get lost.'

'Well, we'll just have to find her and bring her back again.'

Lydia laughed. They went down to the water's edge to join Molly. She beamed at them and waved, her curls blowing about her face like little flames.

'Let's make a sandcastle!' she suggested, her blue eyes bright with pleasure as she skirted out of the way of another wave. 'When was the last time we did that? Hey, look at this shell I found!'

She jogged over to them and held out a round flat shell for their inspection.

'That's a sand dollar, Molly,' Lydia said. 'In perfect condition, too. Isn't it good luck to find one of those?'

'If it's not, it should be,' Cassie replied. 'Make a wish, Molly.'

Molly handed the sand dollar to Lydia. 'You make one for me, Lyd. Something involving a tall, rich Italian man who owns a *palazzo* in Florence. Now, come on, one of you is coming into the water with me!'

She grabbed Cassie's hand and tugged her towards the water. Cassie laughed, squealing when the icy water hit her feet. Lydia smiled, closing her fingers around the sand dollar. I wish the best for you, she thought as she watched Cassie and Molly leaping out of the water's way.

She looked up as a flock of seagulls coasted overhead, their wings outlined fuzzily against the grey sky. The wind pushed undulating waves on to the beach, one after the other, and filled the air with a fresh, salty scent.

*I wish the best for all of us.* Lydia tucked the sand dollar into her pocket for safekeeping and ran down to the edge of the ocean to join her friends.